Enchanted in Edinburgh

Enchanted in Edinburgh

Yvonne Carse

First edition 2022

ISBN 978-1-80227-634-3 (paperback)
ISBN 978-1-80227-635-0 (ebook)

Typeset using Atomik ePublisher from Easypress Technologies

CHAPTER ONE

Marchmont Estate, Wick, Caithness, October 1843

LADY CYNTHIA MARCHMONT leaned against the window in her father's study and let out a shivering sigh. Her breath clouded the glass with a powdery mark that vanished, like a tiny ghost, into the grey blur of mist and rain outside. The weather had been dreich for days now, which had put a stop to Cynthia's habitual morning rides on her cherished horse, Snowy. The wind howled. The pelting rain showed no sign of abating. God, she was bored.

Cynthia pulled her crochet shawl tight around her shoulders. She had on one of her favourite evening gowns: a midnight blue affair with a voluminous skirt and black lace applique detail on its neckline and hem. *All dressed up but nowhere to go,* thought Cynthia, taffeta whispering as she turned to face her father, Lord Joseph Marchmont, engrossed in the *John O'Groats Journal* sprawled across his desk. 'Seriously, Daddy,' said Cynthia. 'How many more days of this miserable weather must we tolerate? I can't go for my usual morning ride or afternoon walk. If I do, I shall be soaked to the bone and will probably catch pneumonia and die. We've been stuck inside for days and I'm so, so painfully bored.'

Lord Marchmont took off his spectacles and half-squinted at his daughter. 'I gather you're a little put out by the weather, my dear?'

'Argh, I shall go insane if I spend one more day cooped up in here.' Cynthia flung her arms wide and flopped onto the chaise lounge in front of the rattling windows. 'There's only so many parlour games a woman can play, and I'm tired of sewing and playing piano, and I'm useless at painting. Reading is becoming tedious, and, as you know, I'm not the type to sleep during the day, and even if the weather *was* fine, there's…' Lord Marchmont's hefty moustache twitched as Cynthia continued to add to her 'boredom' inventory. He was trying not to laugh. She was the most theatrical of his two daughters, a trait Cynthia inherited from her mother, Lady Georgina Marchmont, who not only stole the show in games of charades but also relished a drama or two in quotidian life. In the nicest possible way, of course. '…Well, there just isn't much to do in Wick, and soon it will be winter, and I fear this gloom will never lift and I'll never go out again, and will never find a…'

'Husband?' finished Lord Marchmont, folding his newspaper. 'Indeed, it's about time you and your sister found eligible husbands. Especially you, Cynthia. You really ought to be running a household by now.' Cynthia fiddled with her shawl. Her father had a point. Nearly twenty-three, she risked being classed 'too old' for courtship, let alone marriage, by today's social standards. Her sister Angela, however, being four years younger, was of perfect marriageable age. 'But fear no more, my dear. I have news that might cheer you up. How does a trip to Edinburgh sound? I have several meetings there over the winter season, so it makes sense for us all to relocate there for a few months- you, Angela, and your brother Derek. Your mother too, of course.' Lord Marchmont straightened in his chair, a smug smile quivering below his moustache.

'Edinburgh?' said Cynthia, her tone brightening. Cynthia had not been to Edinburgh since she was a child but her mother, who was born and raised there, spoke fondly of the city. Unlike Wick, there should be lots to do in Edinburgh. There were theatres and dance halls and taverns and a castle even. Lady Georgina's sister Mary lived in the capital with her husband Felix and their daughter Frances, who was a few months younger than Angela. It would be so lovely to see them again, thought Cynthia.

'Imagine, you'll be able to spend time with your cousin, make new friends and go to balls and soirees,' Lord Marchmont added. 'You and Angela. Two beautiful Marchmont debutantes. Aye, you'll both be sure to find husbands in Edinburgh, my dear.'

Cynthia angled her head on one side. 'Och, Father,' she said with a tinkling laugh, 'more likely you want Angela and me out of your hair, right? Let two young Edinburgh chaps whisk us off our feet then bring us to heel and curb our charming high spirits?' Although Cynthia was already picturing a ravishingly handsome man twirling her across a grand ballroom floor to a romantic ballade or polonaise.

'Well, that's true…to an extent, Cynthia, but I also want you to marry a gentleman who will not only cherish you, but who will allow you *some* freedom to indulge your, how shall I put it, more *liberal* points of view?'

'Of course, Father,' said Cynthia, blonde ringlets bobbing about her face as she shot from the chaise lounge and pattered towards the door, stopping to kiss her father's cheek. 'Angela and I know you only want the very best for us. We would love to go to Edinburgh – but only if you can afford it?' While Lord Marchmont was one of the wealthiest landowners in Caithness, Cynthia was also aware that the estate had suffered a substantial loss of late. The crops had failed last summer, and much of the cattle had been rustled by vagabonds who were never caught.

Lord Marchmont laughed. 'Go, run along and tell your sister – if she's not snoring her brains away, that is. You ladies should pack. We'll be leaving in two days.'

'Oh Father, you're the best. I can't wait to tell Angela the good news. I promise we'll try our very best to attract suitable husbands who will take us off your hands.'

Minutes later, Cynthia and Angela waltzed around the younger sister's dressing room, giggling. 'There'll be parties every night for sure,' said Angela, a little breathless. Her corset felt tighter than usual amid all this excitement. 'And we'll have our pick of eligible young men, too. Imagine, we could meet our future husbands. In Edinburgh. How wonderful would that be?'

'Indeed,' said Cynthia. 'That's why Father has arranged this trip – so he can get us married off before we become old maids.' The sisters were now laughing so hard they didn't notice when their maid Margaret entered the room and announced: 'Lady Cynthia, Lady Angela, afternoon tea will be served in the drawing room in ten minutes.'

Until now, Cynthia had abandoned all hope of becoming a Mrs. "someone". She had, of course, come out into society when she was eighteen but, alas, her parents' efforts to find a suitor for Cynthia had been unsuccessful. The young gentlemen of Wick were invariably already married, not financially high-ranking enough for the Marchmonts, or simply didn't fit Cynthia's idea of a perfect husband. Many gentlemen she'd encountered were so dull she struggled to imagine spending one day with them, let alone a lifetime. Others, she suspected, would indeed crush her personality and expect her to become the stereotypical, submissive wife who would sit at home all day looking pretty. Seen but not heard. A wife with no opinions or interests of her own other than to obey her spouse. But who *would* fit the bill as Cynthia's ideal husband? The question whirled in her mind throughout afternoon tea – and supper – when conversation focussed on the Marchmonts' forthcoming trip to Edinburgh. Inspired, that night Cynthia took herself off to the library to compile a list of the qualities she would look for in a husband. Sitting at the bureau, a clean sheet of paper before her, she dipped her pen nib in the inkwell and, after a pensive moment, wrote: *Lady Cynthia Marchmont's future husband is a kind man who understands and respects her desires, quirks and faults. He is:*

1. *Heart-stopping handsome though not conceited*
2. *Generous but not too frivolous with money*
3. *Loving, but not overbearing or domineering (Nobody wants a bossy-boots for a husband)*
4. *Sensitive – although you'll never see him greet in public (unless he's attending the funeral of a close relative or friend)*
5. *Tall, with luscious dark hair, intense eyes and a physique like Michelangelo's* David

6. A man of good wealth and status
7. Adventurous and impulsive. Rebellious at times
8. Romantic but not sickeningly so
9. Intelligent, without being a know-all
10- A considerate lover

Cynthia filled both sides of the paper with her vision of the perfect suitor. She read her list twice then, cringing, scrunched the paper into a ball and threw it into the fire. She would surely die of embarrassment if anybody else in their household, especially Derek or Father, were to happen upon her list. Watching her musings ignite in flames, Cynthia realised she hadn't named her fantasy husband. Was she being too picky? *Maybe that's why I'm not married*, thought Cynthia, *I'm expecting too much, setting my sights too high perhaps?* 'Will I ever find such a man?' she said to herself through a yawn. It was late, the back of 10 pm, according to the grandfather clock tick-tock-ing away behind her, steady and wise. 'Och well,' Cynthia said to the fire. 'Let's see what happens in Edinburgh.'

CHAPTER TWO

A week later, in Edinburgh…

LORD ANTHONY SINCLAIR left his townhouse-mansion on Moray Place with a spring in his step. As Wednesdays went, today was looking mighty fine thus far. The weather was glorious: clement for this time of year, with a clear sky and low autumn sun casting a russet glow upon the city. And Anthony's prize horse, Bluebell, had just won a princely purse race, which added to his chipper mood. Not that Anthony needed the money. At almost 30, and the eldest of three children born to Duchess Rosalind and the late duke, Andrew Sinclair, he was one of Edinburgh's wealthiest aristocrats, with his recent purchase of the Girnigoe Estate in Caithness, complete with a castle, further bolstering his list of assets. Still, a win was a win, and Anthony would later celebrate Bluebell's victory over a gourmet dinner served with as much fine claret he could physically imbibe. But which of his mistresses should he entertain tonight? *Marianne? She likes a hearty meal and can hold her ale, right enough. What about Kathleen? She's fun to be around. Charlotte could do with a good meal down her neck. Awfully thin, her. But Marianne's husband is out of town just now…* Such were Anthony's thoughts as he powered through the New Town to his appointment at Niall Johnstone's shop on George Street. He fancied himself a new riding coat and a suit – and Johnstone was the finest tailor in the capital.

Marianne, she's my safest bet, decided Anthony, as he approached Johnstone's shop. *No, wait a minute, Lady Anne Stewart is also good for…*

'Anthony, old chum, I was hoping I'd bump into you.' Anthony heard Lord William McLean – or Bill as he was known among friends – before he saw him, his voice, loud and jovial, interrupting Anthony's reverie. 'How is my dearest friend on this splendid morning? You're looking very dapper, I must say.'

Anthony's right eyebrow shot skywards, like an arrowhead, spearing the brim of his hat. 'OK, enough with the flattery. What do you want this time, Bill?' Anthony knew only too well his friend's conspiratorial expression. The pair had been pals since childhood and, together with their other close friend Sir Ronald Forbes, was the most talked about and desired rakes in Edinburgh. Debutantes' mothers fought and schemed to introduce their daughters to these men, who avoided such overtures at all costs. Indeed, Anthony had no immediate desire to settle down. Clandestine dalliances with promiscuous women like Marianne, Kathleen, Charlotte or indeed Lady Anne Stewart were more his style.

'I'm offended,' said Bill with a faux wounded look. 'Is it such a crime for a gentleman to compliment his friend – his dearest friend for whom he would do anything for? A friend he would trust with his life. A friend he would give his own life for. A friend who…'

'Alright, enough dramatics, Bill. Cut to the chase – I can't miss my appointment.'

Bill wriggled his chin above his high collar. 'I need a favour of sorts. I really need you to attend Lord Thomas Walker's soiree on Saturday evening. Please Anthony? You know I wouldn't ask unless I was desperate, pal.'

'Sorry Bill. I've already made plans for Saturday,' replied Anthony, slightly confused at Bill's request. 'I promised Ron a night of debauchery and I can't possibly let him down. You know how it is. And besides, why do you need me there? You know how those society women like to throw themselves at me. You'll have a better chance of finding a wife without me cramping your style, old boy.' Anthony swung his cane back and forth, laughing at his own joke.

'No, Anthony, you don't understand. That's exactly what I want you to do.' Bill's expression was deadly serious. 'Lord Walker is introducing his daughter Julianne to society this year, which will undoubtedly be difficult for him after all he's been through.'

'Indeed, poor chap. He'll still be grieving,' said Anthony. Lord Walker's wife, Morag, had died six months ago. Dropped dead as she went about her morning ablutions. A seizure, so said the doctor. 'But I don't see how Lord Walker or his dearly departed wife – or their daughter for that matter – has anything to do with *me.*'

Bill threw his head over his right shoulder, then his left and shuffled closer to Anthony. 'I need a diversion,' he said, lowering his voice. 'As you know my father is a good friend of Lord Walker – and he feels obliged to help him, given his tragic circumstances. Father wants me to support Julianne at her first soiree. He thinks this will increase her chances of being invited to all the high society balls this season, but I know my mother is rather hoping I might step out with Julianne. Then there are all the other mothers who'll be trying to set me up with their daughters. It's relentless.'

'So, you want to use *me* to get yourself off the hook?'

'Not quite,' added Bill. 'All I'm saying is this: if you come to the soiree on Saturday, I won't have to deal with all the mothers and daughters alone. Their attentions will be split between the two of us. What do you say, old chap?'

Anthony shrugged and reached for his pocket watch. 'Sorry, Bill. I'm busy. Why would I swap a night of debauchery for one of purgatory?'

'Because you owe me one, Anthony. Remember three weeks ago, when we were in the book shop – and Marianne walked in, followed by Kathleen?'

'Honestly, talk about terrible timing, eh.' Anthony gave Bill's arm a playful punch, trying to make light of the memory.

Bill nodded slowly. 'Absolutely, but have you already forgotten how I managed to distract Marianne – steering her out of the shop before she came face to face with you and Kathleen?' Bill paused, inhaled deeply before exhaling with a whistle. 'Imagine the cat fight that would have ensued. The scandal? Then Marianne and Kathleen's husbands would have come after you. Swords and pistols and before…'

'OK, Bill, I get the picture,' said Anthony. 'I'll come to the soiree – but only if you can persuade Ron to come too.'

'Good show, my friend, good show.' Bill slapped his friend on the shoulder, beaming. Anthony could smell last night's wine on Bill's breath. 'I'll find Ron just now,' he said, then hurried east along George Street.

'We're not staying later than 11 pm though,' Anthony called over his shoulder as he went into Johnstone's shop.

Johnstone fussed over Anthony as though he were Prince Albert, greeting him with a bow before relieving him of his hat, coat and cane and ushering him into the dressing room. 'Would his Lordship care for a dram?' he asked, already pouring a glass of single malt. Anthony was Johnstone's most frequent customer, returning several times each season for new attire. He would always buy more than one outfit and today was no exception. Delighted with the fit of his riding coat and dress suit, he decided a new frock coat was also in order. After a second dram, Anthony purchased another suit, four waistcoats, a selection of silk neckties, and was fitted for a Chesterfield coat – the latest must-have for the smartly-dressed men of high society. *If I must go to all these balls and soirees, I might as well look the part*, thought Anthony, a little light-headed as he left the shop and headed west to his regular gentlemen's club on Charlotte Square. It was just after noon, time for a bite to eat and a glass of ale. *All this trying on of garments is thirsty work.*

Anthony's uncle, James Murray, was inside the club, nursing a tankard of ale. He spotted Anthony as soon as he walked into the room and called him over. 'My dear boy,' he said with a double handshake, slippery but lingering. James clearly had more than a couple of ales. 'How good to see you. Come, sit down. Lunch is on me. That investment you told me about came up trumps.'

'Glad to hear it, uncle,' said Anthony, shrugging off his overcoat. Despite its stone interior, the club was always warm, the air thick with the smell of stew, pipe and cigar smoke, all curling around the woolly hum of chatter among Edinburgh's elite gentlemen. 'That should keep your head above water for the time being.' The truth was,

James, Anthony's mother's younger brother, was hopeless with money. He relied heavily on Anthony to help him out with sage advice on investment opportunities. James' son Stewart was no different either. Anthony didn't mind helping his uncle as he thought him a kind soul. Stewart on the other hand, was a different kettle of fish.

'So, one good turn deserves another,' said James with a wink.

Anthony proffered his coat to the waiting butler and sat down. "Really? Do enlighten me, Uncle.'

'Well, it's a warning actually,' added James, chuckling as he swigged his ale. 'It's your mother. She's desperate for you to get married. And she believes she's found the perfect wife for you.'

Anthony shook his head, black waves dancing about his shoulders, sleek in the lamplight. 'Honestly, why must she meddle in my love life. What's this obsession mothers have about their children getting married?' Just then, the waiter appeared and took their order: more ale and two fish stews.

'It's Lord Walker's daughter who your mother fancies as your future wife,' said James once the waiter was out of earshot.

'Julianne?' said Anthony, his face breaking into a sly grin. 'That's funny: Bill's mother is also trying to partner him off with Julianne.'

'She's an outstanding beauty by all accounts,' said James, 'Quite a raven-haired goddess.'

'That may be so, but it doesn't mean I have to *marry* her – just to keep Mother happy. I don't even know the girl. Never met her.' The waiter reappeared, placed two tankards of ale on the table and muttered something about the stew's imminent arrival, then, seeing the two men were deep in conversation, swiftly turned his attention to the neighbouring table.

'Och, cheer up, dear boy. Marriage isn't such a bad thing. Look at your aunt Maggie and me. We get along famously. She runs the house and I go to my clubs – between work, of course. It's the perfect set-up, works wonders.

'True, you have a good marriage. But *if* and *when* I choose to marry, I want to share *all* my interests with my wife. I should be able to converse with her about all kinds of subjects other than housework.'

James raised his tankard, his face flushed and jolly. 'Slàinte Mhath [good health].'

Anthony touched his tankard to James', laughing. 'Slàinte Mhath, Uncle. And here's to freedom.'

As the pair gulped their ale, Anthony thought about his day ahead. He was due to accompany his mother to her meeting at the bank in two hours. *Mm*, he thought, I'll set Mother straight about this Julianne business.

'Freedom,' said James. 'Not a word to your mother.'

On that same Wednesday afternoon, in an upmarket townhouse on Royal Circus, Cynthia and Angela fastened their bonnets ahead of their first outing in Edinburgh. The season's grand ball was taking place at the Assembly Rooms in two weeks – and Georgina's sister Mary had kindly arranged for her nieces to be fitted for ball gowns at Débutante, Madame Lafayette's dressmaking boutique. 'I think you'll suit emerald,' Cynthia said to her sister's reflection in the cheval mirror. 'It will match your eyes. I do wish I had such vivid eyes like yours.'

'Nonsense, you're the lucky one,' replied Angela. 'Name one girl who doesn't long to be blonde and pretty with *blue* eyes?' Cynthia and Angela did not look much alike. Angela was a few inches taller than Cynthia, with brunette hair and an olive-y complexion she inherited from her father's side. Whereas Cynthia was fair, like her mother.

'Oh, but I'd rather your exotic looks and…'

'Cynthia! Angela!' That was Georgina, calling from downstairs. 'Do hurry up, our coach will be here any minute.'

The Marchmonts had arrived in Edinburgh the previous evening following their four-day journey from the Highlands. The sisters should have felt exhausted after such a long haul, but they were too excited to surrender to tiredness. And besides, as their aunt Mary had stressed when she'd welcomed the Marchmonts at the Royal Circus abode:

'Nobody sleeps during the social season. *Edinburgh itself* doesn't sleep during the season.' Indeed, the family had already received a host of invites to dances, balls, formal dinners, soirees and afternoon teas. Cynthia and Angela had spent the entire morning helping Georgina organise the pile of invites into date order, with their first event being a soiree held by their father's old school pal, Lord Thomas Walker, next Saturday. The girls chatted enthusiastically about the festivities throughout the short coach journey to Madame Lafayette's shop on Fredrick Street.

Cynthia and Angela gasped when they stepped into Débutante. Upon a vast work bench lay heavy rolls of silk in the most exquisite colours, from sugary pinks and pastel blues to violet, mauve and reds as rich as claret. More rolls of fabric were piled high on shelves that lined the back wall. Two mannequins, each wearing ball gowns made from the shimmering fabrics, stood side by side on the shop floor. Jewelled purses and fans glittered behind the glass fronts of mahogany display cases. Neither Cynthia nor Angela had been in a dressmaker's this fancy before. 'Welcome to my humble abode,' said Madam Lafayette with a mischievous crackly laugh that belied her patrician features. Then, gazing at Cynthia, added: 'I've just taken delivery of some stunning sapphire silk. It'll complement your blue eyes beautifully. How blessed you are with your fair looks, mademoiselle.'

'See,' said Angela, giving her sister's ribs a dainty nudge, 'I told you so.'

All three women had a field day, trying on dress samples and discussing designs and the season's activities with Madam Lafayette and her team of assistants. Georgina's gown was to be made from ruby satin. Cynthia, after much deliberation, opted for the sapphire silk Madam Lafayette had recommended, and Angela would be in lilac velvet. All three gowns were to include embroidery, lace and pearl embellishments.

The Marchmont ladies stepped out of the shop into a glorious sunset; the sky looked to be strewn with silk found in Madam Lafayette's shop. Layer upon layer, roll after roll, unfurling in shades of mauve, violet

12

and claret, blending into tangerine, coral and honeysuckle. They stood still for a moment to marvel at the tableau. At the same time, a grand coach rolled into the street and came to a halt outside Débutante. The carriage door swung open and out stepped a well-dressed young man with hair like liquorice. Next, a billowing gown of pink lace emerged, its wearer an elaborate-bonneted woman. 'Georgina,' she cried, and Georgina clapped her hands to her face.

'Rosalind,' echoed Georgina, and the two women greeted each other with much hugging and kissing and chants of 'so good to see yous' and 'you're looking well', while Cynthia, Angela and the man watched, bemused. Although Cynthia's gaze was rather flickering on the man with the slick hair. *Oh my*, she thought, *he is handsome*, ravishingly *handsome*. Tall, with broad shoulders; beneath that frock coat, Cynthia envisioned the torso of Michelangelo's *David*. His eyes shone like hot tar. His stance was regal yet self-assured. *Hmm, I bet he's a rake. Or married. But, damn it, he's handsome.*

'So,' said Rosalind, when she and Georgina finally disconnected, 'this must be Cynthia and Angela?' Rosalind gently pressed a hand to her bosom as she addressed the sisters. Her middle and ring fingers were wreathed with gold. 'What beautiful young ladies you've become.' The girls giggled, both feeling bashful, albeit flattered. 'You girls probably don't remember my son –it has been an age since we met,' Rosalind continued, motioning at the man beside her, who, as though rehearsed, stepped forwards, removed his hat, and bowed to Cynthia as Rosalind recited: 'May I re-introduce my eldest son, Lord Anthony Sinclair.'

Charmed to meet you,' Anthony said, giving Cynthia a smile that revealed teeth as white and straight as piano keys. 'Please, do call me Anthony.'

Cynthia curtseyed, her legs hollow. Beneath her corset her heart bulged and thumped.

'Lady Cynthia Marchmont,' Cynthia replied. 'I'm honoured to meet you.'

CHAPTER THREE

DUCHESS ROSALIND SINCLAIR was a name oft mentioned in the Marchmont household. She and Georgina went way back. They were best friends in school and had remained close ever since, despite the hundreds of miles that separated them. The pair exchanged regular letters and telegrams on their birthdays. It had been almost eighteen years since the two families had met – when the Sinclairs spent Christmas in Wick – but as the duchess and Georgina stood chatting in Fredrick Street, they agreed it was as though no time had passed. 'Oh, you haven't changed one dot. You're still looking as young as ever,' the duchess told Georgina, who laughed then returned a similar remark to Rosalind.

Cynthia didn't recognise Anthony from the eleven-year-old boy she vaguely remembered playing Blind Man's Buff with on Christmas Day, 1825. She wondered why Mother hadn't spoken more about this dashing gent stood before her. While Georgina and Rosalind chattered on about fashion and shopping – 'You simply *must* go to Kennington & Jenner on Princes Street,' said Rosalind, 'that store stocks the finest linens and silks,' – and gossiped about who was stepping out with who – Anthony struck up conversation with Cynthia and Angela. He asked which attractions they planned to visit.

'Mother's taking us to Duddingston Village tomorrow to see relatives,' offered Angela. 'But we've heard the Royal Botanic Garden Edinburgh is glorious this time of year.'

'Indeed, it is,' replied Anthony, swallowing a yawn. He was feeling the after-lunch slump. Or was it those tankards of ale and drams he'd necked? 'The Scott Monument is also worth a visit. As too is St Giles Cathedral – both shining examples of magnificent architecture.'

'Our brother, Derek, wants to go to the Musselburgh race meeting next Monday,' said Cynthia, 'I'm hoping he'll let me tag along.'

'You're interested in racing?' asked Anthony. He sounded a little shocked.

Cynthia's face broke into a dreamy smile. 'Oh, I adore horses. At home I ride every day – well, when the weather is fine, that is. Recently it was horrid, and we were stuck indoors for days and days, and poor Snowy – she's my horse – was left all alone in her stable and…' The words avalanched out of Cynthia's mouth. The longer Anthony remained silent, the more garrulous she became. *Snowy this, Snowy that.* God, she was nervous. '…And I miss her [Snowy] dreadfully,' she added and felt her face turn ruby. 'Snowy is due to arrive in Edinburgh in a few weeks, so I suppose I'll have to bide my time until then, but Derek says there are some delightful trails around the city which offer views often missed in a carriage.' Cynthia bowed her head, relieved to finally cease talking.

'Well, if you are interested, you could ride one of my horses until Snowy arrives,' said Anthony. His comment surprised him; it wasn't like Anthony to make gallant gestures to young women as he feared his words would translate to, 'Will you marry me?' in their ears. But there was something fresh and modern about Cynthia that appealed to Anthony. She didn't strike him as being precious or conceited like other aristocratic ladies he knew. Plus, he was rather struck by Cynthia's beauty. Her pale face was like fine bone china, framed by light golden ringlets, and her eyes sparkled as she spoke.

Cynthia laughed. It sounded like pins jangling in a crystal glass, thought Anthony. 'But you don't even know if I can ride. For all you know I might be hopeless.'

'Are you?' Anthony asked, raising his left brow.

"No, I'm quite a good horsewoman actually. So, if you're serious, I would love to accept your kind offer.'

'Of course,' said Anthony. 'My mother would have my hide if I did not offer. I shall send word when I have time in the next few days to take you to the stables, if this is convenient?'

'That would be lovely, thank you.' Said Cynthia, her cheeks flushing again.

'Goodness, I don't mean to be rude,' Rosalind cut in, 'but we really must make haste. I have an appointment with my bank manager, and he's staying behind after closing time to accommodate my schedule. I wouldn't want to keep him waiting.'

'Not at all, my dear,' said Georgina, 'Please, hurry along. We'll catch up properly at Lord Walker's on Saturday. I hear his daughter's coming out then, too.'

'Yes,' said Rosalind, 'I hear Julianne's quite a catch.'

'Come along, Mother, dear,' said Anthony, offering his right arm to Rosalind. 'We mustn't keep Mr Fitzsimmons waiting.' He bowed to the Marchmont women. 'It's an absolute pleasure to be reacquainted with you all. I wish you a fine evening.' Then he put on his hat and steered Rosalind downhill towards Queen Street.

'Oh, what a charming, handsome man Anthony has become,' said Georgina as the Marchmonts walked to their awaiting carriage.

'Yes,' said Angela, 'I think Cynthia's rather smitten.'

'I most certainly am *not* smitten,' scoffed Cynthia. But her words and tone betrayed her true sentiments.

'Oh, sorry, sister dear. I thought I saw you blushing while engaging with Lord Sinclair. My mistake. How can you ever forgive me?'

'Very handsome indeed,' added Georgina.

Stanley Fitzsimmons, manager of Saltire Bank welcomed Rosalind and Anthony into his office with an exaggerated bow. 'Lady Sinclair, Lord Sinclair' he said, 'always a pleasure to see you both. Please, do be seated. How may I help you today?'

'I've noticed some irregularities in our account,' said Rosalind, lowering herself sideways onto the settee in her cumbersome skirts. As a widow – the duke had died of consumption two years previous – Rosalind was allowed access to her late husband's account.

'Irregularities? What kind of irregularities?' said Anthony from the other end of the settee.

Rosalind folded her hands in her lap. 'It appears some money has gone missing.'

'How do you mean, missing?' said Mr. Fitzsimmons, his knees clicking as he took his seat in a desk chair. Tall and wire-thin, every movement Mr. Fitzsimmons made was audible. He felt a surge of panic rise in his chest. Was Lady Sinclair, one of his richest customers, suggesting he was involved in the misappropriation of funds?

'Exactly how much money is missing, Mother?' Anthony demanded.

Rosalind pursed her lips and lightly touched the feathers on her bonnet, as though to make sure they were still there. 'Well, it appears to be almost eighty pounds in total – made up of a few withdrawals over the last day or two.'

'And why have you not mentioned this situation to me hitherto?' asked Anthony.

'Shh, keep your voice down. I don't want the whole of Edinburgh knowing my business,' said Rosalind. 'I thought it best to ask Mr. Fitzsimmons to check the account himself before I made a song and dance about it. I might have misread the figures. Which is very possible.'

Mr. Fitzsimmons cleared his throat as he rose from his chair. 'Excuse me, but allow me to retrieve your file, your Ladyship. I do not understand how this could have happened but be assured, I will get to the bottom of it,' he said, and clickety-clacked out of the room.

Twenty minutes later, Mr. Fitzsimmons returned, armed with Lady Sinclair's file, from which he extracted a bundle of cheques. He handed the pile to Rosalind. 'As you can see,' he explained as Rosalind sifted through the cheques, small gasps escaping her lips, 'these cheques were presented for withdrawals of funds – and seemingly signed by yourself, my Lady.'

'It certainly *looks* like my signature,' Rosalind conceded, 'But I assure you, I did *not* sign those cheques. If you compare the signatures on these cheques with a previous document, you'll note my R in Rosalind has two loops. In all of these signatures, the R has just one loop.'

Rosalind passed one of the cheques to Anthony, who agreed the handwriting was very similar to his mother's signature while also recognising that the R was, indeed, not quite as elaborate.

Mr. Fitzsimmons leafed through more documents in the duchess' file and produced another slip of paper. 'Here's a cheque from last year,' he said, 'Let's compare the two.' Anthony passed him the recent cheque and Mr. Fitzsimmons placed them side by side on the table. 'My goodness,' he said at length, 'at a fleeting glance you certainly wouldn't notice the difference. I must say, this is a very good copy.' Mr. Fitzsimmons laced his fingers tightly in front of him. His knuckles cracked. 'But I'm afraid that is exactly what it is – a copy. Somebody has forged your signature, Lady Sinclair. I shall report this to the police immediately.'

'No, wait,' said Anthony, holding his hands up in protest. 'I would like to investigate this matter first.' Until six months ago, Anthony had spent a two-year spell working as an investigator for the Foreign Office, which had seen him lead many covert operations resulting in villains being brought to justice. At least, that was his job according on paper – and according to the general public. In fact, the foreign office title had been a ruse for his real role as a spy for the government. 'If the police get involved, it will alert the culprit and they'll go to ground. And besides, I think our embezzler could be closer to home than we realise.'

Rosalind clapped her hands to her cheeks. 'What are you saying, Anthony?'

'Sadly, I feel the culprit must be an insider, Mother. Somebody who could gain access to your personal effects, for example. Somebody who knows what your signature looks like.'

'I agree,' added Mr. Fitzsimmons. 'Else, it could be somebody here, at the bank. Clearly, our clerks know your signature, my Lady. But I can't think who would do such a thing.'

The three of them fell silent for a moment as they considered the possibilities. Outside, the continuous sound of hooves clopping cobbles. Horse-drawn carriages delivering Edinburgh's finest to soirees. An orange glow filled the office window, signalling that the gas lighters had started work. 'Right then,' said Anthony, rising, straight as a soldier from the settee. The sounds of nightlife warming up had reminded him of the celebratory dinner he hoped to share with one of his mistresses, whom, he'd decided, would be Marianne. Where had the day gone? He hadn't yet confronted Mother over her meddling in his love life. He didn't suppose now was the right time to do so, either. His upbeat mood from that morning seemed a distant memory now. And why did Cynthia's face keep reappearing in his mind? 'Thank you for your time, Mr. Fitzsimmons. If sir permits, I would like to take one of these forged cheques – so I can compare the handwriting to that of Mother's staff.'

'I beg your pardon?' said Rosalind. She sounded horrified and curious in equal measure. 'Surely you're not suggesting one of my loyal staff has stolen from us?'

Anthony shrugged and spread his hands. 'Not everybody is as loyal and honest as you think they are, Mother.'

CHAPTER FOUR

TWO DAYS LATER, Anthony's butler, Graham, delivered to his master's study a list containing the names of Lady Sinclair's staff, from the core servants working at her four-storey townhouse in Edinburgh's Heriot Row, to the extra workers based at her other estates throughout Scotland. All employees were eventually to be questioned concerning the cheques bearing the duchess' forged signature.

The list, which Anthony had instructed his mother to compile, included notes on each worker: their position, how long they'd worked for the family, and the areas to which they had regular access within the properties. Studying the names, Anthony noted that three staff members – a kitchen maid, laundry maid and a footman – had been in the Sinclair household for less than a year, so he underlined their names and made a note to examine references from their previous employers – and to visit those employers if necessary. He thought it unlikely the maids were involved, simply because few women were allowed to bank, but that wasn't to say they hadn't employed a man to do the deed on their behalf. Meanwhile, an hour earlier, Mr. Fitzsimmons had sent word that new information regarding the cheques had come to light after speaking with his employees, so Anthony had sent his secretary, Michael, to the bank to investigate. *This is a mess I could do without*, thought Anthony, folding the list and slipping it in the inside pocket of his frock coat. Then he headed downstairs, where Graham was waiting in the vestibule. He handed Anthony his cane and top hat. 'Does sir require me to make luncheon reservations?' he asked.

'The No 1. Club. I shall meet my good friends Bill and Ron there at half past noon,' replied Anthony, referring to his favourite gentlemen's-only club on Queen Street, where only the elite of Edinburgh's society was welcome. 'But first, send word to Michael. Ask him to meet me at my mother's townhouse on Heriot Row as soon as he's finished at the bank.'

'Certainly sir,' said Graham as he stepped forth and opened the front door. 'And do have a good day, sir.'

Anthony tipped his hat and headed out into the blustery morning. There was no need for a carriage today as it was just a five-minute walk from Moray Place to Heriot Row. However, the weather had turned dramatically in the last two days, and the bracing wind bit Anthony's cheeks. He walked at a rapid pace with determined strides, golden leaves crunching underfoot, his mind awhirl with thoughts of who the thief might be…and luncheon at the No. 1 club.

Anthony had been at his mother's less than an hour when her butler, Gerald, led Michael into the drawing room on the second floor. Michael joined Anthony and Rosalind around the walnut table and, once Gerald was safely out of the room, relayed the information afforded from his meeting with Mr. Fitzsimmons at the bank. 'A cashier has come forward,' he said, his voice an exaggerated whisper.

Anthony grabbed the decanter and filled three glasses with brandy. 'Go on,' he told Michael, pushing a glass of the amber spirit his way.

Michael took a glug, enjoying the warm sensation as it slid down his throat. Drinking fine brandy before noon on a Friday was a rare pursuit for him. He took another sip and continued. 'The cheques. The ones holding the Lady's forged signature…' he paused to gesture politely at Rosalind, who replied with a silent nod and reached for her brandy. She was on her second glass – *Medicinal, for the shock of it all* – and was beginning to feel a little floaty. '…Well, the cashier confirmed it was a man, and not Rosalind, who cashed the cheques. The cashier – a gentleman who's fairly new to the job – was unable to provide much of a description of this man, other than he was of "average height and build".

'Did the cashier not ask for the man's name?' said Anthony, extracting the list from his inside pocket.

'Apparently not. On each occasion the cheques had been signed. The cashier was confident that the signature matched Lady Sinclair's handwriting, so didn't think to query the matter.'

Anthony unfolded the parchment and lay it on the table. 'Well, unless this man was acting on behalf of another – unless he was merely the messenger – I suppose that means we can eliminate any women suspects from our inquiry,' he said, again scanning the list. 'And I think I know who we should question first.'

Anthony got up and rang the internal bell system. Seconds later, Gerald appeared.

'You rang, my lady,' he announced, his chin held at a perfect right angle to his chest.

'Gerald,' said Anthony, 'please fetch me your footman, Keith Watson.' Which elicited a sharp gasp from Rosalind.

'Surely you don't suspect…' she said, her voice shuddering. The door clicked shut and Gerald's footsteps faded along the hallway and down the stairs. '…Why, he's a loyal young man. He has a wife and child, so I'm led to believe.'

Keith Watson walked into the drawing room, his face pale and shiny as a peeled onion. Anthony noticed the footman's bony hands were shaking at the side of his thighs. 'Mr Watson, we have a problem,' Anthony announced. 'Several cheques have been stolen from my mother's desk and were subsequently cashed at the bank.' Keith looked nervously around the room, unable to maintain eye-contact with Anthony. 'Now, only a few people who work in this property has access to Mother's desk – yourself included. So, if you have any knowledge of whom could be responsible for this theft, now is the time to speak up.'

'Erm…I…well…the…' Keith's words caught in his throat. He looked at his shoes.

'Bearing in mind the truth will come out eventually,' added Anthony. Silence. Then Keith's shoulders began to shake violently as his chest and breath heaved in and out.

'Oh sir,' he croaked between hard gulps. 'I'm so sorry. He made me do it. He's holding my wife and child hostage. He came to my door a few nights ago and said he would kill me and my family if I didn't get him the money, then I stepped outside the door, and he punched me here.' Keith pointed to a spot on the left side of his head. 'He must have been wearing a big ring because I have a deep cut, beneath my hair. I was out cold, then when I came to, it was too late. Now he's holding my family hostage in our home. He's barred the door. Please… you must believe me.' The servant dropped to his knees and sobbed into his hands. 'Please believe me.'

'So, you admit you committed this crime?' Anthony's voice boomed around the room, the crystal glasses singing delicately from the vibrations. He shot from his seat and made two forceful strides to where Keith knelt. You *stole* from my mother?'

'Please,' said Keith, his face slick with tears as he looked up at Anthony. 'I took the money to him, but he said he would kill me if I told you. He still has my wife and son. Please, you have to believe me.'

Rosalind drained her glass – *that will help ease the shock* – and addressed the footman. 'Who is this man, and where is he keeping your family?' she said magnanimously. The footman's behaviour was enough to convince her he was telling the truth.

'He's holed up in our digs – on The Canongate – and barred the door. I can't get in to see them, and he won't give me access until I've done the deed. I don't know who he is. His face was covered when he first demanded the money. Then, he would only speak to me from behind the door – from inside my home, where he's keeping my wife, Ruby, and my wee boy, Alan. He made me slip the money under the door.'

'But you've done the deed…you've cashed the cheques. What more does this man want?' demanded Anthony.

'I don't know,' sobbed Keith, 'But he has my family. And I'm stuck. I can't save them. And I couldn't tell you, because I can't lose my job. And I couldn't tell the police as they would put me in prison – and then what would happen to my poor wife and son. I couldn't abandon them. But please, believe me. I am no thief, sir.' Keith rubbed away his tears with the heels of his hands and turned to face Rosalind. 'I'm so terribly sorry, ma'am. But he does have my family. I didn't know what else to do…'

Rosalind nodded. 'I believe you.'

'Right, let's bring this brute to book,' said Anthony, relenting. He turned to his secretary. 'Michael, pour this man a brandy. Then, I'll need a strong team. Fetch me Bill and Ronald. They're due at the No. 1 Club on Queen Street at half past noon. Tell them lunch is postponed due to an emergency.'

'Will do, sir,' replied Michael.

While Michael went to find the two men, Anthony slipped into his late father's study and took from the desk drawer a double-barrelled flintlock pistol. *For protection*, Anthony told himself. *Just in case this escalates into a life-or-death scenario.*

Bill and Ronald arrived, also armed with pistols. After a brief discussion in the drawing room, Anthony, Bill, Ron and Keith set off on horseback to The Canongate. And what happened next happened fast. When they reached the tenement, they jumped off their horses and tied them to posts at the back of the building. Keith led the men into the tenement. Inside it was dark and damp. Pained sounds echoed in the stairwell, coming from above. Muffled screams and sobbing. Anthony was first to charge up the stairs, drawing his pistol from his coat. Keith followed, his heart thumping with fear and dread and hope. Behind him Bill and Ron, also brandishing their pistols. Up to Keith's flat on the second floor. 'The door, it's open,' said Keith, pointing shakily over Anthony's shoulder at the slightly ajar door, emitting a slice of light and the haunting sobbing sounds, which grew louder as Anthony led the way to the flat at the end of the corridor. Then, in one swift movement, Anthony pushed open the door and powered into the flat, his pistol in his outstretched hand, ready to shoot. Keith, Bill and Ron followed Anthony into the sparsely furnished room, where they found a woman and child, bound, gagged, sobbing and shaking violently. They had been tied together with heavy rope and left in a kneeling position on the stone floor. 'Oh my God, Ruby, Alan,' cried Keith. He flew across the room, grabbed a knife that was lying on the table alongside Ruby and Alan – a knife that Keith did not recognise as one of his own – and cut his wife and son free. As the family hugged and sobbed, Anthony's gaze fell upon a note pinned on the wall. A note addressed to *him*. He ripped it from the wall. It said:

ANTHONY SINCLAIR,
THIS IS ONLY THE BEGINNING.
ARE YOU SCARED? YOU SHOULD BE.
I'M WATCHING YOU. SEE YOU SOON.

'What is it, Anthony?' asked Bill.

'What does it say?' added Ron.

Anthony angled the paper so his friends could surreptitiously read the note without alerting the footman and his family to it.

'What does this mean?' said Bill, an expression of puzzlement swathing his face.

'God knows,' said Anthony with a nod towards the Watson family. 'Let's talk about it later.'

After a few minutes, Ruby and Alan had calmed enough to speak about their terrifying ordeal. They couldn't, however, provide much of a description of their captor as he'd kept his face covered with a tied handkerchief. Although Alan, no older than eight, recalled the man had been wearing a gold ring with a 'huge green stone' on his right little finger.

'What will happen now?' asked Keith, still huddled with his wife and son on the floor. 'Will you go to the police? What will happen to my job?'

Anthony slipped his pistol into his coat pocket with a sigh. 'Ruby, Alan, if you remember anything else about this man, do let us know immediately. I see no reason to contact the police. I'd rather solve this case myself. As for your job, Keith, I suggest you speak to my mother but, given the circumstances, I'm sure we'll be able to come to an arrangement.'

Keith brushed away a tear. 'Thank you so much, sir…for everything.'

Anthony, Ron, and William returned to Heriot Row to brief Rosalind on the afternoon's events, although Anthony deliberately declined to tell her about the threatening note. Best not to worry her, he thought. Shocked to discover the trauma Keith's wife and son endured, Rosalind said she would allow Keith to stay on at the Sinclair residence but would deduct the stolen funds, over time, from his wages. 'But who is this man who demanded the money from the footman?' she asked Anthony. 'And what if he tries this again? Or does worse. Are we in danger?'

Anthony placed a reassuring hand on Rosalind's shoulder. 'The matter is in hand, Mother,' he lied. 'We know who this man is, and he will be punished accordingly. Nobody steals from the Sinclairs. Mark. My. Words.'

The truth was, Anthony hadn't a clue who the kidnapper, with his big green ring, could be, but he would make damn sure he found out. On his way home, Anthony called in to see his former handler, Sir John Ritchie, at the basement bureau in St Andrew's Square that masqueraded as the Foreign Office's Scottish headquarters. Bill, who had also worked as a secret agent, accompanied Anthony to the meeting. They discussed cases with which Anthony had been involved and even compiled a list of villains he'd snared – people who might have nefarious contacts willing to exact revenge on him. 'Let me go through some records,' John told Anthony, 'see if we can link this green ring to anybody. In the meantime, I'll put a few men out to watch you and your family, especially your mother.'

'Good idea,' said Anthony.

'This green ring. It does ring a bell,' Bill cut in, 'but for the life of me I can't think why. Maybe it'll come to me over the next few days.'

'Keep me posted,' added John.

The kidnap and theft and the mystery man with a ring on his little finger was all Anthony, Bill and Ron could talk about that evening over malt whiskies at the No.1 club. They scrutinised the note, hoping to glean some clues from it. Later, they were joined by former 'foreign office' colleagues Alistair Murdoch and Grant Thomson, who was still serving as an agent.

'You've bought a lot of land recently, Anthony. Is there anybody you might have upset in your business dealings?' asked Alistair, which sparked much laughter around the table, for Anthony had a reputation for being ruthless when it came to business and money matters, hence he was one of the richest men in Britain.

'I'd be surprised if I hadn't upset a few men over the years,' said Anthony with a wry smile. 'I even upset my own family. Take my cousin Stewart, for example. I'm always putting his nose out of joint.' Indeed, sadly there was no love lost between the cousins. Stewart was profoundly jealous of Anthony's success, even though Anthony had helped his younger relative out of many a tight spot financially. Not that Stewart appreciated being bailed out; he was often found in the city's betting dens and whore houses, squandering the family's money. He was a total wastrel who associated with some very dubious characters.

'Do you think Stewart could be involved?' asked Grant, lighting his pipe.

'Good grief, no,' said Anthony, who recoiled in his seat at the very suggestion. 'Stewart might be a bit of a scoundrel, but he's my flesh and blood. And why steal from us when we're constantly giving him handouts?'

'Hmm,' went Grant, inhaling. 'I see.' He exhaled, his words accompanied by a plume of smoke.

'Another bottle of malt?' said Ron, and so the festivities continued into the night. A pleasant night at that, even in the shadow of the mystery man. The food and malts in the club were second to none, and a few good gents were always willing to hedge their bets on the card tables.

Despite being well-oiled when they left the club, Anthony, Bill and Ron agreed it would be rude not to continue their deliberations over a nightcap, so they retired to Anthony's townhouse in Moray Place. After all, it had been quite a day, and it was the start of the season, and everyone who was anyone in Edinburgh was partying through the night just now. But discussions about the footman, stolen money, hostage situation and even that elusive man were superseded by talk about the season's upcoming soirees – and women.

Graham had left a pile of invitations for Anthony in his study. And could sir possibly peruse said invites and leave a note for Michael indicating which events he wished to attend, Graham had requested. It was just after midnight, and still the three men were deliberating their social prospects over a fine bottle of brandy.

'Right,' Ron had declared, flicking through the invites, 'Let's stick together on this. I say we go to the same balls and soirees as a team. That way, all the fuss from the desperate mamas and their ardent daughters will be divided between the three of us.' He shuddered, visibly and audibly, and they all burst out laughing.

'Honestly, you would think we were facing the guillotine, not an introduction to a potential wife,' quipped Bill.

Ron pulled a face that was somewhere between a smirk and a grimace. 'Well, it feels like it to me. My mother is hounding me to find a bride this season. She thinks I am getting too old to still play the field. Which, seemingly, is fine for my younger brother to do, but not me. My job, says mother, is to produce an heir and her grandchild.'

'Tell me about it,' said Anthony. 'My mother has hinted at fixing me up with a bride – including Lord Walker's daughter, Julianne, who…'

'My mother is also trying to set *me* up with,' finished Bill.

Ron laughed. 'Pistols at dawn, gents?'

'Hey, remember you both promised to come with me to Lord Walker's ball,' said Bill, indicating his two friends with his brandy glass.

'Ha, more likely we were coerced into it,' Anthony shot back.

'Well, we'll need to go to the opening ball at the Assembly Rooms,' added Ron. 'Then there's my sister's coming out ball at our house – I've already accepted the invite for you both.'

'Fine,' said Anthony, 'but I want to go to the masked ball at Bute House. That's always a good night to meet a married lady – because her husband is usually up to no good too.'

A bottle of port was opened. More invites were scrutinised, and

28

suddenly, the events of the day were a distant, brandy-and-malt-tinged blur – for now.

Anthony woke early the next morning with two thoughts on his mind: *Exactly who is this evil sneaksman who dares prey on my family? And why am I still in my study, wearing last night's clothes?*

Anthony was prostrate on the chaise lounge, one leg on it, one leg off it. Right shoe on, left shoe off. His hair was a matted mess and tangled in his usually neat sideburns. He was sweating pure brandy; he could smell it oozing from his pores. Anthony lifted his head – that hurt – and slowly sat up, squinting at the beam of dawn sunlight, sharp as a sword stabbing his eyes through the gap between the shutters. He took a moment to make a mental document of the previous night's activities and to figure out what day it was. Where were Ron and Bill? They must have left but Anthony didn't recall them saying goodbye – or leaving for that matter. 'It's Saturday,' Anthony said out loud. Then he suddenly remembered he'd made arrangements to meet the gents at Holyrood Park for a ride and to exchange updates – if any - on their inquiry into the threatening notes and mystery man. Anthony also recalled he was due to see Cynthia Marchmont this afternoon. He had sent word to the Marchmont household on Thursday, inviting the lady and her brother to his stables, followed by a ride on a horse of her choice. Just as he'd promised to do so when he'd met her on Fredrick Street. His pocket watch told him he had approximately fifty minutes to wash and change, get to the mews and make it to Holyrood Park. He stood up, wearily, and pulled the bell cord. Graham. He needed Graham.

CHAPTER FIVE

AFTER A BATH, a swift dram and a blast of fresh air, Anthony felt decidedly better. He even made it to Holyrood Park with a few minutes to spare. Now he was raring to go – and keen to find out whether his friends, particularly Grant or Alistair, had unearthed any potential leads as to whom this man with the green ring could be.

Riding their horses at a slow trot, the men discussed the case, lowering their voices every time they passed the occasional fellow morning rider or a courting couple strolling in the crisp autumn weather. However, there appeared to be no fresh information to work with as yet. Grant said he'd quizzed colleagues at the Foreign Office about a 'chap sporting a ring with a huge green stone,' only to be greeted with blank expressions. 'Don't worry though,' assured Grant, 'We're still working on this. I've enlisted some men to delve into some of your previous cases, Anthony. You've put away some highly dangerous villains over the years, so we're looking for anyone who has recently been set free from prison.'

Anthony nodded. 'My thoughts exactly.'

'Oh,' added Grant, 'I'm also hoping Ian Robertson, a highly regarded foreign office minister, will shed some light on this case. He's out of town this weekend but he's expected back on Monday. I'll report back to you.'

'A few contacts of mine are also on their way to Edinburgh as we speak,' said Alistair, 'so I'll be asking around for you. I also told my informants there was a reward for any information leading to the identity of this man with the green ring.

'Indeed, money does talk in the Old Town,' said Ron.

Bill laughed. 'Yes, I know folk who'll sell their granny for a bottle of whiskey.'

'Well. Thanks for your efforts, chaps,' said Anthony, 'Let's meet at the club next week for an update.' Then his face suddenly brightened. 'But that's enough work for today. Who fancies a race around Arthur's Seat?'

'Hurrah, let's go,' Bill shot back, already accelerating his mare to a canter.

'Ten shillings a man – winner takes all?' shouted Ron, and the others hollered their assent as they took off, cantering then galloping up the winding frosty path that led to the extinct volcano. A perilous pursuit for some, but the men were expert riders who invested in horses and installs, both in Edinburgh and at their Scottish estates. The steeds they were riding today were by no means their top mounts, but still fine stock who looked magnificent while going full pelt and carrying such handsome gents. The race, as usual, was close and competitive with Anthony and Bill neck and neck at the front of the group, closely followed by Grant, then Ron in fourth place, and Alistair bringing up the rear as they reached the summit. As they began their descent, Ron overtook Grant, but Bill and Anthony were still leading the race – until, from nowhere, Bill and his horse powered ahead to victory. He was delighted; it had a been a while since he'd beaten Anthony, who was quick to delve into his pocket and pay Bill his winnings – as did Grant, Ron and Alistair. The gents were in high spirits when they parted company. Anthony returned to Moray Place to change ahead of his appointment with Cynthia and Derek. He felt rejuvenated, albeit disappointed regarding the progress of the anonymous notes and green-ring-man probe. *I'll get to the bottom of this. Nobody messes with a Sinclair…nobody,* Anthony vowed, as he hurried up the steps to his townhouse.

Cynthia was already dressed in her riding gear when Anthony arrived. Unbeknownst to him, she had tried on four different outfits before finally settling on the one she was sporting now: an ivory and burgundy striped silk skirt, teamed with a bone white blouse with a Prussian blue neck bow that matched her velvet jacket. Beneath her skirt she wore beige wash leather drawers. Kidskin gauntlets and a topper with a plume and ribbons completed her look. She felt her heart race just being in close proximity to Anthony again. It wasn't just his looks – his fine, even features and glossy hair that enchanted her. No, it was more than that. It was the way that he held himself: straight-backed, authoritative, but with so much charisma. Cynthia suspected he'd made love to many women. *What must it be like to make love?* She mused as she watched Anthony step into his carriage. She was all aquiver just picturing his bare chest. However, she quickly pushed those thoughts to the back of her mind. There was no point her falling for a rake. And besides, her brother Derek was accompanying her on this outing.

Derek and Cynthia followed Anthony in their carriage, taking in a ride around Stockbridge village and Inverleith before finally arriving at the mews in Gloucester Square, where Anthony stabled his horses. Anthony helped Cynthia down from the carriage and led her to the first box, inside which was a beautiful black filly. 'This is Misty. She's a three-year-old filly,' said Anthony, beaming. He patted the horse's head and she let out an affectional snort. 'I thought you could borrow her until your horse arrives. But, if she's too lively, I can show you another?' Anthony gestured along the line of stables.

'Oh no, she's beautiful,' replied Cynthia, reaching to stroke Misty's nose. 'I hope she takes to me.'

'I'm sure she will,' said Anthony. 'She's in need of a good ride out. I'll get her saddled-up.' Next, Anthony turned to Derek. 'The horse in box six will probably suit you.'

Derek tipped his hat to Anthony. 'Good show, my friend.'

Soon, the trio were on their way, starting slow, then giving the horses their heads, before slowing to a trot as they rode into Inverleith, via Stockbridge, which was soon to be part of Edinburgh city. Derek suggested they stop at Goldenacre Green as he'd heard of a lovely little tea shop there. 'Good idea,' said Anthony. Over lunch – a delicious spread of triangle sandwiches and velvety cakes, accompanied by pots of Earl Grey tea – Cynthia thanked Anthony for loaning her Misty.

'I love her. She's beautiful to ride,' gushed Cynthia.

Anthony flashed Cynthia a bright smile. 'That was quite a speed you reached back there. I'm impressed. You are, as you say, quite a good horsewoman.'

Cynthia blushed over her lifted cup. 'Well, there's not much else to do in Caithness except horse-riding and walking – depending on the weather, mind you.'

Anthony nodded, and mentioned, in passing, his recent procurement of the Girnigoe Estate, before turning to Derek. 'So, Derek, fine chap. Cynthia says you're going to the race meeting at Musselburgh on Monday.'

'Indeed, I intend to,' said Derek, casting his sister a sideways playful grin. 'Cynthia's been dropping the biggest hints about tagging along too.'

'Well, I have a box I've hired, along with some friends, at the races on Monday. Why don't you both join us for lunch – and your sister Angela, too, if she wishes? There's plenty of space.' The words spilled from Anthony's mouth without thought, which was unusual for him. He was not in the habit of inviting young debutantes- to share his box at the races, but he was rather enjoying Cynthia's company. She didn't appear clingy in the slightest, which made for a refreshing change. Derek seemed like a decent chap, too. And besides, the Marchmonts were close family friends, and he hadn't thought about the threatening note or the man with the green ring in the time he'd been with Cynthia and Derek.

Cynthia put down her cup and clapped her hands, daintily. 'Oh, we should love to come. How very kind of you to invite us.'

'Grand, I shall pick you all up at noon on Monday,' said Anthony.

'Perfect. I'm so looking forward to it,' beamed Cynthia.

After lunch, the trio enjoyed a fast ride for most of the way back to Gloucester Street, where they dismounted and walked their horses through a throng of Anthony's acquaintances and admirers, chiefly females of marriageable age, who batted their eyelashes at him, as their mammas stood by, firing questions at Anthony to find out which balls and soirees he would be attending. Cynthia thought he dealt with the onslaught in the most gentlemanly manner, bowing politely and introducing her and Derek to his admirers. Cynthia was secretly pleased to notice the envious looks the women cast her way. She was even more delighted to hear Anthony's reply to one mama's question: 'Lord Walker? Why yes, I shall be attending his ball this evening.' A tingle of anticipation rippled through the pit of her stomach as they continued forth to the stables, where Cynthia and Derek's carriage awaited them.

'I trust you are going to Lord Walker's ball tonight?' asked Anthony, offering his hand to help Cynthia onto the carriage step.

'Absolutely, Angela and I can't wait. It shall be our first ball of the season,' said Cynthia, and, looking up at Anthony, had a sudden flashback to the list she'd written and burned just ten days ago in Caithness: *Heart-stopping handsome though not conceited. Lucious dark hair. Intense eyes. Gosh*, thought Cynthia, *did I have a premonition?*

'Grand. I look forward to seeing you all this evening,' said Anthony. He bowed his head, then assisted Cynthia into her carriage. Derek followed and closed the door behind him. Anthony waved at the departing carriage, then headed through the gate to the path that led directly to his townhouse. He felt different. A little smitten, dare he say? He quickly summoned to his mind an image of Marianne in her chemise. *Don't be a fool, Anthony. Freedom is everything.* Anthony entered his mansion, handed his hat and crop to Graham, strode down the hall and went into the library. Michael was in there, sitting behind the desk, his face grave as he held an envelope aloft. A sudden heat prickled Anthony's face and travelled downwards, like molten lava flowing through his veins. He stood there wordless, staring at the envelope.

'I think you should read this,' said Michael.

CHAPTER SIX

'OH, ANGELA,' cried Cynthia as she hurried into her sister's bedroom, her face still pinking from her bracing horse ride with Anthony and Derek, 'Angela, quick, wake up.'

'Argh, what time is it?' croaked Angela. She rolled over, blinking, seeing just a sliver of Cynthia's skirt as she half-skipped over to the bed. Angela had been resting ahead of Lord Walker's ball later that evening. Unlike Cynthia, Angela always heeded their mother's advice when it came to resting: *A young woman must always look her very best. Fresh and radiant. Never tired.* Angela rubbed her eyes, sat up and patted the bed. 'Sit down,' she said, yawning, 'do tell all. You're clearly excited.'

Cynthia sat on the edge of the bed. 'Oh Angela, I've had the most marvellous day. Derek and I went riding with Lord Anthony,' she gushed. 'He lent me a lovely horse called Misty. She was just right in temperament. Then we had lunch, with the most perfect little triangle sandwiches and as much tea as we liked. And you'll never guess what happened next?'

Angela shook her head. 'No, do tell.' She was fully awake. No chance of going back to sleep now.

'Lord Anthony has invited us all to the Musselburgh races on Monday – to have lunch with him in his private box. And he's picking us up in his carriage. And, Angela, you should've seen him when we returned. There was a huge crowd of young ladies – like us, with their mamas and they were all vying for the Lord's attention and he looked so dreamy and …'

'Wait, slow down,' giggled Angela as Cynthia's voice rose another octave, her words demi-semi quavers, 'start from the beginning. I want to know every single detail. *Definitely no chance of sleeping now.*

So, Cynthia again relayed the events of the last few hours, in great detail, from their ride through Stockbridge to snippets of conversation shared over lunch, with Anthony's name mentioned at least once in every sentence. 'Anthony says he's got one younger brother called Giles and a sister, Susanne. And you should see Anthony's stables,' Cynthia enthused. 'Anthony has a fantastic success rating with his racehorses, not to mention a healthy return on his stud farms in the borders.' Angela's eyes widened with each revelation. 'And Anthony's just bought an estate in Caithness, you know,' finished Cynthia, clasping her hands over her heart.

'And Anthony is one of Edinburgh's most eligible gentlemen – albeit a rake?'

'Hmm,' replied Cynthia, 'but he didn't strike me as such today. And he is rather handsome, don't you think?'

'He certainly is handsome – and what a body.' Angela blushed at her comment, a conscious thought that escaped her mouth before she could edit it.

'Good grief, Angela, you shouldn't be saying such things.'

'Well, it's true,' said Angela. She pushed back her quilt and moved to the edge of the bed next to Cynthia. 'Don't tell me you haven't noticed.'

'Well,' mused Cynthia, Michelangelo's *David* appearing in her mind again. Only Cynthia's version was alive, with thick black hair and real, warm skin. He had Anthony's face, too.

'But I don't want you to get hurt,' said Angela, her voice serious for a moment. 'Every debutante in Edinburgh wants to marry Lord Anthony Sinclair. And every mother wants him to marry their daughter.'

Cynthia sighed. 'I know, but that's not to say I can't enjoy his company while I can. I can have some fun without falling for him. Just you keep warning me not to fall for him.' The sisters sat in silence for a few seconds, both of them staring at the ornate blue china bowl and pitcher on the washstand.

'Will Anthony be at Lord Walker's ball tonight?' asked Angela.

'Yes, he will,' said Cynthia, her eyes dancing.

Angela giggled. 'Then you best make haste and dress for the occasion.'

Cynthia gave her sister's hand a squeeze. 'I have just the dress,' she said, and then she was on her feet, fleeing the room as fast as she'd entered it.

Cynthia's maid Lily helped her to dress for the ball. She brushed and styled Cynthia's hair, curling it into the neatest, shiniest ringlets which she then adorned with glistening jewels. Next, Lily assisted Cynthia into her dress, which was mint green with a ruffled skirt decorated with light pink satin roses. Her final touch was to spritz Cynthia's gloves, purse and silk handkerchief with Otto of Roses perfume. Cynthia gasped when Lily turned her towards the cheval mirror. She had never looked – or felt – so glamourous. 'Oh Lily,' she said, admiring her blonde curls studded with gems, 'You have excelled yourself tonight. Thank you, you've done a magnificent job. I feel amazing'

'My Lady, you look lovely,' said Lily, smiling. 'You'll be fighting off all the young beaus tonight.'

Just then, Angela appeared in the glass. 'You look like a princess, Cynthia. He'll not be able to resist you.'

'Och, Angela, you look sensational,' said Cynthia, admiring Angela's plum silk dress. The sisters linked arms and headed downstairs to the vestibule, where their butler stood waiting with Derek and Lord Joseph.

'My, my, Derek,' said Lord Joseph, nudging his son, 'Who are these exquisite beauties before us? Not your tearaway sisters, surely?' Cynthia and Angela giggled as Derek helped them into their capes.

'Indeed,' added Derek. 'Beware, Edinburgh society. You ladies will have all the young bucks after you this evening.'

'Oh, and here comes another beauty,' added Joseph, as Georgina made her way down the stairs. 'You ladies could be three sisters.'

'Ha, you devil,' said Georgina, unfolding her fan and waving it theatrically below her chin. 'You never change, Joseph. You always could charm the birds out of the trees.' She laughed but inwardly loved her husband's flattering comments. The Marchmonts went out to their awaiting coach. It was a chilly night, the cobbles sparkling with frost, the sky littered with stars. They were all looking forward to attending their first soiree of the season. Even Joseph felt a twinge of excitement – and he wasn't one for big social gatherings.

The words leapt from the page, the handwriting undeniably the same as before:

DID YOU HEROES ENJOY YOUR MEETING THIS MORNING? YOU'RE EVERY MOVE IS BEING WATCHED. ENJOY THE BALL THIS EVENING.

The note did not frighten Anthony. Moreover, he was furious at the intrusion – and the fact he had no idea who was behind this evil campaign. A former spy being spied on? That was the final nail in the coffin for Anthony. He slammed the offending parchment down on the desk. 'When did this arrive?' he asked Michael. 'Did you see who delivered it?'

Michael shook his head. 'I'm afraid not, sir. What we do know is that it was delivered by hand shortly after you left for your ride earlier. I've questioned all staff, but nobody saw anyone deliver a note. Graham said it just appeared on the side table in the hall. It's all rather strange if you ask me.'

'Indeed, it is very strange,' said Anthony, and asked Michael to send word to Ron and Bill to meet him at the club on Charlotte Square prior to attending Lord Walker's ball. 'And also alert the runners on the High Street. I'm going to need extra back-up if I am being followed. And I *will* find the culprit. Anthony beat his fist on the desk to the rhythm of his words.

Michael made his exit, closing the door with an apologetic click. Anthony stuffed the note in his desk drawer, cursing under his breath. *What the heck is this all about?* Then he powered out of the library. The door slammed in his wake. He had nothing to apologise for.

Two hours later, Anthony was ensconced in the dim corner of the club, sipping a malt. Bill and Ron arrived, both signalling to the waiter for drinks before sitting down opposite Anthony.

'So, Anthony,' said Bill as he took his seat, 'your footman mentioned you received another one of those notes. We need to up our game, old chum.' Bill took off his top hat and ran his hands over his rusty curls, trying to calm them. 'That green ring,' he added, his eyes searching the ceiling, 'I still can't think where I've heard that mentioned before.'

'Well, in the meantime,' said Ron, 'We've got your back, Anthony. We'll find this scoundrel and have him hung, drawn and quartered.' The waiter arrived and poured the gentlemen's drinks.

'I'll drink to that,' said Anthony, 'but, I admit, this is a concern. This man must be watching my every move. Worse still, he must have gained access to my home, for God's sake. I'm worried my mother could be at risk too.'

'Do you think he could be here now?' said Ron, tentatively swivelling in his chair to peer over his shoulder.

Anthony knitted his brows. 'Who knows. But we'll need to be more vigilant. For all we know, he could be at Lord Walker's ball tonight.' Anthony drained his glass and returned it to the table with a thud. 'Damn, it's as though he's toying with me.'

The men continued their conversation during the short walk from Charlotte Square to Lord Walker's Queen Street mansion, where carriages thronged the front steps. Anthony noticed the Marchmonts alighting and thought it only polite to assist them. Ronald and Bill followed. 'Here, allow me to assist,' said Anthony, helping Angela out of the carriage. She had on a velvet cape the colour of black grapes and adorned with dazzling jewels. Her hair was holding a tiara that twinkled like a halo beneath the glow of the gas lamp.

Angela beamed as she took his hand and looked up at the magnificent building ahead. 'Oh, isn't this grand,' she said, her voice light and breathy yet loaded with excitement. A luscious red carpet spilled from the front door, down the steps and onto the pavement. Flanking its route were spectacular floral displays and glass bowls filled with water and floating candles. Anthony smiled and handed Angela to Ronald to escort up the steps, while he turned to help Cynthia down from the carriage. Although determined not to be lured by any single woman of marriageable age, Anthony couldn't ignore the fluttering sensation in his stomach as he looked into Cynthia's eyes. She looked amazing; her blonde hair was curled to perfection and glittering with little jewels. She reminded him of a Greek goddess. And when he took her hand, he swore a shock darted up his arm – a feeling he'd never experienced before.

'Good evening, Lord Anthony,' said Cynthia, smiling into Anthony's eyes as she stepped down from the carriage. 'I am so looking forward to this evening, but what a job I've had keeping Angela's feet on the ground. She's so very excited.' Cynthia stifled a laugh – for it had been she who couldn't contain her excitement.

'Yes, I can tell from Angela's face that she's excited,' said Anthony, 'I hope her first taste of the season won't be a disappointment.'

Cynthia dipped her chin sideways to her collarbone – a coy yet self-assured gesture, she hoped. 'No, I am sure it will not be.' Then she felt a stab of disappointment as Anthony passed her hand to Bill and offered his arm to Georgina. The guests made their way up the steps and into the grand hallway, where a line of servants relieved them of their capes. The ladies' gowns and jewels sparkled beautifully in the candlelight. And the gentlemen too looked splendid in their dark evening suits.

'Remember, out of here by eleven,' Anthony whispered to Bill as they bowed to their hosts. 'These mothers are desperate, and I've had only one small malt.'

'Let's get to the bar,' said Bill through a forced smile.

'Fat chance of that,' said Ron, nodding towards the ballroom ahead. 'Here comes the mamas with their daughters in tow. Keep your wits about you, gentlemen.'

Lord Marchmont, standing behind the three men, caught the tail end of their conversation and chuckled. 'Aha, we have all been there my boys. I quite remember batting off beautiful women myself when I was a handsome young fellow, but you three have it worse. You shouldn't be so damned handsome and rich. What can I say? I wish you luck,' he said and strolled off laughing. He intended to perform quickly his duties of introducing his daughters to a few acquaintances before dancing the first dance with Georgina. Then he'd escape to the cosy confines of the card room for a few games and malts.

Handsome in evening suits with cravats tied fashionably at their throats, ornamented with sparkling tiepins, Anthony, Bill and Ron headed forth to the ballroom to face the onslaught. Women made a beeline for the trio, who were themselves trying to cut a swift path to the bar. No such luck. Lord Walker cornered them first. 'You three, please, you must be acquainted with Julianne,' he said, indicating the timid looking lady, surely no older than seventeen, beside him. 'I'm sure you'll all make her night a veritable success.' She was petite, with chestnut hair and eyes a shade darker, and when Bill bowed to her, Julianne's face appeared to match her fuchsia satin gown. 'Would you give me the pleasure of the first dance?' he asked her. It was only the polite thing to do and, besides, in that moment, seeing Julianne's face flush so brightly, he felt a little sorry for her.

'Don't worry, he can actually dance quite well for a man,' quipped Ron, 'he won't tread on your toes.'

Julianne giggled. 'Oh sir, rest assured, it will be *I* who stumbles. I am so nervous about starting the dancing tonight.'

'Och you will be fine, my dear,' said Lord Walker as he signalled to the musicians to begin. 'Just follow Bill's lead and don't look down at your feet.' A romantic waltz issued from the grand piano. Bill took Julianne's hand and led her onto the dance floor.

'Follow me and keep looking into my eyes. I will take care of the rest,' Bill said, smiling down at his dance partner. He lifted Julianne's arms into position, nodded, and then they were off, gliding around the floor, their feet beating *one-two-three, one-two-three* in time with the music. Everyone watched for a moment until Lord Walker and his sister-in-law, Jennifer, took to the floor. Others followed, and soon the floor was awhirl with dancing couples.

'So, when did you arrive in Edinburgh?' Bill asked Julianne as he steered her north, south, east and west across the dance floor.

'About a month ago,' replied Julianne, her face still flushed, 'to get dresses ordered and made…then there were all the accessories needed for the season. There was so much to buy.'

'Oh, tell me about it,' said Bill, 'I seem never to be out of Niall Johnstone's shop nowadays. One can't be seen in the same suit twice during the season, you know.'

Julianne giggled. 'Oh, I haven't ventured beyond the shops on George Street and Princes Street yet, but that part of town is so beautiful – with all the new buildings and the gardens with the castle towering above them. It's amazing.I hope to see more of the city in the coming weeks.'

'Tell me, do you like horse riding?' asked Bill, quite taken by Julianne's coy demeanour and enthusiasm for Edinburgh.

'Oh yes,' said Julianne, 'I like to watch, but I am not a great rider myself.'

'Then you must join us on Monday to the Musselburgh races. Anthony has a box there and he won't mind my inviting you.' Bill laughed inwardly at his question. He was, after all, supposed to be avoiding romantic scenarios at all costs this evening. Now he was inviting Edinburgh's most talked about debutante to the races.

'Oh Bill, that would be lovely,' said Julianne, 'what a kind offer, but please don't feel obliged to ask me. I know our fathers put pressure on you and your friends to be here tonight – and are angling for you to accompany me to soirees and balls. And I am sure you three would rather be out somewhere else, doing things men prefer to do?' The music ended with a rippling, broken chord. Major and uplifting.

'Nonsense,' said Bill, and released Julianne's arms, 'I insist – and not just to please our fathers. I would like your company. Please, do come.'

Julianne looked up into Bill's pleading eyes and was immediately wooed by his adorable, forlorn puppy expression. 'Well, put like that, how can I refuse. Thank you, I accept,' she said.

Bill smiled and bowed. 'Why, thank *you*,' he said, then escorted Julianne across the room to Anthony, who would partner her for the next dance, which was another waltz, but faster and lest romantic than its predecessor. When that dance concluded, Anthony handed his partner over to Ron, before attempting to escape from the dance floor. He was desperate for another malt but, try as he might, Anthony found it near impossible to make his getaway. A dance with Julianne led to another waltz with Maureen, followed by a ballade with Isobella, which blended into a polonaise with Lady Veronica McLeod's daughter, Violet. Only when his dance with Alice ended did he manage to break free.

Ron and Bill were already at the bar when Anthony arrived. 'Here you go, pal, get this down you,' said Bill, handing Anthony a generous glass of malt, 'looks like you need it.' Anthony downed it in one and gestured to a loitering waiter for more drinks. 'Oh, by the way,' added Bill. 'I invited Julianne to the races on Monday. Told her she could join us in your box. Hope you don't mind. I was being polite – thought she could do with cheering up a little, especially after her mother's passing.' Actually, Bill had quite enjoyed dancing and chatting with Julianne. He wouldn't reveal as much to his friends though.

Anthony laughed. 'Yes, she told me you'd invited her. I like your style, Bill. You drag Ron and me here to divert attention from yourself – then invite an impressionable young debutante on a romantic day out at the races.'

'Argh, my mother keeps forcing me to dance with all these young girls who do nothing but step on my toes and make eyes at me. As if *that* will draw me into their web,' moaned Ron.

'I know,' agreed Anthony, 'I need some air.'

The men headed out to the terrace – and bumped into Ron's sister, Raquel. 'Ronald,' she cried, 'Mama is looking all over for you. She has found a beautiful young lady for you to dance the cotilion with. She's determined to find you a bride this season. Don't think you can escape out here.' Raquel waggled her finger in front of her brother's face. She did so love to tease him – and his friends. Raquel looked at Anthony next. 'I believe your mother's doing the same,' she said, then excused herself, laughing as she made her way along the terrace.

Ron blew out his cheeks. Sweat shone on his brow. 'Good grief,' he said, 'This is getting serious. We need to watch one another's backs. I won't be told who I should spend the rest of my life with. That's absurd.'

'Quite right,' said Anthony, 'We must make our own choices. Oh well, let's just humour our mothers for now. You know they love plotting – and balls. A few more dances then let's get out of here by eleven. I want to discuss this issue regarding the mystery notes at the club later.'

'Once more into the throng?' said Bill.

Back inside the ballroom, Anthony spotted Cynthia dancing with a man he recognised. It was Captain Thomas Reynolds. Anthony leaned against a pillar and watched. Cynthia was a fine dancer who looked completely at ease on the floor. Graceful, just like a swan. As the cotillion progressed, Anthony began to wonder what it would be like to dance with Cynthia. A part of him didn't much enjoy watching her with Captain Reynolds. *I'll have Cynthia as my next dance partner*, he decided.

When the music stopped Anthony pushed away from the pillar and strode over. As Cynthia came out of her curtsy, he took her hand. 'I believe the next dance is ours,' he declared, stepping between her and the captain, who was a little put out by this intrusion. He'd hoped Cynthia would agree to a turn on the terrace with him. Instead, all she gave him was a gracious smile and a polite 'thank you for the dance'. The captain nodded and made his exit, feeling dejected.

The music began, a beautiful, achingly romantic Chopin ballade. 'I do believe you're correct,' Cynthia said, her stomach aflutter. She'd been waiting all night for this moment. *Goodness you're handsome,*' she thought, smiling at Anthony as he swung her into his arms. She followed his lead. They twirled around the room, both enjoying the music and intimacy. Neither of them felt obliged to make conversation. This was all about the moment, and it felt comfortable.

When the music stopped, they stood looking at each other for a few seconds until Anthony realised this would cause people to stare. He bowed over her hand. 'I would carry on dancing, but it is not the done thing to have two dances with the same partner,' he said then, quick as he'd whisked Cynthia away from the captain, he was offering her hand to the young buck hovering behind her. 'Do not stand on this young lady's toes or you will have me to deal with,' Anthony told him.

'Oh sir, that's not fair,' giggled Cynthia. 'Now he's so nervous he's bound to step on my toes.'

'Well, he's been warned,' said Anthony, and gave Cynthia a wink that made her heart rattle in her chest. 'Thank you for the wonderful dance.' Anthony bowed once more and disappeared between knots of dancers, out of the ballroom and down the stairs. In the hallway a hand landed on Anthony's shoulder from behind. He jumped and wheeled around. It was Ron.

'I've got to get out of here,' he said, raking a hand through his damp hair, 'my mother is driving me crazy. It's gone eleven.'

'Let's find Bill and get the hell out of here. We've more than done our duty tonight,' said Anthony, steering Ron along the hallway. Just then, Bill came down the sweeping staircase linking the ballroom to the hall. At 11.15 pm, on the dot, Anthony, Bill and Ron left Lord Walker's home.

They didn't notice the man lurking in the gardens opposite, watching their every move.

CHAPTER SEVEN

CYNTHIA couldn't remember the last time she'd felt so happy. She adored Edinburgh; there was so much to see and do, and the social scene was like nothing she had experienced before. The Marchmonts had been in Edinburgh a little over a week but already they'd attended several events. And they hardly ever went to bed before 4 am.

The family's rented townhouse was magnificent, set over three floors. On the ground floor there was a study and library, both with doors leading to a rear garden bordered by lush conifers. There was also a dining room on the ground floor, and a lounge boasting vast bay windows from which you could watch the comings and goings on Royal Circus. Four spacious bedrooms took over the first floor, and, above that, two guest bedrooms, a music room and parlour, where the ladies could sew or sketch or drink tea. The servants' quarters were in the attic. Although much smaller than Marchmont House in Wick, the townhouse suited the family's needs in the city.

Unlike Angela, Cynthia liked to rise earlyish, around 10 am, sometimes earlier, no matter how late she tumbled into bed after a function. Today, she got up at 8 am as she wanted to take her time preparing for the Musselburgh races. Anthony said he would pick them up at noon – and Cynthia wanted to ensure she looked her very best for him. After much deliberation, she had chosen a pale pink dress with a cerise shawl and parasol, and a wide-brimmed hat, festooned with flowers and set cheekily to the side. Derek whistled his approval when she walked into the lounge just before noon. 'I'm sure you will win the best-dressed female award,' he said, referring to the monthly gong presented by the racecourse owners. Cynthia was touched by Derek's words. *I do hope Anthony thinks the same*, she thought.

Anthony arrived precisely at noon in his open top carriage. 'You both look lovely,' he said, greeting Cynthia and Angela with a bow, 'you will put all the other ladies to shame.' His words were mostly directed at Cynthia, who looked stunning. Her pink outfit complemented her pale complexion and blue eyes perfectly, he thought.

'Oh sir, you're such a tease,' replied Angela, who had on a pastel blue dress with tiered ruffles and royal blue sash.

Cynthia smiled. A coy smile. 'Why thank you, Lord Anthony,' she said as Anthony stepped forward to shake Derek's hand. 'And what a splendid carriage you have. I absolutely love the colour.' She gestured at the carriage, which was a glossy deep apple red with gold trimmings and emblazoned with the Sinclair crest. Michael had advised Anthony against using the new carriage, fearing its conspicuous exterior would make him an easy target if he was being followed. But Anthony disagreed – he wasn't afraid. And besides, he wanted to know who was behind this despicable campaign.

'You like it?' said Anthony, 'I just took delivery of it from Glasgow. I must say, I'm impressed by its workmanship.

'By Jove, Anthony, it's top-notch,' said Derek as Anthony helped the ladies inside his new carriage.

'Well, this is its maiden journey, so let's see how the suspension holds out between here and Musselburgh,' said Anthony, and signalled to his whip, Edmund, to depart.

'Anything will be better than our ride down from Caithness,' giggled Angela. 'Crickey, I still have the bruises from that journey.' They all laughed at Angela's remark as the carriage rolled smoothly along Royal Circus.

Anthony and Derek pointed out places of interest as they made their way out of the New Town and towards Newhaven village, where the girls were entranced by the fishing boats unloading and the fishwives in their bright skirts, filling their baskets to take to the market. From Newhaven they took the coast road past the Leith docks where some large cargo ships were anchored. Anthony explained this was not an area to come to at night or alone as it was frequented by 'prostitutes and drunks.' They passed through Portobello, which, explained Anthony, was fast becoming a holiday destination. 'The beach is a fine place for a picnic and a paddle,' he said. He pointed to the buildings going up along the promenade, painted in bright colours. Tents had been erected on the sand, presumably so people could change into the new style bathing suits, thought Cynthia. Although she couldn't imagine the sea would be warm enough to paddle in at this time of the year. She shivered at the thought.

A busy fishing harbour ringed by fishermen's cottages greeted them at Musselburgh Town. The quaint stone cottages made for a much cosier, pretty harbour than the one at Newhaven, agreed Cynthia and Angela.

They continued to the river Esk and crossed a bridge into the town centre, which was heaving with market stalls selling all manner of food and wares. The girls' attention was immediately piqued. Cynthia and Angela loved shopping. Alas, there was not time to mooch around the stalls as there was a lengthy queue of carriages waiting to enter the racecourse. When their coach driver eventually reached the entrance, he had to use much skill to manoeuvre into a tight space. Once parked, he jumped down and opened the carriage door for Anthony to step down and assist the ladies out.

'This way,' said Anthony, motioning towards a cordoned area away from where the general public congregated. The private section was arranged in squares separated by boxes. Tables and chairs were set up within the squares for people to socialise over drinks. There was also a large marquee housing a dining table set up with fine china and crystal glasses. As Anthony led Derek and the ladies to his box, a servant stepped forward to offer them refreshing glasses of lemonade. They each took a glass and headed into the marquee.

'Please, be seated,' said Anthony.

'This is lovely, Anthony, thank you so much for inviting us,' Cynthia enthused, 'I really enjoyed out trip down and would love to revisit some of the places we passed through, especially Portobello…that looks like such a fun place.'

'We could ride down there one day and have a picnic on the beach,' suggested Angela, taking her seat next to her sister.

'Oh yes,' said Cynthia, 'that would be lovely. We could make a day of it. I am sure Mother and Father would love to go there too – you know how much Mother enjoys a pic…'

'Well, hello there, isn't this a fine day for it?' The booming voice behind Cynthia made her jump in her chair and cut short her sentence.

'Bill,' said Anthony, rising from his chair, a look of confusion flittering across his forehead, 'I'm so glad you could *all* make it.' Cynthia and Angela turned to see a group composed of three men and three women.

Introductions were made; Bill had brought Julianne, which rather pleased Cynthia. She'd noticed the hopeful expression on Rosalind's face when she'd glanced at Anthony outside Débutante and said, 'I hear Julianne's quite a catch.' Which Cynthia had read to mean: 'Julianne will make the perfect wife for Anthony.' Next, Ron introduced the Marchmonts to his sister Raquel and Sir Daniel Friel, whom she was stepping out with, and Lady Claire Wentworth, whom Ronald had begrudgingly invited at the behest of his mother – a decision he now wished he could reverse, for Lady Claire had chattered incessantly, talking over everybody else throughout the journey to Musselburgh. His ears ached. Claire immediately found a new audience in Cynthia and Angela, at which point Ronald shook Anthony's hand and, glancing at Claire, whispered: 'Sorry about her, old chap. Mama's fault. Hope she doesn't spoil everyone's day.'

'What are you talking about?' said Anthony.

'Oh, you will see soon enough,' Ron said, raising his eyebrows, 'You will see.'

'Please, do sit down and have some refreshments,' Anthony announced to the group.

The wine – and conversation – flowed, and, about ten minutes later, Heather and David Fitzgerald arrived. Recently back from their honeymoon, they enthused about their European trip as they chatted away. David had previously worked with Anthony, Bill, and Ron, who always knew their pal would marry his childhood sweetheart, Heather. Anthony politely finished the introductions, then they all took their places for a light lunch and champagne. Being an informal gathering, there was no seating plan, so Anthony sat between Cynthia and Angela. Derek was seated on Angela's other side and Ronald next to Cynthia. Opposite them were William, Julianne, Heather and David, and Sir Daniel and Lady Claire at the end with Raquel.

'Well, shall we all have a small wager on the first race?' Ronald suggested.

'Oh, yes please,' said Angela excitedly, 'Though I've never placed a bet before. You will have to teach me, Ronald.'

'Indeed, I shall,' replied Ron, 'After lunch, I will go and get everyone a programme of today's races and we can all pick our winners".

'Or loser, which is usually the case with you,' quipped Bill.

'Speak for yourself, I have had quite a few good races lately. I won at Hamilton, Ayr and Kelso.' Then, turning to Angela, Ron added: 'I consider it a winning day if I come out of it with coins in my pocket.'

Angela laughed as she sipped her champagne. Goodness, it tasted good. She felt so light and relaxed. 'I will have to be very careful about taking your advice then.'

'Och, it's all about instinct,' Anthony interjected, 'study the horses then make up your own mind. That's my advice. Ron is an expert rider but he's a bit airy-fairy when placing bets. He only picks a horse because he fancies its name.'

Ron waggled his finger at Anthony. 'Now, now, that's not fair. I *do* always look over the horses, but sometimes a name reminds me of a place or person of whom I have fond memories. And that wins me over.' Ron pulled a nonchalant face, and everyone laughed.

Anthony drained his glass. 'Right, let's eat up and go see the horses.'

The party headed to the pre-parade ring to look at the horses and their jockeys. As promised, Ron got everybody a programme and they were all busy selecting which horses to place their bets on.

'So, Angela,' said Ron, 'Have you chosen a couple of horses yet?'

'Oh yes, I think so. I want to place a bet on Mystic Lad and Bluebell,' she replied.

Ron pursed his lips and nodded sagely. 'Good choice. How much do you want to put on?' he asked Angela as they made their way to the betting booth window. Cynthia watched from behind as her sister and Ron chatted animatedly about odds.

'Don't worry about Angela,' said Anthony, reading Cynthia's thoughts. 'Ron will take good care of her. She is in safe hands.'

'Oh, I'm not worried,' said Cynthia, with a dismissive wave of her hand, "I was just observing how attentive Ron is being with Angela.'

'As I said, she's in safe hands,' Anthony reconfirmed.

'Hmm, Lady Claire and Sir Daniel seem to be hitting it off too,' said Cynthia, nodding in the direction of Anthony's box, where the pair stood close together. Whatever Daniel was saying to the lady must be ever so funny, thought Cynthia. *If she [Lady Claire] laughs any harder, her bonnet shall fly off.*

'Yes, they do appear to be getting along handsomely,' said Anthony, following Cynthia's gaze. 'I hadn't noticed until now. I've been paying too much attention to the horses.'

Cynthia shrugged. 'Oh well, maybe they're not interested in the races?'

'Perhaps,' said Anthony, 'but why come to the races, then? The horses are the main part of the day.'

'Absolutely,' replied Cynthia, smiling. 'Oh well, each to their own.'

'Have you decided which horses you fancy?' asked Anthony, swiftly changing the subject, but he did make a mental note to find out why Raquel's suitor was suddenly so interested in Lady Claire.

'Yes, I want Bonnie Lass and Hercules,' breezed Cynthia.

Anthony winced. 'Oh, not Hercules, he is very heavy as the name suggests, and today the ground favours a lighter horse. How about Bluebell?'

'Fine, you win,' said Cynthia, 'I will bow to your greater knowledge.'

Anthony clapped his hands. 'Let's place our bets,' he said.

Back in Anthony's box, the party roared and cheered as Bluebell stormed across the finishing line in first position. Most had placed bets on the winning horse based on Ron and Anthony's advice.

"I won, I won,' clapped Angela excitedly, then looked around the group. 'Did anyone else win?' A chorus of yeses came back, and the group returned to study the horses ahead of the next race. The afternoon progressed and, after six races, Angela had made a tidy profit. She told the others as much as she counted her winnings. 'I can't believe I got so lucky,' she said, her eyes wide with excitement.

'That's grand, Angela. Now you can treat us all to a drink,' hollered Derek, and they all dissolved into laughter as they headed back to their carriages. Anthony had instructed Michael to make dinner reservations at nearby Carberry Tower Mansion House. As everyone boarded the coaches, Cynthia couldn't help but notice how Sir Daniel assisted Lady Claire up into Bill's carriage before helping Raquel into David's. *I would be most hurt if I were Raquel*, thought Cynthia. Puzzled, she made her thoughts known to Anthony.

'Do you think Sir Daniel's paying too much attention to Lady Claire and neglecting Raquel?' asked Anthony.

Cynthia shook her head. 'It's none of my business, really,' she said, 'but something seems amiss to me.'

The group were in high spirits when they arrived at Carberry Tower. They all agreed they'd had a pleasant and lucrative day – and were now looking forward to a first-class dinner – because Carberry Tower was renowned for its fine dining in impeccable surroundings. Any uncertainty among the guests seemed to evaporate as soon as they walked into the elegant castle – and chatted over pre-dinner drinks. However, as Anthony took his seat at the head of the dinner table, he noticed the corner of an envelope, poking out from beneath his napkin. As his guests continued to talk, Anthony surreptitiously moved the envelope and napkin together, and placed them on his lap. The veins at his temples bulged and pulsed. He knew it was another one of *those* letters, but how did the perpetrator know he would be at Carberry Tower? Michael wouldn't have revealed his plans to anyone. With dextrous fingers, Anthony ripped open the envelope and read its contents beneath the table. Sure enough, it was the same handwriting:

DID YOU ENJOY YOUR DAY OUT?
HOW MUCH DID YOU WIN?
ENJOY YOUR DINNER.
IT COULD BE YOUR LAST.

Anthony hadn't noticed that Heather, sitting to his left, had spied the envelope. Cynthia, on his right, had been too engrossed in conversation to see it. But Heather was curious. 'What's that you're reading, Anthony?' she asked him.

'Oh, nothing of importance,' Anthony replied, stuffing the paper into his inside pocket.

'Really?' said Heather, narrowing her eyes, 'strange getting a letter here though, isn't it?'

'It's really nothing,' repeated Anthony, sparking a quizzical smile from Heather.

'Don't tell me you're doing business today, Anthony?' she said in a voice that caught Cynthia's attention. Heather looked at Cynthia and rolled her eyes. 'Men, they can't take a day off. I'm always on at David about that.'

'Oh, absolutely,' added Cynthia, 'my father and brother are exactly the same.'

'I can well imagine,' said Heather, 'but enough about the men, did you enjoy your day, Cynthia?' Anthony reached for his champagne, relieved that the conversation had moved on.

'Oh, Heather, I have had a lovely day,' said Cynthia, smiling sideways at Anthony. The journey from Edinburgh was so interesting. We hope to spend a day at Portobello soon, maybe have a picnic there if the weather's not too cold.'

'Oh, that would be grand,' enthused Heather, 'Please, do count us in.'

'Absolutely,' said Cynthia.

After dinner, the gentlemen retired to the terrace for cigars and port, and the ladies freshened up in the powder room. While Derek chatted to Sir Daniel, Anthony steered David to the opposite end of the terrace for a quiet word about the menacing notes he'd received. Bill and Ron joined them, and Anthony told them about the latest letter he'd found at the dinner table. 'How awful,' said David, 'I'll make some inquiries, ask some contacts, see if anyone can shed light on this. Let's meet tomorrow though.'

'Good idea,' said Anthony, then swiftly changed the subject to horse racing. He didn't want Sir Daniel overhearing his business. Nor Derek, for that matter. He was too close to Cynthia – and such news would surely terrify her.

Meanwhile in the powder room, and out of earshot from the men, Cynthia jumped at the opportunity to subtlety quiz Heather about Anthony. 'How long have you known Anthony?' she asked, adjusting her bonnet in the mirror, trying to sound blasé.

'Oh, forever,' said Heather, rummaging in her drawstring purse. 'We grew up close to one another, and our families often went on picnics and outings to the country or beach. He is like a second brother to me. And David used to work with Anthony at the Foreign Office, so we have all been very close over the years".

Cynthia nodded. 'That's so lovely,' she said, then, lightly touching Heather's elbow, added, 'but please, do tell me about your honeymoon. Where did you go?'

'Oh, we did the grand tour of Europe,' said Heather, her eyes all dreamy and twinkling. 'It was so lovely. My mother insisted we go away for four weeks. She and my father wanted David and I to have a long engagement, and the tour was their gift to us after the wedding.'

'Oh, how super – and romantic,' said Cynthia, 'I would love to do the grand tour. The furthest I've ever been is to London.'

'Well, maybe you should consider the grand tour for your honeymoon?' Heather suggested.

Cynthia felt her cheeks redden. 'Well, I'm not sure I'm quite…'

she began, but her voice dissolved when she noticed Lady Claire approaching.

'Oh, you have your eye on a bridegroom already?' she asked.

'Och, no, I've only just arrived in Edinburgh for the season,' said Cynthia, 'It would be far too soon to think about courtship – let alone a honeymoon.'

Cynthia was expecting Lady Claire to smile or laugh at her comment, but she just looked Cynthia up and down a few times and said: 'I thought you only had eyes for Anthony. You seem to be stuck to his side like glue. Everybody's noticed.' Lady Claire's tone was snidey. Spiteful even.

'Anthony has been very kind to all of us – by showing us around the city,' said Cynthia, 'I thought it only polite to stay with him? Is this not the done thing?'

Lady Claire's hand fluttered to her chest. 'Oh, good heavens my dear,' she said with an exaggerated apologetic smile, 'I do hope I have not offended you. I was merely making and observation.'

'Of course not, Lady Claire, I just don't want to do anything improper during the season – and I bow to your greater knowledge,' replied Cynthia, although she'd seen through Lady Claire's faux apology.

'Well, you have done nothing wrong, Cynthia,' added Heather, linking her arm through Cynthia's and steering her out of the powder room. 'Truth be told, Anthony loves having a pretty girl by his side. Who would not want to be that girl? After all, he is quite a catch.' Heather darted Lady Claire a smug smile then whispered into Cynthia's ear: 'Lady Claire is only jealous because it's not her attracting Anthony's attention.' They both giggled and returned to dining room, where their fellow guests were preparing to leave.

'Heather, my love, where have you been? Our carriage awaits,' said David, helping his wife into her cape.

'Oh, I've had the most marvellous time speaking with Cynthia,' Heather replied. 'In fact,' she added, turning in her cape to address Cynthia, 'Why don't you and I meet for lunch tomorrow. There's this divine place called the Strath Hotel.'

Cynthia smiled. 'Oh, yes, that would be wonderful. Thank you, Heather.'

'Perfect,' said Heather, 'I'll see you at 12.30 pm.'

Farewells were bid and Anthony assisted Cynthia, Angela and Derek into his carriage.

The ladies were quite tired after their long day out and were glad to arrive home.

'Thank you for a grand day out,' Derek said to Anthony as he helped Angela down from the coach.

'Yes,' agreed Angela, 'I had a lovely time – just wait until I tell Mother and Father about my winnings". She turned to Anthony and curtsied. 'Thank you so much Anthony", she said, then turned and headed inside. 'I must go and find them.'

Derek shook Anthony's hand and followed his sister up the steps.

Anthony helped Cynthia down next, and felt a shock dart up his arm as he took her hand. *What's going on?* He thought, unable to take his eyes off Cynthia as she smiled sweetly at him. She had such an inviting smile – one that captured her innocence and mischievous side at once.

This is the second time I've felt this way. Stop it now, Anthony. You're acting like a young, naïve buck who's new to the scene.

Cynthia stepped down onto the pavement and adjusted her skirts. 'Thank you so much for a wonderful day, Sir Anthony,' she said, her face angled towards his. 'I had the best fun ever.'

'Would you like to go for a ride to Holyrood on Wednesday?' As soon as the overture left his mouth Anthony worried that he'd overstepped the mark, but Cynthia's beaming smile looked genuine.

'Oh, that would be lovely, Sir Anthony,' she said.

Anthony performed an elaborate bow, slowly unfurling his arm several times, which made Cynthia giggle. 'Then I shall send my carriage for the lady at 10 am,' he said, 'but, please, don't call me Sir. Anthony will suffice.'

'Well, Anthony, thank you again for today. Your friends are lovely. Heather has invited me to luncheon tomorrow, so I'm looking forward to getting to know her better.'

'Ah, yes, you two will get on famously. I must warn you, though – she loves shopping, so take your purse with you, as I have no doubt you'll end up at the shops. I know what you ladies are like when you get together.'

'I will, thank you". Cynthia said as Anthony kissed the back of her hand and bowed again. His kiss sent a surge of heat through her entire body. Thanking Anthony again, Cynthia turned and hurried up the steps – before he could see her flaming face and neck.

Anthony watched as Cynthia disappeared into the house, then leapt into his carriage, thinking, *I'm very much looking forward to Wednesday.*

CHAPTER EIGHT

A BURST OF BRIGHT LIGHT woke Cynthia. 'Morning Miss,' came a cheery sing-song voice. Cynthia lifted her head to see a fuzzy silhouette in front of the window through which the bright light was streaming. It was Lily, her maid, opening the curtains on what looked to be another fine day in Edinburgh.

'Morning Lily,' said Cynthia, her stomach aflutter as she recalled the sensation of Anthony's lips on her hand. 'Please could you lay out my powder blue day dress for me to change into after breakfast? I'm going out for luncheon later.'

'Indeed, I shall, Miss,' said Lily, 'and, if you don't mind my saying so, you sound very cheerful this morning.'

'Oh, I am,' said Cynthia, clasping her hands to her chest. 'I had the most wonderful day out yesterday. Sir Anthony Sinclair took us to the Musselburgh races, followed by dinner at Carberry Tower. The food was delicious.'

'Did you win at the races?' asked Lily, lifting the bowl and jug from the washstand, 'my Harry loves going to the races, but he is not always lucky.'

'Yes, both Angela and I had a few wins after Sir Anthony and his friends advised us. They clearly knew what they were talking about.'

Lily giggled. 'My Harry could do with such advice.'

'Well, tell him to put his money on Bluebell next time,' said Cynthia, feeling chuffed at her newfound knowledge for horseracing, 'she romped home.'

'I shall, thank you Miss. Now, if you'll excuse me.'

Once Lily had left the room, Cynthia reclined on her pillows, closed her eyes, and pictured herself in the dream she'd just woken from: she was riding along Portobello beach with Anthony. They had both been laughing hard as they galloped along the shoreline, the sun beating down on them. But much as Cynthia didn't want to lose that dream, she realised she was developing deep feelings for Anthony. *I'll have to watch I don't get too carried away*, she told herself.

Cynthia dressed and went downstairs to the dining room, where Lord Marchmont was reading *The Scotsman* over breakfast. He looked up when Cynthia walked in. 'Hello, my dear,' he said, grinning, 'I hear you had a grand day yesterday, according to your brother and sister.'

Cynthia sat down at the table. 'Yes, we all had a lovely day,' she said, 'Anthony was most kind. He pointed out all the interesting sights during our long journey to Musselburgh. We met Anthony's friends, and he had lunch ready in his box when we arrived at the races. Oh, and to top it all off, Anthony took us to dinner at Carberry Tower. It was superb – and so grand. You and Mummy must go there.'

Lord Marchmont lifted his teacup and looked at Cynthia with raised brows. 'Hmm, *Anthony*, is it?' he said, a trace of shock in his voice. 'Are you sure you don't mean *Sir* Anthony Sinclair? Whatever would he say if he heard you being so informal?'

'Oh, but it's all right, Daddy,' said Cynthia, 'he told us not to call him "sir" all the time. He was quite adamant about it, in fact.' Lord Marchmont nodded – his expression still serious. 'Yes, Anthony gave us permission not to use his title,' Cynthia added. Her father's reaction was making her a little nervous.

'Perhaps you misheard him?' said Lord Marchmont. The kitchen maid arrived and placed a steaming bowl of porridge in front of Cynthia.

'But, I swear, Daddy, he definitely gave us permission – and I wouldn't dare to…'

Lord Marchmont's eyes crinkled. 'Well, if he gave you permission, that's another matter,' he said, laughing.

Cynthia sighed and picked up her spoon. 'Oh, Daddy, you are teasing me, aren't you,' she said.

Lord Marchmont dabbed his eyes with his serviette. 'Of course, I'm teasing you dear.' Then he leaned forwards and, in an exaggerated pretend whisper, said: 'Anthony must be the catch of the season.'

Just then, Derek walked into the kitchen. 'Mother says all the mamas are talking about Anthony,' he said.

Lord Marchmont nodded. 'Tell me about it. One mama approached me on George Street only days ago. She'd heard you and your sisters had been riding with Sir Anthony and asked me to introduce her and her husband to him. Seriously, I ask you…spying on the poor chap. He has all my sympathy.'

'Oh lord, he has my sympathy too,' said Derek, 'I know exactly what he's going through.'

'Ha-ha, really?' said Cynthia through giggles, 'don't flatter yourself. You're not nearly as rich or as handsome as Anthony.'

Derek sat down and the maid delivered his breakfast – a plate loaded with cold meats and cheeses and a basket of bread. 'Oh, I take offence at that,' he said, 'I might not be as rich as Anthony, but I am certainly as handsome as him.'

'You won't be as handsome – or as fit – as Anthony if you keep eating like that,' said Lord Marchmont, indicating Derek's breakfast with his unlit pipe. Cynthia almost choked on her porridge.

'Very funny,' said Derek, spearing his fork into a roll of ham, 'And besides, I'll work it off later in the ring. David invited me to join him for a sparring match later. You could watch us if you like?'

Lord Marchmont got up from the table. 'It's a date. But don't tell your mother – you know how she hates boxing.' He walked around the table and patted Cynthia's shoulder. 'Have a nice day,' he said as he left.

'So, what are you doing with Anthony today?' said Derek.

Cynthia stirred her porridge, though she didn't have much of an appetite. 'Oh I'm not seeing Anthony until Wednesday.'

Derek smirked. 'Oh, I see, Wednesday. That's a whole twenty-four hours away from now. How will you cope?'

'Oh, stop it,' said Cynthia. 'If you must know, I'm meeting Heather for lunch. We're going to the Strath Hotel on Charlotte Square.

It opened at the start of the season. Everybody's talking about the Strath Hotel.'

'Yes, I've heard it's *the* place to be,' replied Derek. 'You must let me know how it goes.'

'I shall,' said Cynthia, 'but right now, I have letters to write, and I need to reply to yet more invites – too many invites and not enough days. I suppose I can't help being so popular.'

Derek laughed. 'I'll give you a lift on my way to David's.'

'Perfect,' said Cynthia, and headed to the library.

Cynthia finished one letter and had just started writing another when her thoughts returned to Anthony. *What shall I wear tomorrow? Does Anthony like me in a romantic way? He kissed my hand. I wonder how it feels to kiss his lips?*

'Don't tell me, you're daydreaming about a very handsome 'Sir' of our acquaintance?'

Cynthia jumped. 'Angela, gosh, you gave me a fright.'

'You were miles away there,' said Angela, noisily dragging a parlour chair across the room. She parked it next to Cynthia, and sat down, puffing. 'What's the latest news about Anthony, then? I've never seen you looking so dreamy.'

'Oh Angela, I had the most wonderful dream about him last night. We were riding along a beach – I think it was Portobello. My hair was flowing in the breeze. Anthony and I were going so fast, and we couldn't stop laughing, then we looked at each other, and the sea glistened like a bed of diamonds in the sunlight. And then…' Cynthia shrugged and dipped her nib into the inkwell. 'As I said, it was just a dream. I shouldn't get carried away.'

'My, you do have it bad,' said Angela, 'but I did notice how attentive Anthony was towards you yesterday. And there was something about the way he looked at you – like he couldn't keep his eyes off you, almost.'

Cynthia's heartrate accelerated. 'Really? How lovely of you to say so. Lady Claire made the same observation when we were in the powder room – but she did so in a horrid way. I felt as though I had done something to upset her.'

'Really, how rude,' said Angela, 'I can't think why she would be upset; she seemed very cosy with Sir Daniel. I did not take to him at all. But, never mind them, when are you seeing Anthony?'

Cynthia put down her pen. She was too excited to write anyway. 'Tomorrow. We are going riding – he is picking me up at ten.'

"My, that's very early,' said Angela, scrunching her nose. 'I shall still be in bed.'

'Oh, Angela, I don't know how you can sleep so late. I love going out before the rich, especially here in Edinburgh. The streets get so crowded later and it's hard to manoeuvre. Going through the old town can take an age in a carriage – the streets are so narrow.'

'Yes, but isn't the New Town lovely,' said Angela, 'the streets are wide and there are so many beautiful new buildings. I love wandering along those streets. Oh, and we must visit the villages we passed yesterday. They looked so quaint. And I loved Newhaven – apart from the smell.'

'Yes, we must, and that reminds me – we must organise a picnic at Portobello. You must ask Mummy and Daddy when would suit them. We could also invite a few friends. Heather and David said they'd like to come. Aunty Mary would love to come too, and we could ask Lady Sinclair – so Mummy can catch up with her.'

Angela gave Cynthia's knee a gentle tap. 'And if Lady Sinclair comes, a certain Sir might join her too?'

'Really? The thought never crossed my mind,' said Cynthia with a sly smile. 'Anyway, I must go. I'm going for lunch at the Strath Hotel with Heather.'

'Oh, lucky you. Only the best for Mademoiselle Cynthia,' teased Angela.

'Heather's suggestion,' Cynthia called over her shoulder as she left the room giggling.

The Strath Hotel was a grand affair, with decorative tiled floors and gilded ceilings throughout. A salty aroma of fresh seafood filled the air. The maître de escorted Cynthia into the dining hall, which was humming with chatter and laughter. Heather was already seated but rose to greet Cynthia with a warm hug.

'Cynthia, so lovely to see you. I'm so glad you could make it,' gushed Heather, 'and I do so love your dress. Blue is most certainly your colour.'

'Oh, thank you,' said Cynthia, taking her seat opposite Heather, 'you look splendid, too.' Heather was in a pale-yellow day dress adorned with applique white daisies.

Over a fine lunch of scallops and mussels, followed by tea and fancies, the two women chatted as though they'd been best friends for years. They reminisced over the previous day at the races, and Heather regaled Cynthia with tales from her Grand Tour. Cynthia was engrossed; she loved hearing about the streets of Paris and the ancient ruins of Rome. She dreamed of going on a grand tour herself one day. But somewhere between Heather's exploits in Venice and Florence, Cynthia became aware of a presence at her left elbow.

'Good afternoon, ladies, I'm so sorry to disturb you, but I noticed you throughout lunch and thought it only polite to come over and pay my respects.' The voice belonged to Sir Daniel Friel. He greeted both women with a bow, then said, 'Please, may I join you for an afternoon drink? I would like to buy you two ladies a glass of wine, if you'd allow me to?'

'Why yes, of course,' replied Heather.

Cynthia nodded. 'Yes, absolutely, please do join us.' They felt it was only polite to accept Sir Daniel's offer, especially as they'd spent the previous day in his company.

'Wonderful,' said Sir Daniel, gesturing at the waiter. 'So how did you both enjoy the races yesterday?' The waiter hurried over, and Daniel ordered the wine. 'A jug of your finest claret, please – for myself and these beautiful ladies,' he said.

'Yes, Cynthia and I were just talking about yesterday' said Heather, 'We had a lovely day, thank you. Did you?'

'Hm, not quite my scene, I'm afraid,' said Sir Daniel, and sat down in the spare seat next to Heather, 'I don't like to throw away money fruitlessly,' he straightened his back, and a proud smile filled his face. 'Dinner at Carberry Tower was excellent though. First class food, as always.' He looked directly at Cynthia as he spoke, ignoring Heather when she also commented on the Carberry meal. He placed his forearms on the table and leaned closer to Cynthia. 'So, my dear, are you enjoying Edinburgh?'

'Yes, I am having a lovely time, thank you,' she said as the waiter returned and poured the wine.

'Good, good,' said Daniel. He knocked back his wine in a few glugs and refilled his glass. 'Where have you visited so far?'

'Well, Anthony showed us so many beautiful villages on the way to Musselburgh. Yes, Anthony knows so much about the city and its surrounding areas – it really was kind of him to invite us yesterday. We want to return to Portobello and Newhaven and…'

'*New*haven?' said Daniel, as the Newhaven were a swear word, 'why ever would you want to go there – it's a foul place, absolutely stinks of fish. No, I don't recommend you go to Newhaven – but do go to Portobello and walk the new promenade. It's all the rage just now.'

'Yes, we intend to do so,' Cynthia replied, but thought Sir Daniel's comment about Newhaven was a little harsh. She thought Newhaven seemed like a colourful and interesting place to visit – so what if it smelled of fish. Newhaven was, after all, a fishing village. Wasn't it supposed to smell fishy? Cynthia wanted to state this fact aloud but instead smiled sweetly. *No point being rude*, she thought.

'Have you been to the Botanical Gardens yet?' Daniel went on. Heather sipped her wine and pretended to appear interested in the conversation.

'Not yet, but my family are planning to visit soon,' said Cynthia.

'Good, it really is beautiful, especially this time of the year. You must let me accompany you. I go there often and know my way around very well.'

'Thank you, I'll tell my mother and father. They might well take you up on your kind offer.'

Daniel laughed. 'Oh, my dear, I was offering to accompany *you* there.'

'Oh, right, well that's very kind of you but we we're planning a family day. You're more than welcome to join us though.'

Daniel stared at Cynthia as he finished his wine in one long swig. 'Fine,' he said, and the table rattled as he put down his glass. 'You can let me know when it's convenient.' His chair made a loud scraping noise as he stood. 'Now, if you'll excuse me, I have an appointment.' He gave a curt bow and made for the door.

'Well,' said Heather, peering into the empty jug, 'I suppose we'll have to pay for own wine – and his.'

Cynthia picked up the jug and pretended to pour from it. 'I suppose so,' she said, and they both burst into laughter.

'Oh well,' added Heather through giggles, 'let's go shopping.'

'Good idea,' said Cynthia.

The ladies left the Strath and sauntered along George Street. Their first stop was the jewellery shop, McInnes and Love, where Heather had spied a stunning brooch a few days ago. 'It has a gorgeous emerald – it'll go superb with the green dress I plan to wear for Lady Prudence Weatherspoon's ball in two weeks' time,' said Heather, 'You are going too, aren't you?'

'Oh yes,' said Cynthia, 'I'm very much looking forward to it.' Lady Prudence, widowed and rich, was one of the most prominent figures on Edinburgh's social scene. And her annual ball was one of the highlights of the season.

'Have you a partner for the night?'

'Oh, no, we're going as a family.' Cynthia's stomach twisted as she spoke. She adored her family, but how she longed to shout, 'Anthony, my partner is Anthony,' in a voice loud enough to be heard in Fife.

'Well, we must find you a partner and you can join us for a pre-ball meal. Leave it to me.'

Cynthia hooked Heather's arm with hers. 'Well, please do not invite Sir Daniel, I'll end up paying for his dinner.'

The two women were still giggling when the concierge welcomed them into McInnes and Love – just as Lady Sinclair was leaving the store. She was accompanied by a young man, who looked like a much thinner version of Anthony. *He has the same wavy black hair as Anthony too*, Cynthia noted. 'Oh, Mrs Fitzgerald – and Miss Marchmont, you both seem jovial,' said Lady Sinclair, who had on a teal dress and a bonnet sprouting peacock feathers. Cynthia and Heather sobered immediately and curtseyed. 'May I present to you my son Giles.' She then turned to her son, peacock feathers dancing, 'Giles, you already know Mrs Fitzgerald. -recently wed, of course – but this is Lady Cynthia Marchmont, the eldest daughter to my dear friend Georgina and her husband, Lord Joseph Marchmont. Introductions made, Lady Sinclair asked Cynthia about her mother. 'Oh, I must arrange to meet her again,' she said.

'Actually, we're arranging a day out to Portobello and we were wondering…would you and Lord Sinclair like to join us? Mummy and Daddy would love for you to come.' Cynthia nodded enthusiastically as Heather threw her an incredulous look that screamed, *did you just invite Lady Sinclair to the beach?*

'Oh, that will be lovely, do send me and invite with the date and I'll try my best to attend.' Lady Sinclair then angled her arm ready for Giles to escort her out of the shop. 'Good day,' she said on her way out.

Heather waited for the door to close, then turned to Cynthia and whispered, 'Goodness Cynthia, you are brave speaking to Lady Sinclair. She has a reputation for being quite a dragon, you know. I have known her for years but still find it hard to say even two words to her.'

'She's really not that bad,' said Cynthia. 'Mummy's been friends with her for years. Besides, you can get to know her better at the Portobello picnic.'

Heather patted Cynthia's arm. 'Aye, now I'm an old married lady, I suppose I should make more of an effort to get to know Lady Sinclair. After all, she's one of the most influential people in Edinburgh. Anthony is very easy to get along with, so his mother can't be as bad as the town says. Anyway, I must show you this brooch.'

The assistant produced a tray of brooches in all manner of shapes and sizes for the women to peruse. 'Ooh, this is it,' said Heather, picking one from the top row. The design was a small bouquet, each flower tipped with a diamond with smaller diamonds decorating the stems and ending with a large emerald at the bottom. 'My dress is a deep green and I thought it would sit perfectly on it.'

'Oh, it's adorable. So pretty and delicate. You should buy if you like it,' urged Cynthia.

Heather's eyes glinted in solidarity with the gems. She handed the brooch to the assistant. 'I'll take it,' she said.

Meanwhile, Cynthia was drawn to a little round brooch studded with small diamonds. Simple yet beautiful. 'Isn't this pretty," she said, turning it this way and that beneath the light. 'It would look lovely on my riding habit, which is a deep blue velvet.'

'Oh yes, that will look beautiful – like stars in the night sky,' said Heather, 'I think you should buy it. Frankly, I think it would be an enormous pity if you didn't buy it.'

Cynthia beamed at the assistant. 'I'll take it.'

The assistant wrapped the brooches and thanked the ladies.

'You're a terrible influence on me, Heather,' said Cynthia as they left the shop, 'but I love it all the same.'

'Don't mention it, Cynthia' giggled Heather, and took Cynthia's arm. 'Now, where next, Kennington & Jenner?'

The ladies laughed all the way to Princes Street, fast becoming best friends.

CHAPTER NINE

'YOU'RE LOOKING DAPPER. Who's the lucky lady then?' said Giles, admiring Anthony's new riding coat as he walked into his brother's bedroom.

Anthony rolled his eyes. 'What do you mean, I always look dapper.'

'Hm, is that cologne I smell,' added Giles, sniffing the air theatrically.

'If you must know, I'm going for a ride.'

'Who with? Does her mama know? Do I hear wedding bells?'

Anthony laughed. He and Giles did like to tease one another. 'Calm down, Giles. I'm just going for a ride with Miss Marchmont. It's nothing serious.'

'Which Miss Marchmont?'

'Cynthia.'

'Oh yes,' said Giles, 'Mama and I met her and Heather outside McInnes and Love yesterday.'

'Really? What were they up to? Costing David a pretty penny, no doubt. I know how Heather enjoys to shop.'

They both laughed. 'Probably,' said Giles, 'ladies shopping in jewellery stores is never a good omen for their husbands. Mama spent a small fortune on a new necklace for Lady Prudence Weatherspoon's ball. She claimed she had nothing suitable and did not want to wear any of the family jewels, as they were getting too "old fashioned". Papa would have a fit if he were still here.'

'Nonsense,' Anthony replied good humouredly, 'Papa would have given Mama the earth – all his blustering was just a show.' The brothers shared a knowing smile. Unlike many marriages in Scotland's society, the Lord and duchess' partnership had been a love-match for thirty-five years.

'Anyway,' said Anthony, 'why did you go to the jewellers with Mama? She normally goes with her friends.'

'Because, dear chap, you were busy with business – and Mama wanted me to accompany her to the bank afterwards. She's still worried about her account but Mr Fitzsimmons has assured her that all is in check.'

'Well, hopefully that business is over with.'

'I heard you received another note,' said Giles, 'is there anything I can do?'

'Just look out for Susanne and Mama. I hope they are not the target, it does appear to be me, but lord knows who or why?'

'Well, you probably upset a few people over the years, especially in your line of work. You have no clear idea who's behind this yet?'

'No, and it is damn frustrating,' Anthony said, 'but, listen, I must go, I have to pick Cynthia up at 10.00 am.'

Anthony bid his brother farewell and headed out to his carriage. It was no distance from his house in Moray Place to hers and he was there in ten minutes. He bounded up the steps and rapped on the door and the butler welcomed him inside. Anthony was looking forward to his day out with Cynthia and when she descended the stairs in a dark blue riding habit, adorned with her new brooch, he felt a flutter in his stomach. *She looks exquisite*, he thought.

He took her hand and bowed over it. 'Good morning, Miss Marchmont. How are you on this fine morning?'

'Good morning, Anthony. I'm so looking forward to our ride.' Cynthia had barely slept for excitement, although she didn't mention this to Anthony.

'Me too, and the weather is fine. Let's make haste to the stables.'

Cynthia pulled on her dark blue riding gloves. 'Yes, let's,' she said, and the feather in her hat fluttered as she took to the steps. *She has no idea how good she looks*, thought Anthony. *How enchanting for a woman to be so unaware of her beauty.*

They arrived at the stables to find Anthony's black stallion and Misty, the filly Cynthia rode previously, saddled-up and ready to go. Helping Cynthia into the side saddle, Anthony felt a sudden urge to kiss her, right there in the stable. The same thought played in Cynthia's mind. Her heart thumped when Anthony's hands encircled her waist to lift her. It took Anthony a moment to settle her into the saddle – and he had to resist his urges to taste her lips. *Maybe later*, he thought. He turned and jumped into his own saddle and shook his head. *Goodness, whatever is wrong with me? I feel like a young buck just out of school.* Anthony was confused and excited in equal measure, for it was unusual for women to move him so deeply, especially after such a short acquaintance.

They made their way out of the stables onto Gloucester Street, and as they did so, Cynthia thought about how Anthony had looked at her when he'd lifted her onto Misty. She thought he might have kissed her had they been somewhere more private. *Oh, stop it, Cynthia, you're letting your hopes and dreams invade reality. Really, what rubbish.*

On Heriot Row, they passed Lady Sinclair's house, which Anthony pointed out. From there they ventured uphill along Fredrick Street, crossed over Princes Street, and headed up the Mound to the Royal Mile. Then they enjoyed a leisurely trot downhill and entered Holyrood Park near the palace. Once they were past the palace walls, they let their horses have their heads before beginning the steep climb towards Arthur's Seat. They stopped at a spot close to Duddingston Loch and sat for a while to admire the view, which took in the entire city and stretched to Fife beyond the icy blue Firth of Forth. 'Oh, this is breath-taking,' sighed Cynthia, 'It's truly magnificent. You can see for miles and miles.'

'I never tire of this view, and the history of this area,' said Anthony, 'you know, over fifty years ago, a hoard of weapons dating back to the Bronze Age was dragged from the water over there.' He pointed at Duddingston Loch, still as glass in the mid-morning sunlight. Cynthia listened intently as Anthony pointed out other sights of interest. They sat for a while before remounting. 'Are you hungry, it's almost noon,' said Anthony, lifting Cynthia into her saddle once more. The same amorous feeling he'd experienced at the stables overwhelmed him again.

'Yes, I am rather,' said Cynthia, 'although I didn't think we'd been out so long.'

'Shall we find a nice spot for a picnic?'

Cynthia giggled, 'That would be lovely, but we don't have any food.'

'Hm, that's a good point,' said Anthony, as they trotted on and turned a bend, 'but, aha, what do we have here?' Cynthia followed Anthony's gaze and gasped at the scene. There on the hill, a few yards to their left, was Anthony's groom, standing guard over a picnic rug laden with food and wine.

'Oh my, you had this planned,' Cynthia said, 'what a wonderful surprise.'

Anthony helped her down and the groom took the horses to tether, feed, and water them while his master escorted Cynthia to the picnic. The groom then made haste with discretion but would return later to gather the remains of the picnic – as Anthony had instructed him to do so.

Cynthia sat on the rug and enjoyed the view wile Anthony poured glasses of cool white wine.

'Thank you, this is lovely,' she said as he passed the glass to her. Their fingers touched and she felt a lovely tingling sensation flow through her.

Anthony made up a plate of food for her. 'Tuck in, there is plenty,' he said. There was a variety of cold meats, cheeses and fruits, Anthony's chef had baked fresh rolls that morning, which were delicious. As they ate, Anthony explained his chef was French. 'He likes to make his own bread as he thinks Scottish stuff is tasteless and hard,' he said.

'I agree,' said Cynthia, 'these certainly are the best rolls I've ever tasted.'

After eating, Cynthia reclined on the rug and looked at the sky. 'Did you ever play spot a shape in the clouds when you were little?' she said.

'Oh yes,' said Anthony, gazing down at Cynthia's lips as she spoke. *I must see if they taste as delicious as they look.* Slowly, he lowered his face to hers. She looked into his eyes and, in that moment, they both felt like the only two people in the world. Their lips connected. Anthony kissed Cynthia slowly, wishing he could go further but not daring to. He lifted his head to stare into her eyes. She had a far-away look, and at once he worried if he'd gone too far and frightened her, but she broke into a lovely smile.

'That was nice,' she said. Her words fluttered through a long, breathy sigh.

Anthony smiled. 'I have wanted to do that for an age -but I did not know how you felt.'

'Oh, I felt the same,' she whispered.

"Would you object if I did it again?'

Cynthia lifted her hand to Anthony's cheek. 'Not in the least. Be my guest,' she said. Anthony kissed her again, savouring the taste of her lips. He nudged them apart with his tongue and she responded instantly. She sighed with pleasure as he drew her body towards his, then snaked her arms around his neck. Anthony pulled her harder against his body and heard his own groan of pleasure this time. Then suddenly he pulled away looked into her dreamy eyes. 'We must stop. I'm sorry. I am getting ahead of myself. This is a public place – anybody could catch us.'

'Yes, I suppose,' said Cynthia, 'but I did enjoy it.' She looked into Anthony's eyes. *In a private location we might have taken this further*, she thought.

Anthony dropped a quick kiss on Cynthia's nose, sprung up and helped her to her feet. Then, as though timed, Anthony whistled, and his groom suddenly reappeared with their horses. Only then did the full realisation of what she'd done dawn on her. *What if we had been caught? Society gossips would make a meal of it, surely. One of the most eligible bachelors in Scotland, kissing her in the open…goodness, what gossip.*

With a cheeky wink, Anthony lifted Cynthia onto her saddle then leapt into his own. 'Right, I will race you back down, and the loser buys us a glass of cider on the way home.'

Cynthia spurred her horse forward. *Little minx*, thought Anthony, watching Cynthia gallop back down the hill towards Holyrood Palace. He followed, knowing he could easily overtake her but deliberately holding back – just enough so she didn't suspect he was letting her win. And besides, he enjoyed watching Cynthia. When they reached the palace wall, she turned to him 'I won, the drinks are on you,' she panted. Anthony laughed, thinking how beautiful and flushed Cynthia looked after her fast gallop and their passionate kissing.

'Fine, you won,' he said. 'I know a little inn where I will toast your success.' He kissed Cynthia on the lips. 'The inn also has rooms…'

'I see,' said Cynthia, her lips wet and tingling, 'Is this where you take all your young ladies after a picnic?'

Anthony shrugged. 'Only the ones I want to take to bed.'

'Oh, Anthony, you are awful.'

'And you, my dear, are quite charming,' he said, playfully tapping her nose.

They stood for a moment, gazing into each other's eyes, both feeling the shift in their relationship.

CHAPTER TEN

AS INSTRUCTED BY HIS MASTER, Fred arrived in Royal Circus ahead of Anthony and Cynthia, who rode home at a gentle pace following their downhill race to Holyrood Palace.

Outside the Marchmonts' townhouse, Anthony dismounted his stallion then assisted Cynthia down from her horse. 'Thank you, Fred, you may now take Misty back to the stables,' said Anthony, looking directly at Cynthia as he spoke. Still her cheeks were flushed, and her eyes danced with mischievous merriment.

'Thank you for a lovely day, I thoroughly enjoyed myself,' Cynthia said smiling. Although secretly, she felt disappointed that she would soon be parting company with Anthony. *Oh, if only I could spend the night with him*, she thought.

Anthony gave Cynthia a broad grin, flickering his eyebrows. 'Oh, so did I – we must do it again soon.' Cynthia first thought Anthony was referring to their picnic, but his sustained grin told her otherwise. 'The sooner the better.' *Ah, he's talking about our kissing.*

A burst of heat tingled Cynthia's face, but she looked up at Anthony all the same. 'I would very much enjoy that,' she said, her stomach aflutter with nervous excitement. They stood for a few seconds, gazing into one another's eyes, both relishing the romantic moment. Then, bang, clatter, clatter, Derek came bounding down the steps.

'Anthony, old chap, are you going to the boxing tonight? Sounds like a good bout.'

Anthony sidestepped Cynthia and proffered his hand to Derek. 'A good afternoon to you, Derek. Yes, I shall be going to the boxing.

Would you care to join the chaps for a bite to eat at the No.1 Club before the match?

'Oh, rather, thank you, that would be grand. I hear it is *the* club to join – the place reserved for only Edinburgh's finest gentlemen.'

'Indeed, and present company included. Meet us there at 6.30. p.m. and I'll sign you in.'

Derek nodded vigorously. 'Thanks awfully, old chap. I shall see you there.' Then, regarding Cynthia, he added, 'Hey-ho, Sis, had a good day? Now, if you'll both excuse me, I must dash – I have an appointment with my barber.' He tipped his hat and powered along the curve of Royal Circus, towards Stockbridge.

Cynthia watched her brother, swinging his cane at a furious tempo. 'Typical Derek, always dashing off somewhere. I can't keep up with him,' she said, again smiling up at Anthony. 'Would you care to come in for tea?'

'Oh, no, sorry, I must go and get ready for this evening.'

'Boys' night out?'

Anthony laughed. 'Indeed. Dinner, boxing then a night of debauchery.'

Cynthia giggled back. 'Well, I hope you have a whizz of a night. And while you're galivanting and committing acts of debauchery, you'll be pleased to know that I'll be at home – sewing, reading and sleeping.'

Anthony clasped his hands behind his back and bent forwards, so as his lips grazed Cynthia's ear. 'I hope you'll dream about me,' he whispered, 'because I am sure I will dream about you.'

'Oh, perhaps I will,' teased Cynthia.

'Grand,' said Anthony, straightening his back, 'then I will take my leave and let you dream sweet dreams.' He lifted his hand, performed an exaggerated bow, then took Cynthia's hand in his and kissed her gloved fingers. Then he turned and leapt into his saddle. 'Farewell, my fair maiden,' he called with a firm salute, and kicked his steed forwards.

'Farewell,' whispered Cynthia, and turned. She felt like a paper doll, fluttering lightly up the steps. She could barely contain her excitement.

Angela came pattering along the hallway as Cynthia entered the house. 'So, tell me, I want to know everything. Where did you go? What did you do? Was it romantic?' she gushed.

Cynthia let out a breathy sigh, like descending notes played on a flute. 'Oh, Angela, it was wonderful.' The girls linked arms and headed upstairs. 'Anthony took me to Holyrood Park where he laid on a surprise picnic. It was so lovely.'

'Gosh, how romantic. But I can tell from your face there is more to tell.' Angela opened the door to Cynthia's bedroom and led her sister inside. 'Come,' she added, gesturing at the chaise lounge, 'let's sit and you can tell me all about it. And don't leave out one detail.'

Cynthia touched her forehead in a mock fainting gesture as she sat. 'He kissed me,' she said softly, 'and it wasn't just a peck on the cheek, either. It was a deep, lingering, loving kiss. I loved it – I did not want Anthony to stop kissing me, in fact. But you can't tell anybody that.'

'I promise, I will not breathe a word – but only if you go through the whole day, event by event – and don't leave out any details.'

'Well, Anthony arrived at ten o'clock, on the dot, looking gloriously handsome,' Cynthia began. And, for the next hour, she and Angela oohed and aahed as Cynthia relived her magical day with Anthony – omitting as she did so, not one single detail.

'Wow, that sounds so lovely and romantic, when are you seeing him again?' Angela asked.

'Oh, well, he didn't say, but I'm certain he'll call by the house or send word,' said Cynthia, her voice laced with hope.

'Or you could always bump into him accidentally-on-purpose at his stables if he doesn't call round?'

Cynthia clasped her hands to her chest, her lips flickering into a conspiratorial smile. 'I could do that. Yes, that's possible.' Five chimes from the grandfather clock on the landing jolted Cynthia from her thoughts. 'Oh help, look at the time. I must wash and dress for dinner – and we have the recital tonight, don't we?' In her excitement, Cynthia had forgotten about the Beethoven piano recital the Marchmonts were due to attend at St Giles Cathedral that evening. She stood and pulled the bell cord to signal for their maid. 'Quickly, Angela, do run along and get ready, Mummy will not be happy if we are late.'

After dinner, Lord and Lady Marchmont, accompanied by their two daughters, took a carriage ride to the Royal Mile in the Old Town. The cathedral, statuesque against the navy sky, looked moodily handsome with its gothic ribs and stained-glass windows aglow with oily amber light. At the cathedral entrance, the Marchmonts greeted acquaintances before taking their seats behind Georgina's sister Mary and her family. Minutes later, Cynthia felt a hand on her shoulder. She turned and her eyes widened at the view: Sir Daniel Friel, grinning through his excessive sideburns.

'Miss Marchmont, what a delightful surprise,' he said, 'May I present my good friend, Sir Lucas Mein?' Daniel indicated the man to his left, a bespectacled man with receding hair.

Cynthia gave a polite nod. 'How do you do Sir?'

'Oh, very well,' replied Sir Mein, but he looked totally uninterested as he scanned the seated crowd.

'Have you decided on a date on which to visit the Botanical gardens yet?' asked Daniel, inching forwards in his seat.

Cynthia shook her head. 'No, I have not yet found the opportunity to discuss the trip with my parents. We have all been very busy, you'll understand.'

'Yes, indeed, this is a busy time for us all, but maybe we could discuss it now?'

Just then, the woolly hum of chatter dimmed to silence as the pianist took his seat at the piano. 'Do excuse me, the music is about to start,' said Cynthia, then faced the front, relieved to end her conversation with Daniel there. She didn't much fancy going to the Botanical Gardens with him. *Why is he so obsessed about taking me to the Botanical Gardens?*

The thunderous opening chords of *Sonata Pathétique* echoed in the chilly cathedral. Closing her eyes, Cynthia pictured a stormy seascape: crashing waves frothing and merging into a heavy gunmetal sky, bursting with clouds. She shivered to the tremolo bass. *Gosh,*

I wish I could play piano this well. She did not hear the tut-tutting behind her.

Fortunately, Cynthia managed to avoid Daniel all through the Beethoven recital, instead losing herself in the music. When the pianist played the *Moonlight Sonata*, she instinctively thought of Anthony and imagined lying beneath a starry sky with him. She thought of his warm lips on hers and her heart thudded softly to the beat of the dreamy arpeggios.

When the concert ended, Cynthia further avoided Daniel by weaving rapidly through the crowd towards the exit, arm in arm with Angela behind their parents. Outside, the cobbles were slippery with frost, the sky clear and cold and studded with stars. November had arrived, and Edinburgh's social scene would soon be at its peak.

'Who was that man you were talking to, Cynthia – the one sitting behind you at the recital?' asked Lord Marchmont once settled in their carriage.

'Oh, that's Sir Daniel Friel, we met at the races – he accompanied Ronald's sister, Raquel, that day,' said Cynthia.

'I see, but he was trying to get your attention as we got up to leave the cathedral – and it looked to me like you were deliberately avoiding him. I've never seen you move so fast, darling daughter.'

'Sorry, yes, I was avoiding Daniel. This is quite rude of me, I know, but I cannot take to him. He's pestering me to go to the Botanical Gardens with him. I told him we were planning to go as a family, so he now wants to show us all around, and has asked me to fix a date with you.'

'I see,' replied Lord Marchmont, 'Leave it with me. We'll get to the Botanical Gardens without Sir Daniel Friel.'

'Oh, thank you Daddy. I can't quite put my finger on what it is I don't like about him. It's just a feeling.'

Angela made a noise that was somewhere between a giggle and a snort. 'He is not Lord Anthony Sinclair. That's what it is.'

Georgina became animated at the mention of her best friend's son's name. 'What is that about Lord Anthony?'

'Oh nothing,' said Cynthia, nudging her sister, 'Angela is teasing me because Sir Anthony has taken me out a couple of times. That's all.'

'Well, you watch yourself, young lady,' Georgina warned, 'I know he is very handsome – the catch of the season. Every lady in Edinburgh will have their eyes on him and his fortune. He will have the pick of society. I don't want you getting hurt.'

'Oh, Mummy, I know, but Anthony is delightful company. I thought I would just have some fun.' Cynthia tried her best to sound nonchalant.

'Well, that's fine, my dear, but, please, don't lose your heart to him. Be careful, that's all I'm saying. I don't want you to wind up with a broken heart,' said Georgina as their carriage came to a stop in Royal Circus. The family headed into the house, where the butler came forward with a note for Cynthia.

'Ooh, I wonder who that could be from,' teased Angela, 'could it be from Sir Anthony Sinclair, I wonder?'

Cynthia opened the envelope and scanned the contents of the note:

Dear Cynthia,

Would you be so kind as to accompany me to a dinner on Friday night at the Strath Hotel? Bill would like to take Miss Julianne Walker and asked if you and I would make up a foursome. Miss Walker would feel more comfortable if another couple are present, Bill tells me. Miss Walker is very quiet and not yet at ease in Edinburgh Society, which Bill is dearly hoping to change, as he would like to partner her to some balls.

So, if you would do me the honour, please let me know soonest.

Yours,

Anthony.

Cynthia's stomach fluttered at the prospect of going out with Anthony again, but equally, she felt a little confused. *Does this mean Anthony has feelings for me – or is he simply trying to please Bill and Julianne with a convenient foursome? Maybe Mummy is right? And I'm getting too attached to this handsome devil.*

'Well?' said Angela, 'Is it from Anthony?'

Cynthia nodded. 'Yes, he has asked me to dinner with Lord William and Miss Julianne Walker on Friday.'

'How lovely. Well, you best reply soon – otherwise he might ask somebody else.'

Cynthia's face darkened. The thought of seeing Anthony with another lady on his arm engendered a deep sadness in her chest.

'Cynthia, what's wrong? I was only teasing. I didn't mean in, I…'

Cynthia shook the dark thought from her mind. 'Oh nothing, I was just being silly. I was picturing Anthony with another lady and that thought made me feel jealous. Which is stupid. I barely know him.'

Angela tilted her head on one side and touched Cynthia's upper arm. 'Oh my, you have got it bad. But imagine, you might enjoy yourself. Seriously, Cynthia, just go out and have some fun, that's what it is all about.' Angela always went out and had fun; she did not have a care in the world.

'Yes, you are right,' said Cynthia, already heading for the stairs, 'I will accept Anthony's invite and enjoy the evening. I shall write my reply right away.'

Anthony received Cynthia's note when he returned from the boxing match. Reading the final two sentences of Cynthia's letter – *I would be honoured to join you, Lord William and Miss Julianne Walker for dinner on Friday evening. Yours thankfully, Cynthia* – he felt a buzz of excitement, followed by a wave of relief. In the back of Anthony's mind, he'd feared Cynthia might decline his invitation. After all, he'd only given her two days' notice. This is strange, he thought, *of all my many liaisons with mistresses, I have never felt this way about a woman before.*

The following day, around mid-morning, the Marchmont sisters headed to Lord Walker's Queen Street mansion, their mission being to invite Miss Julianne on a shopping expedition ahead of their imminent dinner at the Strath Hotel.

Miss Julianne was in the library, daydreaming about the forthcoming dinner when Cynthia and Angela arrived. She'd been thinking how delighted she was to receive the invite. She had liked Lord William from the moment she met him. She found him easy to talk to and funny, which was rare for her as most gentlemen made her ill at ease, rendering her flustered and tongue- tied. But Lord William was different and very handsome, so Julianne was looking forward to their night out immensely.

The Walkers' butler entered the library and announced the Marchmont sisters' arrival.

'Lady, Cynthia and Angela Marchmont are here. They're asking if M'Lady is free to go shopping?'

Julianne sprung from her chair and straightened the teal velvet skirt of her dress. 'Oh, lovely, I will come immediately. Please ask my maid to fetch my coat and purse.'

The three ladies greeted with hugs in the front parlour.

'Cynthia, Angela, it's so lovely to see you both again,' said Julianne.

'I hope you don't mind us popping by unannounced,' said Cynthia, 'but I need some new ribbons and gloves for dinner tomorrow evening and thought it would be nice to catch up with you before then.'

'No, not at all,' said Julianne, taking her purse and gloves from her maid, Marian. 'I'm delighted you came. I need advice on what to wear as I have never been to The Strath before, and I don't want to let Lord William down.'

'Gosh, you won't let him down. Whatever you wear, you'll look lovely, I'm sure. And besides, Lord William wants your company, not a figure piece.' Anthony had previously told Cynthia that Bill was very fond of Julianne, so there was truth to her statement.

'Would you like us to look at your choice and give our opinions?' Cynthia asked.

'Oh yes, thank you, how kind. I have two dresses, but I am not sure which one is best,' said Julianne.

Upstairs in Julianne's bedroom, she showed Cynthia and Angela her options. Displayed on the bed was a deep claret satin dress, its short sleeves and hem decorated with paler red ribbons. Lying beside the red choice was a navy velvet dress with cornflower blue ribbons on its long sleeves.

'Oh, they are both lovely,' said Angela, touching the velvet one.

'Yes, they are,' agreed Cynthia, 'but I think the blue velvet would be too warm, as the Strath Hotel gets very crowded. And the red suits your colouring perfectly, Julianne.'

Julianne clapped her hands. 'Right, that's decided, then. I will wear the red dress. But I will need to buy a new shawl to go with it today, so you can both help me choose.'

'Right, let's go then,' said Angela, 'I love shopping.'

The girls scurried down the stairs in a cloud of giggles.

They took a carriage to George Street and started their shopping spree in Madam Martine's shop, which sold ball gowns and day dresses and every accessory from gloves and bonnets to shawls, purses, brooches, and fans. Being a popular store, especially at the height of the season, it was crowded, so the girls browsed as they waited for an assistant. Cynthia was looking at some bonnets and, lifting a beautiful fuchsia one from the stand, she heard two ladies chatting on the other side of the mirror.

'Really, Anne, you are not buying another one, are you?' the first Lady asked.

Cynthia smiled to herself at this comment. The high society ladies of Edinburgh could never have enough bonnets.

'Yes,' said Anne, 'I must look my best to woo Sir Anthony Sinclair back.'

Cynthia's heart dropped into the pit of her stomach. *Who's Anne? And why does she want to "woo Anthony back"?*

'Why what happened?' came the first woman's voice again.

Anne lowered her voice, but Cynthia heard every word: 'Well, Anthony visited me a few weeks ago, and gifted me a lovely bauble, which is adorable. But he was not his usual self. I knew what was coming before he said anything. He said he must end our affair.'

'Gosh, no, why?' asked the first woman.

'Ha,' Anne spat, 'he gave no reason. He just said, "This is so hard for me to do, but I hope you understand and have no regrets." Then, without saying sorry or anything, that heartless rake kissed me on the cheek.'

'What did you say?' said Anne's friend.

'Not much, he didn't give me a chance to speak even. But you know Anthony's reputation. He expects his ladies to accept his decision when he drops them like a hat. He probably went directly to his next mistress' house after dropping me. Well, I'm not standing for his nonsense. I am going to fight for him. I know what Anthony Sinclair likes and I am going to do everything in power to win him back. I've done it before, I'll do it again. I will put everything into action to get him back.'

Cynthia looked down but could no longer see the blush roses on the fuchsia bonnet she held in her hands – her vision blurred with tears.

'So, is the bonnet is part of your plan to win back Anthony?' Anne's friend probed.

'No, not really, but I will order some Italian silk lingerie to reel him in.'

'Oh, he won't be able to resist you, my dear. As you say, he'll come running back again, just like before. Sir Anthony Sinclair will never settle with one woman. He can't stop himself. Sir Anthony Sinclair is the biggest philanderer in Edinburgh.'

The fuchsia bonnet slipped from Cynthia's hands. As she bent to pick it up, Anne and her friend swished past her in their organza dresses.

Sir Anthony Sinclair, the biggest philanderer in Edinburgh? How can that be so? Please don't let this be true.

CHAPTER ELEVEN

CYNTHIA GLIMPSED ONLY THE BACK OF ANNE. At least she assumed the tall figure in a fir green cape to be the woman who spoke of seducing Anthony with Italian silk lingerie. The caped women had an air of haughtiness – a subtle shimmy about her shoulders, head held as high as her overwhelming bonnet would allow. She was headed towards the front of the shop with her pal. As they reached the door, a bell tinkled and in came two other ladies who stopped to observe Anne and her friend as they crossed paths. Cynthia recognised the two new customers as Susanne, Anthony's sister, with her friend Marie.

'Oh, that's a pretty bonnet, Cynthia – I love the silk roses. Why don't you try it on?' Cynthia jumped as Julianne appeared at her shoulder. A few feet away to their left, Susanne and Marie stood by a glass counter displaying reels of satin ribbons. 'Cynthia, are you alright? Cynthia?'

'Sorry,' replied Cynthia, 'I just got distracted with something.' She returned the bonnet to its stand and motioned with her eyes towards Susanne and Marie.

'Oh, isn't that Anthony's sister?' whispered Julianne and Cynthia nodded, yes.

'I don't think they recognise us though,' said Cynthia in a hushed voice. As Susanne and Marie began chatting, Cynthia and Julianne returned their attention to the bonnet stand so they could surreptitiously listen to the conversation.

'Was that woman – the one in the green cape – Anthony's latest you know what?' Marie asked Susanne.

'Yes,' confirmed Susanne, then lowered her voice. 'Lady Anne Stewart. I don't like her one bit. I don't know what he saw in her.'

'Oh, I can guess,' giggled Marie, 'I've heard some terrible secrets about Lady Anne Stewart.'

'Shh, someone will hear you. We really shouldn't say such things, Mama would be horrified. She has told Anthony he must find a bride and settle down. Although she has been telling him that for years now, but you know Anthony, he does exactly how he pleases.'

Cynthia and Julianne exchanged confused looks. Secretly, Cynthia was hoping Susanne would say, 'But my brother has found the woman of his dreams in Lady Cynthia Marchmont.' Gossip was rife in the city just now. *Surely somebody's talking about Anthony and me?*

Marie sighed. 'I wish Anthony would look at me for his bride.'

'Gosh, don't be silly,' laughed Susanne, 'you're far too young for him and, besides, he would never be interested in my friends in that way. Mama wants him to look at Miss Julianne Walker. She is the new beauty in town.'

Cynthia looked at Julianne, whose expression matched hers – one of pure shock. They stood there, wordless. Then: 'Shall we go to Kennington & Jenner? I hear they have some beautiful new silks in.' That was Angela, appearing from behind the mirror where Lady Anne had earlier spoke of her desires for the man of Cynthia's dreams.

'Yes, let's go to Kennington & Jenner,' said Cynthia, a lump forming in her throat. 'Anything to get out of this shop.'

The ladies hurried out of the shop and made their way to Princes Street. Angela chatted away, hoping to lighten the sudden change in mood. They browsed for a while then, in a quiet corner of the store, Julianne broached the subject of Susanne's remark. She looked at Cynthia. 'I swear, Cynthia,' she said, 'I knew nothing about Lady Sinclair's wishes for Anthony – and he has never made any move to approach me on any level. He has always been courteous and friendly but that is all. You must believe me Cynthia. I have no interest in Anthony whatsoever.'

'Yes, of course I believe you,' said Cynthia through a weak smile, 'it was just a bit of a shock to hear. Just before Susanne made that remark,

I'd also overheard another conversation – between those two women who left the store as Susanne and Marie walked in. Did you see them?'

'Yes,' said Angela, 'I remember the woman in the green cape especially as she was very tall.'

'According to Susanne, one of those ladies was Lady Anne Stewart.'

Julianne frowned, nodding slowly. 'Oh yes, the woman in the green cape and elaborate bonnet was Lady Anne Stewart. Her husband, James, has land near my father's farm in the Borders. He is much older than her and rarely comes into town. Anne has a bit of a reputation.'

'What do you mean, what kind of reputation?' asked Angela.

'You know,' Julianne said, blushing as she dipped her head, 'she's known for being with other men. My mother likes Sir James and feels sorry for him for the way Anne treats him. Mother says Anne is a strumpet.'

'I see,' said Cynthia. She began to feel rather annoyed at Anthony – and jealous of Lady Anne, his former mistress. *Although Anthony did end the affair*, she conceded, *but I wonder if he did so before he asked me out?*

'I really like Lord William, Cynthia, you must believe me,' added Julianne, 'and even if Anthony's mother wants this, I do not.'

Julianne's words interrupted Cynthia's thoughts. 'Yes, I do believe you. It's just, I feel funny about all I have heard.'

'What else did you hear?' Angela asked.

Cynthia swallowed hard, then hissed: 'Lady Anne said she had been Anthony's mistress. And now she wants him back.'

'Goodness, are you sure that's what you heard?' Angela said.

'Oh yes, she intends to go after him – fully armed. "I know what Anthony Sinclair likes and I am going to do everything in power to win him back. I've done it before, I'll do it again," is what she said.'

Angela folded her sister's hands in hers 'Well, Lady Anne has nothing on you. Anthony would be a fool to take her back.'

'Oh, but Lady Anne knows Anthony very well indeed, according to what she said, and intimately, too,' explained Cynthia, her face pinking.

'Right, get the fighting gloves on,' said Angela, letting go of Cynthia's hands and pulling her long ivory gloves out of her purse. 'First, you must look your very best on Friday, so let's get shopping. Let's go to Débutante – I hear Madame Lafayette's got some fine new stock in.'

Cynthia and Julianne laughed at the determined look on Angela's face. 'Yes, let's go,' they said in unison.

They all linked arms and headed for the door.

Angela gasped at Cynthia's reflection in the mirror. 'You look beautiful Cynthia,' she said, 'If you don't trap Anthony tonight, he must be blind.'

Thank you,' breathed Cynthia, who had spent the last two hours preparing for that evening's dinner date with Anthony, Lord William, and Julianne. She could not herself believe how good she felt. Cynthia was in a rouge dress, made from a shimmering layer of gossamer over satin, with short, puffed sleeves adorned with pink ribbons. A rouge velvet ribbon tied in a neat bow below her bust, the lengths of the ribbon dangling to her knees. Smaller ribbon bows decorated the hemline. She wore matching satin gloves to her elbows and her maid had styled her pale blond hair into tight curls topped with a glittering tiara. Long diamond earrings and a matching necklace and bracelet twinkled in the candlelight, perfectly complementing Cynthia's outfit. Angela draped a blush satin shawl around Cynthia's shoulders – just as the doorbell rang.

Anthony stood at the bottom of the stairs looking immaculate in his dark dinner suit and crisp white cravat, bejewelled with a large pearl tie pin. Cynthia's breath caught in her mouth when she saw Anthony from the top of the stairs. She stood for a moment just soaking in the sight of him. As she descended, she felt Anthony's eyes on her, and her stomach somersaulted. She had decided to push all thoughts about Lady Anne to the back of her mind this evening. Well, she would try to do so.

God she is beautiful, thought Anthony as he watched Cynthia glide down the stairs. *If we were somewhere private right now, I would do a lot more than just look at her…a lot more.* He extended his hand to her as she came down the last few steps, and when she reached for it, his heart began to race. He bent over her hand and kissed it slowly and for a moment he felt like a young buck just out of short trousers. He wanted her and he wanted her right now. *God, I must get my mind and body under control.* They were in plain view of the butler and footman.

Anthony looked into Cynthia's eyes. 'You look lovely,' he said.

'Thank you,' she replied. She could hardly speak for nerves.

The butler, standing behind Anthony gave a subtle cough. 'Your coats, My Lord,' he said.

'Yes, thank you,' said Anthony, snapping out of his trance. He draped Cynthia's cape over her shoulders, pressing them softly.

Cynthia felt heat surge through her body at his touch. Anthony quickly pulled on his cape, took his gloves, top hat, and cane, and offered his arm to Cynthia before escorting her to the awaiting carriage. 'Goodnight Miss, Sir, enjoy your evening,' the butler said as Cynthia and Anthony walked into the brisk evening.

'Thank-you, we shall,' replied Cynthia.

Anthony helped Cynthia into the carriage then jumped in beside her. 'You look beautiful,' he said and lightly touched her cheek. The carriage pulled away and at once they were joggled from side to side. Anthony lowered his hand, reached behind Cynthia's neck, and drew her into a lingering kiss. Cynthia lay her hand on Anthony's shoulder as they bumped and swayed. When he felt her responding, Anthony explored her lips with his tongue, and when she gave a little gasp, he took the opportunity to plunge his tongue into her mouth. But when she groaned, Anthony suddenly pulled back. 'We have almost arrived, I must control myself,' he said into her ear. 'You drive me crazy and, trust me, I would much rather stay here and kiss you all evening than go to dinner. If I don't stop, I will embarrass us both when the groom opens the door.' Anthony's eyes glowed in the darkness of the carriage as he spoke. Cynthia loved what he'd said to her and how she felt after his kisses, but she knew he was right, they must stop now before they got too carried away.

The carriage pulled up outside The Strath Hotel and the groomsman opened the door. Anthony, now suitably restrained, jumped down and offered his hand to Cynthia before escorting her into the restaurant. He assisted Cynthia with her cape, which sent little frissons down her arms when his hands brushed her bare skin. She sat down just as Bill and Julianne arrived.

'Anthony, Cynthia, how nice to see you both,' Bill said as he shook Anthony's hand and kissed the back of Cynthia's, 'You both know Julianne.' He turned and helped Julianne out of her cape and onto her chair, his face breaking into a proud smile. *Ah*, thought Cynthia, *he's so smitten.*

'Yes, of course,' said Anthony as he bowed over Julianne's hand, 'how are you both?'

'Very well, I have been very busy trying to persuade Julianne to come to my sister-in-law, Diane's country estate, Hopetoun House, with me at the end of the month. It will be very informal, a small gathering of close friends only. No fuss, just an intimate weekend. That way, Julianne can become better acquainted with everyone.' Julianne sat there, smiling shyly into her shoulder.

'Well, has she agreed yet?' asked Anthony as he indicated a good bottle of claret on the menu to the hovering waiter.

'Not quite, but I am hoping if you can get Cynthia to join us also, she will definitely say yes,' said Bill with a wink.

'What's this? asked Cynthia, who had missed the men's conversation thus far. Her mind had again wandered to that wretched Lady Anne Stewart's comments in Madame Martine's shop: *I will order some Italian silk lingerie to reel him in.*

'Diane, William's young sister-in-law, is having her first weekend house party at her newly renovated country estate,' explained Anthony. 'Bill and I received invites yesterday. It is for two evenings and there will be shooting, croquet, archery, riding, and fishing during the day – and a music soiree or cards in the evening. Timothy, Bill's younger brother, has indulged her fully since they got married last year, and she went wild and renovated practically the whole house. Now she wants to show it off to her closest family and friends.' Cynthia nodded politely, unsure how to react. The waiter arrived and nobody spoke for a moment as he poured the claret. 'So, my dear,' Anthony said finally, leaning closer to Cynthia, 'would you like to accompany me to Hopetoun House?'

Cynthia's stomach clenched as anger suddenly rose inside her. Was Anthony only inviting her because Bill had put him on the spot?

'Are you sure you want to ask me?' she snapped back, 'I hear there are a multitude of ladies queuing up for that honour?' Anthony raised his eyebrows, his expression one of puzzlement. He looked at Cynthia for explanation for her sudden change of tone, but she buried her head in the menu.

The waiter returned to take their orders. Cynthia and Julianne requested oysters, while Anthony shrugged and ordered roast beef, still puzzled by Cynthia's astringent remark. Once Bill had given his order, Cynthia got up. 'Excuse me, I must go to the powder room,' she said.

Immediately Anthony rose and helped her out of her chair.

'Wait, Cynthia,' said Julianne, 'I shall come with you.'

When the ladies left, Bill leaned across the table towards Anthony. 'Well, old chap, what was all that about?'

'I have absolutely no idea,' said Anthony, spreading his hands.

'Did she say anything in the carriage on the way here?'

'Well, no, we were otherwise occupied on the way here,' said Anthony, 'there wasn't much time for talking.'

'What about the last time you saw each other? How did she seem then?'

Anthony shrugged. 'She seemed fine. We had a very pleasant day out riding and I thought we had just moved forward in our relationship. I don't understand what's happened.'

'Well, it looks like you have just taken a step backwards judging by her tone,' smirked Bill. 'Who knows what goes on in their pretty little heads at times.'

'Not me, that's for sure," said Anthony.

Cynthia and Julianne entered the powder room and sat in front of the mirrors. 'Cynthia, that was the wrong approach, now Anthony knows something is wrong,' Julianne said to their reflections.

'I know, I could hit myself. We had a lovely ride here – Anthony said the loveliest things, but something just snapped inside of me as I remembered Lady Anne's words just now.'

'Forget her, you must go back in there and be all charming…that's if you really want him?'

'Yes, yes of course I do, I don't know what came over me. I would love to be Anthony's partner for the weekend. I am so stupid.' Cynthia said wringing her handkerchief. 'Maybe he won't want me to go with him now.'

Julianne smiled. 'Rubbish, just go back and accept his invite. You could tell him you just thought you were too soon acquainted for a close family-and-friends-only affair.'

'Yes, you are right I will do that, thank you for your help,' Cynthia said.

The women arrived back at the table and took their seats, both smiling. Cynthia touched Anthony's sleeve and cast him an apologetic look. 'I'm sorry, Anthony. I would love to accompany you to Hopetoun House. It's just, well…I do not know Bill's relatives, so I wondered whether one of your closer lady friends – somebody who knows Diane and Timothy – would be a better fit?'

Anthony squeezed her hand beneath the table. 'I want you there, no one else,' he said.

'So, it's settled. Cynthia will accompany Anthony,' said Bill, gesturing across the table. Then he turned to Julianne. 'So, will you accompany me now?'

Julianne blushed. 'I would love to, but you must stay close to me and introduce me to everyone.'

'Oh, don't worry I intend to stay very close to you, all weekend, day and night,' said Bill, lifting his glass. 'Slàinte Mhath, all.'

'Slàinte Mhath,' they all sang.

The evening progressed, filled with fine food, claret, laughter, and conversation. The foursome created quite a stir in the restaurant: two of Edinburgh's notorious rakes, entertaining two young ladies of the capital's high society. All eyes were on the two couples. Come the morning, the rumour mill would be churning fast as the mamas of Edinburgh asked, 'Who are those two beauties who've captured the hearts of Lord William Mclean and Sir Anthony Sinclair?'

CHAPTER TWELVE

IT WAS GONE 10.30 P.M. when the two couples left the Strath Hotel, but by Edinburgh's High Society standards, the night was young – and the roaring frivolities of the city's music halls beckoned.

Anthony, Cynthia, Lord William and Julianne took their seats at the front of the hall in Leith – the kind of seats reserved for Edinburgh's most wealthy, while middle class patrons sat in the galleries above. The poorest of society stood huddled together on the top floor.

The music halls were all the rage on Edinburgh's society scene. And although the songs were at times crass, they were usually met with good humour. Everybody had fun, which was what the night was all about.

After the show, Lord William escorted Julianne to his carriage while Anthony and Cynthia left in a separate coach. As the carriage pulled away along Leith Walk, Anthony suddenly turned to Cynthia and blurted: 'I'm not seeing any other women just now.' He'd been mulling over Cynthia's comment at the dinner table all evening.

Cynthia flinched. 'Oh, yes, no, good…sorry, I…I don't know what to say to that.'

'It's just what you said earlier,' explained Anthony, 'when we were at dinner, and I mentioned Hopetoun House.' Anthony shifted in his seat. 'Please,' he added, taking Cynthia's hand in his, 'look at me and tell me that you believe me. Please don't listen to the gossip mongers before hearing my say on the matter.'

'Of course, I'm not,' Cynthia retorted, 'I am very capable of making up my own mind.'

'Then what was all that about earlier this evening? I promise you, Cynthia, I only have eyes for you.'

'Well,' Cynthia started, then looked down at her hands.

'Go on.'

'Well, I overheard a conversation – and, I know, before you say anything, Daddy always says, "Don't listen into conversation, because you will only hear half-truths," – but I heard a certain lady telling her friend how she would win you back and how…' Cynthia hesitated, appearing flustered. She was grateful for the darkness inside the carriage as she knew her cheeks were flushing.

'And which certain lady would that be?' asked Anthony. He was sick of all this tittle-tattle.

'Is there that many women?'

Anthony exhaled sharply. 'Yes. I won't lie to you, Cynthia. I have had quite a few liaisons in the past.'

Cynthia regretted her question as soon as it slipped from her lips. Anthony's tone had changed, too, she noticed. *I wish I'd kept my mouth shut.*

'So,' he urged, 'who is she? Or do you not know her name even?'

Cynthia shrugged. 'Well, I do, and I don't know her.'

'What the Dickens is that supposed to mean?' Anthony said, his voice incredulous. He was visibly losing his patience, which was unusual for him. Anthony could keep his head in the most frustrating of incidents, but Cynthia was driving him to distraction with her remarks.

'Your sister and her friend came into Madam Martine's shop the other day, just as that lady in question was leaving. Then I overheard your sister telling her friend how the lady who'd left was your ex-mistress. I later found out that woman was Lady Anne Stewart. Then your sister said your mother wants you to marry Julianne. Oh gosh, it's all too much,' finished Cynthia, holding her temples.

'Oh, you poor thing,' said Anthony, his tone calmer. He lifted Cynthia's hand to his mouth and kissed her delicate skin. 'You must think I'm such a cad. I have no interest in Julianne, I can assure you. And besides, Bill is besotted by her. He would challenge me to a duel if I asked her to marry me, I can assure you – and I do not wish to be killed by my best friend.' He laughed at his joke then smiled softly at Cynthia. 'Seriously, Julianne is not my type – and contrary to society's ways, I would like to marry for love, not at the will of my mother.' He lifted Cynthia's chin and leaned closer to her. Cynthia could smell his woody cologne. 'Do you believe me?'

Cynthia paused a moment, looking into Anthony's eyes, flickering in the amber glow of the coachman's gas lamp. 'Yes, I am sorry,' she said finally.

'Why are you sorry, it was playing on your mind. Now I understand. But, in future if something is bothering you, please ask me directly. Do not let it stew in your mind, that is how big dramas happen.'

Future? So, he wants to see me again? Gosh, I thought I'd spoiled my chances with him. Keep calm, smile, Cynthia. 'I promise, I'm sorry,' she said, 'I didn't mean to cause a drama.'

Anthony replied by pressing his lips to hers in a gentle kiss. Then he snaked his arm around her back and pulled her closer and kissed her harder, the pair of them jiggling like falling skittles as the carriage powered over the cobbles. Breathing deep and fast, Anthony slipped his hand beneath Cynthia's cape and grasped her breast, kneading it softly through the gossamer fabric of her dress. He felt her nipple harden and rubbed his thumb over it. Cynthia gasped at his touch, enjoying the blissful, fizzing heat surging through every cell and vein and artery in her body. No man had touched her so intimately before, and she felt him harden as she ran her hand up his thigh to his groin. Anthony groaned and pushed Cynthia's cape off her shoulder, then bent to kiss her neck, trailing kisses down her throat to her décolletage. She sucked in her breath. *God, I want more.* Cynthia reached up with her free hand and raked her fingers through Anthony's hair. It felt so silky.

Suddenly, the carriage came to a halt. Anthony quickly pulled Cynthia's cape back over her shoulder, closed his own cape and smoothed down his hair. Stepping down from the carriage, Cynthia wondered whether the coachman noticed her blatant excitement. Anthony didn't worry about such matters; servants saw and heard most

95

things, but Anthony knew they would keep their secrets to themselves if they wanted to keep their jobs.

Anthony escorted Cynthia to the door and kissed the back of her hand – just as the first few flakes of winter began to tumble from the sky. 'Be assured, my lady, I want to see a lot more of you,' he said, and Cynthia shivered. 'Do not listen to gossip mongers or overheard conversations without asking me to clarify what you hear. Do not let your imagination run riot. I shall speak to my mother and sister about the conversation you overheard.'

'Oh gosh, no, please don't do that, Anthony. Please don't tell your mother – she will take against me. Plus, everybody says she's a force to be reckoned with.'

'You're not afraid of my mother, are you?' he asked, astounded.

'Och, no, but I would hate to get on her wrong side.'

'You will not. She likes a person with spirit and cannot stand whimpering madams who do not stand up for themselves – and *you*, my lady, are not one of those.'

'Fine, but do not get me in trouble, please,' Cynthia pleaded.

Anthony grinned. 'Well, that depends what kind of trouble,' he said, 'I would like to get you in all sorts of trouble – and if the carriage had not stopped just then, I probably would have got you into untold trouble tonight.'

Cynthia giggled. 'Oh, Anthony, Sir, I am shocked at you. You are no gentleman.'

'Ha, well, I didn't hear you complaining before – and I promise you won't complain next time,' Anthony added, pecking her on the cheek. 'Goodnight, fair maiden, I will see you on Sunday for a ride in the park.' Then he gave Cynthia a dramatic salute, walked down the steps and disappeared into his carriage. The snow whirled magically, hypnotically in the darkness.

Lord Marchmont came out of his study at the end of the hallway as Cynthia entered the house. 'Oh, I trust you had a good evening, my dear,' he said, noting the dreamy smile on his daughter's face.

'Yes, Daddy, it was lovely,' she replied, peeling off her gloves and cape to hand to the butler who had appeared to assist her.

'Good, where did you go?'

'Well,' Cynthia began, 'We had a lovely dinner at the Strath Hotel – then we went to a music hall in Leith, which was highly amusing.'

'A *music* hall?' said Lord Marchmont, lifting his eyebrows in horror, 'can Sir Anthony Sinclair not take you somewhere better than that?'

Cynthia laughed. 'Oh, Daddy, music halls are all the rage and very amusing. Lots of high society faces were there tonight. I even saw your good friend, Sir James Gillespie, so, if it is good enough for him?' she made a questioning gesture with her palms.

'Well, yes, point taken,' blustered her father, 'but I think I will have a word with Lord Sinclair all the same. Dragging my daughter to a music hall indeed.'

'You will do no such thing, promise me?' Cynthia cringed at the idea.

'I will *not* promise. Sir Anthony Sinclair must treat you with utmost respect… or else.'

'Oh, Daddy you are so old fashioned,' she joked, thinking, *If Daddy thinks a music hall is uncouth, heaven only knows what he'd say if he knew about our carriage ride home tonight?* 'Anyway, I am off to bed. Goodnight, Daddy,' she said, rising on her tiptoes to kiss his cheek – then she headed upstairs to dream about Anthony.

Anthony sat in his carriage thinking about Cynthia and how anxious she'd been about another woman liking him. *She seemed a tad jealous,* he thought, *which means she must like me. That's good – but I must speak with Mother tomorrow.* He held that thought as he disembarked from the carriage into the flurry of snow, which was now settling.

Graham was waiting in the hallway. 'Apologies, Sir,' he said as Anthony stepped through the door, stamping on the tiled floor to rid his shoes of snow, 'but I'm afraid another note has arrived.' He proffered the sheet of parchment, patterned with the familiar script. Anthony read it and cursed.

SO, DID YOU ENJOY YOUR DINNER AND SHOW? WHAT A COSY FOURSOME. CONFUSING, THOUGH. I KNOW YOUR DUCHESS MOTHER WANTS YOU TO MARRY JULIANNE WALKER, BUT YOU SEEM TO FAVOUR CYNTHIA MARCHMONT. HOW ODD. I'M WATCHING YOU.

'Tell me, who delivered this?' said Anthony, furiously waving the paper.

Graham rubbed his temple. 'I'm sorry, Sir, but this is the problem – nobody knows. It appeared under the door about half an hour ago. One of the footmen found it, but when he investigated, there was nobody outside. But I must stress, we're all being very vigilant, Sir.'

Anthony studied the note again, sighing. 'Sorry, I know you're all doing your best, Graham. But this is getting out of hand. Did the footman think it was delivered by someone on foot or on horseback? It would help if we knew this.'

'Ah, yes, Sir,' said Graham, 'good point – and I do have some information in this respect.'

'Go on…'

'Well, he said he did not hear a horse, but believes he heard someone running towards Doune Terrace, Sir. This was before the snow started, Sir. The footman thought the footsteps belonged to a youngster as they were light and fast. Might have been a paid messenger?'

'Yes, probably. Whoever's behind this would not risk getting caught red-handed.'

Anthony handed the note back to Graham as he shed his cape. 'Get me a brandy and bring it to the library, please. I shall write to let everyone know this latest piece in the jigsaw – then you can have a boy deliver the missives.' He passed his cape to Graham, retrieved the note, and made his way down the dark hall.

'And make that a very large brandy,' he called over his shoulder.

CHAPTER THIRTEEN

ANTHONY COULD NOT STOP THINKING ABOUT THE LATEST NOTE as he crunched through the snow to his mother's house the following afternoon. He'd spent the entire morning writing letters to contacts, hoping somebody might offer a lead. But so far, his efforts had been in vain. As he turned into Heriot Row, Anthony peered over his shoulder and looked all around, wary that the secret scribe could be watching him. *Who is this letter-writer? And what do they want from me. How dare they.*

Entering his parents' home, Anthony glimpsed the hem of his sister's brunette skirts disappearing into the library. He followed her in there and tapped her on the shoulder. 'So, little sister, tell all.'

'Oh, God, Anthony, you made me jump out of my skin,' said Susanne, whirling around, hand fluttering to her chest. 'What do you mean?' Susanne hadn't a clue what her brother was talking about. Although Anthony was always finding out something or other about her and her friends and the mischief they got up to. Not that they did anything bad, but they did like to plot and scheme about finding husbands for one another or sneak out to soirees and balls they shouldn't be at. Just like all young girls of their ilk. Anthony never snitched on her to their parents, thank goodness, but he would make it clear if he was not happy with her behaviour. That said, she could not think of anything she'd done wrong this time, so she smiled sweetly at her brother, and raised an eyebrow in question.

'What were you saying about me and a certain lady in Madame

Martine's shop the other day?' said Anthony, narrowing his eyes at his sister.

Susanne shrugged. 'Nothing, I was just chatting with Marie about…' Susanne pressed the side of her palm to the corner of her mouth and whispered, 'Lady Anne Stewart.'

'But you know I don't like being the subject of gossip, especially by my own family – as you well know. And what's this you said about Mother wishing for me to marry Julianne? You should not be making this information public, Susanne.'

'Well, I thought we were being discreet – Marie and I were not exactly shouting from the rooftops. Lady Anne left the shop as we walked in. And Mother is embarrassed about your relationship with the woman – because of the wretched way she treats her husband. You know Lady Anne approached Mother at a ball recently? She tried to speak to her, but Mother snubbed the woman. Mother would hate to see you marry somebody like her – but Julianne on the other hand…'

'I shall marry whomever I choose,' stormed Anthony, 'Why does Mother have to meddle?'

'Oh, you know how she loves to gossip,'

Anthony looked at the ceiling then back at his sister. 'Well, what's done is done – but no more tittle-tattle in public, understand?'

Susanne nodded slowly and Anthony left the room. It suddenly dawned on her that she and Marie had been overheard in the shop that day. Indeed, she had spotted Julianne and Cynthia as she left the store, but she was certain they couldn't have heard her and Marie's conversation. But they must have done. How else would Anthony have found out? *Oh well, I suppose he took it quite well. I'll be careful from now on though.*

But Anthony was not happy. He went upstairs to his mother's study, rapped on the door, and entered before she replied. Rosalind was behind her desk, quill pen in hand, wearing a voluminous dress in forget-me-not blue. She looked up, her expression a little startled. 'Anthony, how lovely to see you.'

'You might not think so when I have said my piece,' he retorted.

Rosalind tilted her head and put down her pen. 'Oh, how so?'

'Miss Julianne, Lady Anne Stewart, Susanne…ring any bells, Mother?'

'Oh please, Anthony, whatever do you mean. You're talking in riddles, dear boy.'

'Oh, mother, please, do not try this game with me, you know perfectly fine what I am talking about. I do not like you or my little sister interfering in my affairs. Do not play the innocent with me.' Anthony said curtly.

A frown knitted Rosalind's forehead. 'Do not take that tone with me, I have no idea what you are talking about.'

'Yes, you do. I believe you snubbed Lady Stewart at a ball recently – and you've been telling the whole city of your wish for me to marry Julianne…'

'Honestly, Anthony darling…'

Anthony held up his hand in protest. 'Oh no, do not insult my intelligence by denying this. I know you hate when you are confronted by my mistresses, which is not often, as you and they do not usually go to the same balls, thankfully,' he said and dropped heavily into the chair on the opposite side of the desk. 'As you know, I try to avoid confrontations but this time the gossip has repercussions, and I am not happy about this.' He paused, drumming his fingers on the arm of the chair, then went on: 'Susanne and her friend saw Lady Anne in Madame Martine's shop the other day. They ignored her but then proceeded to have a tete-a tete in the store about her – and you wanting me to marry Miss Julianne Walker. Unfortunately, they were overheard by Cynthia Marchmont and Julianne. As you know I have been seeing quite a lot of Miss Marchmont and Bill is stepping out with Julianne. So, telling people you wish me to marry Julianne has reached their ears, via my sister and her friend. This has caused a lot of problems. Miss Marchmont was most upset – and I have had to explain all to her. So, can you understand why I am not happy?'

Rosalind fell silent for a moment. Was her Anthony falling for Cynthia Marchmont? Georgina's daughter? She'd never heard Anthony talk so passionately about a lady before. He seemed deeply concerned that Cynthia's feelings had been hurt. 'Yes Anthony, I understand why your unhappy,' she said, 'but you cannot blame me for all this. I did snub Lady Anne – because I did not think she was suitable for you. The way she treats her husband is abominable. She's terribly indiscreet, flaunting her conquests in his face. Poor man. Now, I am not a prude, but she is beyond the pale.' Rosalind inhaled deeply. 'I did say, on a couple of occasions, that I would like you to marry Miss Walker, but what is wrong with that? If you had told me you were interested in Miss Marchmont, I would have been more than pleased, after all she is the daughter of one of my oldest friends. I had no idea you were even seeing Cynthia. You tell me nothing.'

'Mother, there is something else,' said Anthony, ignoring Rosalind's dig at him.

'Whatever else could there be? I've been accused of all sorts today,' she said, making a flouncy gesture with her arm.

'Oh please, Mother, stop with the theatricals.'

Rosalind straightened her back and fiddled with the pearls at her neck. She always did this when she felt awkward or overpowered.

'I received another letter last night. In this one the author claims to know of your desire for Julianne and me to marry. So, I need to know exactly who you made this comment to.'

'Oh, gosh, I shall have to think, Anthony. I would only have said it in passing – to friends at a soiree or two, perhaps. I'll rack my brains though. I know how much these letters are worrying you.' And with that, she rose and went around the desk to hug her son. 'I will make a list of people I've spoken to and send it over later,' she promised, 'I am sorry to have caused you anxiety. I did not mean to, but I am still correct about Lady Stewart.'

Anthony laughed. It was so typical of his mother to get the last word in.

That evening, Anthony bumped into Ronald at the No1. Club. 'Anthony, dear chap, I'm glad you're here,' said his friend, steering

Anthony by the elbow to a table in a stony alcove. 'Remember Lady Jane Carruthers, from Caithness?' added Ronald as the pair sat down.

'You mean Lord Alfred Carruthers' daughter? Yes, I met her a few times on my trips to Caithness. Her father was a good pal of my late father.'

Ronald placed his hands on the table and leaned back in his chair. 'I'm afraid she's disappeared. Vanished.'

'Vanished?' echoed Anthony.

'My friend from Wick arrived last night – and delivered the news. Apparently, she's been missing for over two weeks now. Everyone up there has been searching for her with no sightings. It's a damn strange affair. She went to a ball at Wick Assembly Rooms with her parents and sister. She danced most of the night, according to witnesses, then she left with some friends while her parents and sister went home. Lady Jane has not been seen since.'

'Goodness,' said Anthony, 'what else do we know? Have you told Grant about this?'

Ronald signalled for the waiter. 'Yes, Grant knows. He's on his way. He'll be here soon.' The waiter appeared and the gentlemen ordered ale, including a pint for Grant for when he arrived. 'Of course, Lady Jane's family is frantic with worry. Special police constables were drafted in from Inverness but still no sign of her. All sorts of theories are flying around. She was spotted a few times in the days leading up to the ball – with a gentleman. They were on horseback, according to reports, riding across the moors and near your estate, but no one knows who this gentleman is or where he is now. Some people think Lady Jane may have eloped with this chap.'

Anthony pulled back his head in surprise. 'Really? It's not often a woman goes missing without a trace. And Lady Jane did not strike me as a featherbrain who would run off on a whim.'

'Well, she was left a vast fortune by her uncle. He died last year and whoever marries her will have control of that sum. Her parents think she was abducted but thought a ransom note would have arrived by now if so.' The waiter arrived with the drinks, shortly followed by Grant, his black coat speckled with fresh snow.

'Evening gentlemen,' he said, removing his top hat, also wet with flakes, 'Damn, it's blowing a blizzard out there. I take it Ronald's told you about this situation up north, Anthony?'

Anthony nodded yes. 'What's the plan of action, Grant?'

'Well, our office has sent two of our best agents up to Caithness. They're there as we speak.' Grant sat down and reached for his ale – then turned to the waiter. 'Please, fetch us the food menu – and three whiskeys. I need some warmth.'

'So, how goes the case, Grant?' said Ronald.

'Very interesting,' said Grant, then turned to Anthony. 'Do you remember the mention of a man with a large green ring?'

'Yes, but what has that got to do with all this?'

Grant took a long glug of ale then set down his tankard. 'Well, a young stable lad in a riding post near Wick saw a gent changing steads there – and he noticed he had on a very large, green-stoned ring. He could not describe his features as it was pouring with rain and the chap had his head down. But he did notice the ring when the gent removed his wet gloves to put on dry ones. The stable lad said the man seemed in a hurry and left without giving him a halfpenny even. "Mean old bugger", were his exact words.' Grant laughed.

'Anything else?' asked Anthony.

'Yes, he was next seen at an inn near your estate, here in Edinburgh – just days ago. It was the Sheep Heid Inn. They were very busy that night, but he got a room, where he ate dinner. The maid who served him remembered his ring and how bad tempered he was. She said he had a beard but could not see his face that well as it was dark, lit only by a candle on the other side of the room. But she noted that his clothes were modern and well-tailored. She also said she had worked for a grand estate for a few years and could therefore tell the difference from gentry to ordinary well-off men. We got the gist from her explanation, that he was gentry.'

'So, he could be our man?' said Anthony.

'Not sure, I will get another report in the next few days. But it is a bit of a coincidence if it is, don't you think? If he is the same chap who is sending you letters – and with him being in Caithness at the time Lady Jane disappeared suggests he has an accomplice watching your every move. Are you a close acquaintance of Miss Carruthers? Could this be connected?'

'No, I know her but not that well. I don't see any connection between her disappearance and my letters.'

'I heard you got another note?' said Grant. I think I might go to Caithness myself if this next report does not shed more light on things.'

'Use my house as your base, I will send word to expect you.' offered Anthony.

'Thanks, I probably will go up. I love a mystery, especially if I solve it.'

'I'll drink to that,' said Anthony, as the waiter reappeared with the whiskey and menus.

The three gents discussed matters further over dinner, all of them baffled but determined to crack the case of the mystery notes and Lady Jane's disappearance. But time was limited this evening as Ronald and Anthony were due to attend a soiree at the Assembly Rooms. They paid the bill and Grant was first to get up. 'Right, I must go,' he said, 'enjoy your soiree – I'm glad I'm not going,' he chuckled as he left.

Anthony and Ronald stood up. 'I hope we get to the bottom of this,' said Ronald, 'let me know if you need anything.'

'Yes, I will, thanks,' Anthony replied as they headed for the door. 'See you at the soiree, if not before.'

The men parted company in the polar air – air steeped in mystery and anticipation. Anthony pulled his cape tight around his torso as he walked home, his mind racing as fast as the falling snow, but as he tried to make sense of all he'd just heard, there was one image that interrupted his thoughts: Miss Cynthia Marchmont, in the back of the carriage the previous night, her skin luminous and soft in the gas light.

Am I in love? he thought.

CHAPTER FOURTEEN

CYNTHIA SAT AT THE DRESSING TABLE AND DAYDREAMED ABOUT ANTHONY while Lily wound sections of her hair around rags to make ringlets. In a few hours' time, Cynthia would be at Lady Prudence Weatherspoon's ball, dancing with Anthony amid the warm glow of candelabras. She held that picture in her mind as she also thought about her recent encounters with Anthony. *I cannot stop thinking about him.*

She'd had the most marvellous week. On the Sunday morning after their dinner at the Strath Hotel with Lord William and Julianne, Anthony had taken Cynthia on a long ride to Cramond, where they'd stopped at the cosy inn for lunch. Cynthia's stomach flipped and her face reddened as she remembered how she'd asked Anthony, over bowls of steaming broth, 'Would you and your family like to accompany our family to Portobello on Tuesday?' She'd feared she might have sounded too forward, but Anthony had smiled and accepted her invite.

The Portobello trip ended up being quite a crowded affair, with Heather and David joining the Marchmont and Sinclair families. Julianne attended, as did Ronald, who brought a few friends along too. Alas, Sir Daniel Friel also made an appearance. He accompanied Raquel, but Cynthia noticed his sly looks cast in her direction – and the way he seemed always to be hovering around her – and this made her feel uneasy at times. However, nothing could dampen Cynthia's mood. The weather had been crisp yet sunny. They even managed a brisk picnic on the beach and a few games of rounders, organised by Lord Marchmont.

On the way home from Portobello, Anthony had sat with her in his carriage and held her hand – even though Lord William and Julianne were sitting opposite them. Anthony dropped the other couple off first, then took Cynthia home via the longest route possible.

Both Cynthia and Anthony had shared the same secret thought throughout the journey: *I wish this day could last forever.*

'Miss Cynthia, would you please sit still,' chuckled Lily into the dressing table mirror. 'You will never make it to Lady Weatherspoon's ball this evening at this rate – else you'll have wonky curls. You keep fidgeting and moving your head.'

Cynthia met Lily's gaze in the mirror. 'I'm sorry,' she giggled, 'I had no idea I was moving. I promise I'll keep still from now on.'

Lily tutted and grabbed another piece of rag off the dressing table. 'Honestly, you young ladies, I don't know where you find the energy. Always on the go.' Cynthia straightened her back – and then drifted back to her thoughts.

She wondered whether she should feel disappointed that Anthony had not directly invited her to Lady Weatherspoon's ball. Instead, she'd heard the news from Heather during the Portobello excursion. 'Anthony will be taking you to the ball on Saturday night,' Heather had announced as they strolled along the promenade, their bonnets and dresses buffeted by the cool breeze. 'I told him he simply *must* invite you.'

'But…' Cynthia protested, just as Anthony appeared on her shoulder.

'Anthony, my dear,' began Heather, 'I was just explaining to Cynthia that you'll be accompanying her to Lady Weatherspoon's ball on Saturday.'

Anthony stopped and sighed, raising his chin skywards and folding his hands behind his back. 'Heather, dearest, would you be so kind as to give Miss Marchmont and me a moment?' He tilted his head sideways in a shooing movement.

'Of course,' said Heather, a mischievous smile flitting east to west across her face. Then she hurried ahead to catch up with David. Once again, Cynthia and Anthony were alone. They continued walking at a slow pace. 'I'm sorry about that,' said Anthony, his breath visible in the cold air as he spoke. 'I was talking with your father earlier when Heather stormed in and asked him whether he'd mind my accompanying you to the ball.'

'Gosh, what did he say?'

'He said yes, of course. Heather took for granted my compliance – and I'm jolly well glad she did so. 'I apologise. I hadn't asked you thus far as I assumed you were going with your family. I did not want to presume to interfere with that arrangement. But Heather did. I hope you don't mind.'

'Of course, I don't mind. I am glad Heather did ask you. She is quite the organiser, isn't she?'

'Oh yes, and it can be a bit annoying sometimes, but definitely not this time' said Anthony, smiling.

Two days later, Anthony had joined Cynthia and her family to the Botanical Gardens. Thankfully, Sir Daniel Friel did not show his face. *How did Daddy get us out of that situation?* thought Cynthia. After a stroll around the Botanical Gardens, they went for lunch at the Stockbridge Tavern. 'You must come to our house for dinner this evening, Anthony,' said Lord Marchmont, who was becoming quite fond of Anthony as he got to know him as a person and not by reputation alone.

Cynthia was delighted when Anthony accepted her father's offer and, that evening, for the first time, they all sat around the table together in the Marchmont's townhouse. For Cynthia, this felt like another step forwards in their relationship. And the meal was a cosy concern, served in the front parlour, which was smaller and more intimate than the dining room.

'Gosh, what a week it's been,' Cynthia said out loud, patting her neat, knotted hair.

'Indeed. Right, that's you done for now,' said Lily, straightening her apron. 'I'll be back in two hours to untie the rags and help you into your dress. Is there anything else I can do for you, Miss Marchmont?'

'Oh, no, thank you Lily.'

* * *

The doorbell rang as Lily fastened the laces on the back of Cynthia's silk dress. 'Ooh, that'll be him,' gasped Cynthia, 'Please, Lily, do hurry.'

Lily tugged hard at the laces, pulling the corseted bodice tightly around Cynthia's ribs and waist. 'There, all done,' she said, and tied the final bow. 'Now off you go and have a splendid evening.'

'Oh, I shall,' said Cynthia. She glided out of the room.

Downstairs, Howard greeted Anthony in the hallway. 'Good evening, Lord Sinclair,' he said with a gentle bow.

'Good evening, Howard,' Anthony replied, and Howard felt an immediate glow of pride that Lord Sinclair had remembered his name.

'May I take your cape, sir?'

'Och, no need, Howard. Miss Marchmont and I are going straight…' Suddenly Anthony was lost for words as he glanced up and saw Cynthia descending the stairs. She moved with the grace and poise of a ballerina in a swirl of cherry blossom silk.

Cynthia had taken delivery of her new dress the previous day – one of Madam Lafayette's 'finest creations yet', Angela had remarked. Nipped tightly at the waist, dozens of silk roses festooned the hem. The neckline was low but decent, revealing a flash of ample breast flesh. Cynthia's hair, now free of rags, lay in shimmering ringlets that trailed down her neck. She had on one of the family tiaras, encrusted with glinting garnet stones, with matching long drop earrings, necklace, and bracelet. A deep pink velvet purse and matching feather fan fluttered daintily in her hand.

As Anthony watched with admiration, Cynthia, too, was enchanted. Anthony looked gloriously handsome in his navy evening dress suit, swathed in a thick, dark cape. *He gets better looking by the minute,* she thought, her stomach aflutter with excitement again. Anthony extended his hand as Cynthia arrived at the bottom of the staircase. He felt a deep, stirring arousal flood his body. *Goodness, Anthony, do control yourself.* 'You look beautiful, Cynthia. You take my breath away,' he said, bowing as he kissed her hand. He would have enveloped her in a tight hug and kissed her perfect lips if Howard were not standing a few feet away.

'Thank you,' said Cynthia, her voice breathy. *Oh, I wish I could kiss him.*

Anthony noticed Cynthia's face flushing and bent to whisper in her ear. 'My thoughts exactly.' Then, with a broad smile, he stood tall and flashed Cynthia a wink. A wicked wink full of promise.

Cynthia was a little taken aback. *How does he know what I'm thinking?*

'Your carriage awaits, my lady,' said Anthony as Howard handed Cynthia's cape to him. 'We're meeting Heather and David at the Assembly Rooms for pre-ball drinks and dinner.' He swept forth and draped the smooth velvet over her shoulders, squeezing them gently as he did so. Then had crooked his arm for Cynthia to hold. 'Shall we?' he said.

'Oh yes,' whispered Cynthia.

They arrived at the Assembly Rooms at the same time as Heather and David. The two couples greeted in a flurry of hugs and kisses. 'Cynthia, you look lovely,' Heather enthused, admiring her dress. 'You make me quite jealous. All the gentlemen will only have eyes for you.' Heather deliberately raised her voice as she said this. *Hopefully Anthony hea*rd, she thought. *A little jealousy always helps a relationship along.*

'Nonsense,' Cynthia replied. 'Look at you, that lilac is perfect on you.'

The foursome cut elegant figures as they entered the Assembly Rooms, all so handsomely dressed for the forthcoming ball at Lady Prudence Weatherspoon's posh Charlotte Square abode. Other patrons who had not been invited to the prestigious event in Edinburgh's society calendar eyed them with envy. The waiter escorted the couples to the supper room, alive with high society personalities sipping champagne and chatting with much animation. They made their way to a table hugging the back wall, where Lord William and Julianne were already seated. After a champagne reception, dinner was served.

'Odd business going on in Caithness now,' Lord William whispered to Anthony as the ladies chatted.

'Indeed, very strange,' said Anthony. 'But let's not talk about it tonight. We don't want the ladies to overhear us. Such gloomy discussions would ruin their evening.'

'Quite, you're right, Anthony. I'll call round on Monday to see if there are any updates.'

The meal was a lavish affair of seven courses, each one excelling the next. After the final course of apple pie, Cynthia turned to Anthony, sitting next to her, placed her hands on her slender waist and giggled. 'I think I am going to burst. This fashion does not accommodate huge meals like this.'

Anthony laughed, then, leaning closer to Cynthia, said under his breath, 'Well, I could always take you upstairs and help you out of your dress and loosen your corset, if you wish?'

Cynthia blushed, but her heart shook with erotic anticipation. She responded by opening her fan and waving it coyly beneath her chin. 'I see you are in accord with my suggestion,' added Anthony, placing his hand on her thigh beneath the table.

'You know I am,' she whispered and reached for Anthony's leg too, while still fanning her face. They both felt heat surge through their bodies.

'Right, everyone, time for the ball,' Heather announced, clapping her hands as she stood.

'Perfect timing as usual,' mocked Anthony, and Cynthia giggled.

Everyone made their way out to the awaiting carriages. Anthony had offered William and Julianne a lift to reduce the number of carriages arriving together; the queues to get to the ballroom entrance were invariably long and slow. However, Anthony was now regretting this move as he fervently wished he could be alone with Cynthia before the crush of the crowd engulfed them, and greetings became the order of the evening.

The crush inside the ball was intense, made worse by the ladies' bouffant dresses. Progressing up the sweeping staircase seemed to take the women an age. Julianne and Cynthia marvelled at all the beautiful dresses and decorations as they climbed. Cynthia was in grand spirits until she felt an unpleasant presence behind her on the landing. A shiver trembled down her spine. She turned, and there he stood, smiling eerily at her across the floor: Sir Daniel Friel. Lady Claire Wentworth stood beside him, also darting Cynthia a cold look. Sir Daniel's smile slid into a sinister frown that chilled Cynthia's bones, and just then, Anthony appeared at her side. Sir Daniel and Claire turned to speak to another couple then, but Anthony had clocked the wordless exchange between Cynthia and Sir Daniel. 'What's wrong?' he said, touching Cynthia's arm. 'You look glum, all of a sudden.'

'Oh, gosh, no,' said Cynthia, 'I'm perfectly fine. Shall we go through to the ballroom?'

The first waltz struck up and Anthony escorted Cynthia to the dance floor. As they moved, Cynthia felt the warmth of his hands on her arm and waist. And as he stared into her eyes, she thought she might melt like burning sugar on the spot. They floated around the room as one, oblivious to all movement around them. They did not talk, but danced and absorbed the music, both revelling in the joy of their physical connection. When the waltz ended, Cynthia reluctantly moved on to Ronald, her next dance partner. A quirky polka flooded the room, and Cynthia followed Ronald's lead, feeling bereft without Anthony's arms around her.

Anthony was watching Cynthia and Ronald dance when Sir Daniel sidled up to him. 'She is so captivating to watch, isn't she,' remarked Sir Daniel.

'Yes, she is,' said Anthony, his eyes still fixed on the dancing couple.

'Finest woman in the room, I'd say.'

Anthony turned to face his interlocuter and his spine prickled. He had been so engrossed watching Cynthia that he hadn't recognised Sir Daniel's voice. Anthony had taken an instant dislike to Sir Daniel. He found him pretentious and resented the way he lingered around Cynthia. Now, he felt Sir Daniel's comments seemed somewhat inappropriate. *Does he not know Cynthia is stepping out with me? And why did he frown at Cynthia earlier?*

'I think I'll ask her for the next dance,' Sir Daniel added.

Anthony shot him a stony glare. 'That will not be possible,' he said, 'she's promised to me.' He walked away then, pacing determinedly onto the dance floor. *How dare that weasel be so presumptuous.* Anthony reached Cynthia as the closing bars of the polka rang out. He claimed her hand, feeling extremely possessive of her in that moment. He did not see the fury that knotted Sir Daniel's face. Lord William, watching the tableau from a nearby pillar, noted Sir Daniel's disgruntled demeanour with suspicion.

'May I?' said Anthony, reaching for Cynthia's opposite elbow.

'Oh, Anthony, could we please possibly sit this one out? That polka was very energetic – I feel quite fatigued.'

Anthony nodded. 'Very well, of course,' he said, trying to hide his disappointment. 'Let me escort you to a table and we'll order refreshments.' Cynthia took Anthony's arm and he steered her to an adjacent room where guests were seated around small, round tables adorned with vases sprouting lilies and thistles. He found a vacant table and helped Cynthia into her seat. 'Right, you rest here while I fetch us some drinks. Will champagne suit the lady?'

Cynthia fanned her face again, causing her ringlets to sway a little. 'I think the lady would love some champagne,' she said, grinning. She loved that Anthony was making such a fuss of her. *He's attentive as well as handsome.*

'Coming right up, m'lady,' said Anthony.' He disappeared and returned ten minutes later, carrying two glasses of champagne. 'Actually, you do look tired, Cynthia. Do you wish to leave?'

'Heavens no,' smiled Cynthia. I am having a lovely evening. I just need to catch my breath from all the dancing.'

They sat and chatted for a while, then William and Julianne approached their table. 'Oh, Cynthia, so sorry to interrupt, but do you happen to know where the powder room is? I've been searching all over.'

'Oh, I think it's through the ballroom,' said Cynthia, rising. 'I'll come with you.' Lord William took Cynthia's seat and he and Anthony watched the two women as they walked arm in arm towards the powder room.

'Tell me, dear friend,' Lord William began, lightly nudging Anthony's arm, 'whatever did you say to upset Sir Daniel Friel?'

Anthony jerked back his head in surprise. 'Nothing, what do you mean?'

'Well, if looks could kill…you, my friend would have a dagger in your back.'

'How come?'

'I saw the pair of you talking, while Cynthia was dancing with Ronald. When you left and went over to Cynthia, Sir Daniel stared at you with utter contempt. I wondered what had caused such venom.'

'Well, I told him he could not have the next dance with Cynthia as I was her next partner – even though that was a lie. I just don't want him near her. I have taken a dislike to the man.'

'Well, I think the feeling is mutual, old chap,' Lord William laughed. He found the situation quite amusing; he and Anthony were often the target of disdain from other gentlemen – those who were jealous of their families, wealth, connections, reputations and, moreover, the women who flocked to them. Anthony and Lord William invariably took most of this in jest, but this time, Anthony was not amused.

As Julianne and Cynthia walked back to the table, Cynthia suddenly realised she'd left her fan in the powder room. She told Julianne to go ahead while she went back to retrieve her accessory. 'I'll meet you back at the table,' she said. Cynthia found her fan on the washstand and headed back to the table. But just as she neared the edge of the ballroom, she felt a coldness on her elbow. She wheeled round, and again came face to face with Sir Daniel

"Ah, Miss Marchmont, I do hope you will accompany me for a dance, my dear?' he said, his beady eyes beating up and down her frame. He reached for her elbow again. 'Come, the next dance is about to begin,' he persisted.

'I'm sorry, but my friends are waiting for me in another room,' she said hurriedly, trying to remove her elbow from his grip, but Sir Daniel was already steering her towards the middle of the dance floor.

'I'm sure they won't mind. In fact, I was talking to Lord Sinclair earlier. I mentioned I proposed to dance with you, and he did not seem to mind.' Cynthia shuddered as Sir Daniel jostled her into position as a ballade began, soft and romantic. He bowed and took her hand. Cynthia flinched and shivered at his touch. The dance seemed to last forever, Sir Daniel tightening his grip around her waist as the music crescendoed hauntingly around her. She was relieved when the dance finally ended. She curtseyed politely, thanking Sir Daniel, and was just about to make her excuses and leave when he blurted, 'Would you care to take a stroll around the garden?'

'No, she would not like to stroll around the garden.'

Cynthia jumped and turned. 'Anthony,' she said, shocked. She hadn't seen or heard him approaching. He looked calm, but his tone sounded dangerous.

Anthony took Cynthia's hand and glared at Sir Daniel. 'Come on, Cynthia, let's go.'

Sir Daniel let out a derisive laugh. 'Surely the lady can speak for herself. She is not your property, sir.'

'Mind you don't go too far, *sir*, you have already crossed a line. The Lady is under my care tonight, as you well know.' Anthony's voice rattled in a low and icy tone.

'She still has not given me her own answer,' Sir Daniel said, gesturing at Cynthia.

Cynthia swallowed hard. 'Well, Sir,' she said, 'I came here with Lord Sinclair, and we are about to leave, so, no, I do not wish to stroll in the garden with you. Anthony darted Sir Daniel another warning look, then ushered Cynthia towards the staircase at speed.

'Can you please slow down, Anthony, I cannot keep up this pace and people are beginning to notice,' she pleaded, her corset crunching her ribs with every step.

'Sorry,' Anthony muttered, but he didn't slow down.

Anthony left a note with the doorman for Lord William, informing him of their departure. Then he ordered their capes and quickly helped Cynthia into hers before shrugging on his, without as much as speaking. *He's not even looking at me*, thought Cynthia.

It was raining when they left. Torrential rain that hammered the hood of the carriage. Cynthia's heart banged to the same punishing beat. They travelled in silence, Anthony staring out of the window, chin in his hand. 'Are you angry at me, Anthony?' Cynthia asked after a few minutes. For she could not bear this agonising silence any longer.

Anthony wiped away a few droplets of rain from his forehead and breathed deeply. 'Why did you dance with that man, Friel? I thought you disliked him.'

'He gave me no choice. When I left the powder room, he grabbed my arm and practically pulled me onto the dance floor with him. I did not want to make a scene, so I danced with him.' Anger rose in her chest. *None of this is my fault – so why is Anthony using this accusatory tone with me?* 'Anyway, he told me he had asked you earlier if he could dance with me – and apparently, you did not mind one jot.'

'The devil asked no such thing. How could you possibly think I would want you to dance with someone you disliked?' Anthony shot back.

Cynthia's eyes began to burn. 'How was I to know – it's not as though you were there to rescue me. This has ruined my entire evening. It's ruined *everything*. Cynthia looked away, anger and disappointment engulfing her. 'And I was having such a lovely time too.'

'Oh, you poor thing,' scoffed Anthony. 'It's not exactly been an evening of bonhomie for me, either – seeing that man dancing with my partner.'

They slowed to a halt in Royal Circus. Outside, the rain continued, falling harder and faster. The carriage wobbled in the onslaught. Cynthia faced the door and held her breath.

No way will I let him see my tears, she vowed. The groom opened the carriage door, and Anthony assisted Cynthia down, just as Howard rushed to the carriage with a parasol. She ducked beneath the canopy and allowed Howard to walk her to the front door. Anthony followed.

As Howard opened the door, Cynthia turned to face Anthony. His features turned to stone. There was no smile or romantic gestures. He simply nodded, then turned and hurried down the steps and into his carriage. He didn't look back.

The night sky roared with thunder.

CHAPTER FIFTEEN

CYNTHIA THREW OFF HER SOAKED CAPE, her breath juddering and catching in her throat. The staircase blurred in oak and orangey hues as she ran up it, tears bulging her eyes. She powered into her room, collapsed on her bed, and wept the tears she'd held back in the carriage.

The walls pulsated with Cynthia's sobs, as though they were crying themselves. Angela heard the noise as she made her way down from the parlour upstairs. She had hoped to go into her sister's room to hear about all about her romantic evening at Lady Weatherspoon's ball. Instead, she was shocked to see Cynthia sprawled on her bed, her chest heaving as she wept violent tears.

'Cynthia, darling, whatever is the matter?' cried Angela. She sat on the edge of the bed and touched her sister's shoulder. Cynthia sat up, sobbing, and fell into Angela's arms. 'Oh Cynthia, what happened?' Angela pushed back Cynthia's curls. 'Tell me what happened, Cynthia.'

Cynthia wiped her eyes on the back of her hand, her breath still trembling. Then she gulped. 'Oh, Angela, I was having a magical evening until that horrid man, Sir Daniel Friel came along and forced me to dance with him. Anthony saw this happen and now he's angry with me and everything is ruined, and I don't know what to do,' Cynthia began. She paused for a few seconds, worrying at the velvet of her purse, still hooked to her wrist, then she took a deep breath and explained to Angela every detail of her tarnished evening at Lady Weatherspoon's ball. 'Anthony would not listen to my explanation on the way home, so we parted on bad terms. I don't know if I will see him again,' finished Cynthia, bursting into tears again.

'There, there,' said Angela, pulling Cynthia into a tight hug and stroking her back. 'Everything will be fine. It just sounds like a terrible misunderstanding, that's all. You've had your first argument with Anthony, but I'm sure, after a good night's sleep, things will look better in the morning.'

Cynthia sniffed as she looked into her sister's eyes. 'Do you really think so? Anthony was in a frightful rage.'

'I'm sure things will work themselves out. Anthony adores you – and seeing you dance with Sir Daniel made him jealous, which further proves that he cares about you, Cynthia.'

'Oh, I do hope so,' said Cynthia, a weak smile quivering on her wet face. 'I do hope so.'

'Here, let me help you out of your clothes and into bed,' said Angela, reaching for the laces at the back of Cynthia's dress. 'Then I will go down and make some hot milk for us and we will curl up together – just as we used to do when we were wee – when something frightened us.'

Angela helped Cynthia out of her dress and into her nightgown, then went down to the kitchen. She returned with warm milk and cake. Cynthia was still sniffing, so Angela got in beside her. 'Right, sister, dear, blow your nose, drink this, eat the cake, and we will figure out what to do next.'

'Thank you,' said Cynthia, and sipped her milk. She felt better already.

'Tomorrow is another day,' said Angela.

Meanwhile, back in his study at Moray Place, Anthony poured a generous measure of malt, rage pulsing through his veins. His anger puzzled him. Previously, when a gentleman had whisked a lady away from him, Anthony had dealt with it in his usual manner: firm but good-natured. But why this fury over a nobody like Sir Friel? *He's nothing but an irritant.*

Anthony tossed back his malt in fast glugs then poured a refill. Why am I also angry at Cynthia? She was innocent in all of this, yet he'd hardly spoken to her on the way home. He had treated her abominably; he had not even bid her good evening. *Me and Friel both behaved like cads of the first order. Together, we ruined Cynthia's evening.* Anthony slumped onto his chaise lounge. 'You idiot, Anthony,' he said out loud, squeezing his glass in both hands. He groaned deeply, drained his glass, and reached for the bottle once more.

The next day, around 11 a.m., Giles appeared on Anthony's doorstep. Graham ushered Giles inside and he relieved himself of his cape, hat, and cane. 'Where's Anthony?' he said, removing his sodden gloves. 'Gosh, it's really coming down out there.'

Graham hung Giles' wet garments on the hall stand. 'I'm afraid your brother is a trifle out of sorts this morning,' he said. 'He's in his study, drinking himself into oblivion, no doubt.'

'Really? I thought he went to Lady Weatherspoon's ball last night? It's not like Anthony to overdo things at a ball.'

Graham grunted. 'Yes, well, Sir came home last night in a foul mood, slamming doors and the likes. He even shouted at me and…' Graham cleared his throat. 'Pardon me for being so bold, sir, but this is not like the master at all, not since he was a young buck.' Graham shook his head, baffled. He had known Anthony since he was a child – when he'd worked as his personal valet. Therefore, he felt he could speak openly to Giles regarding Anthony's behaviour.

'Not at all, Graham, you know him better than most,' replied Giles. 'Do you know what happened to warrant this sudden outburst?'

'Not exactly, but judging by his mutterings last night, I would say his troubles concern a lady.'

Giles sighed. Today was Rosalind's birthday and he and Anthony were due to be at the family home for a celebratory lunch in just under two hours. The duchess would be most hurt – and angry – if Anthony failed to attend due to a hangover. 'Right, I'll go and speak to him. Send up black coffee and a cold press for his head – he's going to need all the help he can get.'

A cloud of whisky fumes assailed Giles as he entered Anthony's study. He walked over to the window and pulled back the curtains, coughing.' He looked at his brother, sprawled on the chaise lounge, jacket and shoes on the floor alongside an empty bottle of malt. 'For goodness' sake, Anthony. What is all this about. Why must you do this to yourself – and today of all days, too? Have you remembered it's mother's birthday lunch today? She'll have a fit if she sees you in this state.'

Anthony grumbled and yawned into his chest. It smelled of whisky. His face resembled a scrunched sheet of parchment. Giles bent over his brother and gave his shoulder a few shakes and prods. 'Come on, Anthony, you need to get up, now!' Anthony opened one eye and winced. 'That's it, wake up,' added Giles. 'Time to get up and dressed for mother's party.' Giles prodded him once more and Anthony flinched.

'Oh, leave me alone", he groaned.

'No, Mother will go mad if you miss her birthday lunch.'

'Oh, God, I forgot about that.' Anthony tried to lever himself from the chaise lounge, his limbs fluid and floppy. 'What time is it, anyway?'

'Almost midday,' lied Giles. 'So, you have just under an hour to make yourself presentable.'

The footman entered carrying a tray of coffee and a cold press. He set the tray down on the desk and Giles grabbed the press and slapped it on Anthony's forehead, causing him to moan in protest. 'Ouch, that's cold.'

'Stop moaning and drink this,' said Giles, handing him the cup of strong black coffee.

He turned to the footman. 'Thank you. Please get some bacon and bread for him. We will come through to the front parlour for it.'

Giles sat down opposite Anthony and watched him wince as he drank the coffee. 'So, tell all, why did you neck a whole bottle of malt on your own?'

'God knows, I got angry over a stupid incident at the ball. I let my feelings get in the way and things spiralled out of control,' said Anthony. He yawned again, then gave his brother a brief account of the previous night's events.

'It's not like you to react like this over a lady, Anthony,' said Giles.

'You are usually so in control, frighteningly so most times. And this Sir Friel fellow: do you think he likes Cynthia that much as to play with your wrath? If so, he is either a fool or in love, as no one in their right mind would cross swords with you…and I talk from brotherly experience.'

'I am not sure, but he gives Cynthia the creeps. He seems to turn up wherever she goes. It is more than just a coincidence.'

'So, how did you leave things with Cynthia?'

'Not well,' said Anthony, blowing into his coffee. 'We are supposed to be going to Timothy and Diane's this weekend, but I won't blame her is she calls it off. I was a complete cad.'

'Yes, sounds like you were,' agreed Giles. 'But we have to get you sorted and over to Mother's. So, upstairs for a bath and more coffee, then we can think of how you will apologise – because I reckon it'll be a huge one this time.'

Giles laughed as he ushered his brother up to his room. He was enjoying seeing his big brother in such a pickle as it was usually the other way round. Anthony was so sensible and grounded. Yes, this was a first in a very long time.

Miraculously, Anthony emerged from the depths of his hangover looking refreshed and immaculate in a slate grey dress suit. Before leaving for their mother's house, Giles asked Anthony how he proposed to apologise to Cynthia.

'Flowers or jewels?' asked Anthony, as they sat by the fireplace in the drawing room.

Giles laughed. 'Sorry, brother, dear, but I think this one calls for more imagination.'

Anthony buried his head in his hands. 'Argh, I can't think straight today. My brain is scrambled. Why did I overreact?' moaned Anthony.

Just then, Lord William and Ronald were shown in by Graham. 'You have guests, sir,' said Graham.

Ronald took one look at Anthony, still with his head in his hands, and said: 'Whoa, you look bad, Anthony, old chap. Did you go out on the dazzle after the ball last night?'

Anthony looked up, squinting. 'No, I came home after the ball and drank myself into oblivion.'

'Hmm,' said Lord William, rubbing his damp, orange sideburns. 'I noticed your foul mood when you left the ball last night. I think most others did too. Most unlike you, dear chap. What was that all about?'

'You don't know?' said Giles, raising his brows. 'My dear brother has been an utter cad to a certain young lady, who did nothing wrong. But he saw it differently and now will have to pay the price.'

'This should be good, do tell all,' said Ronald, rubbing his hands together. Giles relayed the story, much to Ronald and Lord William's amusement. Ronald sucked in his breath then exhaled loudly. 'Well, Anthony, I don't know how you're going to dig yourself out of this mess. It's colossal.'

All the men, except Anthony, snorted with laughter.

'Alright, joke over,' Anthony said gruffly. 'If you have no ideas or constructive advice, please just leave me alone in my misery.'

'Oh, no, no, no, no,' said Lord William, straightening his face. 'You need to get this sorted promptly, before this weekend; if Cynthia refuses to go to Tim and Diane's, so will Julianne. And you can't do that to me, Anthony. I have done nothing wrong.'

'Fine, Bill, maybe you have some suggestions as to how I can win Cynthia over? If so, I'm all ears.'

'Send her flowers. Take her for a romantic stroll. Buy her a diamond necklace. Go round there and beg on your knees for mercy. Do anything it takes to win her back- because if my weekend with Julianne is ruined due to your foolery, then you will have *me* to answer to.'

'Okay, fine, enough, please,' said Anthony, raking his fingers through his hair. God, his head hurt. 'I will sort this. Don't worry. I shall meet you and Ronald in the club on Monday. I'll update you on my progress then.'

Before leaving for the duchess' birthday lunch, Anthony wrote a note to Cynthia, apologising for his behaviour. He gave the letter to Graham and instructed him to arrange for it to be delivered, along with a huge basket of flowers, to the Marchmonts' home. Then he and Giles made their way to Heriot Row.

Susanne greeted her brothers in the hallway. 'Hello, dear brothers,' she squealed. 'Everyone else is already here, in the drawing room.'

The duchess was sitting in an elaborate high-backed armchair, her clear blue satin dress spilling over and around it like Highland spring water. 'Mother, dear,' said Anthony, bending to kiss her cheek. 'Many happy returns.' He handed her a gift – a sapphire bracelet he'd bought at McInnes and Love.

'Thank you, my dear,' she replied, sniffing theatrically – her way of telling Anthony, *I know you have a raging hangover – I can smell the whisky on you.*

Giles also kissed his mother and wished her many happy returns, and the duchess set about opening her gifts. She knew better than to say anything to Anthony regarding his present state. Instead, she asked, 'So how was Lady Weatherspoon's ball last night?'

Giles laughed. 'Ha, Anthony got himself into a bit of a pickle. A big pickle, actually.'

'Really?' said Susanne. 'Why does that not surprise me?'

'What did you do?' said Rosalind. 'I hope you haven't smeared our family name. People will be talking, you know.'

Anthony cast Giles a look that warned: *Do not say one more word.* Then the butler walked in.

'Ladies and gentlemen, lunch will now be served,' he announced regally.

Anthony made his way to the dining room with the others.

I must apologise to Cynthia tomorrow, he thought. *If it's not too late, that is.*

CHAPTER SIXTEEN

CYNTHIA WOKE AT NOON when Lily opened the drapes and placed a frothy cup of hot chocolate on her nightstand. It was unlike her to rise so late, but she had barely slept for tossing and turning and crying.

'Oh, my lady, are you alright?' said Lily, studying Cynthia's blotchy face and swollen eyes as she looked up from her pillow.

'I'm fine,' croaked Cynthia, 'but I wish to stay in bed today. Please apologise to my parents. Tell them I'm too exhausted after last night's ball.'

'As you wish, Miss Marchmont. I will fetch you up a light lunch on a tray.' Lily fussed around the room, collecting garments, including the ball gown Cynthia had felt so good in less than twenty-four hours ago, then left, just as Angela breezed in.

'Cynthia, my love, why don't we go out for a walk? Look, it's a nice day today. Blue skies and sunny, albeit a frosty nip in the air, but at least the rain has stopped.' Angela motioned at the window.

'No thank you,' Cynthia replied, rolling onto her other side and away from the sunny view. 'I am too tired, and I wish to stay in bed today.

'But it's not good for you. You'll feel better after a bath and a walk. You need to face the world, Cynthia.'

'No, I want to stay here and wallow in self-pity. Please, let me do this, Angela.'

Angela spent the next twenty minutes trying to convince Cynthia to get up, then Lily returned with lunch, as promised. Cynthia sat up.

'Your mother says she is expecting callers at 2 p.m. and if you feel up to it, please join them in the parlour,' said Lily, laying the tray on Cynthia's lap.

'No, I shall just stay here, thank you.'

'Well, miss, I shall run you a bath. That might make you feel better.'

Cynthia plunged her spoon into a bowl of broth. 'Very well,' she said. She knew Lily and Angela were only trying to lift her spirits.

After her bath, Cynthia changed into a light day dress then lay on her bed, determined to remain there. Angela stayed with her sister. She was reading aloud a fashion article in *My Fair Maid* magazine about next season's ball dresses when there was a sharp knock at the door. 'Come in,' she called, and the door opened with a click to reveal their footman, cradling the biggest basket of flowers the girls had ever seen. They both jumped from the bed. 'A delivery for Miss Cynthia Marchmont,' the footman announced, proffering the bouquet to her.

'Oh, Cynthia, what a beautiful basket,' said Angela once the footman had departed.' Quick, read the note.' Cynthia pulled the sheet of parchment from the envelope and read the note out loud. 'My dearest Cynthia, please accept these flowers as part of my apology for my appalling behaviour last night. Could you find it in your heart to forgive me? I would like to call on you tomorrow morning and apologise in person, if you will permit me? I await your reply with much anticipation. Yours, Anthony.' Cynthia folded the paper and stuffed the note back in the basket, her expression flat.

'What a lovely note,' said Angela encouragingly, taking Cynthia's hands in hers. 'It's clear he's desperately remorseful and wants you to forgive him. Why look so gloomy, dear sister? This is good news.'

Cynthia looked down at their joined hands. 'I was hoping he would call around himself today,' she said tearfully.

'At least he sent flowers. And he wants to see you. Surely that's two good signs, no?'

'I suppose so,' Cynthia conceded. Truth was her mind was somersaulting. She wasn't sure what to make of the situation now. 'You're right, I should be happy.' Cynthia plucked the note from the flowers and read it again. Immediately, she felt better.

'Come, I'll help you write a reply,' said Angela, leading Cynthia to the bureau by the window.

Soon after the footman left Royal Circus to deliver Cynthia's note to Anthony, Julianne arrived at the Marchmonts' house. Cynthia was surprised to see Julianne; they had made no previous plans to meet today – not as far as Cynthia was aware, anyway. The pair met in the library. 'Oh, Cynthia, how are you?' said Julianne, her face loaded with concern as she pattered towards Cynthia with outstretched arms. 'We have been so worried about you; we saw you leave last night with Lord Anthony – and Lord William noted he was not very pleased about something, at the very least.'

'I'm fine,' said Cynthia, appreciative of Julianne's concern, which she knew to be genuine.

'We had an argument over my dancing with that awful man, Sir Daniel Friel. Anthony was furious and would not listen to my explanation – do you know Friel practically forced me onto that dance floor against my will.'

Julianne gasped, cupping her mouth. 'But surely Anthony realises it wasn't your fault. He can't punish you – it's that Friel monster who needs taken down a peg or two…honestly, this is unbelievable. What will you do, Cynthia?'

'Well, I'm hoping the matter will resolve itself,' said Cynthia. 'I think, in the heat of the moment, Anthony merely got the wrong end of the stick. It all happened so quickly. But I have just taken delivery of a huge basket of flowers and a written apology from Anthony. He wants to come over to apologise tomorrow.'

'Oh, that's wonderful news. I could not sleep for worrying about you. I'm sure all will be fine from now on.'

Cynthia smiled and took Julianne's hand in hers. 'Please, Julianne, do come upstairs. You must see this basket. It's huge.'

Julianne spent the afternoon with Cynthia and Angela, drinking tea and eating sponge cake in the parlour, while poring over the illustrations depicting the latest fashions in *My Fair Lady*. 'Gosh, look at this,' said Angela, turning the page to reveal an image of a young woman in a green and red tartan dress, with a flash of primrose bodice beneath a beautiful, fitted jacket. The woman held a bouquet of blood red roses as she stood, staring dreamily into the dancing flames of the open log fire. 'The "Charles Dickens tartan gown" is a must-have for all discerning debutantes in Scotland's high-society this coming festive season,' Angela read.

'Oh, Angela, I can just see you in that dress. The warm colours will suit your skin tone. Plus, you have the height to pull off the pattern,' said Cynthia, forking a cube of sponge cake into her mouth.

'Oh, I agree,' said Julianne, 'we should ask Madam Lafayette to make something similar for you. I noticed she had some tartan silk only last week when I was in her shop. Imagine, you could wear it to your "coming out ball", Angela.'

'It is a nice dress,' said Angela, 'but I don't know – I haven't given my coming out ball much thought, to be honest.' That much was true; Angela had been so caught up with Cynthia's dramas that she'd completely forgotten about the joint event for her and their cousin Frances – in four weeks' time. 'But I guess it wouldn't hurt to pop along to…'

Another knock at the door interrupted the girls' conversation. In walked Lily. 'Miss Cynthia, I'm sorry to disturb you, but there is a gentleman downstairs, Sir Daniel Friel, who wishes to call on you.'

The girls exchanged worried looks. 'Please, Lily,' said Cynthia, 'Do tell Sir Daniel that I am not available for callers right now. I am too exhausted after last night's ball. Please, ask him to leave immediately.'

'Certainly, Miss.' Lily disappeared, and the girls fell silent for a moment.

'Can you believe the audacity of that man?' Julianne said finally. But that was not the end of the matter. Lily returned ten minutes later, with a note for Cynthia.

Cynthia unfolded the parchment and read with shock:

My dear Miss Cynthia Marchmont,

I am sorry I called at an inconvenient time. Please accept my sincere apologies. I called to see you to ensure the incident at the ball did not upset you too much. Lord Anthony is quite overbearing, and I hope you were not frightened by his reaction over such a minor misunderstanding. It was just a dance, after all.

My understanding is that Sir Anthony Sinclair likes everyone to bow down to his wishes, so I was very concerned for you when he ushered you out in such a bullish manner. Let us hope you have no lasting bad effects from his actions.

I will call again soon – and hope you are in brighter spirits.

Yours,

Sir Daniel Friel

Cynthia felt an intense heat in her throat. Her heart hammered beneath her corset. 'Oh no, not him,' she cried, passing the note to Angela and Julianne.

'The nerve of that man,' gasped Angela.

'I just hope Anthony doesn't find out he was here,' said Cynthia. She stood up and began pacing back and forth. 'Why does everything have to be so complicated?'

'Let's hope Anthony and Sir Daniel don't bump into each other,' said Julianne. 'Oh, my dear Cynthia, how worrying for you.'

'Hm, it does sound as though Friel is trying to stir up trouble between Anthony and me. I shall not rise to it, though.'

'But what if they see each other sooner?' Angela weighed in.

Cynthia sat back down and blew out her cheeks. 'I wish Anthony had called around here himself today to get things sorted. Why did he not do so, why?'

'Ah, I know,' said Julianne, her voice lively, hopeful. 'Anthony is at his mother's today. It's her birthday. And Lord William said she was having a celebratory lunch party for all the family.'

'Oh, yes, of course, I should have realised,' said Cynthia. 'Mother met Rosalind the other day to give her a present. How stupid of me to forget.'

'Well, that's a relief,' said Angela. 'Shall I call for more tea, ladies?'

The three girls exploded into tinkling giggles.

'God, it feels good to laugh,' said Cynthia.

CHAPTER SEVENTEEN

ON MONDAY MORNING, ANTHONY MADE HIS WAY TO ROYAL CIRCUS, repeatedly rehearsing his apology to Cynthia in his head as he paced – and nervously anticipating her reaction. *What if she rebuffs my efforts to make peace? Maybe she doesn't have eyes for me after all? Perhaps she's in love with Sir Daniel Friel?*

Those thoughts had kept Anthony awake the previous night; he just didn't know how Cynthia was going to react. All he had to go on was the note she'd sent in response to his flowers and written apology. Short and polite, her letter had revealed little emotion, if any. In fact, Cynthia's note was so brief he could remember it by heart:

> *Dear Anthony,*
>   *Thank you so much for the huge basket of flowers – they're lovely. I will be home tomorrow if you wish to call in around 10 a.m.*
>   *Yours,*
>   *Cynthia*

Damn, I'm going to have to work hard on this apology, thought Anthony as he passed his mother's house on Heriot Row. He looked up at the shuttered windows. The building was still sleeping, along with its owner. Which was not surprising; the festivities had been in full swing when Anthony had slipped away from his mother's birthday party at midnight, just as more guests arrived, and the drunken parlour games got underway. Knowing the duchess, the party would have been a riotous affair ending no sooner than dawn. Anthony walked on, turned left into India Street, which felt quiet and abandoned in the damp morning. More rain had fallen overnight, leaving a slippery sardine sheen on the cobbles, but the air smelled fresh and earthy.

Anthony cut across Circus Gardens, his heartbeat quickening as he spied the curve of Royal Circus ahead. *Oh well, there's no going back now.* On the doorstep of the Marchmonts' townhouse he pulled back his shoulders, took a deep breath and rapped three times on the door, using a force he hoped sounded confident yet polite. Howard answered. 'Ah, Lord Sinclair, we have been expecting you,' he said with a knowing smile that unnerved Anthony. 'Please, do come in.'

Cynthia was waiting for Anthony in the library overlooking the back courtyard. She'd woken early and had changed her mind multiple times as to which outfit to wear. Eventually, she'd opted for a pale blue satin dress with three rows of wide white ribbon circling its hem. Subtle yet feminine. Her dress complemented her eyes and the royal blue velvet settee on which she perched, trying to look nonchalant. A vase of ivory roses sat atop the rosewood jardiniere to her right. The montage depicted the epitome of elegance and innocence. Such was the atmosphere Cynthia hoped to create.

The door opened with an arthritic creak. 'Miss Marchmont, Lord Anthony Sinclair is here to see you,' Howard announced.

Cynthia stretched up from her waist, lengthening her neck. 'Do send him in,' she said.

Anthony advanced into the room, his expression a little sheepish. His hair was damp, and a tad dishevelled from the drizzle, but this added to his handsomeness, thought Cynthia. *Damn, he looks rugged. I could ravish him here and now.*

'Cynthia,' he said, and bowed slowly as he kissed her hand and looked into her eyes. Then he sat down in the armchair facing Cynthia and began his speech. 'Cynthia, you look enchanting, my dear. And I do hope you'll accept my sincere apologies. I acted like a cad towards you, and I have no excuse for my abominable behaviour. It was, I can

132

assure you, completely out of character.' He waited a few seconds, hoping for a reply, but Cynthia just gave a little insouciant shrug. 'So,' he went on, mesmerised by the cool hue of Cynthia's eyes. *They're even bluer than before.* 'I was hoping you would allow me to make amends by taking you out for the day. I know an enchanting little inn – Mrs Forman's in Musselburgh – where we could go for lunch. Or we could go elsewhere? Whatever your heart desires, Cynthia.'

'Yes, well, I am not sure I could possibly accept that feeble excuse for an apology,' said Cynthia after a long pause.

Anthony pulled back his head in shock – then he noticed Cynthia's lips twitching and the cheeky twinkle in her eyes. 'Oh, I see, you're jesting with me,' he said and laughed briefly at the ceiling before straightening his face. 'Well, I can always withdraw my offer.'

'Oh, no, no, don't do that,' blurted Cynthia, panicking.

Anthony laughed again. 'Good, you had me worried there for a moment.'

'You were teasing me?'

'Oh, but you started it, you little minx,' said Anthony, rising and extending his arms. "Now, come here and let me apologise properly.'

Cynthia sprung from the settee like it was on fire and fell into Anthony's arms. When his lips touched hers, she made no protest. They kissed passionately; no further words were needed. A kiss so lengthy they didn't hear the door groan open or Angela's footsteps.

Angela cleared her throat. 'Excuse me,' she said, and Anthony and Cynthia jumped apart, both flushed. 'Lucky it's only me – but Mummy's on her way.'

Cynthia sat back down beside the roses, hoping she did not look as hot as she felt. Anthony winked at Angela and sat in the seat opposite – just as Lady Marchmont appeared.

'Lord Sinclair, how pleasant to see you,' she said, presenting her hand to Anthony as he stood.

'Lady Marchmont,' he said, bowing over her hand. 'Please, forgive the early hour, but I was hoping for your permission to take Miss Cynthia out for lunch to Musselburgh.' He hesitated for a moment, then added, 'And if so, would you care to join us?' Anthony motioned at Lady Marchmont and Angela, secretly hoping they would decline his offer.

'Oh, of course you may take Cynthia to lunch,' said Lady Marchmont. 'But unfortunately, Angela and I will not be able to join you. We've already arranged a lunch date with my sister. We were going to take a hackney over there – but you could give us a lift in your carriage if that's not too much trouble? Lord Marchmont will pick us up after his business meeting later.'

'It will be my pleasure,' Anthony replied.

'I would love to join you and Cynthia for lunch,' Angela said.

'Gracious, no, Angela,' said Lady Marchmont, knowing full well what her youngest daughter was doing – causing mischief as usual. 'Let your sister enjoy her day. And besides, your Aunty Mary is expecting us both to discuss arrangements for your and Frances' coming out ball. You *must* be there.'

'Oh, very well,' sighed Angela, her tone playful.

Anthony was relieved. He wanted an intimate day with Cynthia. *I still have a lot of grovelling to do.* 'Well, your carriage awaits, ladies. Shall we make haste?'

'I'll fetch my bonnet,' said Lady Marchmont.

Anthony's carriage was a modern concern, with velvet padding, sturdy springs for comfort over bumps, and pre-heated stones to keep you warm.

'Oh, I must say, this is far more comfortable than a hired hackney,' Lady Marchmont exclaimed as they headed smoothly along Royal Circus. 'I must get Joseph to look into buying a new carriage; ours was quite comfortable on the way down to Edinburgh, but not nearly as good as this. I am not looking forward to our return journey at all.'

'When do you plan to return?' Anthony asked, feeling a sudden stab of panic in his chest. He did not want Cynthia to leave.

'Probably by the end of next month. The season will be ending then, and Joseph wants to get home before the heavy snow comes.

He also needs to see how things ran in his absence. You know what it's like running an estate, don't you, Lord Anthony.'

'Please,' said Anthony, smiling, 'just call me Anthony. And yes, I have not long acquired the Girnigoe Estate in Caithness. I plan to visit at the end of the season, so if Lord Marchmont has not purchased a new carriage by then, please allow me to offer you a lift home in mine. I have another carriage just like this which I plan to take up and leave on my estate.'

'Oh, that would be grand. Thank you, Anthony,' said Lady Marchmont, grinning. It would be so much more comfortable than their old carriage, she thought, and Joseph would be easier convinced to buy a new one once he'd travelled in Anthony's.

Cynthia glanced out of the window. *I'd love to travel alone with Anthony to Caithness.*

Minutes later, Anthony helped Lady Marchmont and Angela down from the carriage and, finally, he was alone with Cynthia.

An open fire crackled in Mrs Forman's inn, where Anthony and Cynthia sat side by side at a table in a cosy corner next to a window boasting a view of Musselburgh Links. After they'd ordered food, Anthony lifted Cynthia's hand and kissed her fingers. 'Alone again,' he whispered. 'I cannot tell you how sorry I am about my behaviour towards you. I do hope you can find it in your heart to truly forgive me.'

Cynthia leaned close to Anthony – then daringly kissed his cheek. 'I do forgive you,' she said. 'I was so upset at the thought of not seeing you again.' She looked into Anthony's eyes, and he held her gaze.

'If we were somewhere private, I would not be able to control myself just now. You are beautiful,' he said, rubbing his thumb over Cynthia's palm. She shivered with excitement. She felt wonderful.

'Anthony, you must stop, I am quite overwhelmed with feelings,' she murmured.

He smiled, lifted her fingers to his lips, then leaned back in his seat, beaming. 'If you wish, but later", he said, raising an eyebrow.

They had a lovely lunch. The claret flowed, as did the conversation.

They chatted and laughed, brushed hands and knees while gazing passionately at one another. By the time they returned to Anthony's carriage, neither of them could contain their desires. Anthony pulled the canvas curtains across the windows and immediately pulled Cynthia into his arms, kissing her passionately. He kissed her neck, then pulled wide her cape to devour her décolletage. She smelled, and tasted, of violets. Cynthia breathed hard as he then kneaded her breast. Even through the heavy velvet of her dress and corsetry, she could feel the heat of his touch. No man had ever touched in such a way. She crowned his head with her hands, pulling his face into her cleavage. 'Oh, Anthony,' she moaned.

Anthony lifted his head and returned to Cynthia's lips, kissing her hard as he pulled up her skirts and caressed her inner thighs before slowly tracing a path to the opening in her drawers. She felt soft and moist against his fingers. And he loved how Cynthia responded to his touch: panting and writhing while saying his name over and over, until she climaxed in glorious waves.

As the carriage rumbled into Royal Circus, Anthony opened the curtains while Cynthia readjusted her cape. Then Anthony walked her into the Marchmonts' townhouse.

'So, you're home. I thought you had got lost,' said Angela, who just happened to be in the hallway when her sister and Anthony came through the door. 'Mummy says you must stay for tea, Anthony. Giles is here too – he popped by to see Derek. Unless you have a prior engagement, of course.'

Anthony took off his top hat and held it against his chest. 'How kind. And no, I have no prior engagements. I am all yours.' He glanced at Cynthia as he said this and gave her a discreet wink.

Cynthia hid her pinking face as she turned to remove her cape. They made their way into the drawing room, where Lord and Lady Marchmont, Derek and Giles were engrossed in a lively conversation.

'Welcome, come and sit down, children,' said Lady Marchmont. 'Did you have a nice lunch?'

'Oh yes,' enthused Cynthia, 'the food was delicious.'

'Especially the dessert,' Anthony whispered to Cynthia as they sat down, and her heart quickened as she remembered their passionate tryst in the carriage.

'So, I trust everything is well now between you and Miss Cynthia,' Giles said under his breath as Anthony sat down on the settee between his brother and Cynthia.

'Yes, thank you,' Anthony hissed back.

'Good, I can go out tonight with Derek and not have to worry about a repeat performance?'

'This is not the place for such talk, Giles,' said Anthony, then turned to Derek. 'Where are you two going tonight?'

'There's a new greyhound racing track on the edge of town,' said Derek. 'We thought we'd give it a go. Would you like to join us, Anthony?'

'Oh, thank you for the invite, but I really must catch up on some paperwork this evening.'

'Anyone for cake and tea?' said Angela, as Lily wheeled in a wooden trolley loaded with teapots and cups and platters holding cakes.

'And where are you girls off to this evening,' Derek asked, glancing from sister to sister.

'There is a music night at the Strath Hotel for ladies only,' said Cynthia. 'We plan to attend that with a few other ladies.'

'Yes,' said Angela, 'Frances is joining us – and staying over tonight.'

Lily served tea and cakes as Lady Marchmont spoke about the Italian opera she and her husband were attending that evening at the Theatre Royal. 'It's a Verdi opera – and the reviews have been fantastic,' she gushed.

'Let's hope it doesn't go on for too long,' added Lord Marchmont, chuckling as he sucked on his pipe. 'These things do tend to drag on. Greyhound racing sounds like much more fun.'

'Oh, stop being a philistine,' Lady Marchmont shot back, and the whole room started laughing. But Lady Marchmont hurried her husband out of the room some twenty minutes later – just in case he had a change of heart and decided to join the boys at the racetrack.

Soon after the lord and lady left, Anthony rose. 'Well, if you'll excuse me, I must take my leave also, I am afraid. Thank you for tea, Angela, and do enjoy your evening.' Next, he turned to his brother and Derek. 'I hope you two don't lose too much at the races.'

Giles laughed. Don't worry, brother, dear. I know who to come to for a loan.'

Anthony laughed and shook his head and walked into the hall with Cynthia.

'Would you care to go riding tomorrow?' he said, glancing sideways at Howard, waiting at the door with Anthony's cape. He lowered his voice. 'I would kiss you goodbye, but your butler is watching me like a hawk.'

'Yes, he is very protective,' whispered Cynthia. 'Thank you for a glorious day. I shall dream about it tonight.'

Anthony gave her hand a discreet squeeze. 'Me too,' he said, raising her hand to his lips. He kissed her fingers. 'Thank you for a wonderful afternoon, Miss Cynthia. I enjoyed every moment.' They shared a knowing smile, both thinking about their earlier carriage ride. Then Anthony reclaimed his cape and swung it around his shoulders. 'I bid you adieu…until tomorrow,' he said, and a waft of icy air filled the hall as Howard opened the front door.

'Adieu,' said Cynthia, then climbed slowly up the stairs to change. Briefly closing her eyes, she could still feel Anthony's hot breath on her skin, his fingers lightly caressing her. She went into her bedroom.

'Until tomorrow,' she whispered.

CHAPTER EIGHTEEN

ANTHONY SAT IN HIS STUDY, trying to read paperwork relating to his purchase of the Girnigoe Estate, but unable to focus. The words blurred on the page, meaningless compared to the thoughts that distracted him: Cynthia: her warm lips, her soft skin, the way she had quivered beneath his touch in the carriage that afternoon. *Cynthia, Cynthia, Cynthia.*

He got up and walked over to the window, still thinking about Cynthia. The way she had responded to his advances confirmed to Anthony that Cynthia was a passionate woman. *I can't wait to take her to new heights.*

Tomorrow could not come sooner for Anthony.

The following morning, Anthony and Cynthia set out on their ride to the Pentland hills. Anthony knew an inn en route, where they'd stop for lunch. As they rode swiftly, enjoying giving their horses full head to gallop fast across the open fields, Cynthia felt totally exhilarated. She was a fine horsewoman, Anthony acknowledged, so he let her gallop. He loved how she enjoyed riding at full pelt, especially as many society ladies only wanted to travel in carriages or sedate rides. He observed how Cynthia's blonde hair escaped from her net and fluttered in the wind as she pushed on further. *She looks a picture,* he thought.

They arrived at Flotterstone Inn for a late lunch. It was a quaint, white-stone inn, steeped in history at over 200 years old. The atmosphere inside was cosy, with a low ceiling and a roaring fire. They chatted and laughed over a lunch of roast beef and potatoes, washed down with warm, giddying wine. By the time Cynthia and Anthony left, the sky was a flat gunmetal grey, strewn with charcoal clouds. 'Ready for a fast gallop back to Edinburgh?' said Anthony, looking skywards. 'Looks like the heavens are about to open.'

'Oh, I can manage a fast gallop,' said Cynthia. They mounted their horses and headed off amid the misty beginnings of a storm. Fifteen minutes later, as they rode through farmland just outside the city, thunder rumbled above. Lightening veined the sky with painful cracks, then at once, torrential rain fell, turning the landscape into an atmospheric scene reminiscent of a Turner painting. They slowed their pace; it was difficult to see through the rain. 'Let's take shelter in that barn,' said Anthony, pointing to a ramshackle building on his left.

'Yes, let's do that,' replied Cynthia, her teeth chattering.

Anthony dismounted, then helped Cynthia down. They settled the horses and went into the barn, which smelled of wet mud and hay. The rain thrummed rhythmically on the timber roof. 'Here, drink this. It'll warm you up,' said Anthony, handing his hip flask to Cynthia as they sat down on a bundle of hay. 'It's an excellent brandy. Just what you need on a day like today.' Cynthia lifted the flask to her lips.

'Slàinte Mhath,' she said, giggling, then took three generous gulps, enjoying the warm sensation as the amber liquid travelled down her throat. She gave the flask back to Anthony. 'I saved you a drop,' she said, then shivered. Anthony put the flask on the ground, winged his arm over Cynthia's shoulder, and pulled her close against his chest. She gazed up at him, and his heart raced. Slowly, he lowered his head and kissed her gently. She reached up and lay her hand on his shoulder, and he kissed her deeper, faster. She groaned and moved her hand behind his head, and, in one movement, he eased her down onto the straw bail and plunged his tongue into her mouth.

He touched her breast, kneading it softly at first – then harder as he unbuttoned Cynthia's riding jacket with his other hand. He felt Cynthia's nipple harden through the fabric of her blouse and she moaned as he rubbed it firmly. He unbuttoned her blouse and lifted her chemise to expose her breasts, taking her right breast in his mouth and flicking his tongue over her ripe nipple. Cynthia gasped loudly, grabbing Anthony's hair in her fists as he moved on to her second breast. Cynthia thrusted her body against him, and whispered, 'I want you, Anthony.'

He needed no encouragement.

With speed, Anthony lifted Cynthia's skirts above her knees then, slowly, he traced his fingers up her inner thigh until he reached the moist spot between her legs. He paused, then massaged her gently. Cynthia groaned loudly, drowning the rain hammering the roof. She reached down, unfastened his trouser flap, and took his erection in her hand, feeling it throb as she rubbed it hard – until Anthony too was groaning with passion. They gazed into each other's eyes, panting, their hearts beating fiercely until they both climaxed. Time stood still in that moment, the rain now a gentle patter on the roof. Anthony pulled Cynthia into his arms and kissed her at length. He kissed her neck. 'Darling, that was wonderful,' he breathed into her ear.'

'I did not… could not… imagine how I would feel, but I'm floating on air,' she sighed back. He knew how she felt. In all his affairs, with ladies far more experienced than Cynthia, he had not enjoyed climaxing as much as he had just now. She bewitched him.

'You are beautiful, every bit of you. I could lay here all day with you but, unfortunately, we still have a long ride home, and the rain has eased, so I am afraid we must start back.'

'I know, we must,' said Cynthia, suddenly feeling very shy as she lay there dishevelled, her body exposed to the elements. She bent her head and started to reassemble her outfit.

'Here let me help,' Anthony offered as he brushed her hands away and started buttoning up her blouse. 'Cynthia, look at me.' She raised her eyes to his, blushing. 'Never feel shy with me, I think your body is beautiful and I thoroughly enjoy seeing and touching it. Honestly, you have no reason to be shy with me, okay?'

'Yes, Anthony, thank you,' she replied.

'No, thank you for sharing it with me,' he smiled and gave her nose a playful tap. 'Now get up, you lazy wench.'

She smiled and got up quickly, brushing straw off her skirts.

Once they'd dressed, Anthony twirled Cynthia around, checking for bits of hay in her hair or clinging to her outfit. 'Ah, you will pass muster" he said, then he helped her onto her horse before jumping on his stallion.

'Race you back?' Cynthia called over her shoulder as she bounded off.

'Fine but loser has to pay a penalty.'

Anthony passed her as they reached the Old Town, just as they slowed their pace to negotiate the busy streets. 'You lose,' he said.

'I did not.'

'Yes, you did, so I will have to give you a penalty to fulfil.'

'Fine – what is it? Dinner?' she asked.

'No, I want another day like today,' he said, eyes gleaming.

'Sounds good to me – just let me know when.'

'Now, right now,' said Anthony, laughing.

'I'm afraid you'll have to wait a little…but soon, Anthony, soon.' Cynthia tossed back her head and jiggled Misty's reins.

Back in Royal Circus, as they stood between their horses, Anthony covertly looked around then, confident nobody could see them, plucked a tiny piece of straw from Cynthia's hat, touched her nose with it, then kissed her softly and swiftly on the lips. As he led her up the steps to the house, Derek ambled into Royal Circus.

'Hello Anthony, glad you're here,' he said.

'Hello Derek, just home?' said Anthony, and Derek grimaced.

'I have been with Giles all night. He took quite a tumble at the races, and I had to help him home and get a doctor to him. Of course, he was quite shaken. The doctor says he's cracked a bone in his foot, poor soul.'

'Goodness, you must go to him, Anthony,' urged Cynthia.

Anthony nodded and jumped back on his horse. 'See you soon,' he said, then gave a brisk wave as he trotted off.

CHAPTER NINETEEN

'WHAT AN EARTH HAPPENED TO YOU?' Anthony said, eyeing Giles' bandaged leg as he sat on his bed, pillows propping his back against the headboard.

Giles shrugged, then grimaced as he tried to move his injured leg. 'I think somebody pushed me down the stairs last night,' he said. 'I won a fair amount on the last race, so maybe somebody was trying to rob me? But then again, I cannot confirm this as there was quite a crush leaving the stadium – and I still have my wallet.' Giles chuckled, then winced. 'Ouch, that hurt.'

'But Derek was with you – did he see anything?' said Anthony, taking a seat in the armchair beside Giles' bed.

'Oh, Derek reckons I drank too much wine and ale and fell over – but I know my limit and I had not reached it. I am pretty sure I was pushed.'

'Hm, how odd. But you don't look too bad. Could've been worse, brother dear. An injured leg won't spoil your handsome looks. I'm sure all the ladies will want to fuss you back to health.' Anthony laughed as he rose. 'You'll be inundated with callers. Mark my words.'

'Oh Lord, please save me from do-gooders,' Giles said, rolling his eyes.

'I will pop in and let Mother know how you are – she will be right over to make a fuss of you.'

Giles groaned. 'No, please don't let her come over.'

'No stopping her, I'm afraid,' Anthony called over his shoulder as he left Giles' room.

* * *

It was early evening by the time Anthony arrived home, tired but also exhilarated after his earlier frolics with Cynthia. Graham greeted Anthony at the front door, as usual, and handed him a few notes. 'Thank you, Graham. Please can you send tea to my study? I have a lot of work to do this evening.'

'Certainly Sir.'

In his study, Anthony leafed through his correspondence, stopping when he again recognised the familiar yet sinister writing on a coarse piece of parchment. He unfolded the note, anger rising in his chest. This anonymous letter was lengthier than usual – and explicitly unnerving.

I HEAR YOUR BROTHER HAD A FALL? BUT DID HE REALLY FALL? I THINK NOT.

IT'S SO EASY FOR ME TO GET TO YOUR LOVED ONES, ANTHONY. EASIER THAN YOU THINK.

I ENJOYED WATCHING YOUR ROMANTIC SCENE AT ROYAL CIRCUS EARLIER. THOUGHT NOBODY SAW YOU? HA, THINK AGAIN …

NOW THAT I HAVE YOUR ATTENTION, THIS IS WHAT I WANT FROM YOU:

YOU WILL SIGN OVER THE NORTH LODGE AT YOUR CAITHNESS ESTATE TO YOUR COUSIN, STEWART. YOU WILL ALSO SIGN TO STEWART ALL FOUR FIELDS TO THE WEST OF THE LODGE. DO IT NOW, WITHOUT DELAY.

Anthony reread the note, fuming as he paced erratic circles. *Who is this evil person, watching my every move? I will not be blackmailed.* Still gripping the note in one hand, Anthony marched to the door and flung it open with such force its handle smashed into the study wall. 'Graham,' he yelled into his vast house, 'Graham, I need to speak to you.'

Graham's shoes clattered hurriedly over the hall tiles. 'Yes, my lord, what's wrong?' he asked.

'Who delivered this?' said Anthony, beating the note in the air.

'I don't know, Sir – honestly, I haven't a clue. I came downstairs after arranging your attire for tomorrow and the mail was on the stand in the hall. Nobody called at the front door, I can assure you.'

Anthony exhaled loudly and slammed the note down on his desk, causing a few drops of ink to spill from the well. 'Ask all staff if they saw anyone,' said Anthony, his voice low and menacing. He then ordered Graham to send word to Bill, Ronald, his former Foreign Office colleague Alistair Murdoch and his good friend Patrick Braid, the chief inspector of Edinburgh Police Force. 'And forget the tea.' he added, 'I'll take a large brandy instead.'

An hour later, all the gentlemen were seated around Anthony's desk. 'I want this blighter found and dealt with accordingly,' Anthony growled.

Chief Inspector Braid removed his helmet and ran a hand over his bald head, as though smoothing down imaginary hair. He crossed his bushy brows. 'We're making inquiries but, so far, there's no indication who's behind these sinister notes.

'Anthony, where is Stewart?' asked Bill.

'No one has seen hide nor hair of him for weeks,' said Anthony, reaching for his brandy. 'Which, now I think about it, is strange- and goes against his modus operandi. Under usual circumstances he would have surfaced to tap one of us for money by now. I'll speak with his father, James…find out whether he's heard anything.'

'Right,' said Ronald, 'I'll check out Stewart's haunts – if you can get a full list from your uncle, Anthony?'

Alistair nodded vigorously. 'I'll come with you, Ron.'

'Well, you could start with all the gambling holes and brothels in Leith,' said Anthony. 'Stewart's a heavy gambler. All half- decent gaming houses in the city have banned him on James's orders – after he paid off Stewart's debts at those establishments. I will get you a list of Stewart's cronies tonight but take some strong lads with you for protection. Leith can be dangerous and…'

Chief Inspector Braid cleared his throat and raised his hand. 'Excuse me, Sir,' he said politely, 'With all due respect, I think it'll be best for my men to make inquiries at the gaming establishments. Folk there will clam-up if they see gentry.'

Anthony nodded his assent. 'Good idea,' he said. 'Ron, you and Alistair concentrate on Stewart's cronies, please?'

'And I'll try some of the brothels,' added Bill. 'The madams there will blow the whistle on anybody if you grease their palms enough, I'm sure.'

Inspector Braid put his helmet back on. 'Well, I'd better get going,' he said, standing. 'Be careful, gentlemen. I will send over a couple of my undercover men to assist.'

'Thank you, inspector,' said Anthony. 'Right, gentlemen, let's get to work. We will find this villain no matter what it takes.'

'Yes, let's crack this,' said Bill.

Anthony stood up. 'I'm off to see James now.'

Anthony arrived at James' house and the pair sat in the library. Anthony did not hold back. 'I need you to look at this,' he said, thrusting forth the threatening note. James studied it for a few moments, frowning, then looked up at Anthony. 'I don't understand,' he said. 'Why would you sign any of your estate over to Stewart? Do you think Stewart is behind this?'

'No, I don't believe so. But I do think someone is pulling his strings, manipulating him. How he got mixed up in this is anyone's guess. Do you happen to know Stewart's whereabouts – or who his associates are?'

James handed the note back to Anthony, 'I will ask around the relatives, see if they know of his whereabouts. You know what Stewart's like… always so elusive. But wait a second, there was one man…' James' voice trailed off. He bent his head and massaged his temples, then looked up again, clicking his fingers. 'Humphrey McPearson, that's his name. He's

146

a good-for -nothing wastrel whom Stewart was seen with not so long ago. Yes, Humphrey McPearson. Chances are you'll find him drinking himself into a stupor at the White Hart Inn, down in the Grassmarket. And there's a barmaid, Margaret, I've heard Stewart mention her a few times too.' James grabbed his nib pen, plucked a sheet of paper from the tray on his desk, then scribbled down the two names. 'If I think of anyone else, I'll be straight over,' he said, proffering the paper to Anthony.

'Thank you,' Anthony said, folding the note.

'No, I'm sorry my wayward son is causing you problems.'

'It's not your doing, uncle. I'll keep you posted.'

Next, Anthony met Ron at the club – and gave him James' list. 'Are you going to sign over the lodge and land?' Ron asked, pocketing the note.

Anthony shook his head. 'Absolutely not,' he said. 'I will *not* be blackmailed. The sooner we find out who's behind these notes, the better. My cousin is a wastrel, but he does not have the brains to pull this together. I think more than one person is involved –and I intend to bring them all to justice.'

'Hm, I think you're right,' said Ron. 'I'll see what I can find out. Let's meet back here tomorrow night?'

The gentlemen drained their glasses and headed out into the blustery, raven dark night.

The following evening, Ron returned with constructive news. Stewart had indeed been spotted in the White Hart of late, he explained to the other gentlemen. According to the locals Ron spoke to, Stewart was accompanied by a 'well- dressed gent with an arrogant demeanour'. 'I tracked Margaret down today, too,' said Ron. 'She [Margaret] said she had been stepping out with Stewart for a while. He would regularly spend the night at her lodgings – but he suddenly became very nervous and said he needed to leave town.'

'Did he give any indication as to when he'd be back?' asked Anthony.

Ron shook his head. 'No, he wouldn't even tell her where he was going. "He just took off," were Margaret's words.' But what I did find out, from a local, was that Stewart apparently got himself into huge debt at Leith's notorious gambling house. His debt was sold to an agent, but nobody seems to know the agent's name.

'I see,' said Inspector Braid. 'I wonder is the agent is the same gent seen with Stewart in the White Hart Inn? Actually, the well-dressed gent sounds similar to reports we received of a similar gent frequenting Danube Street a few months back. The madams in the brothels reported this chap, said he wore a huge green ring on his right hand – and had unusual sexual tendencies. He would beat them with his right hand so the ring caused them more pain, the women claimed.'

'Sounds like the gent from Caithness,' said Bill. 'The man with the green ring.'

'Yes, I concur,' said Anthony. 'But it could just be a coincidence.'

'Oh, I heard from Grant today too,' said Alistair. 'Apparently our green-ringed gent has since disappeared from the Sheep's Heid Inn and the trail has gone dead.' Just then, James walked into the club. 'Anthony,' he called, approaching the men's table. 'I have news,' he added as he sat down. He lowered his voice. 'Stewart loaned of a grey dapple horse from Angus's stable.' James paused and gestured at the other gents. 'Angus is James and Anthony's cousin,' he explained. 'Anyway, Angus says Stewart was heading to Perth.'

'Right, I will send men after him,' said Alistair as he got up to leave.

'Keep us up to date,' Anthony called after him. Then the men sat for a while, re-examining the evidence thus far. Inspector Braid said he'd deploy one of his men to watch the White Hart Inn. 'See if we can spot this "well-dressed gent",' he offered.

'Indeed,' said Anthony, 'I think he could be the key to solving this mess.'

The following day Anthony received word from his estate manager, Bernard, in Caithness, reporting sightings of a stranger seen roaming around the north lodge in the last few weeks. 'Has Lord Sinclair sent a man to stay or inspect the old lodge?' asked Bernard. 'I'm inquiring as the lord usually sends word of such visits.'

Anthony wrote a note back to Bernard, verifying he had not sent anybody to Caithness. He penned Grant a note, asking for his men investigate. *This is too coincidental*, thought Anthony, then hurried out of his study – and almost collided with Graham, who was about to knock the door. 'Sir, I'm terribly sorry but…' he began, taking a polite step backwards. And as he did so, Anthony noticed the ivory folded sheet of parchment, aquiver in Graham's hand against his thigh. '…I think this is another of those notes, sir.' He handed the parchment to Anthony, who opened it swiftly and began reading. The message was shorter this time:

YOU HAVE NOT DONE AS I ASKED.

WELL, YOU WILL BE SORRY IF IT IS NOT COMPLETED BY TOMORROW!

BE WARNED, SINCLAIR. BE WARNED!

CHAPTER TWENTY

WITHOUT HESITATION, GRAHAM ASKED HIS MASTER, 'SHALL I CALL FOR YOUR MEN, SIR? RONALD OR LORD WILLIAM, PERHAPS?' Anthony threw the note on his desk, like the parchment was diseased. He stood for a moment, head bowed and pinching the bridge of his nose, thinking.

'No, we must try to flush out the culprit,' Anthony said finally. 'Right, this is our plan.' Anthony began pacing back and forth, his stride flitting between determined and frantic, beating his fist in the air as he spoke. 'First, ask Michael to contact my legal team – have them send a lawyer to me immediately. And get one of the footmen to take a note to my uncle James – I'll write it now.' Leaning over his desk, Anthony wrote a brief note to James and handed it to Graham.

'Certainly, Sir,' said Graham, bowing. 'I shall fetch Michael right away. Will that be all, Sir?'

'Yes, thank you,' Anthony replied. 'But do stress to all concerned to be discreet. The perpetrator of these notes clearly knows everything about my family and friends. They're watching my every move, God damn it.' Anthony was at the window now, clunking the shutters over the glass. 'And do bring an extra oil lamp for our meeting. It's awfully dark in here.'

Graham nodded. 'Understood, Sir.'

James and Samuel, a senior legal clerk, arrived at noon. Anthony explained the scenario to them, stressing he did not believe James' son was the author of the notes. 'But the thing is, Samuel,' he said slowly, 'whomever is behind these notes *knows* who's who in our family,'

Samuel shifted in his chair. 'So, what do you propose, Sir?'

'Do you intend to sign the lodge and grounds over?' asked James.

'No, I will not sign *anything* over. But I suggest we call the author's bluff – put on a show of signing over the lodge.'

'Interesting,' said Samuel. 'But what if the culprit asks for proof? How will you fool him – or her?'

Anthony clapped his hands together. 'Ha, that's where you come in, Samuel. Could you go to the White Hart Inn tonight, with a trusted friend or colleague – or better still, I'll find somebody to go with you – and put on an act?'

'Well, I suppose, yes. What do you have in mind?'

Anthony shot to his feet and began pacing again. 'Pretend to be drunk. Sit with your friend and talk loudly. Tell your companion about how foolish you think I have been by just handing over the lodge and lands to a wastrel like Stewart. Make sure you are in earshot of the bar and locals. Let them hear how your firm has been charged with finding Stewart to get the deeds signed over. Make a great play of it – say how you think Anthony Sinclair is most unwise and you did try to talk me out of it…can you do that?'

'Yes sir, who will come with me?'

'I will send word over. In the meantime, when you leave here today, as you walk back to the office, be sure to shake your head in disbelief – as though you failed to stop me signing over the lodge – because, rest assured, somebody will be watching you.'

Samuel stood up. 'Right I will go to the White Hart Inn about 8.30 p.m.' he said, then Graham escorted him to the front door.

'Why did you need me here?' James asked once he and Anthony were alone in the study.

'I thought it might look like I was trying to find Stewart. I also want you to warn the family to be very vigilant. Remember that last note I showed you – the one that said, "It's so easy for me to get to your loved ones, Anthony?" If this does not work, the guilty party could turn very nasty.'

'Right, I will go and do the rounds. Anything else – except strangling my stupid son, that is.'

'No, just be wary,' said Anthony, shaking James' hand. 'I'll arrange for runners to watch the family, including you, Mother, Giles and Susanne.'

'But what about you? You could be in grave danger, Anthony.'

'I will get Bill, Ronald and Alistair to stay close. Between us we have the finest swordsman, boxer, and sharpshooter in Edinburgh, and we all have undercover experience, so we know how to handle most situations.'

'Indeed, but, please, do be careful.'

'Do not worry, uncle. I'm going to solve this – and whoever is behind those poisonous notes is going to pay for it. Mark. My. Words.'

As James left, Anthony again recalled the evil words of his blackmailer: *It's so easy for me to get to your loved ones, Anthony.* Then Anthony's bones turned to ice as another thought crept in.

Cynthia. Please don't let anybody hurt my beautiful Cynthia. Please God, no.

Cynthia stabbed her embroidery needle into the canvas. She was cross-stitching a thistle design, but her mind was distracted. She had not heard from Anthony in two days, and she wondered whether the weekend trip to Hopetoun House was still on. They were due to leave on Friday. *That's… tomorrow*, Cynthia realised. She needed to pack today if they were leaving tomorrow morning, as Anthony had suggested. Maybe he would just show up – and expect her to be ready, thought Cynthia. *But he would have sent word of confirmation by now, surely.* Oh, how she hated feeling in limbo. How could she find out whether the trip was going ahead without appearing too presumptuous or forward? She sewed another cross – just as Derek sauntered into the room.

'Hullo sister, dear,' he said, grinning. 'You're very quiet in here. Are you not going out with the lord today?'

Cynthia dropped her embroidery into her lap with a sigh. 'Well, I should be packing for a country weekend at Diane and Timothy's with Anthony, but I have not heard from him since the other day when he rushed away to see Giles after his accident. So, I don't know what to do. I'm not sure if we are going, even. I don't know what to pack – that's if I need to pack at all.'

'My, what a dilemma,' teased Derek, and Cynthia shot him a dangerous look. 'But fear not, dear sister, I might be able to help you.'

Cynthia's face softened. 'Really, how so?'

'I could nip round to Anthony's – to ask how Giles is. I was going to do so anyway. While I'm there I could covertly inquire about his plans for the weekend. How's that for an idea?'

'Oh, Derek, could you?' Cynthia pressed a palm over her heart. 'Could you come straight back and tell me what he said – and try and find out what I should pack?'

Derek beamed, proud of his idea. 'Yes, I will go right now,' he said, and headed for the door.

'Oh, and if you could subtly ask about the itinerary, so I can pack appropriate dresses, that would be…'

'Cheerio, Cynthia.'

Graham led Derek into Anthony's study and announced him.

'Derek, old chap, how are you?' Anthony said in a bright voice that betrayed his mood. He rose to greet Derek. Can I get you a drink?'

'Yes please, a small scotch would be grand,' said Derek. Graham poured them both a large malt then left. Anthony gestured at the chaise lounge and Derek sat down. 'So, how is Giles getting along after his tumble?'

'Hm, I'm not certain he fell. I believe somebody pushed him. I received a note alluding to as much.'

'Good grief,' Derek exclaimed. 'I thought he was just mixed up, you know, shaken after the fall, so I did not take much head of his thoughts on someone pushing him. Who did it – and, more importantly, why?'

Anthony took a seat in his desk chair and looked at the ceiling, swirling his glass. Then, directing his gaze at Derek, said, 'I am being blackmailed by this anonymous fiend. I've received notes. Threatening notes. I have several police and runners out trying to find out who's behind the letters. No luck so far but everyone is on the lookout for clues. My cousin Stewart appears to be mixed up in it all, somehow, too.'

'How long has this been going on?' Derek asked.

'Several weeks,' sighed Anthony. 'The threats were mainly towards my business and family's safety. But I'm afraid the threats have stepped up a pace in the last few days. So, I have been warning all my family to be on their guard.'

Derek took a long swig of malt then leaned forwards, elbows resting on his knees, still holding his glass. 'Is there anything I can do?' he said.

'Well, keep an eye on your sister, Cynthia. Whoever is watching me saw me with Cynthia the other day – according to the recent notes. But please don't alarm her.'

'Of course, goes without saying. I will tell my father – and our staff.' Derek paused. 'But while we're talking about Cynthia, she mentioned you might be going away this weekend. Although I think she's unsure what to pack – if she needs to pack, that is.'

Anthony banged his palm against his forehead. 'Oh, lord, I completely forgot we leave tomorrow for two nights at Hopetoun House. Cynthia must think I am totally without manners, not to have been in touch sooner. Knowing ladies, she must be frantic about what to pack. With all the comings and goings over the last few days, I have just been so busy. But, no excuses, I must go immediately and put her mind at rest.'

Derek smiled. 'Thank you, Anthony. But one question, if I may. Cynthia isn't in danger, is she?'

Anthony's chest rose as he inhaled, then deflated slowly as he breathed out. He looked Derek directly in the eye.

'I will not let anything happen to Cynthia, Derek. I promise.'

CHAPTER TWENTY-ONE

THE FOLLOWING MORNING ANTHONY AND CYNTHIA left for Hopetoun House. As promised, Anthony had called in on Cynthia straight after his meeting with Derck and confirmed their plans for the weekend, apologising profusely for his delay in doing so. 'I am so sorry for my tardiness,' he'd said, kissing Cynthia's hand. 'Unfortunately, an urgent business matter arose that I could not ignore. But I am very much looking forward to our weekend away – if you still care to join me, of course?'

'Oh, absolutely,' Cynthia had replied. 'But I must make haste and pack.' Anthony had then explained the itinerary for the weekend – then explained he had more business to address and bid his farewell.

'I shall pick you up at 8.30 a.m., my dear,' he said.

Anthony arrived at Royal Circus at 8.30 a.m. on the dot. Howard helped the groom load Cynthia's luggage onto the coach, and, twenty minutes later, they were en route to Hopetoun House.

'I must apologise again, Cynthia,' said Anthony as they passed Haymarket Station, engulfed in fresh steam. The Edinburgh to Glasgow train link had proved most popular since the station opened the previous year. 'I have neglected you the last few days – but I will make up for that this weekend. I promise.'

'Oh, it's fine,' replied Cynthia, gazing out the window at the crowd thronging the station, 'I spent yesterday packing – and the day before that I caught up with friends. I am really looking forward to this trip".

'So am I,' said Anthony, reaching for Cynthia's hand. 'So am I.'

Frissons of excitement coursed through her body. 'Who else will be joining us?'

'Well, I don't know everyone, but Heather, David, Bill, Julianne and Ronald, for sure. And, of course, our hosts, Diane, and Timothy. Bill says they're expecting around thirty guests, give or take a few. I am sure you will know more, but I will introduce you to everyone, don't worry.'

He smiled and kissed the back of her hand.

'It's fine – as long as I have some close friends to talk to when you go off shooting or fishing or whatever. And besides, Julianne and I will keep one another company; she is as nervous about this as I am.'

'Och, Bill will stick by her side like glue, I am sure of that,' Anthony laughed. 'I have never seen him so enamoured by a lady before.'

'Ha, I think the feeling is mutual. Your mother will be disappointed,' teased Cynthia, smiling.

'Probably, she had high hopes for Julianne and me.' Anthony smiled back at her and, with a mischievous wink, added, 'I am, of course, quite devastated.'

'Really, your Lordship? My heart bleeds.'

'Yes, quite broken hearted,' he quipped back. 'So, you will have to help me get over this trauma. Do not leave my side.'

'I am sure I'll manage that,' Cynthia said softly, and leaned in to kiss Anthony's cheek.

Desire flooded his whole being. *Cynthia has not taken the lead before.* Seizing the moment, he enveloped Cynthia in his arms and kissed her at length. They continued kissing throughout the journey – until the coach rolled through the gates of Hopetoun House.

'Oh, my,' gasped Cynthia when she glimpsed the stately home ahead: The driveway appeared miles long, flanked by lawns iced pure white in the December chill.

'Yes, it cost Timothy a pretty penny. He used his inheritance from the death of his aunt. She left it to him knowing he wouldn't inherit all his family's estate – because he's the second son. His aunt had no children of her own to leave her fortune to. I must say, it was very decent of her.'

'Well, the house and gardens look magnificent – money well spent, I'd say.' Cynthia remarked.

'Yes, so long as the estate farmers and tenants work well – the last owner let everything fall into disrepair. Timothy has his work cut out.'

Diane and Timothy greeted Anthony and Cynthia as they alighted from the carriage.

'It's so lovely to see you again,' said Diane, hugging Cynthia and Anthony in turn. 'I am so glad you managed to come.'

'Please, this way,' added Timothy, gesturing at the steps leading up to the grand entrance. 'Ladies first.' Diane led the party inside, and Cynthia stopped in the magnificent hallway to admire the view.

'Oh, you have such a lovely home,' she said. 'And the gardens are lovely, it must have taken a lot of work.'

Diane smiled and Cynthia thought how elegant her host looked. She had on a plum dress and fine black lace gloves and shawl. 'Yes, but well worth it,' said Diane. 'I will show you around later once everyone has arrived.'

Timothy nudged Anthony and said in a loud, jocular whisper, 'And it cost a fortune too.'

Anthony laughed. 'What we'll do to keep our ladies happy, hey?'

Timothy raised his eyebrows. 'Wait until you're married, dear chap – then you'll know just how much you need to do – or spend, rather.' He laughed again, then led the way to the drawing room, where other guests – including Lord William, Julianne, Heather, and David – were gathered.

'Anyway, I reckon he'll be next,' added Timothy, indicating Lord William as he approached to greet Anthony and Cynthia. 'Mamma will be pleased. She had all but given up hope on my rake of a brother.'

'Yes, my mother has been pushing for me to marry Julianne, she wanted our families to unite,' said Anthony under his breath.

Timothy shot Anthony a confused look. 'Really? I did not have Julianne down as your type.'

'That's why I let Bill have free reign,' laughed Anthony as Bill extended his hand.

'What are you two laughing at?' he said, glancing across the room at Julianne, who was deep in conversation with Heather, David and Diane's friends, Jane, and Christina.

'Oh, just your impending marriage doom,' joked Anthony.

'Ha, I don't think I'm the only one,' said Bill, nodding at Cynthia. 'Too soon to tell, my friend.'

'Come, say hello to everyone,' said Timothy, his tone diplomatic.

Soon, the drawing room was heaving with guests. The staff weaved among them, serving champagne and malts. Anthony stood by Cynthia's side and gave her a running commentary of who was married to who – and introduced her to gents 'I've known since I was five'. Bill and Timothy's sister, Margaret, arrived, shortly followed by Ronald and Phoebe Thomson, a debutante he'd started stepping out with. A flurry of introductions ensued, with laughter and lively chatter filling the room. When the luncheon gong struck, they all headed to the dining room for a feast of assorted meats and fish, served with fresh vegetables.

After lunch, Diane and Timothy gave their visitors a guided tour of the house. 'It's such a beautiful day – we should take a stroll in the gardens too,' suggested Diane. 'Then we can all retire to freshen-up before pre-dinner drinks in the conservatory.'

They caught the last rays of winter sunshine, walking in small groups around the vast grounds. The grass was crunchy with frost underfoot. Cynthia, Julianne and Phoebe walked together. Anthony, Bill and Ronald were a few yards behind the women but slowed their pace when Bill asked Anthony, 'So, any further news on our mystery?'

Anthony looked over his shoulder. 'No, I have warned everyone to be on their guard. And I've sent an undercover man to the White Hart Inn – to see if he can surreptitiously lure information from locals. My biggest fear is the culprit might target one of the ladies – so we must all be doubly vigilant.' Anthony's words steamed the cold air. Then, as though snapping out of a trance, he plunged his hands into the deep pockets of his Chesterfield coat and pulled his head back with a broad smile. 'Anyway, let's relax and enjoy the weekend. Who fancies a shooting or riding jaunt tomorrow?'

'Well, I'll need to see what Julianne wants to do first, but possibly, yes.'

Anthony and Ron looked at each other for a second, then burst out laughing.

Like all the other unmarried guests staying at Diane and Timothy's, Cynthia and Anthony were to sleep in separate bedrooms. When the walking party returned to the house, Anthony showed Cynthia to her room. 'Gosh, we couldn't be further apart,' said Anthony, as they climbed the sweeping staircase. 'You're in the east of the house but my bedroom is on the west side.'

'Hm, that's a pity,' said Cynthia as they walked along the first-floor oak-panneled landing, adorned with oil paintings and tapestries. When they reached the door to Cynthia's room, she looked up at Anthony, her expression expectant yet sultry.

'Well, I'm sure we'll find a way to be alone later,' he said – and gave Cynthia his best rakish wink.

'Good, I'm looking forward to that,' Cynthia whispered, then she pushed through the door, throwing Anthony a replica wink over her shoulder.

At 7 p.m. another gong echoed through Hopetoun House, signalling half an hour until evening drinks. Cynthia had arranged to meet Julianne in her room, so they could then go downstairs together. Peering over the bannisters on the landing, Cynthia spied Anthony and Bill in the hall below. She scuttled on to Julianne's room, a nervous excitement fluttering in her stomach as she anticipated the evening ahead.

Julianne also appeared nervous, firing a volley of questions at Cynthia as she welcomed her into her bedroom. 'Oh, when are we supposed to go downstairs?' 'Have the gents gone down yet?' 'Is this dress too casual?' Julianne gestured at the flounces and ribbons on her tiered royal blue dress.

Cynthia giggled. 'The gentlemen have gone down, so we should follow. And you look stunning Julianne.' Julianne looked at the corniced ceiling, her brunette ringlets jiggling as she shook her head.

'I'm so foolish for being nervous,' she said, blushing. 'But there are so many grand people here. Cynthia smiled linked her arm through Julianne's.

'Not as grand as us, Julianne. Shall we?'

The two ladies descended the staircase and entered the conservatory, which was already packed with mingling guests. Bill and Anthony sprung to life when they saw Cynthia and Julianne. 'Ladies, you both look enchanting,' enthused Bill as he stepped forward to greet them.

'Yes, I must totally agree,' Anthony said – and offered Cynthia his arm to escort her around the room for more introductions and champagne. Bill and Julianne joined them.

The second gong sounded just as the front door chimed. 'Oh, that must be more guests. Do excuse us,' Diane said. She and Timothy left the room and returned a few minutes later with the new arrivals. When Anthony saw the new guests, he lowered his head and turned towards Bill. 'Damn, who invited *her*?' he said.

Bill spread his hands. 'Nothing to do with me, old chap.'

Cynthia and Julianne, facing the gents, could not see who was behind them, but they heard her. A familiar voice: loud, bright, and haughty. Unmistakable. 'Anthony darling, I did not know you would be here this weekend. Cynthia turned around slowly, as a plume of white satin whooshed past her. 'How lovely, we will have such fun,' said Lady Anne Stewart, gushing forth and planting a kiss on Anthony's cheek. 'You look handsome as ever, you devil.' Anthony grimaced and looked past Lady Anne's cheek, trying to catch Cynthia's eye. But Cynthia's gaze was on Lady Anne's dress, which was as elaborate as Queen Victoria's wedding gown and trimmed with Honiton lace and pearls. Cynthia's face burned. Her insides curdled. Suddenly, she was back in Madam Martine's shop, listening to Lady Anne's vows to 'win Anthony back'.

I've done it before, I'll do it again. I will put everything into action to get him back.

I will order some Italian silk lingerie to reel him in.

160

'Lord William, you are also here,' added Lady Anne, and kissed him too. 'Oh, we shall all have a grand time together.' Then, to Cynthia's horror, the woman threaded her arm through Anthony's, as though to steer him away. Another gent approached then. 'Ah, Sir John McIvor,' trilled Lady Anne, 'do let me introduce you to Lord Anthony Sinclair.' She nodded sideways at Anthony, smiling, then gestured with her free hand at Bill, 'And this is Lord William McLean. Gentlemen, Sir John McIvor is Diane and Timothy's neighbour to the north of their estate.' She totally ignored Cynthia and Julianne.

Anthony bristled and untangled his arm from Lady Anne's – then, addressing the third gent, said, 'A pleasure to meet you, Sir McIvor. Please, do escort Lady Anne Stewart to the champagne bar. She must be parched after her journey here.'

'Oh, of course, how thoughtless of me,' blustered Sir McIvor, offering his arm to Lady Anne. She smiled reluctantly and took his arm.

'Yes, of course, lead on,' she said. As she walked away, she shot Anthony a determined look. 'I'll see you later for a proper catchup.'

The foursome stood in silence for a moment. Then three other couples approached, and more introductions were made. But Cynthia couldn't concentrate. The names whizzed past her- The Honourable gentlemen, Peter Cruikshank and Ralph McGregor (army friends of Anthony and Bill), Fiona Clements, Louise Wilson…Cynthia would need reminding of their names later. Her mind was instead on Lady Anne Stewart. *How dare she link arms with Anthony. How* dare *she. How dare she appear and ruin our weekend?*

Anthony noticed Cynthia's silence and felt relieved when the dinner gong chimed – until Bill nudged him once more and nodded at another couple walking into the room. 'Oh God, that's all we need,' groaned Anthony.

Cynthia turned, and came eye to eye with Sir Daniel Friel, who was arm in arm with a raven-haired woman in a shell pink dress.

'Dinner is served,' the butler announced.

Cynthia wanted to scream. She was gobsmacked. *First that horrible woman shows up – and now creepy Sir Daniel Friel? Are the gods against me?*

CHAPTER TWENTY-TWO

CYNTHIA FELT THE HEAT of Sir Daniel Friel's penetrating stare and quickly looked away. Next, she heard Lady Anne Stewart's loud squawking laugh as she headed to the dining room with the other guests. The sound alone gave Cynthia pins and needles all over. She watched as Lady Anne, still on the arm of Lord McIvor, tipped her head over her shoulder and shot Anthony a teasing smile, to which Anthony did not respond. Instead, he offered his arm to Cynthia and bent to speak into her ear. 'Please,' he said, 'Do not let Friel or that woman ruin our weekend together. I have absolutely no feelings for that woman.' Anthony squeezed his hand over hers to affirm his words. 'Cynthia, look at me, you do believe me, don't you?'

'Yes, yes, of course,' whispered Cynthia. 'It was just a shock to see her here and watch her rude display.'

'Oh, just ignore her. And cheer up – let's enjoy tonight,' said Anthony.

'Yes, I will,' Cynthia said through an unconvincing weak smile. They followed the guests into the dining room and took their seats opposite Peter Cruickshank and Louise Wilson. The meal was a feast of soups followed by roasted pheasant, hare, and venison – all hunted by the estate's gamekeepers – served with vegetables and thick stocks. Elaborate desserts included an array of rich jellies and iced puddings. As the courses were served and the wine and conversation flowed, Cynthia began to relax. She enjoyed chatting with Peter and Louise – a welcome distraction from Lady Anne, who was fortunately seated at the opposite end of the banquet table to Cynthia and Anthony. *Good, best place for her*, thought Cynthia.

After dessert, Diane announced the next event of the evening. 'We ladies shall adjourn to the drawing room and leave the gents to their port and cigars,' she said, and the ladies gathered their skirts and stood. As Cynthia rose, Anthony took Cynthia's hand and looked up at her with a reassuring smile. She smiled back and squeezed his hand. *Good,* he thought, *Cynthia seems far more relaxed.*

The ladies congregated in small groups around the drawing room. Cynthia and Julianne sat with Phoebe. Cynthia immediately warmed to Phoebe, who relayed, with palpable excitement, details of her romance with Ronald.

'I had no idea you two were stepping out until today,' said Cynthia. 'Mind you, Anthony has been busy with business and, well, you know what the gents are like for not passing on *relevant* news.'

'Oh gosh,' said Phoebe, 'I know but, to be fair, we've only been stepping out for two weeks. Although, that said, we've known one another for over a year now – through a mutual friend.'

'Do tell us how you got together,' enthused Juliane, 'I do love to hear a fine romance story.'

'Well, I'd love to regale you with an enchanting love story, but the truth is, Ronald and I got chatting over a game of cards at a party. The next day he took me for a walk around Holyrood Park, followed by a lovely dinner at the Strath Hotel. We've seen each other almost every day since. And I must say, I'm rather smitten.'

The women were still chatting – mainly gossiping about who was stepping out with who and exchanging thoughts on which dresses to wear for upcoming functions – when the gentlemen arrived.

Diane stood and clapped her hands. 'Oh good,' she said. 'Now we can now have some entertainment. I have set up card tables next door – and there's also a pianoforte if anyone wishes to play for us? And Timothy took delivery of a billiards table yesterday. It's set up down the hall, but I warn you, this is not a gentlemen's-only domain; I play a mean game if anyone would like a challenge?' The room rumbled with polite laughter. 'Please,' finished Diane, 'Do find your own way to which ever entertainment takes your fancy.'

Anthony asked Cynthia if she would like to pair up for a game of whist.

'Yes, that could be fun, do any of you want to make up a foursome?' she said, gesturing around their satellite group.

'Oh yes,' said Phoebe, 'I would like that. She looked up at Ronald. 'Yes, let's do it,' he said.

The foursome went into the card room, found a table, and started playing. All was well until half an hour later when Lady Anne appeared on Anthony's shoulder. She leaned over him; her face close to his as she examined his fanned cards. 'Oh, darling, no. No, no, no, no, no,' she said, then tutted. 'No, darling, you do not want to play *that* card,' said Lady Anne, pointing at two of hearts Anthony had isolated to the right from the rest of his cards.

Anthony turned and pulled his head away from Lady Anne's. 'Excuse me, I am quite capable of deciding which card to play,' he snapped.

A sour smile played on Lady Anne's lips. 'Well, I was only trying to help.' Then, glancing at Cynthia, added, 'You know how distracted you get when I am near you, Anthony, darling.'

'It's not even my turn,' said Anthony, as Ronald played his next card – the queen of spades.

Anthony tensed, wondering what Lady Anne was talking about. He wished she would go away. But she seized Anthony's shoulders, her hands the talons of a vulture, pouncing on its prey.

'See, I told you,' she sneered. 'Ronald clearly has a better hand than you, my love. I would give up now if I were you – you will only loose if I hang around.'

'Then I suggest you move on,' Anthony growled under his breath as he shook himself free from Lady Anne's grip. But still she persisted with her flirtation act, now tracing a finger over Anthony's cheek.

'Oh, Anthony, that's not what you usually say,' she said brazenly.

Cynthia's blood boiled. She wanted to physically remove Lady Anne from the room – and scream at her. *How dare she humiliate Anthony and me in this disgusting manner.*

Anthony grabbed Lady Anne's hand and looked her straight in the eye. 'Please, go and find Sir McIvor, I am sure he will be looking for you,' he hissed.

'Hm,' sighed Lady Anne, 'Actually, Lord McIvor is outside – he wanted some air. Perhaps I should join him. But, you know, it's awfully dark outside – and I would hate to stumble.'

'Right, fine,' said Anthony, placing his cards face-down on the table. 'I shall escort you to Lord McIvor – then we can continue our game in peace.'

'Actually, we might move on to the billiards table,' said Ronald.

'Oh yes, let's do that,' agreed Phoebe. 'Will you join us, Cynthia?'

'Oh no, I think I'll stay here and wait for Anthony, thank you,' Cynthia replied, glowering at Lady Anne.

Anthony bent to kiss Cynthia's cheek. 'I shall not be long,' he said. 'I will take her to find Sir McIvor and be straight back.' Cynthia began gathering the cards, not daring to look up. *I very much doubt that… if Lady Anne gets her claws into Anthony.*

Cynthia sat in the drawing room, stewing. At least fifteen minutes had passed but still Anthony had not returned. *What were they doing?* She waited another five minutes then, fuming, decided to head upstairs. *Lady Anne has clearly succeeded in her ploy to win Anthony over*, she thought.

As Cynthia opened the door to her bedroom, Anthony returned to the drawing room. His heart dropped when he saw the empty cards table. 'Damn,' he muttered under his breath. He had found it harder than he anticipated to shake off Lady Anne Stewart. She had explicitly told Anthony how she wished to reignite their romance. 'Remember the fun times we had, darling,' she'd said as Anthony led her outside. 'Cynthia need not know about us. You know how discreet I am, Anthony. And you should see my new silk lingerie. You'll not be able to resist me once…'

'No, stop this now,' Anthony had told Lady Anne. She was quite upset, her eyes brimming with bitter tears. They had walked on then, into the cold night, searching for Lord McIvor. It had taken some time to find him in the grounds, hence Anthony's delay.

Anthony headed to the billiards table down the hall – then into the piano room, but Cynthia was nowhere to be seen. People were moving from room to room. He went back into the hallway and bumped into Ronald and Phoebe. 'Have you seen Cynthia?' he asked.

'Yes, she went upstairs, only minutes ago,' said Phoebe.

'Damn,' he mumbled again.

'What's wrong with you?' asked Ronald.

'Lady Anne Stewart is the problem,' said Anthony.

'Yes, she was rather forward at the cards table,' said Ronald. 'But everybody knows Lady Anne Stewart is a troublemaker – loves nothing better than to stir.' Ronald gave Anthony's shoulder a firm squeeze. 'Good luck,' he added, then walked on with Phoebe.

Anthony knew he had to explain himself to Cynthia. And he must do so, now. He powered along the hallway to the grand staircase, zigzagging past puzzled guests as he did so. He bounded up the stairs and through the corridor to Cynthia's bedroom. He tapped on the door, a gentle, apologetic knock, followed by a firmer rap when she did not answer. 'Cynthia, please open the door,' he said to the door, but still, nobody answered. He knocked once more. Nothing. Begrudgingly defeated, Anthony shambled westwards through the mansion which, despite the bonhomie and laughter warming its walls, felt cold and lonely to Anthony in that moment.

Cynthia had been sitting on her bed when Anthony knocked. She had heard his plea but had been too afraid to answer the door. She had convinced herself Lady Anne Stewart had won him back.

She listened to the steady soft thuds of Anthony's shoes on the carpet, receding into silence. Tears welled then trickled down her face.

'Please God,' she whispered. 'Please don't let that horrible woman steal Anthony.'

Downstairs, the party was just beginning.

CHAPTER TWENTY-THREE

THE NEXT MORNING PHOEBE made her way to Cynthia's bedroom. 'Would you like to come to breakfast with me?' she said as Cynthia answered the door. Ronald had explained the history of Lady Anne Stewart and Anthony's affair to Phoebe – and she knew if she were in Cynthia's shoes, she would appreciate the kindness and support of a friend. So, Phoebe decided she would do everything in her power to help Cynthia over the weekend.

'Oh, yes please,' said Cynthia, stifling a yawn. Cynthia had barely slept for worrying. 'That'll be lovely.'

As Cynthia and Phoebe reached the stairs, Julianne came out of her room. 'Oh, mind if I join you ladies?' she said. Cynthia offered her other arm to Julianne, and they followed the smell of sizzling bacon.

Anthony shot to his feet when the ladies entered the breakfast room. He made a beeline for Cynthia. 'Please, let me assist you, my dear,' he said softly. Knowing it would be rude to refuse, Cynthia allowed Anthony to take her arm and lead her to her seat.

'I am so sorry,' he whispered as he pulled out the chair. 'I should not have left you last night. But I knew she would make a scene if I allowed her to stay in the room. Please, do accept my apology.'

'Fine.' Said Cynthia, her tone flat and nonchalant.

Anthony noted her insouciance. *I shall have to work hard to convince her there's nothing going on between Lady Anne Stewart and me.* 'Would you care for tea?' he asked.

Cynthia nodded and gave a taut smile. 'Yes, thank you.'

Phoebe and Julianne sat opposite Cynthia. 'That's it,' whispered

Phoebe once Anthony's back was turned, 'make him work.' But equally, Cynthia was touched by Anthony's attentiveness. He returned with a pot of tea and began to pour Cynthia a cup. He hadn't needed to go to such bother – the servants were there to execute such tasks. She began to wonder, *Maybe I've got it all wrong about Anthony and Lady Anne? She clearly wants Anthony back, but that doesn't mean he feels the same way, does it?* And besides, Cynthia hated being at odds with him. She looked into his eyes as he poured. They were so dark she could see the reflection of her teacup in them. 'Are you going riding today?' she asked.

'Only if you'll join me,' he said.

'I would like that very much.'

'Good, it's glorious weather for a ride, too.'

After Breakfast, Cynthia returned briefly to her room to change into her riding habit – a forest green jacket, apron skirt and matching hat festooned with peacock feathers. Anthony was right; it was a beautiful day, sunny and crisp but not as frosty as the previous day. She headed out to the stables, where Anthony was already waiting alongside two saddled horses. He couldn't help but notice how subdued Cynthia still seemed. *Hm, this is all Lady Anne Stewart's fault*, he thought. *But I will double my efforts to cheer up Cynthia.*

'Hello again,' he said as she approached. He smiled and lifted her chin with his finger. 'Can I not have a smile, please?'

Cynthia smiled weakly – although she found Anthony hard to resist.

'Now that's better,' he said and at once he planted his hands around her waist and lifted her sideways into the saddle of the smaller of the two horses. Anthony's swift movement surprised Cynthia, who became a little flustered. She arranged her skirt and adjusted her position in the saddle, while Anthony jumped onto his horse. 'Ready?' he said brightly.

'I'm ready,' said Cynthia.

They trotted out of the stables, gathering pace towards the edge of a field, where they galloped north, towards the hazy ice-blue expanse of the Firth of Forth. When they reached a hill by the water, they stopped and admired the view. The sky was clear but for a few wispy clouds, tinged apricot by the low winter sun.

'Oh gosh, it's beautiful,' said Cynthia, squinting in the light.

'Almost as beautiful as you,' replied Anthony, and Cynthia darted him a bemused look.

'Are you trying to soft-soap me, Sir?'

Anthony pressed his hands to his heart and pulled a wounded expression. 'Who me?'

Cynthia gave him her best haughty smirk. 'Yes, *you*. I was not lovely enough last night for you to return quickly to my side, was I?'

'I know…but…she…I mean you…you were lovely…I mean you *are* so lovely…Oh, anyway…' Anthony ran his hands through his hair and looked helplessly at the sky. 'I'm mincing my words here,' he added and spread his hands wide. 'That's the effect you have on me. See what you do to me? I can't manage a coherent sentence even. Please, let me start again.'

'Go on, I'm listening,' said Cynthia.

'That damn woman…'

'Lady Anne Stewart – your former *mistress*,' Cynthia interjected.

'Look, I know I should have come straight back last night, but she would not take no for an answer. Eventually, I had to be quite brutal in my response, but I hope she has now got the message and will leave me – leave *us* – alone. Please, Cynthia, please forgive me?'

A few seconds silence followed, then Cynthia looked up at Anthony, pursed her lips and replied, 'I suppose so. But I'm watching you.'

'Thank you, my dear.' He bent to kiss Cynthia on the lips. 'Lucky we're on these steads, or I might be tempted to show how very sorry I am,' he added.

'Well, we must head back for lunch.'

'My dear, that sounds like a plan. Race you back?' said Anthony.

They galloped back and were in high spirits when they arrived at Hopetoun House. Anthony helped Cynthia down from her horse – then, as they made their way out of the stables, he suddenly pulled her into an empty stall and kissed her. She melted in his arms.

'I love kissing you,' he murmured, nuzzling her neck. Cynthia snaked her arms around Anthony's back.

'I love kissing…' A loud voice interrupted Cynthia.

'Charlie, lad, come and give me a hand, will you? That was the groomsman, calling for the stable boy.

Cynthia and Anthony waited, holding their breath as Charlie scuttled past the stall.

'I'm on my way, Bob.' Then they both burst out laughing.

Anthony took Cynthia's hand in his and led her out of the stall. 'That was a close call, you little minx.'

'Ha, that was *your* fault,' teased Cynthia, and they bounded into the house, giggling.

After a buffet lunch with wine, the guests mingled in the recreation rooms and corridors. Cynthia and Anthony joined Bill, Julianne, Ronald, and Phoebe around the billiards table in the hallway.

I challenge you to a match,' Cynthia said to Anthony, and the others clapped and agreed.

'Oh, yes, that'll be fun,' said Phoebe. 'Then the winner can choose their next opponent. Although, we all know that will be Cynthia.'

'Hm, we'll see about that,' said Anthony. He picked up a cue and inspected its leather tip. 'I'm quite the expert at billiards.' But as the game got underway, Cynthia took the lead; at home, Cynthia loved to play billiards with Lord Marchmont – and she'd honed well her skills over the years. Now she was having so much fun she didn't even notice Lady Anne Stewart staring at her from along the hallway.

'C'mon Anthony, old chap, surely you can do better than this. It looks as though the lady's going to beat you,' said Ronald, grinning, as Cynthia lifted her cue to take her shot. If she potted the final red ball, she'd win the game. She positioned her hand on the table to support the tip of the cue, which she drew back in her other hand. As she did so, Anthony pretended to sneeze – in a bid to distract her. Cynthia straightened her back, glared across the table at Anthony and resumed her pose. And just as she was about to hit the ball, Ronald coughed – a fake cough.

'Stop it, you're both being totally unfair,' said Phoebe, wagging her finger at Anthony and Ronald. 'You're both trying to put Cynthia off.'

'Yes, I agree,' said Julianne, and Bill placed his hand on her shoulder.

'You're quite right, my dear Julianne,' he said, 'I declare Anthony disqualified and Cynthia the winner.' And with that, Cynthia flashed Anthony a smug smile, returned to her shot – and laughed when the red ball tumbled into the righthand pocket.

Everybody burst into fits of applause and laughter.

'Right, Cynthia, who will you play next?' asked Ronald.

'Oh, I think I'm done with billiards,' Cynthia replied. 'I'll let somebody else play.' She put down her cue as Anthony sidled up to her, took her hand to his lips and bowed ceremoniously.

'You won fair and square. I am humbled, I was trying to put you off as I knew you would win,' he said with a smile.

'Oh, you're a true gentleman, accepting defeat so gallantly.'

'Come, let's go for a walk around this grand house,' said Anthony. As they progressed along the hallway, Cynthia noticed through the door to the ballroom, Sir Daniel Friel and Lady Anne Stewart. They were alone – and talking very covertly, it seemed. Cynthia walked on, chatting gaily to Anthony while secretly hoping Lady Anne had forgotten about Anthony and had instead found another victim to sink her claws into.

'Would you like some tea?' Anthony asked.

Cynthia jiggled her head as she smiled. 'Why, yes, that would be nice. But you really should be toasting my win with champagne.'

'You are right, of course, but I am not that good a loser. Tea will have to do.' He steered Cynthia into the drawing room, where other guests were already seated. Anthony found them two seats by the window. Minutes later, as the maid served them tea and cake, Cynthia noticed a movement through the glass, over Anthony's shoulder. When she looked closer, she saw a man, tall and stocky with sideburns that swamped his already wide face. He was loitering by the bushes outside. It was Sir Daniel Friel. She inched forwards in her seat, craned her neck and, at that point, Sir Daniel Friel disappeared into the bushes.

'Gosh, how odd,' said Cynthia.

Anthony turned, following Cynthia's gaze over his shoulder. 'What is it?' he said, turning back to Cynthia.

'I just saw Sir Daniel Friel duck into those bushes,' she said, pointing at the window. 'He was in the ballroom a short while ago, talking to *that* woman. He must have rushed outside.'

'How did you know they were talking in the ballroom?' asked Anthony. He knew very well that the woman to whom Cynthia was referring was Lady Anne Stewart.

'Oh, because I saw them as we walked past there – just moments ago. Did you not see them?'

Anthony shook his head, but a worrying thought suddenly crept in. *I'm supposed to be extra vigilant this weekend.* 'Indeed, how odd,' he agreed.

'I didn't know they were so close.'

'Me neither. He doesn't seem like Anne's type to me.' Anthony regretted those words as soon as they spilled from his mouth.

'Of course, and you would know all about that, wouldn't you,' snapped Cynthia.

'Oh, please don't start again, I didn't mean anything by it.'

Cynthia drained her teacup, then returned it to its saucer with a tinkle. 'Right, I'd better go and change for tonight's soiree.'

'I shall come along for you at 7p.m. and escort you down.' Anthony said, rising to help Cynthia out of her seat.

'Fine, I'll see you then, loser.'

Anthony laughed. 'I will never live this down, will I.'

'No,' she said, and pivoted dramatically before walking out of the room. As she made her way down the hall, she bumped into Lady Anne Stewart.

'Ah, if it isn't the little billiards champion,' she trilled, looking down her spindly nose at Cynthia. 'It's not often Anthony lets somebody else win.'

'Oh, I won fair and square – and Anthony agreed as much.'

'Ha, nonsense,' said Lady Anne with a flick of her wrist, 'Anthony was not playing his best. I have seen him play on numerous occasions and he plays much better than his performance today. But of course, you don't know Anthony like I do.'

Cynthia smiled, determined not to rise to Lady Anne's pathetic attempt to make her jealous, but also furious that she knew about the billiards match. *Did she spy on us? Argh, walk on Cynthia…don't get involved.* 'If you'll excuse me,' she said finally, still smiling, 'but I must go and freshen up for tonight's soiree.' But as Cynthia went to leave, Lady Anne touched her arm.

'I know everything about Anthony,' she sneered. 'I know his favourite drink, his favourite food and all his intimate habits and pleasures. You know *nothing*, nothing at all. He is playing with you. He likes women with experience. Women like *me*.' Lady Anne almost spat her venomous words, then threw back her head and let out a demonic laugh. 'Go along,' she said, making a brushing action with her hands,' run along and get changed. Put on your fanciest dress – because you're going to need all the help you can get to hold on to a man like Anthony.'

CHAPTER TWENTY-FOUR

CYNTHIA FLOUNCED PAST LADY ANNE STEWART, hoping to appear unfazed by her threatening diatribe. She stomped on, her face boiling with rage. *What an evil, disgraceful woman. What did Anthony ever see in Lady Anne Stewart?*

Back in her room, Cynthia called for her assigned maid, Agatha. *I must look my finest. I will show that woman. Anthony will have eyes only for me tonight.*

Cynthia spent the next two hours getting ready. Agatha styled Cynthia's hair into tight ringlets – then pinned a section of the curls high upon her crown and added ribbons and diamante combs. Next, Agatha helped her into a sugar pink evening gown of shimmering silk layered with twinkling, diamond-studded gauze. A crimson ribbon tied in a neat bow beneath her ample bosom, and matching bows decorated the puffed, off the shoulder sleeves. Cynthia pinched her cheeks and pursed her lips tightly for thirty seconds to create a rosy glow – then checked her reflection in the long gilt mirror. 'Och, you look a picture, Miss Marchmont,' said Agatha. Cynthia twisted this way and that in front of the glass before adding the final touches to her outfit – diamond earrings and matching bracelets worn over her long, pale pink gloves. 'A bonny picture indeed.'

'Thank you, Agatha, but I do hope it's…' A firm knock at the door interrupted the ladies. 'Oh gosh, that'll be him, Lord Sinclair,' said Cynthia, her voice laced with nerves.

'Allow me, Miss,' Agatha and scuttled to open the door. 'Evening my lord,' she said as Anthony stepped into the room, tall and sleek in a black dinner suit and bow tie.

'Thank you,' Anthony replied, barely glancing at Agatha. His unblinking gaze was on Cynthia. *She looks ravishing*, he thought. 'You may leave now, thank you.' Agatha curtseyed and wished Anthony and Cynthia a pleasant evening as she left. The door clicked shut, and Anthony stood for a few seconds, his eyes caressing every inch of Cynthia. 'You look amazing, quite breathtaking,' he said, walking slowly towards her. She raised her hand for Anthony to kiss.

'You look rather dashing yourself,' she said with a nervous smile.

'But your outfit is sorely lacking something,' added Anthony, and suddenly Cynthia's heart turned to ice. She spun round to check her reflection. She had put all her effort into getting ready; indeed, Agatha had excelled herself. Disappointment welled heavy in Cynthia's chest and, try as she might she could not erase Lady Anne's wicked remarks from her mind. *You're going to need all the help you can get to hold on to a man like Anthony*. Then he was behind her, holding her gaze in the mirror. He smiled as he leaned down to kiss her naked shoulder. 'I think your beautiful outfit needs this,' he whispered. Cynthia turned to face him – just as Anthony produced from his pocket a slender midnight blue box embossed with "M&L" in bronze. 'Please, open it.' Cynthia felt a little overwhelmed.

'What is this?' she said, even though she recognised the packaging and initials; the box was from the jewellery shop, McInnes and Love, on George Street.

'Open it and see.'

Slowly, delicately, Cynthia lifted the lid – and gasped at its contents. Inside, nestled in blue velvet, was the most exquisite diamond necklace. 'Oh Anthony, it's beautiful,' she said.

'Not as beautiful as you.' Cynthia felt quite faint, her stomach awhirl with butterflies. Lady Anne and her cruel words had all but vanished from her mind. 'Here, let me put it on for you,' offered Anthony, lifting the glinting jewels out of the box. Cynthia turned towards the mirror again and watched as Anthony tenderly fastened the clasp at the back of her neck. The diamonds felt cold against her décolletage – a coldness soon thawed by the sudden heat that rushed over her when Anthony caressed her shoulders and pulled her against him. She felt his hardness even through the bouffant layers of her dress. 'Perfection,' he whispered into her ear, and kissed her neck, down to its nape, then spun her round and kissed her hard on the lips. Cynthia felt breathless, but she wanted more. At that point, Anthony drew back.

'I want you here and now. That's the effect you have on me, Cynthia,' he said.

Cynthia felt his desire; she saw it sparkle in his glossy eyes. She knew that if the pre-dinner drinks gong had not sounded at that moment, this would have gone a lot further.

'Walk away from me", he ordered. 'I need to get myself under control before we go downstairs.'

'I don't want to,' she said and leaned against him. He pushed her back.

'Cynthia, please, move away,' he rasped. 'I have little control at the moment and do not want everyone downstairs to notice.'

Cynthia looked down and noticed Anthony's hard erection straining against his trousers. 'Right, I need some air,' he said. He marched over to the window and pushed up the bottom sash, filling the room with an Arctic draught. Cynthia giggled and Anthony threw her an exasperated look over his shoulder. 'I'm glad this amuses you so much.'

'Oh, Anthony, dear, you are always so much in control – I did not realise I could have so much power over you.' She giggled again.

'Ah, woman, you go too far,' said Anthony, closing the window. He turned, straightened his cravat, and blew out his cheeks. 'So, shall we go downstairs now before I lose *all* control?'

Cynthia lifted her shoulders. 'I suppose so,' she said.

Cynthia could not stop smiling as she entered the drawing room on Anthony's arm. She loved her necklace and would treasure it forever; she was also delighted at Anthony's arousal in the bedroom. *My outfit must have done the trick*. The footman approached and offered them champagne. Anthony lifted two flutes from the footman's tray, handed one to Cynthia with a wink, and they joined Bill and Julianne by the fireplace.

'Oh my, what a stunning necklace, Cynthia,' said Julianne.

Cynthia's hand fluttered to the diamonds as she glanced sideways at Anthony. 'Isn't it lovely? It's a present, from Anthony.'

'It goes beautifully with your dress – I so adore that pink on you. You look perfect as usual.'

Cynthia blushed. 'Oh Julianne, you're far too kind. You look lovely yourself – as always. And that plum silk is simply divine against your skin.'

'And look at your gloves. They are exquisite. Did you get those from Madame Martine's?'

'Yes, I did, but tell me, where did you get that beautiful purse? I adore the beadwork – and is that crocheted silk underneath.'

'Gosh, yes, I found this in Madam Lafayette's only a few days ago. I simply couldn't leave the shop without buying it.'

'I would have done the same,' gushed Cynthia, 'It's so, so adorable.'

The men exchanged bemused looks as the two women continued to compliment one another's outfits and accessories. Then Ronald and Phoebe arrived.

'Cynthia, you played an exceptional game of billiards this afternoon,' said Ronald. 'You were quite a match for Anthony.'

'Och, thank you, but I'm sure he let me win,' said Cynthia.

'Nonsense, you deserved to win,' said Ronald, giving Anthony's shoulder a sympathetic squeeze. 'Bad luck, old chap.'

'You're right, my friend,' said Anthony. 'Cynthia won fair and square.' A coy smile played on Cynthia's lips. Ronald and Anthony's kind remarks filled her with pleasure – especially after Lady Anne's hurtful comments earlier. But it wouldn't do to be heard gloating in company, so instead she turned to Phoebe.

'Phoebe, you look glorious,' she said, and so another round of compliments ensued among the women – interrupted by the second gong as the butler, George, called the guests for dinner.

Smiling, Cynthia took her seat at the dinner table next to Anthony, but her heart dropped when she saw who was sitting on his other side: Lady Anne Stewart. Likewise, Anthony was annoyed and perplexed in equal measure at this arrangement. Diane and Timothy knew Lady Anne was Anthony's ex-mistress. *Why would they make such a social faux pas?* Then, all became clear as he sat down.

'Anthony, dear, I hope you don't mind but I changed the seating arrangements so I could be close to you,' Lady Anne said in a loud whisper. 'I thought it would be good for us to chat. I noticed you avoided me today, which is really quite rude of you, wouldn't you say?'

'Yes, I have been avoiding you,' Anthony hissed, hoping Cynthia couldn't hear. 'Intentionally so, too. You had no right to change the seating arrangements.'

'Oh, but Anthony, dear,' Lady Anne went on. She touched his arm and he flinched. 'I need to talk to you. I miss you so much. And you cannot be getting satisfaction from that young chit next to you.'

'That is none of your business,' Anthony growled, glancing at Cynthia, who was chatting to Ralph McGregor to her left. He hoped she hadn't heard Lady Anne's cruel words. But although Cynthia seemed engrossed in conversation, she knew Anthony and Lady Anne were talking. She'd noticed Anthony leaning close to her, speaking in a hushed voice. *What were they talking about?* Disappointment, jealousy, and rage swelled in her chest. How could things have changed so drastically? Less than an hour ago, Anthony had been unable to control himself as he'd lovingly kissed her neck. She nervously fingered the diamonds at her throat as waiters served bowls of fine onion soup. Suddenly, Cynthia's appetite had all but vanished. Then finally, Anthony turned away from Lady Anne and spoke to Cynthia. 'So, was Ralph saying anything interesting?' he said.

'Oh yes, very. He was asking all about me and my family,' she lied. The truth was, Ralph hadn't stopped talking about a horse he'd just purchased. 'Lady Anne clearly had riveting things to say too. I saw you talking, your heads close together.'

'Cynthia, please, there's no reason for you to be jealous. The seating arrangements had nothing to do with me.'

'Oh, I really couldn't care less about anything that woman has to say,' she lied again, then shook her head as another of Lady Anne's vile remarks looped in her mind. *He is playing with you. He likes women with experience. Women like* me.

Anthony smirked, secretly a little flattered by Cynthia's jealousy. But, he conceded, sitting between the two women could make for a very awkward dinner indeed. He tried to ignore Lady Anne, but her persistence knew no bounds where Anthony was concerned. 'So, do you intend to ignore me all through dinner?' she asked as the main hog roast dish was served.

'If possible,' he said through gritted teeth. 'As much as I can without looking rude in everyone's eyes.'

'Well, I will not allow it,' she added. 'I miss you and think we should talk about our situation.'

'Please, understand, we don't have a *situation*.'

'Oh yes we do,' insisted Lady Anne. 'I have received threatening letters… about *you*.'

Anthony looked at Lady Anne, scanning her face for clues she was bluffing, but her expression was serious. 'What letters – and what do they say?'

Lady Anne shrugged then forked a chunk of pork into her mouth and chewed slowly, thoughtfully. She swallowed the meat then reached for her champagne glass and took a lingering sip. 'The letters say I must persuade you to sign over some deeds to your cousin, Stewart, or there will be trouble,' she said, still holding her glass. 'I don't know what to do. The letters say harm will befall me if I do not comply. I am at my wits' end.'

Anthony glanced at Cynthia, worried she had overheard their conversation. Fortunately, Cynthia was now chatting to Julianne, sitting opposite her. He quickly turned back to Lady Anne. 'Do you have these letters here with you?' he asked.

'No, I burned them.'

'Why?' Anthony said incredulously.

'I thought it was a joke at first, but now they are getting ugly. And do not get angry with me. This is *not* my fault. We need to talk privately and decide what action we should take.' Lady Anne took another sip of champagne.

'Fine, we'll speak later,' he said, and flinched again as Lady Anne rubbed his thigh beneath the table.

'I knew I could count on you,' she purred. Cynthia saw this and Lady Stewart caught her eye, smirking. Anthony removed her hand but did not notice the look between the two ladies.

Cynthia turned to resume speaking to Ralph. Anger and hurt raged inside her, but she tried not to let it show by smiling. *How dare that woman touch Anthony. How dare she?*

Over dessert, Anthony turned his attention back to Cynthia. 'Can I have your attention for a bit?' he said.

'Of course, your lordship. What would you like to talk about?' Cynthia said sarcastically.

'How are you enjoying the food?'

Cynthia laughed, 'It's very tasty, how's yours?'

'It would taste much better if you were not in a mood with me,'

'I am not in a mood with you.'

'Yes, you are. Stop pretending you are not.' Anthony smiled at her as he said this, hoping to bring her round. He reached into her lap and took her hand. 'Please, talk to me properly.'

'Fine, I was annoyed at you talking to Lady Anne Stewart,' Cynthia said while smiling at the other guests. 'She is trying to cause mischief between us.'

'Well, she is succeeding then, isn't she? Frankly, I don't want to give her the satisfaction, do you?'

Cynthia sighed, still smiling. 'No, you're right.' *I must stop jumping to conclusions*, she thought. 'Let's go for a stroll after dinner – and maybe you can continue what you started upstairs.'

'Now, there's an invitation I can't possibly reject,' he said.

After dinner, the gents stayed in the dining room for their cigars and brandy while the ladies went to the drawing room for tea. Cynthia sat with Phoebe. 'That woman is causing mischief again,' she said, eyeing Lady Anne, laughing animatedly with a woman in a sombre black dress. 'I wish she would just leave us alone.'

'I noticed,' said Phoebe. 'She was vying for Anthony's attention all during dinner. I would want to slap her face if she targeted Ronald.'

'I know. I feel the same, but Anthony and I have agreed the best thing to do is to simply ignore her. We're going for a stroll soon.'

Alas, Cynthia's planned romantic walk with Anthony would have to wait a while; when the gents returned to the drawing room, Diane announced the 'musicians' had arrived and were ready to perform in the front parlour. Anthony sat next to Cynthia while the orchestra played a beautiful Baroque repertoire, from Pachelbel's "Canon in D Major" and gigues by Handel and Telemann to Bach's famous "Suite in D, Air and Gavotte". Fortunately, Lady Anne was not sitting close to Anthony for the performance; he held Cynthia's hand throughout the hour-long concert, seductively stroking her palm with his thumb, which sent waves of excitable anticipation through her. She had almost forgotten about Lady Anne and her attempts to woo Anthony. By the end of the session, Cynthia couldn't wait to be alone with Anthony. 'Hurry, go and get your wrap and we'll go for that stroll,' Anthony said to her as everyone applauded the musicians. 'I'll meet you in the library.' Cynthia smiled.

'I'll not be long,' she said as they left the parlour. She hurried along in her satin slippers – then practically flew up the stairs. No sooner had Cynthia left than Lady Anne pounced on Anthony again. She crept up on him as he walked into the library.

'Right, we need to talk, *now*,' she said forcefully. Anthony turned slowly, an exasperated expression swathing his face.

'Can't this wait?' he said.

'I'm worried…about these letters. You must help me, Anthony.' Lady Anne moved in close to Anthony, looked him in the eyes, then quickly brushed past him into the library. She marched over to the desk and leaned against it, facing him. She untied her purse and withdrew from it a folded sheet of paper, which she placed on the desk next to her hips, tonight wearing venomous, blood-red velvet. 'So, I wrote down all the details I could remember from the threatening letters,' she said, again searching Anthony's face for a reaction. Her lips began to quiver; her nostrils fluttered too. She looked as though she were about to cry, thought Anthony. 'Please, read it,' she said, indicating the paper with a tilt of her head. She had on an elaborate headdress comprising black lace and jewels cordoned by velvet ribbon and roses in the same colour as her dress. Anthony sighed as he walked over to the desk and grabbed the sheet of paper. He didn't need this right now. Cynthia would be here any minute.

'So, you didn't keep any of the original letters?' he said as he began reading Lady Anne's spiky handwriting.

Lady Anne Stewart, you must tell Lord Anthony Sinclair to sign over the deeds to his cousin, Stewart, with immediate effect. If you do not do so, your life could be in danger.

'No, none. I was too scared. But I swear, what you're reading now is what was said in those notes.'

'I see,' said Anthony. And he did concede, the words on the page were like the threats he'd received. Lady Anne pushed away from the desk and lay her hand on Anthony's arm.

'Oh Anthony, please help me,' she said, her eyes watering. 'You can see how upsetting this is for me. I'm so frightened.' And in that moment, Anthony felt sorry for the woman.

'Yes, of course, I am sorry you've been brought into this.'

'Please, help me, Anthony. Tell me what to do.' Tears tumbled down Lady Anne's face. Crying came naturally to her.

'There, there,' said Anthony, drawing Lady Anne into his arms and gently patting her back. 'I will sort this. Try not to worry.' Lady Anne lay her chin on Anthony's shoulder, enjoying the warmth of his embrace – and the view in the doorframe behind his back: Cynthia, cloaked in raspberry cashmere, her eyes wide with shock. She sniffed and, tears fast evaporating, shot Cynthia a winning smile. A smile drenched with bitterness.

'Oh, Anthony, I knew you wouldn't let me down. I knew you would take care of us – as you always have done,' she said, knowing Cynthia could hear every single word.

Anthony, unaware of Cynthia's presence, said, 'Yes, I will take care of you. Don't worry, I'll not let anybody hurt you.'

Tears burned Cynthia's eyes. *How could he? What's going on? Has Anthony been lying to me all along?* She felt nauseous, devastated. With a sharp gasp she turned and fled along the corridor, her mind awhirl. *How could he? How could Anthony do this to me? He is the worst kind of rake ever, going so easily from me to her, I believed him. How could he?* Cynthia ran through the empty conservatory, then out into the gardens, the air frosting her lungs as she gasped. She kept running until she reached the arbour festooned with winter roses. She dropped onto the seat, buried her face in her hands and cried hot, loud tears into the ice-cold night. Cynthia wept and wept. Minutes passed and she began to shiver – and hyperventilate. *How could he, how could he, HOW COULD HE?* Then a male voice cut through hers. The voice did not belong to Anthony. She didn't recognise the voice even. She didn't care who it was.

'There, there,' he said. 'Here, take this handkerchief.' The man dangled the handkerchief in front of Cynthia's shoulder. She took it gratefully, not looking up or behind her, and covered her face with the white linen. She tried to blow her nose but couldn't do so for panting hard. Her breath accelerated. *I'm dying, I can't breathe*, she thought. Then suddenly, the man behind her clamped his hand over her mouth and nose, forcing the handkerchief into her mouth. Cynthia attempted a cry for help, but she could no longer breathe. She looked skywards, glimpsed a few stars, then drifted into blackness. She did not hear the words of her attacker: 'I have your prize, Lord Sinclair. She is all mine now.' Likewise, she was unconscious when her assailant's men appeared, wrapped her in a blanket and carried her away and into a waiting carriage.

Inside Hopetoun House, Lady Anne had since retired to the drawing room, where she was seen hooting with laughter with Sir John McIvor before leaving the room some ten minutes later. Meanwhile in the library, Anthony paced impatiently.

Where the hell is Cynthia?

CHAPTER TWENTY-FIVE

WHEN CYNTHIA FAILED TO APPEAR, Anthony left the library to look for her. *Maybe she's suddenly fallen ill*, he thought. *Or fallen asleep. Or become engaged in a lengthy conversation with another guest?* He certainly couldn't think of any other possible reason for her not showing up. She had, after all, been looking forward to their evening stroll. She'd told Anthony as much, too.

Anthony searched the hall, but Cynthia was not there. There was no sign of her in the drawing room either. Deciding she must still be in her bedroom, he ran upstairs and rapped on her door. Agatha answered. 'Oh, Miss Marchmont was in and out in a flash. She was here about twenty minutes ago. She picked up her wrap and said she was going for a walk – with you, Sir. Miss Marchmont headed downstairs after that. Maybe she's in the…' Anthony didn't catch the end of Agatha's sentence. He raced back downstairs. Maybe Cynthia had misunderstood him and thought they were meeting in the garden? He cut through the conservatory and stepped outside into the brisk air. He couldn't see Cynthia, so he walked around the grounds for a while, calling her name and becoming more and more annoyed. *What the devil is she playing at? Is this some kind of joke? Where* is *Cynthia?*

Anthony went back inside and again searched the main rooms. He asked his friends, 'Have you seen Cynthia?' but nobody had seen her since she left the music room.

'What do you think has happened? Did you two have another row?' Bill asked.

'No, we were going for a stroll. She went upstairs to fetch her wrap... and never appeared in the library, where we'd agreed to meet,' said Anthony rubbing his temple.

Bill creased his forehead. 'How strange. She's probably got chatting to someone – you know how easily ladies get distracted, but I'll check with the servants.'

'And I'll check the powder rooms,' offered Julianne.

'Thank you,' said Anthony. 'This is deeply concerning. Cynthia wouldn't hide – or run away.'

Soon, everybody at Hopetoun House was looking for Cynthia – servants and guests alike. They checked all the rooms and corridors. A further search of the grounds was conducted and, an hour later, one of the footmen dashed inside and approached Anthony in the drawing room. 'I found this, Sir,' he said, proffering a raspberry pink wrap. 'It was on the seat of the small arbour. Does it belong to Miss Marchmont, Sir?'

'Well, it matches her dress, but...'

'Oh, my goodness, that's it. That's Miss Marchmont's wrap,' cried Agatha as she walked into the drawing room.

'I found it by the arbour outside,' the footman repeated. Agatha clapped her hands to her face. 'My Lord, what has happened to her? Miss Marchmont would not wander about in this cold dampness without her wrap, surely?'

Anthony nodded. 'My thoughts exactly, it is damp, cold and dark. Her dress is too thin for this weather. Ronald, fetch lamps and organise search parties with the staff. We must do a thorough search of all the grounds.' Anthony turned back to the footman. 'Get all the gents' capes, we could be out for quite some time. Bill, can you organise everyone. Julianne, can you organise the ladies to conduct a thorough search of the house from top to bottom?'

'Absolutely,' they said in unison.

The searched continued and, just before sunrise, everybody convened inside to exchange notes. Nobody had seen Cynthia. After refreshments, the search parties headed outside again while Anthony, Bill, and Ron headed to the library for a private meeting. 'Oh God, what has happened to her?' said Anthony, raking his fingers through his hair.

'Do you think this could be connected to those letters you've received?' asked Ron.

Anthony's face darkened at the thought. 'I hope not, but the longer this goes on, the worse it looks.'

'Shall we dispatch word to Cynthia's family?' said Bill.

'Yes, we best had,' said Anthony, his voice low and grave. 'Could you please also send word to my house, asking my staff to look out for further letters? Bill nodded. Anthony walked over to the window. 'This is all my fault,' he said into the glass. 'I should have taken more care of Cynthia.'

'You've done nothing wrong, Anthony,' said Ron.

Bill nodded his assent. 'Right, let's get these notes written – then I'll organise for the fastest horsemen to dispatch them.'

'Thank you,' said Anthony. 'I must find Cynthia. I simply *must* find her.'

As Bill took care of the admin work, Anthony and Ron headed outside where the search had resumed in daylight. Stan, one of the footmen, called them over as he walked through the gardens. 'Come quickly, my lords,' he said, crouching to examine something on the ground next to the arbour. Anthony and Ron quickened their step. 'I believe these are footprints,' added the footman, his face aglow with enthusiasm. 'We did not see them in the dark.' Anthony and Ron bent down to study the prints with Stan.

'Yes, you're correct,' said Anthony. 'And look, some are different in size – there looks to be more than one set of prints.' He pointed to a series of treads leading towards the pathway. 'Those are deeper, too, which suggests the person was either very heavy – or he was carrying something that added to his weight.'

'Indeed,' said Stan, and rose to point out more prints behind him. 'And these head back towards the house. But I suppose they could have been made by anybody in the search party.'

'Hm, it's difficult to confirm,' said Ron.

'It looks damn like it though, don't you think?' hissed Anthony.

'Do you think our suspect is here in our company? Could there be more than one suspect?'

'Yes, I bloody well do think the suspect is here with us – and yes, there's every chance he'll not be acting alone. And I will kill him.' Anthony shot to his feet and started marching towards the house. 'I will kill him.' With Ron on his heels, Anthony slammed into the conservatory and barrelled through the hall, almost knocking over the stunned butler, George. 'Get everybody into the drawing room – guests *and* staff,' he roared. Diane heard the commotion and came pattering from the drawing room to the hall.

'Goodness, Anthony, what has happened?' she asked, but looked at Ron as she spoke.

Anthony balled his hands at his sides. 'Cynthia has been abducted,' he said, trying to remain calm. 'And I believe somebody in this house was there when this happened.'

'Anthony, really, whatever are you saying?' said Diane, holding her clasped hands to her chest. 'That you believe one of our guests had something to do with Cynthia's disappearance? Surely not.'

Anthony relaxed his hands, a hint of helplessness present in his expression as he looked directly at Diane and said, in a slow voice, 'Cynthia is missing. I fear something terrible has happened to her. I must find her, Diane. I *must* find her.' Diane lifted her chin, then turned to the butler.

'George, gather all guests and staff, please. Have them all come to the drawing room – as a matter of urgency.'

With no time to waste, Anthony kept his address to guests and staff brief. There were gasps and cries of 'oh gosh, please let her be safe', and 'no, please don't let this be so,' fluttering around the drawing room as Anthony voiced his worst fears: 'We believe Cynthia Marchmont was abducted from the gardens last night. Now, if anybody knows anything about her disappearance, you must inform me, Ron, or Bill. Do not withhold information. If any one of you noticed anything suspicious in the last few days, I want to know. If any of you saw strangers loitering in the grounds – again, I *want* to know. Your information could be vital to finding Cynthia.' There was a succession of serious nods and mumbled vows to assist. Then Anthony turned and walked out of the room, signalling for Bill and Ron to follow.

Moments later, as Anthony, Bill and Ron headed into the library, Sandra, one of the housemaids, appeared behind them. 'Excuse me, gentlemen,' she said, her demeanour flustered, 'but I have some information, please.'

Anthony turned, frowning. 'What is it?'

'It's Lady Anne Stewart, Sir. She wasn't present at the meeting in the drawing room. I'm her assigned maid for the weekend, Sir. Would you like me to check her bedroom?'

'Yes, please do, right away,' said Anthony.

'Absolutely, Sir.' Sandra curtseyed then hurried along the hallway towards the staircase.

'That's strange,' said Bill. 'We called everyone to the meeting.'

'Wait a minute,' Ron interjected, 'I don't recall seeing Sir Daniel Friel in the room either, do you?' He looked from Anthony to Bill in turn.

'No,' they replied. Alarm bells immediately sounded in their heads.

'Right, we need to act fast,' said Anthony. 'Ron, can you please check Friel's room? And Bill, please do check the stables – see if their horses are there.'

The next hour was fraught as more information came to light about Lady Anne Stewart and Sir Daniel Friel's last whereabouts. Another footman reported serving Sir Friel a whiskey shortly after the musicians departed Hopetoun House around 10 p.m. the previous night. Ron checked Sir Friel's room, which looked to have been abandoned. And a female guest recalled seeing Lady Anne leave the drawing room, where she'd been seen laughing with John McIvor, and head to the powder room 'sometime between 9.30 and 10 p.m.' Nobody saw Lady Anne thereafter. Then, Sandra returned to the library, where Julianne and Phoebe had since joined Anthony and Ron. 'Lady Anne has gone,' said Sandra. 'She has left nothing in her room, but nobody saw her pack or leave.'

'Damn, that woman must have set Cynthia up,' Anthony cursed once Sandra had left the room.

'How, what happened?' asked Julianne.

'Last night, Lady Anne cornered me, in this room,' Anthony began. 'I was supposed to meet Cynthia here…she had gone up to her room, to fetch her wrap…we'd planned a romantic walk and…' Anthony shook his head, silently berating himself as he recalled how he'd comforted Lady Anne.

'Go on,' said Phoebe. And so, Anthony explained to the women how Lady Anne had wept on his shoulder.

'She [Lady Anne] said she'd received threatening notes. She said her life was in danger – so I put my arms around her…a sympathetic act, you'll understand. My back was to the door, which was open. Maybe Cynthia arrived, saw me embracing Lady Anne, and got the wrong impression,' said Anthony. 'Lady Anne has been trying to cause mischief between Cynthia and me for months, and now I fear she has succeeded. But why…why would she do such a thing?'

'Oh, Anthony, I know Cynthia has been upset over a few things regarding you and Lady Anne Stewart. Anne has been stirring things at every turn,' said Julianne. 'Both Phoebe and I couldn't help but notice how she upset poor Cynthia.'

'Yes,' agreed Phoebe, 'And if Cynthia saw you and Anne together, she might very well have taken it out of context. Perhaps fled out into the garden?'

'Yes, I fear so,' said Anthony, a mix of emotions vying heavily in his chest: guilt, fear, rage, but also hope – hope that Cynthia was still alive and not in danger. Hope, that whoever had taken her had done so merely to use her as a bargaining tool. He tried to remain calm and convey this hope to the ladies. 'I will find Cynthia – mark my words,' he told them. As thoughts whizzed in his mind about who he should ask to join him on his quest to rescue Cynthia, Bill blustered into the library.

'There are three horses missing from the stable,' he announced, his face flushed almost as red as his hair. 'A groom helped a lady and gent to saddle them. The groom said the third horse was for their luggage. The gent had tipped him very well and said they were going on a romantic tryst – then told the groom to "keep this a secret". The groom only came forward when I explained we're investigating a possible abduction. Unfortunately, he didn't see the "couple" leave – he just prepared the horses for departure.'

'The couple must be Lady Anne and Friel – and we must assume they are totally involved in Cynthia's disappearance and the letters I have received,' said Anthony.

Bill and Ron agreed while Julianne and Phoebe, not knowing about the 'letters', exchanged puzzled looks. But there was no time for explanations – the sound of approaching hooves crunching over gravel told them help had arrived from Edinburgh. 'Right, gents, let's get ready – we're going after Friel and Lady Stewart. We shall find them – and Cynthia.'

Alistair Murdoch and chief inspector Patrick Braid were the first of the Edinburgh contingent to arrive at Hopetoun House. They came with further news, too. 'A letter arrived at your solicitor's, informing him that your cousin Stewart is ready to sign the deeds you are offering,' Alistair explained. 'And Margaret, the barmaid at the White Hart, also received a note telling her to go to your solicitor, collect the deeds, and take them back to her lodgings.'

'Although Margaret is terrified,' added Inspector Braid. 'She fears someone has been following her. Her lodgings were turned over the other night, but she has no idea where Stewart is.'

'I have left men watching her to see if he appears,' added Alistair.

Inspector Braid cleared his throat, then continued. 'So, it also appears a gent with a large ring is trying to take over the gambling establishments in Leith. He's been getting heavy with the owners and clients by all accounts. This could spark a gang war in Leith. Unfortunately, we are still no nearer to finding out who this gent with the ring is.'

'Well, as you know, it appears Cynthia has been kidnapped,' said

Anthony. 'Bill, Ron and me, are going after Sir Daniel Friel and Lady Anne Stewart, as we believe they are involved.'

'Right, we will come with you,' said Alistair. Just then, Cynthia's family arrived. Anthony greeted them in the drawing room – and explained the situation to them, trying not to worry them too much in the process. But Georgina and Angela were in floods of tears.

'Please, Anthony,' pleaded Georgina, shivering with shock. 'Please find our Cynthia.'

'I will find Cynthia. I promise you all,' said Anthony. 'I am leaving imminently with my team of men. And we shall find Cynthia and bring her home to you.'

Derek stepped forward, eyes watering, and shook Anthony's hand. 'I will come with you – and we *shall* find my sister.'

CHAPTER TWENTY-SIX

ANTHONY AND HIS TEAM OF MEN SET OFF ON HORSEBACK, galloping towards Edinburgh in the fading light of day. By the time they reached South Queensferry, it was dark. At the town's stables, a groom told Anthony that a lady and gentleman of similar description to Lady Anne Stewart and Sir Daniel Friel had met a coach there in the early hours of the morning. 'The gent said they were taking the ferry across to Fife,' said the groom.

'That makes sense,' said Anthony. He thanked the groom and the men headed to the harbour, where they caught the next service across the Firth of Forth to North Queensferry. Onwards they trekked, heading towards Perth, following the route Anthony assumed Cynthia's captors would have taken to Caithness. They pushed their horses hard and arrived at Glenfarg Inn later that evening. A groom rushed out to meet them and relieved the gents of their horses.

'Has a coach from Edinburgh passed through here today?' Anthony asked the lad.

'Yes, Sir. Earlier this afternoon,' he replied.

Anthony reached into his pocket, pulled out a few coins and handed them to the groom 'Did you see the occupants?'

The lad's face lit up – he'd never received such a generous tip before. 'Oh yes, Sir. The gent was a big chap – tall and heavy, with big sideburns too.' He jiggled his cupped hands at the sides of his face to demonstrate. 'But I didn't catch his name I'm afraid, Sir.'

'And what about the woman, what was she like?' urged Anthony.

The boy scrunched his nose. 'She was also tall, with a long, bony nose that poked beneath the veil of her riding hat. She had brown-ish hair and was dressed head to toe in black, like she was in mourning, y'know?' Anthony nodded. 'Anyway, they went inside for refreshments while me and Henry – the stable boy – changed the horses for a fresh pair.'

And there was nobody else with them?'

The lad bit his lip, thinking. 'Ah, yes,' he replied. 'Their coachman, but that is all. They left at dusk.'

'Anthony handed the groom another coin. 'What about last night and earlier today? Anybody else pass through here?'

'Just two lone riders, Sir. They stopped here just before lunch – said they were going to Aberdeen. But nothing else has passed here since yesterday when the mail carriage stopped.'

'Thank you, you've been most helpful,' said Anthony, and the party went inside for food and ale and some much-needed rest before continuing their journey north. The host divulged more information about the couple who'd passed through that day. 'They left around 4 p.m.,' he said. 'The gentleman told me they planned to stay in Perth overnight.'

Over dinner in a private room, the men discussed their next course of action. 'Well, it looks like Sir Friel and Lady Anne Stewart are not too far ahead of us, but the coach that's carrying Cynthia – if indeed this is the case – may not be heading this way,' Anthony said.

'Should we backtrack – try to find it?' Derek suggested.

'Maybe some of us should, while the others focus their efforts on catching Sir Friel and Lady Stewart?' said Bill.

'Good idea,' said the inspector. 'I will go after the two of them if the rest of you want to try to find the coach?'

'Yes, I agree,' said Anthony. 'The rest of the team will start backtracking. We will split into two groups and spread east and west – then make our way towards Perth. Leave word at The Salvation Inn if we don't arrive together. I will also send word to Grant – ask him to head to Wick. We'll need somebody on the ground there if the coach is headed that way.'

The following afternoon, Anthony, Ron and Alistair arrived at The Salvation Inn. They had stopped at as many inns and stables as possible that morning, again quizzing staff about their clientele over the last day or two. Another stable boy at an inn in Forteviot confirmed four people had visited with a coach. 'Three men and a lady who was very ill. She needed much assistance,' he told Anthony.

'And the woman, the one you say was unwell, what did she look like?' asked Anthony.

'Oh, I couldn't tell you, Sir,' the boy replied, 'One of the men carried her into the inn and I didn't get a look at her face, I'm afraid. Then they left early this morning. I think they were heading to Dalwhinnie, Sir – although please don't quote me on that.'

Anthony left word of this new information for the other search group (Derek and Bill), and Inspector Braid had also left word for both groups. In his note, the inspector said he was following the coach he believed Lady Anne Stewart and Sir Friel were travelling in. He also said he would leave further word, if possible, at the inn at Loch Ericht, near Dalwhinnie. Anthony relayed this information in the note he left for Derek and Bill, then he and his group travelled on.

It was late evening when Anthony, Ron and Alistair arrived at the inn at Loch Ericht. The windows glowed amber in the sooty darkness. The gents dismounted and walked around the side of the inn to the stables. There was one carriage parked outside and several horses in the stalls. They tied their own horses to posts and entered the inn. The door gave way to a lounge, where a weakening blaze was still aglow in the fireplace. A solitary, flickering candle sat on the window ledge. At the back of the room, a maid was cleaning debris – mainly broken glass and food – from a table. She looked up as the men walked in. 'Good evening, gentlemen? Are you looking for rooms?' She put down her rag, adjusted her mobcap and exhaled at length. 'Och, it's been quite eventful in here tonight, that'll be right.'

'We're looking for a police officer – Chief Inspector Patrick Braid, of Edinburgh Police. Have you seen him?'

The maid planted her hands on her hips. 'Aye, I've seen him alright. The gent's a hero if you ask me. Somebody would have been killed for sure in here tonight if it wasn't for that officer.'

Ron stepped forward. 'Why, what happened?' he asked.

'Oh, there was quite a commotion,' the maid went on, eyes dancing. 'The inn was packed, everybody enjoying their ale and the like – the usual evening jovialities – when this gent and lady started arguing. Oh, you should've seen it. The woman was quite well-to-do, too. You could hear from her accent that she wasn't from round here, if you know what I mean?' The maid confirmed that statement with a brisk nod of her head. Anthony, Alistair, and Ron exchanged knowing looks. 'Anyway, it was all getting heated, people jostling. Glasses getting broken and the like. Then your man, erm…'

'Chief Inspector Patrick Braid?' said Anthony.

'Yes, that's the one. Well, he intervened. Drew his pistol, right enough, but he didn't fire it. When he tried to arrest the couple, they put up quite a fight. But he managed to overpower them. Och, I'll never. The inspector arrested the man – *and* the well-to-do woman and locked them in the cellar. Two men are guarding their prison as we speak – just in case, you know.'

'Hm, interesting,' said Anthony. 'And where might we find the inspector now?'

'Och, upstairs sleeping, as far as I know.' The maid picked up her cloth. 'Would you like some cold meat and ale?'

Anthony nodded. 'Yes please. And a few blankets, please. We will bed down in here for the night if that's OK?'

'Yes, I will tell the master you are here, and return shortly.' She curtsied, then pointed at the archway in the wall to her left. 'The stairs are just through there, Sir – if you'd like to check on the inspector? His room is the second on the left at the top of the stairs.' Then she curtseyed again before skittering through a door at the back of the room.

'Right, I'm going to speak with the inspector – get the full story, if he's awake,' said Anthony.

'Do you want us to come with you?' offered Alistair.

'No, no. You two get some rest. I'll not be long.'

* * *

196

Anthony's knuckles had barely touched the bedroom door when it flew open. Standing on the threshold was Inspector Braid, gun in hand, sword on his waist, ready to shoot or strike. His head glistened with sweat. 'Oh, Sir, sorry. I did not realise it was you,' he said lowering his gun and stepping sideways. 'Please, do come in.'

'So, what do you know, what happened?' asked Anthony, walking across the sloping floorboards that croaked with every step. He and Inspector Braid remained standing as there was nowhere to sit aside from on the bed.

'Well, I found Lady Anne Stewart and Sir Daniel Friel, arguing in the bar. Not a covert look, if you ask me. They're both locked up here, in the cellar.'

'So I hear. Did you speak with the lady and Friel? Did you get anything out of them?'

'Yes, but it's all very strange. It appears they had both been black-mailed into doing a gent's bidding. Neither of them knew this chap's name or where to find him. Their instructions – and "threats" always came third party, they claim.'

'Do you believe them?'

'Yes, she was apparently blackmailed over an illegitimate child she had. And Friel, it seems, passed on some highly sensitive information to the enemy during the war – so the blackmailer used this against him. Imagine if these scandals became public knowledge? They're both so arrogant – they would be ruined and neither of them would want that.'

'Very true,' said Anthony, although he was confused. He knew nothing about Lady Anne's 'illegitimate child'.

'The other piece of news is they were carrying the false deeds for Stewart,' added Inspector Braid. At that point the inspector turned towards the bed, slipped his hand beneath the pillow, and produced a bundle of paperwork. 'Here they are, the false deeds,' he said, handing the document to Anthony. 'The coachman picked them up in the old town before picking the lady and Friel up in Queensferry. Seemingly, some rough necks overpowered my men, broke into Margaret's and stole the papers. They were to deliver them to Wick.

'So, Friel is our man after all,' sneered Anthony. 'I will kill him.'

'No, no, no – not so fast. Friel thinks Stewart is also being black-mailed, although he's not sure why. This so-called "gent" obviously wants your land. But why?'

'So, what next? Do we let them go or use them to find Stewart?

'I think we should get them to lead us to Stewart. I'll get one of my men to drive their coach and another to sit with them. We can follow the coach at a distance. Meanwhile, Anthony, you can ride on and look for the other coach – hopefully the one carrying Cynthia. The inn keeper said a coach passed earlier today but didn't stop, which is unusual as it is pretty remote here and almost everyone stops for a meal and a rest. He surmises it must be stopping at Newtonmore tonight.'

'Right, we shall leave at dawn. Get some sleep now. I will see you in Wick,' said Anthony, then shook the inspector's hand. 'Great work today, Sir.'

Anthony went back down to the lounge. Bill and Derek had since arrived, so Anthony briefed the group on the latest events in the ongoing mystery before they all bedded down. But Anthony could not sleep for worrying about Cynthia. *Please God, let her be safe. Please let me find her – then I will look after her forever.* He was surprised at that last thought, but he meant it. *I have fallen in love with Miss Cynthia Marchmont,* he realised. *And I shall tell her so when I rescue her.*

The night stretched on, cold, haunting, and lugubriously slow. Anthony lay awake, watching the dying embers in the fireplace, thinking of his love, Cynthia.

The dawn cannot come sooner.

CHAPTER TWENTY-SEVEN

THE MEN SET OFF AT FULL GALLOP, pushing their horses hard all the way to Newtonmore. They arrived at the inn just before 8 a.m. Inside, breakfast was still being served in the lounge, which was busy with guests and bedecked with festive fir and holly garlands. Anthony spoke to the innkeeper, who confirmed the mail coach – plus another carriage carrying three gents – had stopped the previous night. 'There's not much to say,' said the innkeeper. 'The three gents stayed for dinner – then left.'

'Do you remember seeing a lady with them at any point?' asked Anthony.

'No, no, Sir, I do not recall seeing a lady.'

'But what about the three gents? Did you notice anything unusual or suspicious about them? What did they look like? What were they wearing?' Anthony pushed.

The innkeeper pulled back his head in disbelief. 'What's all this about? Look, I was too busy in here to notice such details. You're best asking the stable lads. Now, if you don't mind, I have work to do.'

Anthony muttered an apology and headed back outside, where Bill and Derek were waiting for him beside the stables. 'We've just spoken to one of the lads in there,' said Bill, ushering Anthony and Derek away from the stables.

'Yes, and he said a gent paid him to get a basket of food and keep quiet about it,' Derek weighed in.

'Really? That's interesting,' said Anthony.

'Yes, I paid handsomely for that information,' said Bill, tapping his nose. 'I don't think he would have mentioned it otherwise, the little beggar.

'So, it is probably the carriage we are after as the inn keeper said three gents were in for a meal. If they got more food, it might have been for Cynthia?'

'That's what I'm thinking,' said Bill. 'The stable lad said they left around 9 p.m. It was dark, but the full moon and lanterns on the carriage would have made it possible for them to carry on.

'And the road from here to Ruthven Barracks is fairly easy to navigate by all accounts,' said Derek.

Anthony rubbed his hands together. 'Right, no time to waste. Let's go.'

'Ron and Alistair are arranging fresh horses and food for the journey,' said Derek.

'Great work,' said Anthony, and gave Derek's shoulder a firm pat, then, casting him a sincere look, said: 'We will find Cynthia.'

After two days' traveling, the men were north of Inverness and believed they were close to the coach carrying the three gents – and possibly Cynthia. They called in at Garve Lodge and were told three men had stopped there an hour previously but had since moved on in their carriage. With renewed determination, the men galloped on. It was early afternoon, but soon it would be dark. Then, as they rode through Strathpeffer, Ron spotted a carriage parked alongside Loch Kinellan. A black, brougham carriage with red trimmed wheels, which matched the description of the coach that had stopped at Garve Lodge and the inn at Newtonmore. 'Look, over there,' he called, pointing at the carriage as he slowed his horse to a trot. Anthony, Derek, Alistair, and Bill followed, and they all dismounted.

Stealthily, Anthony, Ron and Derek approached the carriage while Alistair and Bill guarded the horses – in case they took flight. Ron and Derek crept up to one carriage door and Anthony went around the other side. The coach looked abandoned. The curtains were drawn and there were no horses accompanying the carriage. Wielding their pistols, Anthony and Ronald each pulled open a carriage door – then looked at each other across the seat, both bewildered. The carriage was empty. Anthony kicked the wheel of the coach, causing it to wobble. 'Where are they?' he growled, turning to survey the surrounding area, still holding forth his gun, finger poised on the trigger.

'Anthony, wait,' said Ron, reaching into the footwell of the carriage and extracting a folded piece of parchment. 'It's a note, look.' He unfolded the paper. 'Looks like the same handwriting as before.'

'Let me see,' said Anthony, marching around the carriage. Ron held out the note so the three men could read it together.

SO, YOU THOUGHT YOU HAD FOUND US?

**IF YOU DO NOT SIGN THE DEEDS AND
HAND THEM TO STEWART, I WILL HARM
MISS MARCHMONT – AND YOU WILL NEVER
SEE HER AGAIN.**

BE WARNED.

**STEWART IS WAITING FOR YOU IN DORNOCH,
AT THE EAGLE INN.**

'Damn the bastard to hell,' fumed Anthony.

'What are we going to do?' said Derek, his voice thick with panic. 'He might kill my sister.'

Anthony looked around as he put his pistol back in its holster, then combed his fingers through his hair, trying to focus and look calm, but he felt frantic with fear for Cynthia. 'I will sign over the land and lodge to Stewart,' he said.

'Let's go then,' said Derek and they headed back to their horses, breaking news of their plans to Alistair and Bill as they swung into their saddles.

'We're off to Dornoch to rescue Cynthia – whoever has her wants to kill her,' said Derek.

'I'm signing over the land and lodge to Stewart,' added Anthony. 'But we must make haste – time is against us.'

The men galloped their horses at full pelt, all the way to Dornoch.

Anthony entered the Eagle Inn, his face blank of all emotion, a trick he had learned in his secret service days: never let your enemy see your reactions. In a leather bag, strapped diagonally across his chest, were the false deeds to the Girnigoe Estate that Inspector Braid had secured when he arrested Lady Anne Stewart and Sir Daniel Friel. Anthony spotted Stewart, sitting side-on in a small alcove in the corner of the lounge, nursing a tankard of ale. After scanning the room and covertly noting the other patrons, Anthony strode confidently towards Stewart, aware his men were guarding the premises. Alistair had followed Anthony into the lounge and was surreptitiously waiting by the door. Derek had gone to check the stables. And Bill and Ronald were keeping watch outside. Stewart turned and smiled at his cousin. 'I have the papers that you have asked for,' sneered Anthony, his tone cold as ice. He reached into his bag, pulled out the fake deeds and slammed them hard on the table. 'I have signed them. Now, tell me where Cynthia is.'

Stewart placed his hands on the deeds. 'I don't know where she is,' he said flatly. 'I was told to get the papers and deliver them to Wick – and you must not follow me or "she will die".' He grabbed the papers and went to leave. As Stewart rose, Anthony grabbed his arm and growled into his ear. 'I will kill you and everyone involved if one hair on her head is touched. Tell *that* to the devil who has her. I don't know why he wants my land, but I will find out. Crossing me is a big mistake.' Stewart shivered at his cousin's threat.

'I must go,' he said. 'The man behind all of this is dangerous. And I must warn you, do not follow me. If he finds out you have done so, he *will* kill Cynthia.'

Anthony let go of Stewart's arm with a shake. 'Go away. You make me sick.' As Stewart scudded towards the door, Anthony nodded at Alistair to follow him. Then he went over to the bar and ordered a much-needed whiskey. Alistair slipped out quietly; Anthony watched him in the mirror behind the bar. Nobody followed Alistair outside. Knowing his friends would follow Stewart at a safe distance, Anthony ordered food and sat down facing the door.

Stewart stuffed the paperwork in his canvas saddlebag and rode to Wick, unaware anyone was following him. Anthony's friends were all experts at this, having all – Derek aside – served in the secret service at some point. As they approached Wick, the men split up and entered the town from different directions. Ron and Bill followed Stewart as they thought they would be the least recognisable if seen. Derek and Alistair took a cross-country route to the right of Stewart but still managed to keep their target in sight.

Stewart stopped at a large stone house in the middle of the town, where he dismounted and tied his horse to railings. Looking around, he did not see anyone suspicious. He did not see his four pursuers who, after tying up their horses, were now hiding at various locales surrounding the house – in the foliage, behind the crumbling dyke wall, watching from a safe distance. Nor was he aware of Gordon Ogg's craggy face framed in the upstairs window of the bedroom, where he stood, staring out while shining the bulky green stone in his ring with a silk handkerchief. His henchman, Tam Morris, sat in an armchair behind him, puffing a pipe. Stewart walked to the front door and rapped on it three times. An elderly lady with gnarly arthritic hands that looked too big for her answered. She opened wide the door for Stewart to enter, then told him to wait in the parlour. Inside, the house was dark and smelled damp and grassy. Clutching the deeds Anthony had handed to him, Stewart sat down on one of the few wooden chairs that lined a wall in the parlour. Against the wall to his right stood a small desk complete with an ink well and a small china jug sprouting a few nib pens. No flames danced in the empty fireplace.

A few minutes later, Gordon Ogg walked into the room, his footsteps slow, heavy, and sinister. His expression matched his gait. 'Well, did you get the deeds?' he asked. Stewart stood up and gave a nervous bow.

'Yes, I have the deeds,' he said, proffering the paperwork to Gordon. 'Anthony has signed them over to me.'

Gordon grunted, receiving the deeds in his left hand while motioning at the desk with his right. The ring on his little finger glowed through the dim early afternoon light. 'Good. Now you can sign them over to me.' He grunted again then shouted over his shoulder, his voice travelling through the open door and along the hallway, 'Chalmers, are you there, Chalmers?' A flurry of steps followed, light and panicked compared to those of Gordon Ogg. 'Chalmers here is a solicitor,' added Gordon as a gnomish-looking man with a pointy face and piercing eyes enlarged behind spectacles pattered into the room. 'He will deal with the handover.' Gordon handed the paperwork to Chalmers, who placed the deeds on the desk before pulling up a chair.

'Right then,' said Chalmers, his voice high and tinny. 'Let's study these deeds and get them signed, Mr Ogg.' Chalmers began reading the deeds aloud as Gordon sat beside him, unaware of the activity happening outside the house. All three men were so engrossed in the deeds that they did not notice Ron's head as he fleetingly peered into the parlour window.

Ron quickly ducked his head and crouched outside below the parlour window in the right side of the house, hoping the men inside had not seen him. He waited a few seconds, then turned and signalled to Bill, crouching in a row of conifers, to join him. Bill shot from his hiding place, hunching as he ran, then dropping to crawl the last few paces. Anthony and Derek were hiding in foliage about a hundred yards away from the house. The group had agreed they should hold back for now while the others assessed the layout of the house and tried to gain entry. 'Stewart is in there,' whispered Ron, pointing at the window. Bill nodded and they both crawled along and round to the back of the house, where Alistair was waiting for them, his back pressed against the wall next to the back door to the property.

'That's the kitchen,' said Alistair, indicating the door with a quick nod. 'I looked in the window. The elderly woman who answered the door to Stewart is in there.'

'Let's get her out so we can go in,' said Ron.

'Yes, I'll do it. Stand back.' Alistair knocked gently on the kitchen door and the woman answered. 'I have a delivery out here – can I bring it in?' he said.

'What delivery, we're not expecting a delivery,' said the woman. But she stepped outside to look – and saw Bill and Ron waiting to the side of the door.

'It's in the lane,' added Alistair. 'It's very big. Come and take a look.' The woman seemed reluctant at first, but Alistair managed to persuade her. He guided her to the gate at the bottom of the garden. When she stepped through the gate he quickly closed and locked it behind her. 'Go and find somewhere safe, quickly,' he said through the wood. 'Please, do not hurry back. Believe me, this is for your own safety.' The woman gasped and walked rickety steps along the lane, while Alistair hurried back to the house.

The three men slipped into the kitchen, then crept into the hallway, where they heard muffled sounds, groans, coming from behind a door. 'I think this must be the cellar,' said Bill as he tried the door handle. 'And it's locked.' He pressed his ear to the door and again heard the subdued moans, accompanied by rustling sounds. He knocked on the door while Alistair and Ron kept guard in the hallway. 'Miss Marchmont, are you down there,' he said softly. Another muffled cry issued. 'Let's see if we can find a key,' he said.

As the trio turned the corner of the long L-shaped hall, they heard voices coming from a room ahead, opposite the stairs. They stopped, just as another voice boomed from upstairs. 'Who the devil are you?' And what happened next happened fast.

Tam Morris bombed down the stairs and started fighting with Alistair. At the same time, Gordon flung open the parlour door, and was immediately greeted by Ron and Bill, who both lunged forth and, between them, tackled Gordon. Seconds later, two thugs, who'd been alerted by the elderly lady, pounded in through the back door and a mass brawl ensued, raging throughout the house. Then Anthony and Derek, having heard the commotion from a distance, rushed through the back door. Anthony grabbed one of the thugs and punched him square in the face, knocking him out. Then, pulling his sword from its sheath, swung his weapon at the second thug, wounding his arm as he fled. Derek caught the thug as he made for the back door and thumped him on the head with his gun butt – just as Alistair knocked out Tam. Meanwhile, Bill and Ron overpowered Gordon, wrestling the brute to the floor while Stewart and Chalmers cowered in the corner of the parlour, hands raised in surrender. 'Please, don't hurt us, Anthony,' pleaded Stewart. 'We were forced into this.' But Anthony was not listening to his cousin as his focus was on Gordon, pinned to the floor, and the huge, green-stoned ring on his right little finger. Anthony wasted no time. Stepping forwards he dropped to his haunches and grabbed Gordon by his lapels.

'Where is she? What have you done to her? What have you done to Cynthia?' he raged.

'I have absolutely no idea what you are talking about,' Gordon said in a strained voice.

'I think she's locked in the cellar, around the corner in the hall,' said Bill. Anthony let go of Gordon's lapels, pushing him to the floor as he did so. 'If anything has happened to her, I will kill you,' Anthony growled, then shot to his feet and charged along the hall to the cellar. Derek followed while Alistair and Ron restrained Gordon, Stewart, and Chalmers. Tam was still out for the count. Steadying himself on the doorframe, Anthony repeatedly booted the cellar door until it burst open. He raced down the stairs and there, tied to a bed, lay Cynthia, gagged and pale in the flickering lamplight. 'Oh my god, Cynthia. I'm so sorry,' he choked as he quickly untied her and removed the cloth gag from her mouth. He enfolded Cynthia in his arms. She felt cold and thin but never had he felt so relieved to see her. 'Are you OK? Did they hurt you, my love?' he asked as he took her face in her hands and looked into her eyes. Cynthia rattled as she started shivering uncontrollably. She couldn't speak for shock and her chattering teeth. In one swift movement Anthony took off his cape, wrapped it around

Cynthia's shoulders, then scooped her in his arms and carried her upstairs, where Derek was waiting, his face etched with fear.

'Is she fine?' he asked anxiously.

'She seems to be,' said Anthony. 'But get her a brandy.'

In Anthony's absence, Bill, Ron and Alistair locked Gordon and the other men in the parlour. Anthony took Cynthia into a bedroom on the ground floor. His friends followed, bombarding Anthony with questions: 'Is she OK?' 'What happened?' 'Was she in the cellar?' 'Is she hurt?' Anthony lay Cynthia on a small bed, propping her back against pillows.

'I found brandy in the kitchen,' Derek announced as he strode in holding a glass filled to the brim. Anthony took the drink from Derek and held the glass to Cynthia's lips for her to drink the warming spirit. She managed a couple of sips, but she was still so pale and shivering.

'Somebody send for a doctor. I will take her to the Gunn Inn at the end of the street,' Anthony said to nobody in particular as he lifted Cynthia from the bed and carried her out of the room. 'Oh, and somebody find Grant, please,' he added over his shoulder. 'He should be here by now – and we'll be needing his help.'

'I'll ride ahead and secure the rooms at the Gunn,' said Derek.

'And I'll find Grant – and send for the local magistrate too,' said Alistair.

Outside, Cynthia swooned as soon as the cold air hit her. Anthony patted her face and managed to bring her round to lift her onto the horse with him, but she drifted in and out of consciousness during the ride to the inn. 'God,' cursed Anthony as he looked down at Cynthia. Never had he felt so helpless.

As promised, Derek rode ahead and secured rooms at the inn, where a maid greeted Anthony and Cynthia. 'This way Sir, we have a room ready,' she said, leading the way upstairs. 'Och, the poor wee lassie must be frozen to the bone – but she'll have the warmest room in the house. There's a good fire burning in the hearth already.' The room was indeed warm; the Marchmonts were well known in the town, so the staff made a huge fuss of Cynthia, bringing her jugs of warm water to wash the dust from her face, neck, and arms.

Soon after, the town's Dr Andrews arrived at the Gunn. He harrumphed when he entered the bedroom and saw Anthony standing over Cynthia. Dr Andrews maintained strict rules of conduct; as far as Dr Andrews was concerned, a gentleman's presence in a lady's bed chamber was out of bounds out of wedlock. Recognising the doctor's unease, Anthony stepped back from the bed.

'Please, Dr Andrews, do excuse me, but Miss Marchmont is my fiancée and the future Lady Sinclair of Girnigoe. I do hope this assuages your concerns on the matter,' he said.

Dr Andrews placed his bag on the washstand. 'Of course, your lordship. I had no idea,' he said. 'But, if you please, the maid and I shall carry on from here.' Dr Andrews indicated the door – as the maid arrived with fresh water.

Anthony went downstairs, where Grant was waiting for him in the hall with the local magistrate, Archibald. They all shook hands then found a quiet table in the corner of the lounge.

'Gordon Ogg is our man,' said Grant, his tone conspiratorial. 'His green ring matches the one described by so many people.'

'But why does he want my land and lodge?' asked Anthony.

'We are not sure yet, but we will interrogate him and the others down at the jail, and report back,' Grant assured him.

'Fine, I will stay here tonight to be near Cynthia. If she is fit to travel tomorrow, I will take her home to her father's estate. Can you send word to her family, please?'

At that point Derek walked in. 'How is my sister?' he said, his voice loaded with desperation. 'Doctor Andrews made it quite clear I was not to hang around and be a hindrance.'

'He's with Cynthia just now,' said Anthony. 'Dr Andrews dismissed me with a flea in my ear also.' The gents laughed at the absurdity of Anthony's comment; the idea of a local doctor dismissing Lord Sinclair with a 'flea in his ear' was unheard of. Not that Anthony minded on this occasion. He was far too concerned about Cynthia to care. 'Here he comes now,' added Anthony, rising as Dr Andrews neared the table. 'How is she, doctor?'

'Your fiancée is fine, Sir. She's very shaken, understandably. She's a little bruised, thirsty, and hungry, but otherwise she's in good health. Once the shock of her ordeal has worn off – and after some good food and rest – she will make a good recovery.'

'Can we take her home tomorrow?' Anthony asked.

'Yes, provided she feels up to the ride, she should be fine,' said Dr Andrews, then he tilted his top hat, bowed, and left.

Anthony exhaled at length. 'Well, that's a relief – at least Cynthia's on the road to…'

'Fiancée?' interrupted Derek, his forehead concertinaed with confusion. 'Cynthia's your *fiancée*? When, what, how…'

'Well, maybe that was a little fabrication on my part,' said Anthony, spreading his hands. 'To keep your sister's reputation intact. You see, Dr Andrews was jumping to all sorts of conclusions when he saw me at Cynthia's bedside. I was so preoccupied with Cynthia's wellbeing and safety that I totally forgot how society would view my being in her bed chamber. But, talking of which, now the doctor's gone, I must see her.'

'I'll come with you,' said Derek, and the pair headed for the stairs.

Cynthia's face was as pale as the white pillows that propped her up in the large bed. She had on a borrowed nightgown that swamped her. A flicker of a smile trembled on her lips when Anthony and Derek walked into the room.

'Cynthia, how are you?' Derek asked as he rushed forward and knelt at the bedside. He grasped her hand, his face tight with anxiety. Anthony drew up a chair for Derek, then took another seat for himself and sat on the other side of the bed to Derek.

'Thank you for coming after me, I was so afraid,' Cynthia whispered, glancing from side to side at them both.

'We've been beside ourselves with worry,' said Derek, squeezing Cynthia's hand. Mother, Father and Angela will be home here in Wick soon. Gosh, they're going to make such a fuss of you, sister, dear. I shall be quite jealous.' He winked at his sister, trying to lighten the mood. Tears glistened in Cynthia's eyes.

'I can't wait to see them, too. And I'm sorry for causing so much worry,' she said, her voice delicate as fine lace. She looked at Anthony then quickly moved her gaze back to Derek.

'Do not apologise,' said Anthony. 'None of this is your fault.' Anthony wondered, as he said that, whether Cynthia was still annoyed at him for giving Lady Anne Stewart so much attention. That evening at Hopetoun House seemed an age ago now but he understood Cynthia's pain at witnessing the unfortunate scene in the library. *Will Cynthia ever forgive me?* A momentary silence was broken by a whining creak as the door slowly opened.

'I've brought some broth and roast beef for you, Miss Marchmont, my dear.' The voice belonged to Annie, one of the maids, whom Cynthia and Derek knew well. She advanced with careful steps, carrying a tray laden with food. Derek and Anthony stood up to make way for her.

'I think we should leave you to eat and rest now, Cynthia,' Anthony said gently. Annie positioned the tray on Cynthia's lap and sat down on one of the chairs to assist her. 'Derek is in the next room and I'm along the landing.'

'Yes, if you need anything, you just call us,' added Derek. 'Annie will sleep in here with you tonight, so you will not be alone.'

Cynthia nodded, her eyes heavy and weary. Annie fed her a spoonful of broth, but Cynthia was struggling to stay awake.

'Nobody will hurt you from now on, I promise,' added Anthony. 'Sleep tight.'

'Sleep well, Cynthia,' said Derek, and the two men crept out of the room.

'Thank you,' whispered Cynthia, already falling asleep.

CHAPTER TWENTY-EIGHT

ANTHONY WAS EATING BREAKFAST WITH ALISTAIR and Ron when Derek came into the lounge.

'Good morning, Derek, how's Cynthia this morning?' said Anthony over the brim of his teacup.

Derek pulled out a chair and sat down next to Alistair. 'She is still sleeping. Annie will let me know when she wakes up.

Anthony nodded sagely. 'Well, hopefully Cynthia will be fit enough to travel today. I have arranged for my carriage to transport her. It will be comfier than a hire coach, that's for sure.'

'That's very kind of you, Anthony,' said Derek, reaching for the coffee jug in the centre of the table. 'I think we should get her home as soon as possible and get the family doctor to check her over. My parents and Angela will soon be here. They will be very anxious to see Cynthia. They must all be worried sick.'

'We'll leave as soon as Cynthia feels up to it,' said Anthony, his voice calm and measured.

'Well, I'm off to see Grant,' said Alistair, rising. 'See if he has more information for us.' Alistair glanced down at Anthony. 'Will you join me?'

'No, I would do but I wish to remain here for now – until I know that Cynthia is well.'

Half an hour later, Annie arrived at the gents' table. 'Good news, gentlemen,' she said. 'Miss Marchmont is feeling better this morning. She will take a bath, but needs a fresh outfit to travel in.'

'No problem. I'll send word to our estate for one of Cynthia's dresses to be sent here,' Derek said.

'Thank you, Mr Marchmont. She will definitely need a new gown. The one she arrived in is totally ruined.' Annie held the sides of her face and shook her head. 'Oh, my goodness. What that poor lady has been through. It's shocking. Absolutely shocking.' Anthony and Derek exchanged worried looks. 'But at least she's on the mend.' Annie's tone brightened. She clasped her hands over her heart. 'Thank goodness she's on the mend. Now, if you'll excuse me, gentlemen.'

By late morning, Cynthia confirmed she was fit to travel, albeit not able to walk more than a few paces. Anthony carried Cynthia to his carriage. He couldn't help but notice Cynthia seemed agitated when he helped her into her seat. *Perhaps she's frustrated at being so weary?* Derek got into the carriage and sat next to his sister and off they went, Anthony, Bill, and Ron on horseback, riding alongside and behind the carriage, watching for any rogue thugs still lurking.

They arrived at the Marchmont's estate in time for lunch. Molly, the Marchmonts' housekeeper made a huge fuss of Cynthia, as did the family's butler Geoffrey, and Margaret, Cynthia and Angela's maid at their home estate. 'Oh, Miss Marchmont, you poor thing. What a frightful time you've had. We're going to take good care of you,' gushed Margaret as she helped Cynthia into bed where the waiting family medic, Dr Thompson examined Cynthia.

'You indeed have been through quite a shocking ordeal,' he told Cynthia. 'Now you must rest. I suggest four days' bed rest – at least. You need to recoup your strength.'

Cynthia rolled her head across the pillow, too tired to protest.

Later that afternoon, Anthony at last went upstairs to visit Cynthia. He pulled a chair up to her bedside while Margaret sat in the corner of the room, sewing. Anthony felt frustrated at Margaret's presence, but understood etiquette demanded Cynthia be chaperoned.

'How're you feeling?' he said softly.

'I'm fine,' replied Cynthia, but Anthony detected annoyance in her tone. 'I'm just a little tired and weary of all this fussing.'

'Well, they all want to see you recover and will fuss for a while.'

212

'Hmm, I know, and it will be worse when my parents and Angela arrive. I hope I am up by then.' Cynthia finished with a weary sigh.

'I expect you will. If I know you, after a couple of days you will be bored witless of this room.' Anthony took Cynthia's hand in his and gently massaged her palm with his thumb. Her skin felt cool and delicate. He felt something was on her mind. 'Was your ordeal awful?' he asked.

'Yes, but it could have been far worse.'

'Do you want to talk about it?' asked Anthony.

'No, not really. I know mother and Angela will want every little detail, but I really don't want to go into it yet.'

'Well, the good news is this. Those thugs have all been locked up – and I have sent word to Grant for an update on the case. He'll be here shortly. Cynthia pursed her lips, anger flashing in her cobalt eyes.

'Good. I hope they throw away the key,' she said. 'Especially Sir Daniel Friel's. He tried to suffocate me. He could have killed me.'

Anthony bowed his head. 'Oh Cynthia, I'm so sorry. I did not know that.'

Cynthia looked into Anthony's eyes. Try as she might, she could not shake the image of Lady Anne, locked in a tight embrace with Anthony in the library. She felt her eyes burn, then tears spilled, cutting hot trickly paths down her cheeks. *Does he have feelings for Lady Anne? Can I trust him?* Anthony leaned forward and touched Cynthia's face, wiping fresh tears away. He now guessed Cynthia was still rankled after seeing him with Lady Anne.

'We need to talk,' he offered. 'I know what you thought you saw, but you are wrong, Cynthia. It was not how it looked.'

'Really?' Cynthia tried to stop crying but her eyes were flowing helplessly. She felt she could flood the entire room with her tears.

'Please, Cynthia, you must believe me. That women [Lady Anne] set it all up, knowing you would come back and see us together in the library. She gave me a sob story about receiving threatening letters. She said she was afraid and needed my protection. She started crying and I felt sorry that this was happening to her. Somehow, I thought it was my fault she was getting harassed. I was only comforting her when I presume you saw us? Am I correct?'

Cynthia swallowed, lips aquiver. 'Yes,' she said in a brittle voice.

'I was doing nothing more than comforting Lady Anne. You must believe me. She tricked me.'

Cynthia turned her head away, sniffing. 'I will try. But Lady Anne has been after you for weeks. And I know you two were very close before, and...' Cynthia began to sob.

Margaret looked up from her sewing but did not intervene. *Cynthia will ask for my assistance if she needs it*, she thought.

'Please, Cynthia. Please believe me.'

'And I cannot give you what Lady Anne gave you.' Cynthia pulled her hand away from Anthony's grasp. Suddenly, her tears subsided as anger presided her sorrow.

Anthony sighed. 'Cynthia, I am not interested in ever seeing that woman [Lady Anne] again. She is nothing to me, absolutely nothing. Please look at me, you must believe me.'

'Please, just go.'

Anthony rose reluctantly. He did not want to leave Cynthia this way, but he respected her wishes. 'I will wait for you,' he said. 'Whenever you feel ready to see me, I will be here for you,' Anthony turned and walked out of the room, his heart dense and aching in his chest.

As the door closed, Cynthia burst into tears again. Margaret rushed to Cynthia, handed her a handkerchief. 'There, there, miss, don't upset yourself,' she said.

'Oh, Margaret, I am so confused. I wish Mummy was here.'

'She will be here soon, Miss. I will go and make some sweet tea.' Margaret scuttled out of the room – just as Derek arrived. He'd heard Cynthia's sobs from his room along the landing. He rushed to Cynthia's side

'Cynthia, sweetie, what on earth is the matter?' He sat on the edge of Cynthia's bed and enfolded her in his arms. 'It's understandable you're upset after all you've been through, my dear. But you will feel better soon. You're still in shock.'

'No, you don't understand,' Cynthia began, her voice catching in her throat. She took a deep breath, wiped her eyes, then told Derek the whole story of how she'd walked in on Anthony and Lady Anne, tears streaming as she then relayed how she'd fled into the garden, only to be kidnapped by Sir Daniel Friel. 'I thought he [Daniel Friel] was comforting me. Everything turned black, and when I awoke, I was a prisoner, tied to a bed.'

'There, there, sweetie,' Derek stroked his sister's back. After a pause, Cynthia told Derek Anthony's version of events. She explained how Anthony claimed Lady Anne had set him up. 'Anthony said he has no feelings for that woman [Lady Anne],' said Cynthia.

'Well, sis, I believe him,' said Derek, holding Cynthia's shoulders at arm's length. 'I saw how frantic he was when you disappeared. He did everything to find you. Anthony has barely slept a wink since you went missing, so, believe me, he cares a lot for you.'

Cynthia tilted her head. 'Are you sure?'

Derek's eyes widened. 'Yes, absolutely. You should have seen Anthony. He was threatening everyone he would kill them if they touched a hair on your head. I have never seen him so provoked. If that does not prove to you how much he cares, then what does?'

Cynthia gave Derek a watery smile as he again pulled her into a tight hug. 'Anthony cares for you deeply, I'm sure,' he said.

Anthony spent the next hour pacing the Marchmonts' drawing room, going over and over in his mind his conversation at Cynthia's bedside. *What can I do or say to make her forgive me?* He thought about going back up to her room, but that intention was interrupted when Grant and Alistair arrived at the house.

Anthony, Ron, Bill and Derek greeted Grant and Alistair in the drawing room, anxious to hear the latest news. Cynthia, having felt strong enough to be helped downstairs by Margaret, sat on the chaise lounge, listening intently to Grant, her stomach churning as he revealed the dark web of deceit spun by Gordon Ogg and his cronies.

'Sir Daniel Friel, Lady Stewart, and Anthony's cousin, Stewart, have all been charged and are locked up in Inverness jail, awaiting sentencing. They all confessed to helping Gordon Ogg,' explained Grant, sipping a malt. 'As you know, Gordon Ogg is our man with the green ring. Under intense questioning, he admitted killing Lady Jane Curruthers – he tried to marry her, to get to her money. But Lady Jane turned down Ogg's offer. He lost his temper and hit her. Lady Jane fell and cracked her skull. Ogg claimed it was an accident.'

Cynthia cupped her mouth, gasping. Anthony shot from his seat and rushed over to sit beside Cynthia on the chaise lounge. 'Are you sure you want to hear all this?' he asked, taking her hand, his voice and features loaded with concern.

'Yes, I am just a bit shocked he could do such a horrible thing,' said Cynthia.

'Believe me, he's more than capable,' said Grant. 'He buried Lady Jane on your land, Anthony. One of his henchmen confessed to helping him dig her grave. That is why Ogg was desperate to get the deeds, Anthony. He thought, if he owned your land, Lady Jane's body would never be found. Fortunately, Ogg's henchman did not want to be implicated in Lady Jane's murder, hence his confession.' Grant paused as he drained his glass.

'Go on,' said Derek, standing to refill Grant's glass.

'So, Ogg put his plan into action,' Grant continued. 'He found out Anthony's cousin Stewart had large debts and bought them from the gambling house in Leith. He needed people in society close enough to you to help him, hence Sir Friel and Lady Stewart. She has a secret, illegitimate son, but society does not know about him. If news of that illegitimate son got out, it would have ruined her. But that's not all. Ogg sold information to the enemy during war times. He will be charged with treason and faces the gallows.'

'Bloody Hell,' Derek exclaimed. 'Anything else?'

Grant nodded as he gestured at Anthony. 'He hates you for putting his brother, Simon, in jail, Anthony, during your time in the foreign office. He was planning to bring you down somehow. Lady Jane was part of that plan, but we cannot see how that fits in yet.'

'May I?' That was Alistair. 'Lady Jane's father, Alfred, told people he planned to marry Jane off to Lord Sinclair. This kept the debtors from his door. Although Jane had been left a fortune by her uncle, Alfred had spent his fortune on bad investments – and he could not touch her money. Alfred hoped his debtors would show him a little grace and persuade Lord Sinclair he would be a good match for his daughter, as their lands join in the east. Lady Jane would inherit that land, which Alfred thought would benefit Anthony.'

'So, when Gordon Ogg heard of this, he thought it was true – then tried to get one over on Anthony?' said Ron.

'Exactly,' came Alistair's reply.

'Therefore, if Ogg knew you and Cynthia were serious about each other, Cynthia had a lucky escape. He might have tried to force her to marry him,' added Grant.

'Oh, no, what a horrible thought,' said Cynthia.

'There, there,' said Anthony, giving Cynthia's hand a reassuring squeeze. 'He will be hanged. You will never see that evil man again.'

Anthony draped his arm over Cynthia's shoulder. And in that moment, Cynthia instantly felt protected.

Perhaps Derek is right, she thought. *Maybe Anthony is telling the truth after all?*

Cynthia leaned into Anthony's embrace.

'Thank you for rescuing me,' she said.

CHAPTER TWENTY-NINE

A FEW DAYS LATER, CYNTHIA'S PARENTS AND ANGELA ARRIVED. They greeted Cynthia with hugs and tears in the conservatory where she had been chatting with Derek, Bill and Ron.

'Oh, my baby girl. Thank God you are safe,' said Georgina, smothering her eldest daughter's face with kisses, while Lord Marchmont thanked the men for their 'heroic efforts' in rescuing Cynthia. Then, over tea and cakes, Cynthia, helped by the men, relayed her kidnapping and the details of Gordon Ogg's evil plot. Angela and Georgina cried when Cynthia told them how Anthony had burst into the cellar and untied her. 'Oh, he really is your knight in shining armour, Cynthia,' choked Angela. Cynthia gave her sister a hesitant smile, then continued talking about Gordon Ogg. 'So, he buried Lady Jane on Anthony's land,' she said.

'Anthony, Alistair and Grant are there just now,' explained Derek, arranging for Lady Jane's body to be returned to her mother ahead of her funeral. It's so sad.'

'Shocking, just shocking,' said Georgina.

When Anthony returned to the house an hour later, Lord Marchmont thanked him profusely for rescuing Cynthia – and insisted he should stay with them for dinner and another night. Anthony accepted; the more time he could spend with Cynthia the better. Although her mood had softened in the last few days, he still sensed Cynthia did not fully trust him. 'So long as my staying isn't an inconvenience to you all,' said Anthony, taking a seat next to Ron in the conservatory.

Lord Marchmont laughed. 'Good heavens, not at all. You are a hero, not an inconvenience.' Angela followed Cynthia's gaze out of the conservatory window. The lawn was blanketed with snow, tinged peachy by the low winter sun. Like Anthony, Angela picked up on Cynthia's frostiness and later, as the two girls dressed for dinner in the bedroom, Angela quizzed her sister. Derek had told Angela all about the mix-up between Cynthia and Lady Anne, so she was well versed on the matter.

'Right, now we are alone, tell me what is wrong" said Angela, fastening a sapphire brooch to her navy shawl.

'I don't know what you mean,' said Cynthia, twisting this way and that in front of the full-length mirror. She had on an emerald green, two-tiered checked dress but was now wondering whether to change into her cerise ruffled dress. 'Do you think this looks too plain? Maybe my pink gown is more suitable for dinner?' Cynthia turned to face Angela, perched on the edge of her bed.

'Derek told me you're still not speaking much to Anthony?' said Angela, ignoring Cynthia's question. 'From what Derek said, it sounds like Anthony has more than explained himself to you. It sounds like a silly misunderstanding to me. Anybody can see that Anthony adores you, Cynthia.'

Cynthia gave her ringlets a dainty pat. 'Anthony has been distant with me, too. Or did Derek not tell you that?'

'Yes, he did. He said you have both been polite to each other – but he says you two are not as close as you were before the kidnapping. Do you not like Anthony now?'

'Of course, I do. Too much, if anything,' Cynthia sat down next to her sister. 'Oh, Angela, what am I to do?'

'Can you not forgive him?' Angela asked, taking Cynthia's hand.

'Yes, but it's not that easy.'

'Why not?' Cynthia noted a hint of irritation in Angela's voice.

'I don't know how he feels … About me.'

'Maybe he does not know how *you* feel? Derek says you've avoided being alone with him. Is that right?'

Cynthia nodded, her throat tightening as she held back tears.

'But, why?'

'Because I'm afraid he doesn't feel the same way about me as I do towards him.'

'And how do you feel?' Angela's voice calmed to a gentle tone.

Cynthia let out an exasperated sigh. 'I love him. I love Sir Anthony Sinclair. I love him.' The words avalanched from Cynthia's lips, came from nowhere. She turned and looked directly into her sister's eyes. 'I love him,' she said.

'Well tell him so,' urged Angela.

'I can't. I don't even know if he wants to be with me.'

Angela snorted. 'Sorry, but I think you're wrong, sister, dear. Anthony never takes his eyes off you. He looks sad just now. I feel sorry for him.'

'Really? I haven't noticed.'

'No, that is because you are avoiding looking at him.' Angela rose, pulling Cynthia up with her. 'Honestly, I could knock your heads together. Right, we are going downstairs, and you are going to give the poor man a break and talk to him.'

Cynthia giggled. 'But should I wear the pink dress?'

Angela shook her head. 'No,' she said firmly.

Unbeknown to the sisters, while they'd been chatting in the bedroom, Anthony had a near-identical conversation with Bill in the library. 'Anthony, you really need to talk to Cynthia, old chap. She looks so lost and forlorn. I know you are the cause,' Bill had said. 'You're leaving here tomorrow. Do you really want to leave with this unease hanging between you and Cynthia?'

'No, I don't. But what can I do if she won't speak to me?'

'I'll try to engineer an opportunity for you to speak to Cynthia this evening,' Bill had promised. As it turned out, that opportunity arose sooner than Anthony had imagined – a few minutes later, in fact, just as he and Bill entered the drawing-room for pre-dinner drinks.

Cynthia and Angela were standing alone at the far end near the window. Her parents were sitting on the sofa talking to Ronald, Alistair and Derek.

Bill nudged Anthony's arm 'Go on, now's your chance,' he said under his breath.

They both took a whisky from the footman's tray and approached the sisters. Angela was first to seize the moment.

'Sir William,' she trilled, 'I would like your advice on a horse I'm interested in buying.' She threaded her arm through Bill's and steered him towards a small, round table, leaving Anthony and Cynthia alone.

'That was not obvious – by any stretch of the imagination,' said Anthony, the corners of his lips twitching into an amused smile.

Cynthia giggled. 'Not at all obvious,' she quipped back.

'I think they want us to talk, don't you?' Anthony surveyed Cynthia's features – the sparkles in her eyes as she smiled. *She has a beautiful smile.*

'I think so, yes.'

'Then, please, let us oblige them. I am truly sorry for my actions. I should have seen through Lady Stewart's ploys. I miss you, Cynthia.' Anthony paused, then rubbed the back of his neck. 'I miss our easy-going conversations. I miss our rides and picnics. I just really miss being with you. Can you ever forgive me? Can't we go back to how we were before all of this mess?'

Cynthia's eyes began to mist. *Don't cry, Cynthia, this is just what you'd hoped to hear.* 'I miss you too. And I would love to go back to how we were,' she said, smiling up at Anthony.

'Were we not in company I'd take you in my arms and …' Anthony joggled his eyebrows. Cynthia continued smiling. *I can't take my eyes off you, Sir Anthony Sinclair,* she thought. Somewhere in the room behind her, the butler announced, 'Dinner will now be served.'

'Shall we?' asked Anthony, proffering his arm to Cynthia.

Throughout dinner, Anthony and Cynthia covertly touched each other's thighs beneath the table, sending shocks of heat through their bodies. Cynthia wondered, *Why didn't Anthony and I clear the air sooner?* At last, the chemistry between her and Anthony had returned.

After dinner, Anthony led Cynthia into the conservatory while the others headed to the parlour for drinks and games. 'What are you doing?' giggled Cynthia when Anthony quickly shut the conservatory door behind them. Anthony responded by taking Cynthia in his arms. Then he lowered his face to hers and kissed her lips, slowly and gently. It was the loveliest kiss they had shared. When their lips finally disconnected, Anthony lifted his palm to Cynthia's cheek, stared into her eyes, and whispered, 'I love you.'

Cynthia's legs turned hollow. She felt faint, giddy with happiness. 'I love you too,' she said after a pause. Then she reached for Anthony's face and again they came together in a lingering, passionate kiss until Anthony, reluctantly, pushed Cynthia away.

'Enough, I will forget myself and where we are if we do not stop now,' he said smiling at her. I shall go to speak to your father right now,' he added, and strode off purposefully.

Cynthia hugged herself, bursting with excitement. 'He loves me, he loves me, he loves me,' she whispered, clapping her hands.

The parlour fell quiet when Anthony entered the room, head held high. Everybody turned to look at him with expectant eyes. He stopped in his tracks. 'What?' he said beaming.

'Well, did you ask her?' said Angela.

Anthony frowned. 'Ask her what?'

'To marry you, you ninny.' Angela flung her arms wide in frustration.

'Please, dear chap, do tell us you and Cynthia will live happily ever after?' Derek weighed in.

Anthony cleared his throat and blinked at Lord Marchmont. 'Well, actually, I…well…the thing…'

'Well, did you or did you not?' said Lord Marchmont.

'Erm, yes, yes I did ask Cynthia, yes.' Derek smiled to himself. He had never seen or heard Anthony nervous before.

Lord Marchmont spread his hands and jabbed his chin towards Anthony. 'And, what did she say?'

Anthony's face flushed. He was hoping for a quiet word with Lord Marchmont. Instead, he felt like an actor on stage – one who hadn't learned his lines. 'Well,' he began, eyes fixed on Lord Marchmont, 'she said yes.'

Cheers filled the room. Lord Marchmont bounded forth, shook Anthony's hand, and slapped him on the shoulder. 'Good show, good show, welcome to the family. We are so pleased,' he said. Anthony was stunned at such a liberal reaction from his father-in-law-to-be. Then, behind him, more cheers as Cynthia walked into the parlour. Georgina, tears of joy glistening in her eyes, rushed over to congratulate her daughter. 'Oh, my darling, congratulations, I've never felt prouder. We're so happy for you both,' she cried, enveloping Cynthia in her arms.

Cynthia was equally shocked as Anthony. She caught his eye over her mother's shoulder. He was shaking hands with Derek. Anthony flashed her a smile and a shrug then moved on to accept Bill's handshake.

The room was abuzz with chants of 'Congratulations' and squeals of delight. Angela was next to hug Cynthia. 'We knew he'd ask you,' she said. Then Lord Marchmont called for the butler.

'Time for champagne,' he bellowed.

More well wishes were bestowed upon the happy couple. The butler arrived and, while he poured the champagne, Anthony sidled up to Cynthia. 'I did not have to ask your father's permission,' he said.

Cynthia laughed. 'No, it looks like they all expected it. How disappointed they would have been if I had sent you away with a flea in your ear.'

'Now, that's what I have so missed – you can bring me right down to earth with just one quip,' Anthony said, and leant to kiss his fiancée's cheek.

The champagne flowed; toasts were made, and at once, Cynthia and Anthony's anxieties evaporated. They both conceded, 'We've never felt happier.'

CHAPTER THIRTY

WITHIN DAYS, CYNTHIA AND ANTHONY'S ENGAGEMENT was the talk of Edinburgh's society scene.

Anthony and his friends arrived back in the city ahead of Cynthia and her family and began planning his upcoming nuptials. He posted an announcement in *The Scotsman*. They were to marry at St Giles Cathedral in a month's time. The wedding would be the highlight event of the season.

Anthony was inundated with congratulatory messages. Ian Robertson, minister of foreign affairs was one of the first callers to his townhouse.

'Anthony, allow me to congratulate you on your up-coming marriage.' Ian said as he strode into Anthony's study.

The gentlemen sat down on the chaise lounge. 'Thank-you,' Anthony replied.

'I also come with grave news. Gordon Ogg is to be hanged for murder and treason. We found plenty evidence of his betrayal, so the hanging goes forth immediately. Within days.'

'He deserves everything he gets, the blighter.' Anthony said gravely.

'Indeed,' said Ian. 'But, on a cheerier note, tell me about you and Miss Marchmont. I didn't realise you two were that serious?'

'Yes, well this whole sorry episode made me realise I could not live without having her in my life. When Cynthia was abducted, I was beside myself with worry.'

'Well, I am glad, about time you settled down. I will miss having you around to call on though.'

Anthony laughed. 'Well, I'm about to be a married man, so my reckless days are over. I don't mind you calling on an advisory capacity though.'

'I should think so too, after all the hours of training I put into you.' Ian said, laughing as he stood to shake Anthony's hand. 'I will expect an invite to the wedding,' he shouted over his shoulder on his way out.

Anthony stood for a moment, listened to the hurried thud of Ian's footsteps down the stairs. *Wow, end of an era,* he thought. Bill, Ron and he had enjoyed their days working undercover for the Foreign Office and, while Anthony felt a pang of regret that those days were over, he was looking forward to settling down with Cynthia. He poured himself a malt and smiled to himself. *Lord Sinclair, Edinburgh's most notorious rake is getting married. Who would've thought it?*

Cynthia and her family arrived a week later to arrange the wedding. Their first evening back in the capital was spent celebrating the engagement with Anthony's family at their home in Heriot Row.

Anthony greeted the Marchmonts outside the house. Cynthia, on her father's arm and jittery with nerves at the prospect of meeting her future mother-in-law again, thought Anthony looked glorious. He looked the epitome of an upper-class lord. Handsome in a dark evening suit and crisp white cravat adorned with a diamond that glimmered in the gas light. Cynthia's heart hammered hard. She felt breathless. *He'll soon be my husband.*

In the vestibule, Anthony helped Cynthia out of her cape. 'You look absolutely beautiful,' he whispered into her ear, hands grazing her shoulders. Waves of arousal shot through Cynthia's body. As she looked up over her shoulder, Anthony gave her a quick kiss then winked. A wink loaded with promise. Cynthia took Anthony's proffered arm and he led her and the other guests into the drawing room.

Cynthia's nerves dispersed a little as Rosalind rushed forward to greet her. 'Cynthia, my dear,' she said, kissing Cynthia on both cheeks. 'We are so pleased to welcome you into our family. Anthony has made a wonderful choice for his wife.'

'Thank you so much,' said Cynthia. Rosalind then moved on to greet Georgina while Susanne stepped forward and embraced Cynthia warmly. 'It will be lovely to have a sister, you have no idea what I have had to put up with all these years with those two" she said, indicating Anthony and Giles.

Giles pulled a mocking face. 'Now, sister, dear, you give as good as you get. But I must say, it will be most pleasant having another sister, if only to distract Anthony from looking into my every move – and getting Susanne out of my hair. You can take her shopping and the likes, then I will at last get some peace.'

Cynthia was relieved. The Sinclairs were a close family who were welcoming her with open arms. But her stomach fluttered with excitement when she caught Anthony watching her. He was observing Cynthia as if she would suddenly disappear. Her abduction had affected him badly. He just wanted to keep her with him all the time, out of harm's way.

Cynthia felt the intensity of Anthony's stare. She wished they could be alone, but Anthony's mother and sister wanted to know all about her and Anthony's romance and the forthcoming wedding. 'Where did he propose?' asked Susanne.

'Have you thought about your dress yet?' said Rosalind.' Oh, you will make such a beautiful bride.' They wanted every detail – bridesmaids, flowers, music.

After dinner they discussed who to invite to the wedding. Anthony said his secretary would draw up a list of people that must be invited and they could add friends to it. So, they decided the ladies would all meet at Anthony's the following morning to continue discussing the wedding arrangements.

Towards the end of the evening, Anthony pulled Cynthia aside in the hallway. 'We need to find a day alone soon,' he said, 'It is driving me crazy being in your company but not being intimate.'

Cynthia laughed. 'I don't see how we can get away with all this wedding to prepare.'

'Leave it to me,' he said, kissing her hand.

Everyone said goodnight and departed. Anthony decided to walk home, but he took a detour to his club for a nightcap. When he arrived, everybody congratulated him. Luckily, Ron was there to share a whisky with him.

'Well, congratulations again,' said Ron, handing Anthony a glass of whisky. 'Here, you will need this malt to keep you going.'

'God, yes, if tonight is anything to go by, this is just the start. Heaven help me.' Anthony laughed, and the two of them settled down to enjoy their malt.

The next morning Graham announced the ladies and ushered them into Anthony's study.

Cynthia was wearing a pink outfit that complemented her blonde hair. Anthony wanted to whisk her away and enjoy her company alone, but he just stared at her – and Cynthia felt desire soar through her.

'Please, take a seat,' Anthony offered the ladies, and went over to hold Cynthia's chair for her, giving her shoulders a swift squeeze as she sat down. Nobody noticed, but she felt the heat of his touch. *Goodness, how could such a light touch affect me so much?*

All during the planning of the invitations they kept glancing at one another. Anthony's gaze held so much promise. Cynthia had to shake herself to concentrate on the conversation in the room.

By lunch time the guest list was finalised. Rosalind suggested a late lunch at the Strath Hotel, which the ther ladies readily accepted. Anthony had other plans.

'Thank you, Mother but I have a surprise for Cynthia, so, if you will excuse us today, another time would be better' he said politely.

Rosalind smiled. 'Oh, that's fine. I do hope it is something nice. We shall take our leave.'

The ladies left, leaving Anthony alone with Cynthia. He took her hand. 'Come, I have a surprise, this way.' He led her upstairs to the drawing room, a beautiful space with a table set for two below tall sash windows overlooking Moray Gardens. The décor was Regency blue, with mahogany furniture and velvet cushioned settees and dark blue drapes. Although it was a large room, the setting felt cosy. Anthony ushered Cynthia into a seat by the table and poured her a glass of Claret. Then Anthony's footman and maid served them a decadent lunch of oysters, followed by beef bourguignon and a French tart for dessert. Anthony's chef had excelled himself.

'That was delicious,' said Cynthia when the maid cleared the table. 'Far better than any restaurant.'

'Come, let's adjourn to a comfier seat,' said Anthony once the footman and maid had finished clearing up and left the room. As they settled on the velvet sofa, Anthony reached inside his dinner jacket and produced a small green box festooned with silky gold ribbons. 'This is for you,' he said, handing the box to Cynthia.

'Oh, what is it?'

'Open it and see.' Cynthia untied the ribbons and lifted the lid to find another, smaller box, also green with a metal clasp. Slowly, she prised the box open, then gasped at its contents: a platinum ring with a huge diamond set on beautiful little arms studded with smaller diamonds.

'Oh Anthony, it's amazing,' cried Cynthia, easing the ring out of the box and examining its design with awe. She slipped it onto her third left hand finger. 'I love it.' She breathed deeply, admiring the jewellery on her hand, looking at it from all angles. 'Thank you.' Cynthia leaned forwards and kissed Anthony, who pulled her into his arms. She lifted her arms around his neck and moved closer. He pulled her onto his knee and ran his hand down her side, then back up, grazing her breast. Then his hands snaked around her back, fingers unpicking the ribbons of her dress until it loosened. In one movement, Anthony tugged the bodice down to Cynthia's waist. She gasped as he ran his thumb over her nipple before passionately kneading then kissing her breast through her chemise. Cynthia raked her fingers into Anthony's hair, breathing sharply, revelling at the warm touch of his mouth. She had never felt such passion before now. 'Anthony, I want you so badly,' she whispered breathlessly, and Anthony lifted his head and pushed her down on the sofa, kissing her mouth and raising her skirt as he did so. They pleasured each other slowly at first, then increased the rhythm, all the while kissing, until they climaxed together in a flurry of gasps and hot breath.

They lay on the sofa for a while, embracing their love for one another. Cynthia felt as though she'd burst into a heaven of shooting stars. Anthony had reached a peak he'd never experienced with another partner. He kissed Cynthia softly. 'I love you with all my heart,' he said, and tears of joy began to pattern Cynthia's cheeks.

'I love you too – so much that it hurts,' she replied.

CHAPTER THIRTY-ONE

ANTHONY ESCORTED CYNTHIA HOME LATER THAT AFTERNOON. Cynthia burst into the house and ran into the drawing room, where her parents and Angela were gathered for afternoon tea.

'Mummy, Mummy, look,' she cried, shunting her left hand at her mother. Georgina's hands flew to her cheeks.

'Oh, my, that is just beautiful. You lucky girl.'

'Let me see,' said Angela, springing from her chair and excitedly taking Cynthia's hand to examine the ring. 'Oh, it's lovely,' she gasped.

Lord Marchmont nodded his approval at Anthony. 'Forget the tea, let's have champagne to celebrate,' he said.

Again, the champagne flowed, but this time, the toast was official.

The next few days whirled by. Cynthia went for fittings for her bridal gown at Madam Lafayette's boutique. Angela and Susanne, her two bridesmaids, were also fitted for their dresses. Georgina and Rosalind joined the ladies and carefully chose their outfits to avoid any clashes of colour or style. Cynthia was in her element. The atmosphere inside the boutique was one of fine bonhomie, with fellow customers congratulating Cynthia on her engagement.

The social scene was in full swing; around shopping and organising the wedding, there were afternoon teas to attend, lunches and dinners with friends, balls, and evening soirees.

Cynthia had recovered well after her kidnap ordeal. She was back to full health and felt truly grateful for all her blessings – Anthony, her family and future in-laws, the upcoming wedding, and most of all, she was so thankful to have survived her recent trauma. Although she had shivered when she heard about Lady Jane's funeral and Gordon Ogg's execution two days ago. 'He was hanged in public in Inverness,' Anthony had told her. 'Seemingly there was a good crowd of spectators at the gallows. It was a grim day up north, but at least we can all move on now.'

Meanwhile, Anthony was becoming increasingly frustrated. He desperately wanted to spend more time alone with his fiancée, but their busy schedules were an obstruction. He had planned to whisk Cynthia away to Girnigoe for a few days, but his estate manager, Bernard, soon thwarted that idea. Bernard sent word to Edinburgh, saying the land was in a sorry state after inspectors dug up Lady Jane's body. Then a freak rainstorm flooded the field, said Bernard. Anthony replied to Bernard via a messenger. He wrote: 'Employ staff to get the grounds and house ready for our arrival. I want everything sorted for her ladyship's first visit. We shall return to Girnigoe after our honeymoon, and I want it finished whatever the cost.'

Three weeks later, at an afternoon tea at Georgina's friend's house, Cynthia found herself drifting into another reverie about Anthony. She had not seen him since the evening before last and felt quite bereft without him. As the women chatted about the wedding, Cynthia relived the afternoon she'd spent in his townhouse. She pictured the moment he presented the engagement ring to her, and the ensuing time spent in his arms. *Oh, those arms.* Cynthia recalled the list she'd made in Caithness outlining the qualities her future husband should possess. *Tall, with luscious dark hair, intense eyes and a physique like Michelangelo's* David. And she suddenly realised, *I've found him. That man is Anthony. Gosh, I cannot wait for our wedding night.* In the meantime, Cynthia would need to wait until the evening to be reunited with her love. Off she drifted again. *Eyes like hot tar. Lips, curvy, warm and soft on my skin and…*

'Cynthia, Cynthia!' Georgina's voice cut through her daydream. 'Lady Katherine wants to know which flowers you've chosen for your bouquet?'

* * *

At last, it was evening, and Cynthia and Anthony were sitting side by side inside Surgeons Hall, listening to a Mendelssohn string quartet. Anthony held her hand under her fan, and she felt her skin goosebump as his thigh pressed against hers. Their wedding was due to take place in just five days' time. *Not long now*, Cynthia thought.

When the concert ended, Anthony helped Cynthia into her cape, lightly caressing her shoulders and blowing gently on the back of her neck as he draped her in fuchsia velvet. The sexual chemistry between them was palpable. They walked quickly to the carriage and climbed inside. Then Anthony rapped on the roof with his cane, indicating for his coachman to drive on.

As the carriage bumped along Nicholson Street, Anthony and Cynthia fell into an embrace, kissing passionately. Soon, articles of clothing were loosened and dishevelled and they again pleasured one another with rhythmic strokes throughout the short ride to Royal Circus.

'You are beautiful,' said Anthony as the carriage swayed on.

'I love you so much,' breathed Cynthia. 'I wish we could stay like this forever.'

'Soon, my love. Soon we will be able to spend the whole day like this, and there is so much more to come, I promise.'

Outside the Marchmonts' townhouse Anthony kissed Cynthia goodnight. 'You should go straight up to your room,' he said, smirking. 'Your hair is well out of place and your dress is hopelessly crumpled.'

'I know, you are terrible getting me in such a state,' giggled Cynthia.

'Oh, but you love it.' Anthony kissed her cheek again. 'Goodnight my love.'

'Goodnight" she replied, wishing she did not have to go inside. She pouted up at Anthony, hoping he'd whisk her away in the carriage again. But he grabbed her shoulders and turned her round, adding a comedic shove.

'Go, before I can't leave you.'

Cynthia looked over her shoulder, fluttered her lashes.

'Go,' Anthony groaned.

Cynthia crept into the house, then ran upstairs, undetected. In her bedroom she quickly changed into her nightgown and brushed her hair – then soaked her dress and chemise in the bathroom. 'I spilled a drink over my dress,' she explained when Lily popped her head around the door. 'I'm soaking it before it stains.'

'Oh, don't you be doing that. I will get your dress cleaned up, Miss,' fussed Lily. 'Did you have a nice evening?'

'Oh yes, it was perfect, Lily,' said Cynthia, then she floated back to her bedroom while Lily dealt with her dress. Cynthia climbed into bed and drifted off to sleep, thinking about the erotic carriage ride, replaying Anthony's words in her head. *Soon, my love. Soon we will be able to spend the whole day like this, and there is so much more to come, I promise.*

CHAPTER THIRTY-TWO

AFTER BREAKFAST THE NEXT MORNING, CYNTHIA, ANGELA, AND HEATHER took a carriage to Madam Martine's boutique on George Street, the purpose of today's shopping expedition being for Cynthia to choose her wedding trousseau.

For Cynthia, picking her trousseau was the highlight of all the wedding plans. In Madam Martine's shop she would select several outfits for her honeymoon – outdoor suits and ball dresses, riding habits, a variety of bonnets, gloves, and shoes and, most importantly, underwear.

However, Cynthia's flesh prickled slightly when she walked into Madam Martine's shop and suddenly remembered her awful encounter there months ago. Argh, Lady Anne and her vile vows to win Anthony back. The shop bell dinged cheerily as the words tolled a death knell in Cynthia's mind. *I will order some Italian silk lingerie to reel him in.* Then Madam Martine hurried across the shop, her face as bright and welcoming as her rose satin skirt. 'Oh, Miss Marchmont, soon to be Lady Sinclair. Many congratulations to you. I have some beautiful outfits to show you,' she said, kissing Cynthia on both cheeks.

'Thank you,' said Cynthia, inhaling Martine's perfume, which she recognised as Otto of Roses. 'I can't wait to see them.' Cynthia pulled herself together. She didn't need to worry about Lady Anne now. *That witch is in jail. Today is my day. Today I'm the one picking the lingerie – and I don't need to 'reel Anthony in'. He's all mine.*

Indeed, Cynthia had a wonderful morning at Madam Martine's. She chose some beautiful dresses, elaborate bonnets, and silk slippers.

But the pièce de la resistance, the lingerie, filled Cynthia with erotic excitement, evoking flashbacks of her carriage ride with Anthony the previous night. Sifting through delicate stockings with frills and bows – her stomach sizzled as she pictured Anthony's reaction when he saw her in them. The ladies giggled and winked at one another as Cynthia made her selections. What fun they were having. Cynthia found a pale pink chemise and matching stocking garters, laced with cerise ribbons. Her face flushed just thinking how she would stand before Anthony and slowly lift the hem of the chemise to expose the garters.

Once the ladies finished shopping and arranging delivery of their purchases to Royal Circus, Heather suggested lunch at the Café Royal, to which the sisters readily agreed. 'Oh, yes, the oysters are to die for at Café Royal,' gushed Angela.

Instantly recognising Cynthia as the future Lady Sinclair, the maître d' fawned over her and led the ladies directly to a table by the window, even though the restaurant was extremely busy, with others also waiting to be seated.

During lunch Cynthia was approached several times by well-wishers, which warmed her heart. She thought it adorable how so many people were genuinely happy for her and Anthony. Until she visited the powder room and happened upon a most unsavoury character.

Cynthia was pulling on her gloves after washing her hands when she heard the woman's voice, sour and catty. 'Well, well, well, who do we have here?' Cynthia wheeled round to face a woman with bulging chestnut eyes and fat black ringlets. Her dress was rather low-cut at the neck, exposing a deep cleavage. 'So, you're the lucky lady to snare the most eligible bachelor in Edinburgh?' The woman leaned closer to Cynthia as she said this, those imposing eyes popping.

'Excuse me, do I know you?' said Cynthia. She could not place this rude person.

'Ha, no, I don't believe I've had the displeasure of an introduction, but let's just say, I know your future husband well.' The woman sucked in her breath, hands planted on her waist. 'Oh, I know Anthony Sinclair very well. Very well indeed.'

Cynthia was taken aback. Who was this lady who, judging by her remarks and expressions, knew Anthony intimately?

The woman exhaled, pushing her face closer still to Cynthia's. 'You are young and naïve,' she snarled. 'Anthony will soon get bored and look elsewhere – and I will be on the side-lines, awaiting his pleasure.' She then grabbed fistfuls of coarse black fabric at the sides of her skirt, turned and stomped out of the powder room, leaving Cynthia astounded. She waited a moment to compose herself, then returned to the restaurant.

'Goodness, Cynthia, whatever is the matter?' said Angela as Cynthia took her seat at the table. 'You have turned quite pale.'

Cynthia looked at her two companions; she felt on the verge of tears.

'I have just had a very unpleasant encounter with a lady in the powder room who claims to know Anthony intimately,' she whispered.

'Goodness, who?' said Angela.

'Yes, who was she? Do you know her?' added Heather.

Cynthia shook her head. 'No, I've never met her. She just implied she would be waiting for Anthony to grow bored of me and go to her.' Cynthia pressed her lips together and looked at the ceiling, trying not to cry. 'Please, can we leave now?'

'Of course,' said Angela and Heather in unison.' The ladies paid the bill and hastily headed to their awaiting carriage.

'So, what did this woman look like, Cynthia?' asked Heather as they travelled along Princes Street.

Cynthia stared at Heather for a moment. 'She had huge chestnut eyes that looked like they were about to pop out of her head. And jet-black hair. She was slightly taller than me, and her dress was low cut – too low, especially for the daytime. She looked like a lady of the night to me. She was horrible. Do you think you know her, Heather?'

'I'm not sure, but if you see her at the theatre tonight, do point her out to me,' said Heather. A group of twelve couples, including Cynthia and Anthony, were due to attend a play at the Theatre Royal that evening. Cynthia had been looking forward to the event but now the prospect of bumping into that woman again turned her stomach maggoty. For the rest of the short journey home, she stared out of the window, mulling over the woman's vile words. Dangerous thoughts began to whirl. *What if Anthony does get bored quickly? After all, he has a reputation for being a notorious rake. And he's good looking and very wealthy.* She could feel tears welling. Heather knowingly patted her hand.

Heather dropped the ladies off and immediately went home to tell David about the encounter. She was sure she knew who the woman was but needed confirmation. Based on Cynthia's description, Heather suspected Cynthia had bumped into Lady Lydia Hamilton, but she had not wanted to upset Cynthia further by saying so. Lady Lydia Hamilton, herself married, had a reputation for stealing other women's husbands. She was also an ex-lover of Anthony.

'Oh yes, that sounds like Lady Lydia Hamilton to me,' David confirmed. 'But do not meddle. Anthony is quite capable of putting Hamilton in her place. He let her down not too gently when he found out she'd lied to him about her husband being accepting of her affairs. That was not the case. Anyway, we don't even know if the woman who accosted Cynthia is Hamilton. It could be somebody else. So, do stay out of this.'

Heather sighed. 'Well, she best not be upsetting Cynthia again.'

That evening, as planned, the twelve couples met for dinner before going to the Theatre Royal. Taking their seats for the *Arabian Nights* play, "Ali Baba and the Forty Thieves", Anthony noticed Cynthia seemed a little quiet this evening. *Must be pre-wedding nerves*, he thought.

Heather, seated to Cynthia's right, patted her friend's hand. 'Don't be so worried,' she whispered. Do not give that woman the satisfaction of seeing you upset. There is nothing to worry about. Anyone with eyes can see Anthony is besotted with you – she doesn't stand a chance. And besides, you may never see that woman again. There's no guarantee that she's…'

'Look, that's her,' interrupted Cynthia, nodding diagonally ahead. She leaned towards Heather. 'Second row, fourth seat from the right. The one with the red feather in her bonnet.'

Cynthia could not concentrate on the play for watching the woman ahead. Although she tried hard not to be too conspicuous with her actions. At the interval, the woman stood up with her partner, turned and gave Cynthia a deliberate nod. Heather noted this exchange and quickly ushered Cynthia out with the gentlemen for refreshments. She had sensed how tense Cynthia had been throughout the play.

Once in the vestibule, Heather steered Cynthia towards a table away from the gents, who were deep in conversation among themselves while ordering drinks. As soon as they were seated Cynthia asked Heather if she knew the woman. 'Yes, unfortunately I do. Her name is Lady Lydia Hamilton. She eats men for breakfast. Oh, how her poor husband suffers so.' Heather lifted her fan to hide her face and leant into Cynthia. 'She is also an ex-lover of Anthony, sorry.

'I see, well, that explains her comments,' Cynthia whispered back. The women did not notice David watching their tete-a-tete. He sensed they were speaking about Lady Hamilton, so he took Anthony aside to enlighten him about the situation. *Best warn the chap*, he thought.

'Damn, I knew Cynthia was upset about something, but I thought it was pre-wedding nerves,' said Anthony after hearing David's explanation for Cynthia's mood. 'That bloody woman [Lady Hamilton] needs taken in hand. Her poor husband.'

'I bet you wish you had not been such a rake in the past. It would make your current situation far easier. I talk from experience with Heather's moods over my past liaisons.' He laughed at Anthony's pained expression.'

The gents collected the drinks and joined Cynthia and Heather at their table. Anthony gave Cynthia her drink with a smile and a wink, hoping to lighten her mood. She smiled back but he could tell it was forced. He fervently wished he could speak to her privately, at least to put her mind at rest.

Cynthia sat through the second half of the play wondering how her mood could sway so drastically from near ecstatic in the morning to one of utter misery this evening. *First Lady Anne, now this?* Making matters worse, that horrible woman, Lady Hamilton, pounced on Anthony as they were leaving the theatre.

'Anthony, darling,' she trilled, looping her arm though his. 'Darling, it's been an age. I have missed you so. We simply must meet up soon.' Anthony wanted to tell Lady Hamilton to go away but society dictated manners on this occasion, so he politely smiled through gritted teeth and extracted her arm from his.

'Lady Hamilton, you catch me on my way out to escort my fiancée home,' he said, emphasising the word fiancée and indicating Cynthia, standing to his right with Heather.

Lady Hamilton turned slowly towards Cynthia. 'Aye, yes, the future Lady Sinclair,' she said, looking Cynthia up and down with disdain. Then, nudging Anthony's arm, she sneered, 'Going for the young, naïve ones nowadays, I see, Anthony? Well, when you decide you want a real woman, do call upon me.' She pivoted swiftly and marched away before Anthony had a chance to riposte a cutting put-down. He no longer cared about manners after Lady Hamilton's abhorrent tirade. How dare she insult his fiancée? He glanced at Cynthia, who looked visibly upset.

'Cynthia, I'm so sorry. That woman's evil, but you have nothing to worry about,' said Anthony, reaching for her hand.

Cynthia opened her mouth, but no words formed. Then she spotted Derek on Anthony's shoulder. 'Hey sis, I didn't know you were here tonight.' He smiled at her and then at Anthony. 'Anthony, dear chap, could you take pity on me and give me a lift home? My carriage axle has broken – and I presume you're escorting sister here home?'

'Of course, no problem,' said Anthony. What choice did he have? 'Let's make a move then.'

Derek chatted happily all the way home about the evening's play. Anthony was happy to let him, but he kept an eye on Cynthia the whole journey home. She barely said a word and stared glumly out the window. He did not know what she was thinking but guessed it did not bode well for him.

When they arrived at their house, Cynthia jumped down from

the carriage without waiting for assistance. Anthony sprang down from the carriage, unwilling to let her run into the house, as was her intention. He caught her arm and gently spun her round to face him.

'Look, I know you're upset. And I understand why you're upset. But let me assure you, she means *nothing* to me, absolutely nothing.'

Cynthia's face twisted into a scowl. 'That is not how *she* sees it, I can *assure* you.'

Derek saw this exchange and felt it prudent to go inside. 'Thanks for the lift, old chap, much appreciated,' he said and bounded up the steps where the butler stood, holding open the door.

I need to talk to you, can I come in?' Anthony pleaded.

'If you will excuse me, *sir*. I am exhausted and need to go,' she said loudly so the butler would hear – and it would be most ungentlemanly of Anthony not to respect her wishes.

'Very well,' Anthony replied, resigned to the fact she would not let him in to talk it over tonight. 'I will call round in the morning and hopefully you will be rested by then.' He lifted her hand and kissed the back of it, then turned and alighted the carriage.

Cynthia walked up the steps feeling miserable and exhausted.

CHAPTER THIRTY-THREE

CYNTHIA HAD A THOROUGHLY RESTLESS NIGHT, tossing and turning, her mind aching as she dissected the events of the day and pictured Anthony with his ex-lover. She rose early, around 7 a.m. and went down to the breakfast parlour, where Lord Marchmont was at his habitual place at the table, sipping his breakfast tea and reading *The Scotsman*.

Lord Marchmont looked up from his paper and did a double take. 'Cynthia, dear, you look so drawn. Whatever has happened? And where's my smile? You don't look like a happy bride-to-be to me.' Lord Marchmont folded his newspaper and patted the seat next to him. 'My dear, come and keep your old father company. I have not seen much of you these last few days – I'm in desperate need of your company.' Cynthia sat down with a sigh. Her father could see she was very upset about something. 'Now, tell your old father what is troubling you.'

'Oh, nothing, I am just tired from all the wedding arrangements and visitors,' she lied.

Lord Marchmont rubbed his moustache, thinking of a new tact. 'How was your shopping yesterday? Mother says you almost bankrupted me,' he laughed then, hoping to lighten Cynthia's mood.

'It was fine,' said Cynthia, staring at the table. 'Thank you for letting me buy all those pretty things.'

'Goodness, Cynthia, I was joking. You know you can spend all you like.' Lord Marchmont felt bad – Cynthia had obviously taken his joke to heart. He patted her hand. 'You also went for lunch at Cafe Royal. Was it enjoyable? Their oysters are to die for.' Cynthia looked into her lap, fighting back tears as she remembered Angela saying exactly the same about Café Royal's oysters yesterday. At that point she'd still been dancing on cloud nine. Now she felt gloomy as hell. 'Cynthia, darling, whatever is the matter? Are you having second thoughts about marrying Anthony? He looked at her intently, then took her hand. 'If you are, just say so. I will stand by you, whatever you decide.' In that moment he felt desperately sad for Cynthia. 'Has Anthony done you harm or ill-treated you?' he asked, a fierceness in his usually calm intonation. 'If he has, I will knock his block off.'

Cynthia laughed, imagining her little old father squaring up to Anthony. 'There, that's better, a smile. Now, tell me, do you not want to marry Anthony?' he coaxed gently.

'I do, yes, but I don't. Oh I don't know," Cynthia cried, sprung from her chair and ran out of the room, leaving her father even more confused than ever – and furious. *Anthony must be at the route of this,* he thought. *I shall call on Anthony.* Lord Marchmont folded his napkin and lay it on the table, just as Derek breezed into the room.

'Derek, son, do you know what the devil Anthony has done to your poor sister? Lord Marchmont's chair wobbled as he rocketed off it, hands balled at his sides. Derek was shocked at Lord Marchmont's anger. It was rare to see his father in a rage.

'Gosh, I don't know, Father. I did overhear a bit of a set-to between Anthony and Cynthia last night, just outside the house – when we arrived home from the theatre. But I made myself scarce. I didn't feel it was appropriate to intervene. Although Cynthia had looked keen to run into the house,' said Derek.

Lord Marchmont nodded slowly. 'Well, how did Anthony and Cynthia seem at the theatre?'

'I don't know. I wasn't sitting with them. I only bumped into them at the end – then Anthony gave me a lift home.' Derek was confused. He thought Cynthia and Anthony had put all their troubles behind them since leaving Caithness. 'Listen, why don't I speak to Angela. You know what she and Cynthia are like – they share everything with one another.'

'Yes, yes, go at once. I'll see what your mother knows too.'

Derek knocked then entered his younger sister's room on hearing her sleepy reply. Angela sat up in bed, bleary eyed. 'What is it, Derek? I'm not awake yet. What time is it?'

'Father sent me. Do you know what's upsetting Cynthia?'

'Oh, oh no.'

'What is it? You need to tell me, Angela. Cynthia is in a terrible state. Father's about to call on Anthony. He's raging.'

'OK, shut the door and sit down. I'll tell you what I know,' said Angela, yawning. Derek followed his sister's orders and listened, still confused, as Angela told her brother the events of the previous day involving Cynthia's encounter with Lady Lydia Hamilton in the powder room. 'Cynthia feared Lady Hamilton would be at the theatre last night,' she finished.

'Hm, I reckon she [Lady Hamilton] must have been there – I caught a carriage back with Cynthia and Anthony. Cynthia didn't say a word all the way home. Then she and Anthony had words outside. It didn't sound good.'

'Well, for what it's worth, I don't think Anthony is to blame,' said Angela through another yawn. She'd been to a dance at a music hall in Leith the previous night – and had not arrived home until gone 4 a.m. 'Whatever happened between him and Lady Hamilton is in the past. I think this woman is just making mischief.'

'Right, thank you. Well, that all makes sense.' Derek bounded downstairs and relayed the Lady Hamilton story to his father.

'So, do you think there's a chance this Hamilton woman is still Anthony's lover? Lord Marchmont demanded, crossing his brows.

Derek lifted his shoulders. 'I don't think so. Anthony does have a previous reputation as a rake – along with Ron and Bill. They are, after all, Edinburgh's most eligible bachelors. So, we can presume Anthony has had many mistresses over the years. But I think all of that is now behind him. He's besotted with Cynthia. When we are at balls and she is dancing with another partner, he never takes his eyes off her, and he always looks out for her comfort. He was beside himself with worry when she was kidnapped and would not leave her side until you and mother arrived after the rescue.'

Lord Marchmont's features softened. 'Fine, that is your mother's thoughts also. She thinks I should talk to him, but he might resent my interference?'

'No, I think Anthony would see you as the concerned parent that you are.' Just then, the butler walked in to say Sir Anthony was in the front sitting room and asking to see Miss Cynthia Marchmont.

'I shall see him,' replied Lord Marchmont then, turning to Derek, 'You go to Cynthia. And fetch your mother too.'

Lord Marchmont entered the sitting room to find Anthony pacing around the settee, his posture rigid, agitated. He stopped when he saw Lord Marchmont. He was expecting Cynthia, not her father. 'Lord Marchmont, good morning to you,' said Anthony as he bowed. 'I was hoping to see Cynthia.'

'Please, do take a seat.' Lord Marchmont indicated one of the armchairs in front of the fireplace. 'Cynthia is a bit indisposed today, out of sorts, you know?' he stammered, and lowered himself into the armchair opposite Anthony. 'She came down to breakfast with me this morning looking very pale and upset. I have since found out from her sister she had a bit of a run-in at the Cafe Royal and possibly last night?' He raised his brows at Anthony.

'Yes, sir, it appears a certain Lady Hamilton accosted her at lunch saying some rather unpleasant things. Lady Hamilton also came up to me in the foyer last night and I could see Cynthia was upset. Cynthia would not let me speak with her last night, and I promised to come by today to sort it all out,' Anthony explained. 'But I can assure you, sir, there is nothing, absolutely nothing, going on between Lady Hamilton and myself. Not now, or in the future.' Anthony sat on the edge of his chair, his face a mixture of hope and fear. He bowed his head briefly, then returned his gaze to Lord Marchmont. 'I will admit, I did have a past affair with Lady Hamilton, albeit a brief affair. But that is definitely over and will never happen again.

'Please believe me, sir. Since meeting Cynthia, I have changed. I have not even looked at another woman since I've been with Cynthia. Sir, I promise. I love your daughter with all my heart. I would never do anything to purposely hurt her. She means too much to me. All I want is to love and care for your daughter, sir.'

Lord Marchmont leaned back in his chair, satisfied Anthony's words were sincere. 'Well, my boy, unfortunately for you it is not me you have to convince. I, for one, can see you are genuine and this so-called lady appears to be out to cause mischief between you and Cynthia. Hopefully you can put an end to her meddling. Cynthia is another hurdle you will need to cross, that is down to you.' He stood and offered Anthony his hand. 'Good luck.'

The butler reappeared as the men shook hands. 'M'lord, Miss Cynthia is ready to receive Sir Anthony Sinclair in the conservatory.' He gestured at Anthony, 'If you'd like to follow me, sir?'

Anthony closed the conservatory door quietly and observed Cynthia as she stood forlornly, gazing at a beautiful yellow rose in a single-stem vase. His heart went to out to her. How he longed to rush over and take her in his arms but knew he must tread carefully. He walked up behind her, but she continued to stare at the rose. 'Cynthia, please look at me?' he said softly. She shrugged her shoulders.

'Please?' Cynthia turned slowly but did not lift her gaze to meet his. 'I can assure you, as I assured your father, there is, and never will be, anything going on between that woman and me. I love you and want to marry you with all my heart. Please believe me, please?'

Cynthia's lips quivered but still she didn't respond.

Anthony shook his head. Had he lost Cynthia? Was this the end? His heartrate quickened. *I can't lose her.* 'God damn it, woman' he blurted. 'Do you not hear what I am saying? I love you, and I want to spend the rest of my life with you. Is that not enough?'

Cynthia's eyes welled. 'My darling, I'm sorry, I didn't mean to raise my voice,' said Anthony. He grabbed Cynthia's shoulders and pulled her into his chest. He rubbed her back as she wept. 'I didn't mean to hurt you, my love. I will not have an affair with that woman. Please believe me. She means nothing to me, but you mean the world to me,' he whispered into her hair. She rattled in his arms. 'Come, let's sit over here.' Anthony led Cynthia to a bench a few feet away. As they sat down, he drew her close and let her weep. She had been through so much with the kidnap, wedding arrangements and now this stupid woman trying to get between them. Who could blame her for feeling venerable and weepy?

They sat for a while. Anthony handed Cynthia his handkerchief and, once she'd stopped crying, he put his finger under her chin, lifted her face and kissed her gently on the lips. 'Now, will you please give me a smile and talk to me?' he pleaded. 'Your father will think me an utter cad getting you into this state – and your brother will surely call me out. Pistols at dawn.'

Cynthia gave him a weak smile. 'Don't be silly, Derek knows you are an excellent shot, so he would go for swords at least,' she teased.

'My God, not that, please. You will have to get yourself sorted out immediately if you do not want your future husband to get a blade through his heart,' he said dramatically. Cynthia laughed as she pictured her poor brother, facing Anthony, one of the best swordsmen in Scotland.

'That's better, now I know your sense of humour has not escaped you. Can I start again?' he said as he leant forward and kissed her. When Cynthia responded he deepened the kiss and pulled her closer. She moaned gently as he slipped his tongue into her mouth. He did not want to push her too quickly, but Cynthia dug her fingers into his hair and kissed him back with passion. Anthony groaned, 'Oh God, we must stop now, or I will not be able to stop. Then your father will challenge me at dawn.' He slowly pushed her back and gazed into her eyes. 'I meant everything I said. I love you, truly. That woman is just causing mischief. I don't want you fretting over her. If she ever approaches you again, come directly to me. I will not have her upsetting you. You are my love and I only have eyes for you, is that crystal clear?'

Cynthia nodded. 'I love you too,' she said.

'Right, tonight is our last night together as single people,' said Anthony. 'We will go out and have a lovely night. Agreed?'

'Yes, let's, where shall we go?' she asked.

'I will book a meal at the Strath Hotel – your parents, Angela and Derek should come if they can make it – then we will attend a ball at the assembly rooms. We'll leave early – then go to a private gaming club. You can bet away all of my money.'

'Ha, you will be sorry, my lord. I am hopeless at cards.' Anthony smiled and gave his future bride a tight hug – then the door burst open. Derek stood on the threshold, grinning.

'Father sent me to see if it was pistols at dawn or a celebration drink in the parlour?'

Cynthia and Anthony looked into one another's eyes, smiling.

'A celebration drink in the parlour,' they said in unison.

CHAPTER THIRTY-FOUR

ANTHONY AND CYNTHIA ARRIVED FASHIONABLY LATE at the Strath Hotel, making a grand entrance into the dining hall where family and friends were already seated. The engaged couple looked radiant. Cynthia wore a beautiful pale pink silk dress, a ruby velvet cape and pink roses in her hair. Anthony, sleek in a black dress suit and crisp, white shirt. They looked the epitome of Edinburgh society.

The meal was excellent. Everyone had a splendid time, chatting about the forthcoming wedding. Later, most of the couples – including Cynthia and Anthony, Bill and Julianne and Heather and David – headed to the ball at the Assembly Rooms. As they entered the packed ballroom – the group deliberately stopped to survey the room, and to allow the room to observe them, Edinburgh's finest people – and the talk of the town. Then the men assisted their partners down the steps, onto the dance floor, and into a lilting waltz. Anthony and Cynthia flowed around the room, gazing into each other's eyes, lost in their own little world. Everyone watching whispered how much in love they looked, which was quite unusual as most of society matches were for titles, lands, and wealth rather than the love-fit this pair seemed to be.

As they danced, Anthony smiled down at Cynthia. 'You know every gentleman in this room is envious of me just now,' he said.

'I think you mean every lady is – and every mama has daggers out, aimed at me for taking Edinburgh's most eligible bachelor off the marriage market,' she smiled back.

'Probably, but I will shield you with my body should they take aim … although I can think of many more things I would like to do to your body.' Anthony's statement made Cynthia go hot all over. Anthony sensed this and squeezed Cynthia's hand.

He bent his head and whispered in her ear. 'Only two more nights, then I will satisfy you thoroughly.' He winked knowingly. Cynthia thought everyone in the room must know what he was doing to her, and a pink hue stained her cheeks.

Anthony laughed, thoroughly enjoying her discomfort but equally loving that he'd aroused her.

At the end of the waltz, the couples switched partners, and so, the night flowed on. Anthony and Cynthia danced with all their friends before reconnecting with one another for the last dance of the evening. Anthony continued whispering sweet nothings into Cynthia's ear. She had never been so happy – a far cry from her mood that morning.

Anthony usually got bored quickly at balls, so he was surprised when he realised he was reluctant to leave, he was so enjoying himself. 'So, your Lordship, are we off to the gaming club now?' said Cynthia as they departed the ballroom. 'I'm yet to lose all of your money.'

Anthony laughed. 'So, my Lady, you wish to bankrupt me before we are wed? Most ladies save that until they have a wedding ring safely on their finger. I could always change my mind if I run out of funds – then leave you at the altar.'

'You would not dare, sir. My brother and father would roast you alive if you did such a thing.'

'So, you would still have me, even if I do not have a penny left to my name?' he teased.

Cynthia pulled a serious face. 'Anthony, I would have you if you were a pauper with no title or land.'

'I know, sweet pea, said Anthony, kissing Cynthia's cheek. 'Now, let us be off before I change my mind.'

They all left in separate carriages and made their way to a new club on Queen Street, an upmarket affair with two imposing gentlemen dressed in red and gold livery guarding its doors. The guards' duty was to allow only the best of society into the club – and to politely send folk packing if they didn't pay their bills. The doors opened to a splendidly furnished foyer with a spiral staircase leading up to several gaming rooms. They all discarded their capes, hats and gloves and were ushered into a plush lounge where champagne or whisky was served. In the far wall, there was a discreet hatch where the gentleman exchanged money for chips. After a short time, the gents returned to escort the ladies upstairs. Before going into the first gaming room, Anthony handed Cynthia a velvet purse. 'There, my dear, all my worldly funds.' He laughed at the look on Cynthia's face.

'Gosh, this purse is very heavy,' she said.

Giles, standing next to his brother, laughed. 'If that is all your worldly goods, there would be no point me coming by tomorrow for a loan, which I'll probably need after tonight.'

'I would say no point at all, Giles, I always loose,' quipped Cynthia.

'Let's see. Shall we proceed,' said Anthony. He took Cynthia's arm and led her into a large room furnished with four roulette tables. Cynthia gasped as she walked into the room.

'This looks interesting,' she said, then turned to the ladies. 'Shall we?' The ladies were all excited as they had never been to such a place; casinos were typically a male's domain.

Julianne turned to Bill. 'I am not sure how much I should bet. I would hate to lose.'

'Choose your favourite number or place your bet on odd or even – that way you'll have a better chance of winning,' Bill advised. They gathered round a table.

'Right,' said Cynthia, 'let's go.' She placed a few coins – one on odd, another on a long line, and two straight-up on four, her favourite number. The croupier spun the wheel and the ball clattered round the rim before falling on number three.

Cynthia clapped her hands and squealed with delight. 'I won, I won, I never win,' she said as she turned to Anthony, who handed her another (empty) purse.

'Wonderful, now put some of your winnings in this empty bag and some on another option. That way you might take something home with you,' he said.

Cynthia thought for a moment, pursing her lips. 'Yes, but I will put *all* my winnings in the bag – then I will see if I win or lose at the end of the night.'

'Ladies and gentlemen, please place your bets,' announced the croupier.

Cynthia reached into the heavier bag, placed two more bets. This time she chose even numbers, including four again. She watched as the wheel turned hypnotically. The ball slowed – then landed in the number four groove. 'Ooh, look, I won again,' she cried. 'Look, Anthony, isn't this lovely.'

'I know, I was watching,' he said smiling. 'You must be my lucky charm.' Anthony was so pleased to see Cynthia happy that he didn't bother playing himself.

The hours slipped by – Cynthia ecstatic when she won, but totally offended if she lost.

Anthony was thoroughly enjoying his evening; he usually chose to play cards, but he could not bear to leave Cynthia. He left her side only a couple of times to get drinks for them. He would even say it was quite a turn on, standing behind her, rubbing her shoulders and arms and feeling her leaning into him when she was watching the ball spin round the wheel. Each time she won he gave her a peck on the cheek. He could not wait for the carriage ride home.

By 3a.m., Cynthia leant into Anthony and whispered softly, "Let's leave, I want to be alone with you.' He needed no persuasion. They all left, comparing their winnings and losses. The gentlemen gave Anthony jovial slaps on the back, all saying they would see him the following evening for his stag night. The ladies hugged each other and promised to keep Cynthia company during Anthony's stag festivities. Everyone thanked Anthony for a splendid evening before alighting their carriages.

It was a short ride from Queen Street to Royal Circus, but Anthony intended to make the most of it. As soon as he sat down next to Cynthia, he pulled her into his arms and kissed her passionately, pushing her back against the velvet swabs. His hand went to her chest, and he kneaded her breast through her silk dress, rubbing his finger over her nipple. 'God, you are lovely,' he whispered as he nibbled her ear and trailed kisses down her neck onto her ample bosom. He quickly pulled her breast out of her dress and chemise and sucked on her nipple as it's bud rose in his mouth.

Cynthia pulled on his hair and gasped, 'Anthony I want you so much.' Without hesitation, Anthony pulled up Cynthia's skirt and felt between her legs. He found her spot and rubbed her whilst plunging another finger deep inside her. Cynthia groaned with pleasure as Anthony moved back to her mouth, and they kissed passionately until Cynthia climaxed – just minutes before the carriage hit the cobbles in Royal Circus. 'Just in time,' said Anthony with a smile and a wink. He rearranged her skirt while Cynthia re-covered her breasts.

'Well, being an experienced rake comes in handy in such occasions,' she joked quietly and smiled at him.

'Quite,' he said – just as the coachman opened the carriage door. Anthony helped Cynthia down from the carriage and escorted her to the front door. He kissed the back of her hand. In two days, they would be husband and wife. He was truly looking forward to that. 'Goodnight, my love,' he whispered, staring into her eyes.

'Goodnight,' she replied breathlessly. Cynthia thought the whole street must be able to hear her thumping heart. She turned and entered the house, then watched Anthony leave and reflected on how wonderful the day had turned out. It had started so badly she thought he might have called off the wedding, but after the way Anthony had been all evening, she was sure he did love her very much. *If I ever encounter that woman (Lady Hamilton) again I shall put her in her place, for sure.*

During his carriage ride home, Anthony also pondered on how the day had turned out. Thank goodness he'd assuaged Cynthia's awful fears regarding Lady Hamilton – and hopefully put those anxieties to rest. But what if other ex-lovers were to come crawling out of the woodwork? There were, after all, plenty of women who could do so. The first three years of marriage are the hardest, Anthony's friends had told him. 'It takes a while to adjust to one another,' one friend had said. 'And If the marriage is to survive, the husband must understand the need to share decisions about things with his wife – and not just go their own merry way.'

Anthony hoped fervently his marriage with Cynthia would be one that crossed every hurdle and survived all.

CHAPTER THIRTY-FIVE

CYNTHIA OVERSLEPT THAT MORNING but woke to the sound of loud, joyous voices and clattering sounds seeping through the floorboards. She called for Lily, who arrived minutes later with a breakfast tray.

'Good morning, Miss Marchmont,' she said, smiling, 'and how is the bride-to-be today?'

'Gosh, Lily,' said Cynthia, swinging her legs over the edge of the bed. 'What an earth is going on downstairs?' The floor vibrated, tickling the soles of her feet.

'Oh, miss, people are arriving in droves, then being dispatched to various rooms or directed to your father's friens' homes, where they will be staying for the wedding,' explained Lily, pouring the tea. 'Your mother is in a proper tizz and the housekeeper has lists and lists of things that need doing. It's quite chaotic – we staff are running about, trying to keep up. It's all very exciting.'

'Oh, I can imagine the commotion. I'm a little nervous now, Lily,' said Cynthia, rubbing her stomach. She felt jittery inside.

'Your dress will arrive at noon, so I have to clear room in your wardrobe, miss, so is there any dresses I could put away into storage?' added Lily.

Cynthia took a sharp intake of breath. 'Oh dear, there's so much to do. I must greet our guests, but I need to pack for my honeymoon – oh, that will clear space in the wardrobe for my wedding gown.'

'Very well, miss. And do not worry, all will be fine.'

Cynthia drank her tea, washed, and dressed quickly, then headed downstairs, into the hubbub. Her parents were in the lounge, greeting guests with hugs and kisses. Cynthia walked in and was immediately greeted by her father's brother, her uncle Albert, and his wife Eileen. 'Ah, here comes the bride,' he boomed, stepping towards her with outstretched arms. 'My dear, you look lovely – and so grown up since I last saw you. He wrapped his arms tightly around Cynthia. Then her aunty Eileen wrestled her husband off Cynthia. 'Och, out of the way, you big oaf,' she said. 'Let me see my lovely niece.' Cynthia laughed. Albert and Eileen lived in Perth, and she hadn't seen them in over a year. But they hadn't changed – they always had rough banter with each other, but it was always in good humour.

'Cynthia, let me look at you, your mother told me all about your awful ordeal at the hands of that horrid man, how did you fair?' Eileen asked as she hugged her niece.

'I am fully recovered now, but I do not like to dwell on it,' she replied, hoping she did not need to go into every detail, especially as this should be a happy time. Fortunately, her father appeared on Eileen's shoulder.

'Right, let's get you settled into your room, Eileen, Albert. Cynthia was just going in to have a very late breakfast as she was up out most of the night, so plenty time to catch up later,' said Lord Marchmont, winking at Cynthia.

While Lord Marchmont guided the couple upstairs, Cynthia greeted more guests in the lounge then headed to the breakfast room, where more relatives and friends were still sitting around, chatting and eating breakfast. Although it was nearing 1 p.m., late breakfasts were common during the season, what with all the late-night balls and soirees. Cynthia made her rounds, welcoming everyone cheerfully. It was lovely having everyone here for her wedding, but her nerves were almost at breaking point. She didn't feel like eating even. Unlike Angela who loved entertaining and chatting to people, Cynthia preferred observing to leading. But today was different as the guests were all here for her and Anthony.

After breakfast, the butler arrived with a note for Cynthia. The note was from Anthony. 'I'm in your garden. Why don't you slip away and meet me, now? Love, Anthony.' Cynthia's heart and stomach fluttered as one. She shot from her seat, into the library and out through the garden doors. She found Anthony, sitting on a bench in an alcove by the conifers at the bottom of the garden. When he saw Cynthia, holding up her skirts and hurrying along the path in her satin slippers, Anthony stood up, beaming. Cynthia flew into his open arms and tilted her head to receive his lips. They kissed deeply for a long minute before Anthony broke away. 'I would love to take this further but who knows who could be viewing us from the many windows of the house,' he said.

Cynthia gazed up at Anthony. *God, he's so handsome. I can't believe we'll be married in two days.* 'I don't really care, kiss me again,' she urged. Anthony laughed and pecked her cheek.

'No, I daren't, your father would skin me alive if he caught us. Now, sit down and open this. Anthony reached into the inside pocket of his dress coat and pulled out a green velvet box.

'What's this?' said Cynthia, accepting the box.

'Open it and see.

Cynthia lifted the lid and drew in her breath. Nestled on a velvet cushion was a beautiful pearl necklace with a diamond clasp. 'Oh, Anthony, they are exquisite,' she breathed, lightly running her fingers over the pearls.

'Just like you,' said Anthony. 'I know the tradition of wearing something old, something new, something borrowed and something blue – so, I thought this could be your "something old". Those pearls have been in the Sinclair clan's coffers for two generations.'

'Oh, how lovely,' said Cynthia.

'And this can be your something new,' added Anthony, producing another, smaller box.

'Oh, Anthony, you are spoiling me.' Cynthia opened the second box and again, gasped. Inside, was a three-strand pearl bracelet, also with a diamond clasp. 'Oh, this is beautiful – and it matches the necklace perfectly.' She turned and lightly kissed Anthony on the cheek. 'I love them both, and I can't wait to wear them on our wedding day.'

'Well, I hope they will match your dress. If not, I could get you something else?' he replied anxiously.

'They are perfect, as you will see for yourself shortly. I cannot believe there are only two days left, time has flown in one respect but dragged in another.'

'I know, I will not see you tomorrow as I'm told it's bad luck for us to meet on the day before the wedding. Our mothers will string me up if I dare show my face. So, how about a turn in my phaeton carriage before I head off to my stag night?'

Cynthia grinned. 'Oh, yes please, the house is bedlam, and everyone wants to ask me all about the kidnapping and how we got engaged. I have repeated both events so many times I could scream at the next person who asks.' Anthony laughed as he stood, pulling Cynthia up with him. 'Come on, let's go.' As they left the alcove, they bumped into Lord Marchmont. He rolled his eyes.

'God, give me strength,' he said. 'Your mother is driving me crazy. I have come out here to escape. What are you two up to?'

'Look, father, Anthony gave me these beautiful jewels to wear on my wedding day.' Cynthia opened first the small box containing the bracelet then passed that box to Anthony to show her father the necklace.

'Oh, my, my,' said Lord Marchmont, his moustache twitching. Your fiancé has done you very proud. You'd better go and put them somewhere safe.'

'Yes, I will meet you out front in five minutes,' she said to Anthony as she rushed off. And then the two men were alone for a moment.

'Well, my boy, enjoy your stag night this evening, and I will see you at the alter on Saturday. Thank-you for making my daughter happy, I can see you are a very good match, Lord Marchmont said as he patted Anthony's shoulder and walked off up the garden for some peace and a cigar. Anthony watched him go. *I'm going to get on so well with my new in-laws. What a lovely family.* He turned and went to meet his fiancé.

* * *

Anthony helped Cynthia up onto his phaeton then sprang up beside her, gave her a wink and guided his pair of greys along the arc of Royal Circus, across Stockbridge, and out into the open space towards the Firth of Forth. Once they were trotting along nicely, he took her hand. 'Happy?' he called above the clip-clopping of hooves.

Oh, I am on seventh heaven right now. Thank-you so much for the jewels – they are exquisite.' Anthony and Cynthia revelled in each other's company over the next two hours, enjoying the silences as much as their conversation. Anthony had never felt so at one with a lady in his life. He did not want to leave Cynthia when he dropped her back at Royal Circus, but the gents were waiting for him.

'Enjoy your stag night and I will see you on Saturday at the altar,' Cynthia giggled.

'Yes, thank-you, I will,' said Anthony, bending to kiss her cheek. 'I love you,' he whispered. 'See you on Saturday.' Then he turned and bounded into his phaeton and heaved the reins.

'See you on Saturday,' Cynthia repeated as Anthony disappeared round the corner of Royal Circus. 'I can't wait.'

CHAPTER THIRTY-SIX

CYNTHIA STOOD IN FRONT OF THE CHEVAL MIRROR, admiring her reflection. She was entranced. Never had she felt so beautiful. Her white lace wedding gown was encrusted with pearls, with long, wide, flowing sleeves. Cynthia twisted to marvel at the gown's long train, also pearl-encrusted and and hemmed with flowers. The neckline of her gown was square and edged with lace flowers, and the veil, crowned by Cynthia's grandmother's diamond tiara, trailed to the floor. The dress was a simple, elegant design which suited her to perfection.

'Oh, Miss, you look like and angel,' said Lily, bending to straighten Cynthia's train.

'She does,' agreed Angela and Susanne in unison. Cynthia's brides-maids were in lilac satin dresses, with little puffed sleeves and trimmed with flowers matching those on Cynthia's gown. Two flower girls, Julia and Hilary – both second cousins to Cynthia and Angela – were in white dresses trimmed with lilac bows and flowers. They held baskets of lilac petals to sprinkle in front of Cynthia when she walked down the aisle.

'Right, girls, your carriage awaits. Off you go,' said Lord Marchmont as he walked into the bedroom with Georgina. The couple stopped suddenly as they looked at Cynthia, tears misting their eyes.

'Oh, my dear,' said Georgina, 'how beautiful you look.' She stepped forward and kissed Cynthia's cheek. 'I know you will both be so happy. Anthony is a lucky man. He clearly adores you.'

'Right, Mother, off you go with the girls,' said Lord Marchmont, guiding his wife, the bridesmaids and flower girls out the door. Then he marched over to Cynthia and offered his arm. 'Shall we go?' he said.

Cynthia nodded. 'Yes, I'm ready.'

'Not had a change of heart? Last chance to change your mind.' Lord Marchmont lifted his brows at Cynthia.

'No, definitely not,' she laughed.

'Good, let's get you to the altar, then.' They made their way downstairs, where staff gathered to wish her well. 'Well, miss, you do look a picture, if you don't mind me saying so,' the butler said with a smile. 'We wish you all the happiness in the world.'

'Thank you all,' replied Cynthia. I am very nervous, I must admit.'

The housekeeper, Joan, stepped forward. 'You look lovely,' she said. Allow me help you into the carriage.' Cynthia handed her bouquet to Lily while Joan, Angela and Susanne lifted her train for the short walk to the carriage. The staff, and neighbours, gathered in Royal Circus to wave off the bride.

Cynthia arrived at St Giles Cathedral to find a huge crowd of well-wishers on the forecourt. 'Goodness, I did not expect so many people,' she exclaimed.

'Well, Sir Anthony Sinclair is a well-known, respected member of Edinburgh society. Naturally, people are curious to see who his wife is – and to see high society dressed up in their finest,' said Lord Marchmont.

'Gosh, I hope I live up to their expectations.' Cynthia's stomach swirled with nerves.

Lord Marchmont smiled at his daughter and gave her hand a squeeze as the coachman swung open their carriage door. 'You are beautiful, kind and caring. All that matters is that you and Anthony are happy together. Just smile, wave, and enjoy yourself. This is *your* day.'

Lord Marchmont, aided by Angela and Susanne, helped Cynthia out of the carriage. Angela handed Cynthia a huge bouquet of white roses, festooned with lilac ribbons. Cynthia touched the necklace Anthony had given her then turned to her father, took a deep breath, and nodded. 'I'm ready.'

They walked ceremoniously, up the steps and into the cathedral, Cynthia's arm threaded through Lord Marchmont's. A string quartet played Pachelbel's *Canon* as they progressed along the candle-lit aisle behind the bridesmaids and flower girls. Garlands of white and lilac roses decorated the pews, while vases throughout the cathedral sprouted more flowers. *This is stunning*, thought Cynthia. Then she saw Anthony, waiting at the altar. His brother Giles at his side. *He's here. He showed up.* Anthony turned round then, and Cynthia thought her heart might stop. *Oh, look at my handsome man.*

Anthony knew Cynthia would make a beautiful bride, but still he was stunned when he assimilated the view as she reached the altar. She looked an absolute picture. She smiled sweetly at Anthony through her veil and stood beside him. He lifted her veil, smiled, winked then took her hand. She was shaking like a leaf.

Cynthia felt as though she was on the ceiling, looking down at herself as she recited her vows. Her voice trembled. *Is this really happening?* The ceremony passed in a nervous blur, then she heard the minister's voice. Loud and clear: 'I now pronounce you husband and wife.' Anthony looked into her eyes, then lowered his lips to hers for their first kiss as a married couple. After they'd kissed, they turned, and the cathedral erupted with cheers and applause. Anthony and Cynthia exchanged smiles, then advanced along the aisle to more applause. *I'm married to Sir Anthony Sinclair*, thought Cynthia. *I could weep with joy.* But there was no time for tears. Once the certificate was signed, Anthony and Cynthia headed outside, waving at the cheering crowd as they walked to their carriage, which would take them to the Strath Hotel for their wedding breakfast. Before alighting, Anthony emptied his pockets of handfuls of pennies and performed a traditional 'poor-oot' to the waiting children, who scrambled to retrieve the scattered coins. Then, at once, the newlyweds were on their way, waving to the crowds lining The Mound and Princes Street before arriving at Charlotte Square.

A small crowd of Sinclair staff awaited Anthony and Cynthia at the Strath Hotel, including Anthony's butler, Graham. And as tradition dictated, Anthony performed another pour-oot before they entered, this time emptying a purse full of pennies that he'd stored in the carriage. 'Congratulations, Lord and Lady Sinclair,' said Graham with a bow. Anthony thanked his workers for all their good wishes as he and Cynthia headed inside.

With their guests yet to arrive, Anthony pulled his new bride into his arms and kissed her tenderly. 'You took my breath away. When I saw you entering the church, I just wanted to whisk you off somewhere private, I still do,' he said, lightly cupping Cynthia's face as he broke away from the kiss.

'Well, my Lordship, you will just have to wait. We have a long day ahead of us,' laughed Cynthia, rising on her tiptoes to kiss her husband again.

'Woman, you tease me to distraction.' A huge grin split Anthony's face.

'That was my intention. I shall keep you on tenterhooks all day.' She gave him a playful push. 'Now, help me look respectable for our guests.'

Anthony groaned but straightened his bride's tiara and veil.

Ten minutes later, they stood with their families in the dining hall, greeting an interminable line of guests. This seemed to take an age, but at last they could sit for the wedding breakfast – a veritable feast of stewed oysters, galantines, roast beef and fowl, a selection of game, followed by ices and jellies and confectionary. They drank champagne amid several toasts to the new Sinclair couple, who ended the celebratory meal by cutting their wedding cake to a cheering room.

After the breakfast, the wedding party headed to the Assembly Rooms, which took some time while carriage upon carriage queued to transport guests to the next venue. Some younger guests and single males decided to walk there instead.

Once everyone had arrived at the Assembly Rooms, the orchestra struck up the first waltz. Anthony twirled Cynthia around the room, and as they gazed into each other's eyes, everyone could see they were in love. They only had eyes for each other.

Many dances – and more champagne – later, Anthony drew Cynthia aside. 'My carriage is waiting outside to take us to Melville Castle. Say your goodbyes quietly to your parents so nobody else sees us leaving. We'll sneak through the red door beneath the staircase. I'll meet you there and we'll slip out the side lane and into my carriage,' he said with a conspiratorial wink.

'Oh, how controversial,' The idea of slipping away unnoticed excited Cynthia. Traditionally, Cynthia would toss her bouquet over her shoulder – then the guests would wave them off. 'I'll speak to Father, then I'll see you at our secret meeting place.' Cynthia wandered across the ballroom to where Lord Marchmont was chatting with her uncle Albert over a malt. She asked Albert to excuse them for a minute, then she surreptitiously revealed Anthony's plan to her father.

Lord Marchmont drew back his head and he sucked in his breath. 'Ooh, don't tell your mother,' he warned. 'She will foil Anthony's ploy for a secret getaway, for sure. But I don't blame you. Off you go. Don't worry about your mother. I'll calm her down when she discovers you've thwarted her big send off. So long as you don't mind missing out on the farewells?'

Cynthia shook her head. 'Oh, Daddy, how can you ask such a thing? You of all people know how I hate big fusses.'

Lord Marchmont smiled and kissed his daughter's cheek. 'I know, I know. I was just checking. Now, quick, off you go – before your mother gets wind of this.'

'Thank you, Daddy – for everything,' said Cynthia and skittered to the exit and through the corridor until she came to the door beneath the stairs. She pushed through the door – and into the arms of her waiting husband.

'Darling, are you sure you're OK with this arrangement,' Anthony asked.

Cynthia giggled. 'Absolutely. Let's go.' They alighted the carriage and sped off through Edinburgh, towards Lasswade, where Melville Castle awaited them. In the back seat of the trundling carriage, Anthony drew Cynthia towards him, laughing at their escape.

'Tired?' he asked.

'No, not at all. I think the excitement of our escape has perked me up,' she laughed.

Anthony took Cynthia's hand and looked at her. She twinkled all over with diamonds and pearls. 'Good, I want this to be a night you will remember,' he said. He kissed her tenderly at first – and then with more passion. She leant into him, devouring his kisses.

'I love you, Lady Sinclair,' he said between kisses, his breath warm and ardent.

'And I love you, Lord Sinclair.'

Anthony smiled. 'But I'll stop kissing you now. If I carry on, I'll take you here and now. And, much as I want to do that, I want to savour tonight.' He winged his arm over Cynthia's shoulder, and she snuggled into his chest.

'Right, let's talk of mundane things, then. Have you visited Melville Castle before?' she asked.

'Yes, General Henry Dundas, the 3rd Viscount Melville served with Bill and I in Canada during a government mission, so we all got to know each other well. He was there today, but you might not have registered him among the many people you were introduced to. For our wedding present he has given us free reign of Melville Castle for as long as we wish. He's staying at the Moray Place townhouse until we leave for our honeymoon.'

'Oh, how kind of him. Are we the only guests?'

'Absolutely. I want you all to myself tonight and for the next few days.'

'When do we leave for our honeymoon?'

'I have booked passage to France in a weeks' time. We will have several stops on our way to Dover, spend a couple of weeks touring France then on to Italy, Austria, Switzerland, Luxembourg, and back to Calais. We'll be away for three months, all told. I gave your father a copy of our itinerary and his present to us is three nights in Venice, where he once took your mother.'

Cynthia let out a long 'Ooh' sound. 'Oh, Anthony, I did not know all of this. I thought we were just going to the south of England then Wales.'

264

'Well, I do like to surprise you, darling. Get used to it – there'll be plenty more surprises to come over the years.' Anthony hugged his wife closer. 'Plenty more.'

'Oh, thank you. It all sounds wonderful – and Daddy did not let the cat out the bag either. If Angela had got wind of this, I would have got it out of her as I can tell when she is keeping secrets.'

'Ah, that is why we told no one else, not even your mother.'

Cynthia laughed. 'Wise decision.'

At last, the carriage turned into a winding drive. As they turned Cynthia caught sight of Melville Castle, majestic and lit by gas lamps. 'My, it is lovely,' she breathed. 'I am so looking forward to our time here and the peace and quiet after the last few hectic months in Edinburgh.'

'I am definitely looking forward to my time here and at last having you all to myself,' Anthony whispered into her neck. He blew softly into Cynthia's ear, sending shivers down her spine in anticipation.

The butler, who introduced himself as 'McLeod', was standing at the front door with two footmen, waiting to assist Anthony and Cynthia into the grand front hall.

'My Lord", he bowed, "My Lady, welcome to Melville Castle, we have everything prepared for you. Your luggage arrived earlier, and our maids have unpacked everything for you. Please, allow me to show to your rooms,' he said. As they entered the grand hall with its huge fireplace and elaborate oil paintings adorning the walls, Cynthia sighed. 'Oh, how beautiful and welcoming this is.' Although used to grandeur, she was enthralled by her new surroundings.

'That is Henry,' said Anthony, pointing at the portrait above the fireplace. 'The next portrait along is of Henry's father, then his father's father – and so the sequence continues through the hall and to the top of the stairs, where a portrait of Henry's mother resides.

Cynthia's eyes followed Anthony's arm as he rattled off names of the portraited men. They followed McLeod up the impressive staircase, then along the hallway before stopping outside double doors at the turret end of the building. 'My lady, my lord, may I present your rooms,' said McLeod, throwing open both doors.

The view was breathtaking: a large sitting room with an inviting fire blazing in the hearth and large windows overlooking gardens to the east. Positioned in front of the windows was a table laden with a cold buffet, champagne on ice and a large vase blooming with red, pink, yellow and white roses of. Encircling the fire, a settee and two grand armchairs. Anthony and Cynthia followed McLeod to another set of double doors at the back of the sitting room. 'And through here is your lady and lord's bedrooms,' he said, pushing open the mahogany gates to reveal a four-poster bed, draped with crimson velvet curtains, its mattress strewn with red rose petals.

Anthony shook McLeod's hand. 'Thank you, McLeod. I will take it from here,' he said. Then he swooped Cynthia into his arms and carried her over the threshold.

She squealed with joy.

CHAPTER THIRTY-SEVEN

'I BELIEVE CARRYING YOU OVER THE THRESHOLD WILL BRING GOOD LUCK TO OUR MARRIAGE,' said Anthony, smiling down at Cynthia as he expertly booted the doors shut behind them with two dexterous backward kicks.

Cynthia laughed. 'So they say.' Anthony caried her across the room and set her down by the window. He then took her face in his hands and kissed her at length. 'I have been waiting all day to do that,' he breathed when their lips finally disengaged. Then he grabbed Cynthia's hand, whirled her round, and headed for a further set of doors in the right-hand wall. Cynthia almost lost her veil as she turned.

Through to a further inviting room housing another four-poster bed, also adorned with crimson curtains and rose petals – and surrounded by lit candles in elaborate, tall holders. A fire glowed in the hearth, and a beautiful Queen Anne dressing table and matching wardrobe hugged the back wall. On the other side of the room, a full-length mirror stood beside a huge window overlooking the gardens. Two velvet chairs and a small table, topped with another vase of roses, surrounded the fire.

'Oh, this is beautiful,' said Cynthia as Anthony turned her into his arms.

'Not as lovely as you.' He kissed her slowly and gently. 'I love you, my precious,' he said softly. He grasped her shoulders, pivoted her round to face the mirror and stood behind her, gazing at her reflection. 'You look stunning in that dress, my love,' he added, lowering his face to Cynthia's neck and nibbling her earlobe. 'But I think I'd like to see you out of it now.' He kissed her neck, a trail of fluttering kisses down to her shoulder. At the same time, Anthony began unfastening the ribbons and buttons at the back of Cynthia's wedding gown. She groaned and rolled her head backwards, leaning into Anthony's touch, shivers travelling down her neck with his warm lips. Her dress loosened and he swept her veil aside, then slowly slipped down one shoulder of her dress, followed by the second sleeve, planting more kisses across her neck and the tops of her arms. Cynthia gasped as she watched their erotic reflection in the mirror, a moistness forming between her legs. Next, Anthony looked up and, staring intently at Cynthia in the mirror, he eased her dress down further, exposing her hard nipples beneath the delicate fabric of her chemise. Cynthia closed her eyes, her breath catching in her throat when Anthony cupped her breasts, then rubbed her nipples and kissed her neck.

Cynthia reached behind her and massaged Anthony's erection through his trousers. Then she felt a rush of air over her chest when Anthony pushed the straps of her chemise over her shoulders. The garment slithered south. 'God, you're beautiful,' said Anthony moving to face Cynthia. He caressed her breasts again, then lowered his lips to her right nipple, licking gently at first, then sucking it hard. Cynthia watched his bent head in the mirror and thought, *This is the most erotic moment ever.* Her breath came hard and fast as Anthony then circled round her and unfastened the final buttons on her gown until it fell to the floor with a rustle.

Cynthia stepped out of the sparkling white circle of fabric while Anthony shouldered off his jacket and threw it on the floor. Then he looked at Cynthia, naked but for her stockings, heels and veil. 'You look like an angel,' he whispered, stroking her upper arms. 'An angel I am going to thoroughly seduce tonight.' At once, they were kissing again, harder and urgent. 'You are everything I want and more tonight.' Fingers working rapidly, Anthony unbuttoned his shirt, discarding it on the floor next to his jacket while Cynthia unfastened his trousers and pulled down his undergarments. 'Face the mirror,' he told Cynthia, stepping out of his clothes.

Cynthia did as she was told and watched as Anthony held her naked body against his and reached between her legs, rubbing her spot gently while massaging her breasts with his other hand. She arched her back, panting loudly as he rubbed her harder, while looking directly at her husband in the mirror, the image flickering in the candlelight. 'Anthony, Anthony, Anthony,' she said breathlessly, her entire body convulsing through her orgasm.

Cynthia's breasts lifted lightly as she breathed in and out, her skin damp and smooth as marble in the glow of the candles and fire. Slowly she turned to face Anthony, rubbing his hard penis as he kissed her again. They danced as one shape across the room, kissing, touching each other all over, groaning and panting and turning until they fell onto the bed. Then Anthony rolled on top of Cynthia and gently eased his penis into her. She tilted her hips. 'I love you,' they both said over and over as they made love for the first time in a carpet of rose petals, their encounter ending with a mutual climax that left them gasping for air.

They lay side by side for a while, limbs entangled, Anthony stroking Cynthia's hair (she'd lost her veil and tiara in the throes of passion). 'I love you. That was sensational, you are sensational,' he whispered.

'So are you,' said Cynthia.

'Now, let us eat. I'm ravenous,' added Anthony, springing forth from the bed. 'Come on.' He held his hands out to Cynthia.

'But I don't have my robe,' she said, suddenly self-conscious of walking around the room naked. 'I can't see it anywhere.'

'Oh, don't worry about a robe. It'll only come off again.' Cynthia sat up, looking around for her robe. 'I'd just feel more comfortable with…'

'Here, take this, my love.' Sensing his wife's unease, Anthony retrieved his shirt from the floor and handed it to her. 'It will keep you warm.' Cynthia slipped on the shirt, and they sauntered through to the buffet table in the next room. 'God, you look adorable in that shirt,' he whispered into her ear as she sat down. He gave her ear and neck a nibble as he helped her into her seat.

'Sit down, your lordship, and eat – I thought you said you were hungry.'

'I am now – but not so much for food.' Anthony sat down, draping a napkin over his groin. He felt aroused again.

Cynthia giggled, picked up a chicken drumstick and licked it seductively.

'Stop it, you tease me beyond reason,' laughed Anthony.

They had a playful, seductive supper. Although Anthony could not resist his desires and, before their meal was over, made love to Cynthia again – this time over the back of the settee in front of the fire.

It was 3 a.m. when they finally tumbled back into bed, tired but both content in their love for one another.

'Sleep now, we can start all over again in the morning,' said Anthony, pulling Cynthia towards him beneath the covers.

'Goodnight, my love, my husband,' whispered Cynthia. 'Today was the best day of my life.'

Anthony kissed his wife's forehead. 'You *are* my life,' he said. 'Sleep tight, my angel.'

CHAPTER THIRTY-EIGHT

AFTER THEIR HONEYMOON, CYNTHIA AND ANTHONY RETURNED TO EDINBURGH for a few days before heading north to the Girnigoe Estate in Caithness, which would become their permanent home.

They had enjoyed a delightful honeymoon. They'd visited all the major sites, dined at the finest restaurants, and stayed at the most beautiful hotels by the sea or in the cities. But the highlight, for both Anthony and Cynthia, had been the many passionate moments shared, making love at night – or during the day at siesta time. Their love for one another was palpable.

Now in Edinburgh, the happy couple were reunited with friends and family who were all thrilled to see them and hear about their European adventures. And to celebrate their homecoming, Cynthia and Anthony organised a ball, which would take place at the city's Assembly Rooms two weeks later, giving Anthony and Cynthia time to return to Girnigoe in the interim.

After a whirlwind few days, the newlyweds set off on their long carriage ride to Caithness. Cynthia slept for most of the journey. Anthony noticed how tired his wife had been of late. *I do hope she's not sickening for something*, he thought.

Anthony's butler Graham, who had relocated to Girnigoe in the honeymooners' absence, greeted the couple on their arrival at the estate. He was joined by a twelve-strong line of fellow staff members, who all welcomed the new Lady Sinclair with bows and curtseys.

'My lord, my lady, welcome home. I trust you had a pleasant holiday?' said Graham.

'Yes, we had a wonderful time, thank you, Graham,' said Anthony, his arm around Cynthia's waist. 'And I trust all was well here and in Edinburgh while we were away?'

Graham gave a regal nod. 'Of course, my lord. I hope you and her ladyship will approve of all the work that has been carried out throughout the estate.'

'I am sure we will. Now you may formally introduce the staff to their new mistress,' Anthony instructed.

Graham bowed again before Cynthia. 'My lady, if you please,' he said, guiding Cynthia towards the housekeeper. Anthony stood back and observed his wife as she moved along the line of servants, noting how she had a kind word for each of them. She also asked pertinent questions regarding their duties on the estate. Then, introductions over, Graham led the couple inside for tea and cakes, followed by a tour of the grand house.

During the tour, Anthony was quite happy to let Graham and Cynthia walk ahead of him. He watched with great admiration how Cynthia's hips swayed with her step as she marvelled at the rooms housing numerous paintings. Anthony particularly enjoyed observing how Cynthia's pert bottom protruded when she climbed the sweeping staircase that led to the bedrooms. *I hope I never tire of looking at my lady.* As Graham showed them around the turret bedroom, Anthony drifted into a reverie about his wedding night at Melville Castle. Then…

'Anthony, Anthony, I'm talking to you.' Cynthia's voice interrupted his woolgathering.

'Sorry, my dear, I was not quite listening. I was daydreaming about our honeymoon.' Anthony gave his wife a wink. Graham flushed and cast his gaze to the view through the window – the dramatic cliff faces falling into the gunmetal waters of Sinclairs Bay. 'What were you saying, my dear?'

Cynthia sighed. An amused sigh. 'Am I boring you with all my questions?'

'Gosh, no, you could never bore me, my love. It is just that I know this house inside out. Please, do repeat your question.'

Cynthia crossed the ends of her shawl across her chest. 'Very well. Do you know when our first guests arrive?'

'Oh, I apologise. Of course. I've invited your parents to return here with us after our Edinburgh trip. Then, the following month, my mother will join us for a while. But there are sure to be other visitors in between. I know Bill and Julianne wish to come for a few days … actually, I promised I would send word to Bill regarding dates – shall I go to my study and do that now? I can leave you to finish the tour with Graham.'

Cynthia could tell Anthony was bored with traipsing around – and there were still several rooms yet to see.

'Yes, you go down,' said Cynthia, stifling a yawn. 'I will find you when we are done.' She smiled at the relief on Anthony's face. She was getting to know her husband's moods and proclivities quite well already.

'Thank you,' he said, then kissed her cheek before turning to flee to his study. Cynthia laughed and turned to Graham.

'I knew he was bored,' she said with a twinkle in her eye.

'Just so, my lady,' said Graham, extending his arm towards the door. 'Now, let's move on to the first-floor parlour.'

Anthony sat at his desk, sorting through his correspondence. He had a lot of paperwork to get through ahead of their four-day carriage journey back to the capital, and they had only five nights at Girnigoe. His mind began to wander again, thinking of the fun he'd have while alone with his wife in their new home. At once, hurried footsteps approaching the door stirred him. The door burst open and in came the lady of his dreams. 'Finished the grand tour,' he asked, laughing.

'Yes, it was very interesting. Your house is beautiful,' she said.

'This is *our* house,' said Anthony. He stood up and walked around the desk to join Cynthia. Placing his hands around her

273

shoulders he looked into her eyes. 'This is our house,' he repeated. 'And you are free to change anything you don't like without asking permission.'

Cynthia shook her head, ringlets bobbing and glistening in the shaft of morning sunlight streaming through the window. 'No, everything is perfect. I love it, although…'

'Although what?' said Anthony, raising his brows.

'Well, we maybe could change one room. Just a small change, mind you,' said Cynthia, rolling her lips inwards as she eyed him coyly through long lashes.

'Ha, I knew it. Women always want to change something. My sister and mother are always saying the décor at the Moray Place townhouse is too masculine. But I did try for a feminine look here at Girnigoe. I got professional help on the colours even.'

'Oh, darling, sorry, everything is lovely. Please don't look so down-hearted. It was not a criticism of your excellent taste,' she said, as she rushed forward and hugged him.

Anthony kissed Cynthia's head, then pulled back to look into her eyes. 'Don't be silly. Really, I'm not upset. Tell me, what would you like to change? I will redecorate the whole place if you ask me. I love you and what you want is all that matters.'

'Oh Anthony, how kind you are, but I just want to change one or maybe two rooms, if you really don't mind? Just the small room in the turret – the room neighbouring the master bedroom, the one with the round windows and little adjoining room.'

'Fine, they are yours,' said Anthony, a look of confusion swathing his face. 'Does that mean you wish to move into your own quarters? I had hoped we would share all quarters, but I quite understand if you want your own space.'

'Oh, Anthony,' said Cynthia, laughing. She gave his arm a playful slap. 'Of course I want to share your rooms. Is it not obvious how much I enjoy your company? Have I not proven how much I adore making love to you?' She blushed then and placed a hand on her middle, lightly twisting at the waist. 'Those two rooms are not for me, silly. Rather …' she paused, still holding her stomach. 'Well, I thought the smaller room could be for another member of our family.'

Anthony raised his brows. 'OK, that's fine. Have you invited Angela or Derek to stay with us?'

Cynthia rolled her eyes. *How has he not realised?* She nodded down at her hand, still holding her stomach.

'I mean, I don't mind them visiting,' Anthony continued. 'But do you really want your sister or brother sleeping in the next room to us. Heavens, I thought that would be your last wish. As you know, we do make quite a racket when we…'

Cynthia rattled with laughter. She couldn't stop. 'What, what's so funny?' said Anthony, frustrated with Cynthia now. 'Fine, don't tell me.' Anthony turned to leave.

'Oh, don't go. I'm sorry – I have ruined the moment.' Anthony's reaction had quickly quelled her giggles. 'You weren't supposed to get angry. Please, hug me again. I have something to tell you.'

'OK,' he sighed, and pulled her into his arms. It was not in Anthony's nature to be in a huff for long. Cynthia squeezed him tight then let go and stepped back. She pressed both hands to her midriff.

'My lord. Anthony, darling. The reason I wish for the rooms, truly, is for this little bundle.' She glanced down at her middle, then looked up at Anthony's beaming face.

'Really, you are with child so soon?'

Cynthia gave a succession of hurried nods. 'Yes, I am, we are going to have a baby" she laughed. 'We must be very fertile.'

'Oh, my love, this is wonderful news,' said Anthony, wrapping his arms around his pregnant wife. 'I love you so much.'

'Yes, I saw Dr. Munro when we were in Edinburgh. He confirmed I am with child. Possibly two months' pregnant already. I wanted to wait until we were in our new home to tell you. Are you happy?'

'Oh, my love, I'm delighted, thrilled.' Now it was Anthony's turn to laugh. 'So, if my calculations are correct, you must have conceived while we were in Venice?'

Cynthia giggled. 'Yes, I think it was that night when you seduced me in…'

A rap at the door. Anthony composed himself. 'Enter,' he called. The door opened and Graham stepped into the study.

'My lady, my lord, lunch will be served in the drawing room at two o'clock, if that suits your schedule?'

'Absolutely, we'll be there,' replied Anthony, smiling at Cynthia. 'Oh, and please arrange for the painters to return tomorrow. The lady has requested some changes.'

'Yes, My Lord.' Graham bowed and left the room, clicking the door behind him. Then Anthony and Cynthia took one look at each other and burst out laughing.

Ten days later and back in Edinburgh, Anthony and Cynthia broke their baby news to Lord and Lady Marchmont at their townhouse in Royal Circus. Then they informed other relatives and friends at their celebration ball the next day. Everybody was overjoyed to hear such wonderful news.

Anthony was like a dog with a new bone throughout the ball. He fretted over Cynthia all night, worried that she would overexert herself and harm the baby.

Cynthia's father stood at the edge of the ballroom, chatting to Lord Walker while watching Anthony and Cynthia on the dance floor. He noticed Anthony, pausing intermittently to check that Cynthia was OK – and protectively placing his hand on her middle. 'Goodness, he [Anthony] wears me out just watching him,' said Lord Marchmont, laughing.

'Yes, we were never like that,' agreed Lord Walker, his tone wistful as he pictured his late wife Morag when she was pregnant with Julianne. The truth was, both men had been equally attentive as Anthony throughout their wives' pregnancies years ago.

'It will be good having a little one around again,' added Cynthia's father. 'I loved teaching mine to ride and hunt, although Cynthia's mother never thought hunting a sport for young ladies.'

'Ha-ha, no, neither did Morag, God rest her soul.' Lord Marchmont was about to offer comforting words to his old school pal when Derek crept up behind them.

'Hey, Pa,' said, 'What are you two plotting now?'

'Oh, nothing, son. I was just telling my good pal here how much I'm looking forward to being a grandpa – all the fun without the responsibilities.'

'Oh, yes. I just know you'll spoil that grandchild something rotten,' laughed Derek. 'Anthony won't like that – you know how serious he is.'

'Hmm, unlike you, son, taking no responsibilities and living off your dear old parents,' joked Lord Marchmont. 'It will be you next, Derek. I will get your mother onto it, she loves matchmaking.'

'Oh, no,' groaned Derek.

When the waltz ended, Anthony joined the men while Cynthia chatted with Julianne at a table by the bar.

'What are you lot laughing at?' said Anthony, grinning at Derek.

'Oh, nothing. Just this one,' he jabbed a thumb in his father's direction, 'throwing me into the lion's den. Father thinks Mother will try to marry me off with her matchmaking meddling.' Anthony laughed and the men chatted for a while – until Cynthia appeared.

'Excuse me, I have come for my husband for a dance,' she said, proffering her bent hand aloft to Anthony.

'My dear, you must take it easy, are you sure more dancing is…'

'I can always choose another partner,' Cynthia interrupted, her head on one side.

'Very well, my love, let's dance.' Anthony took his wife's hand and they stepped onto the dancefloor, bathed amber in the candelabra light. They took their positions, Anthony's hand resting gently on the small of Cynthia's back, his right hand clasping her right. Then the opening bars to Chopin's "Grande Valse Brilliante" issued from the piano, bright and rapid, but heart-achingly romantic. Anthony led Cynthia, making fluid circles across the floor, all the while gazing into one another's eyes. And all eyes in the room were on them, the most romantic couple of Edinburgh's high society. Other couples stopped dancing to admire Lord and Lady Sinclair, who were blissfully lost in the moment. The music flurried and crescendoed on, reverberating around the hall, through windows and doors, out onto George Street, where passers-by stopped to listen.

Standing arm and arm on the north periphery of the dance floor was Lady Georgina Marchmont and Duchess Rosalind Sinclair. The women gazed lovingly at Cynthia and Anthony, eyes glazed with tears. They both sighed.

'Oh, look at our babies,' said Georgina, turning to face her friend. Then they returned their gaze to the dance floor.

'What an enchanting couple,' they said in unison.